NOT THINKING OF DEATH

Also by Alexander Fullerton:

SURFACE!
BURY THE PAST
OLD MOKE
NO MAN'S MISTRESS
A WREN CALLED SMITH
THE WHITE MEN SANG
THE YELLOW FORD
SOLDIER FROM THE SEA
THE WAITING GAME
THE THUNDER AND THE FLAME
LIONHEART
CHIEF EXECUTIVE
THE PUBLISHER
STORE
THE ESCAPISTS
OTHER MEN'S WIVES
PIPER'S LEAVE
REGENESIS
THE APHRODITE CARGO
JOHNSON'S BIRD
BLOODY SUNSET
LOOK TO THE WOLVES
LOVE FOR AN ENEMY

The Everard series of naval novels

THE BLOODING OF THE GUNS
SIXTY MINUTES FOR ST GEORGE
PATROL TO THE GOLDEN HORN
STORM FORCE TO NARVIK
LAST LIFT FROM CRETE
ALL THE DROWNING SEAS
A SHARE OF HONOUR
THE TORCH BEARERS
THE GATECRASHERS

The SBS Trilogy

SPECIAL DELIVERANCE
SPECIAL DYNAMIC
SPECIAL DECEPTION

NOT THINKING OF DEATH

A Novel

Alexander Fullerton

LITTLE, BROWN AND COMPANY

A *Little, Brown* Book

First published in Great Britain in 1994
by Little, Brown and Company

A CIP catalogue record for this book is available from the British Library.

ISBN 0 316 91017 1

Typeset in Times by Solidus (Bristol) Limited
Printed and bound in Great Britain by
BPC Hazell Books Ltd
A member of
The British Printing Company Ltd

Little, Brown and Company (UK) Limited
Brettenham House
Lancaster Place
London WC2E 7EN

And nothing to say and the glasses are raised, we are happy
Drinking through time and a world that is gentle and helpless
Survives in the pub and goes up in the smoke of our breath.
The regulars doze in the corner, the talkers are fluent;
Look now in the faces of those you love and remember
That you are not thinking of death.

From *Pub* by Julian Symons

Chapter 1

JUNE 1941

At Hatfield she left the Anson in the care of the ferry pool's maintenance crew, who'd been waiting for it, and accepted a lift in their pickup to the ATA women pilots' Mess. It was getting on for 9pm on this pretty summer evening when she handed in her flight chits at the office; the light was dying out there, and the sunset which she'd had as a blaze behind her left shoulder during the flight from White Waltham had melted into a darkening peach-tinted glow with the hangars solid black against it. There'd been a weight of anxiety in the back of her mind all day, and it was in the forefront now: nothing to do with the flying, simply whether or not there'd be a message here from Chris. There hadn't been last night when she'd 'phoned in from the hotel at Banbury. She'd 'phoned home – which was in Scotland – too, and her mother had had nothing for her, had told her 'Don't *worry* so much, Suzie darling! He'll be back in good time, I'm *sure*!'

Stupid damn thing to say. And – all right, Mama meant well, wanted only to calm her down, but she'd been thinking solely of the wedding, not for a moment of the fact that if Chris's submarine was overdue – well, for Christ's sake, you could postpone a damn wedding, but—

Biting her lip. Calming *herself* down. Telling herself *Get cleaned up, then a snack* ... And please God there *will* be a message ... Not necessarily here, he could have left one with her landlady, in the village. But he'd be more likely to call here, to the Mess: and she'd eat here anyway because (a) the old bag wasn't too hot on providing meals; (b) if you left your own rations there they tended to disappear, the stock excuse being 'Oh, that went off, dear, I had to throw it out.' Pushing into the changing room, she could hear Churchill's voice coming from somewhere along the corridor – that now familiar, rasping tone ... She'd thrown the door shut behind her but it jerked open again and Winston's voice boomed more loudly: 'We shall fight him by land, we shall fight him by sea, we shall fight him—'

'In the air, presumably. Must say I thought some of the chaps had been doing so, quite successfully ...' Jill Blessington shoved the door shut with her heel. 'Hi, Suzie.'

'Hi. Our Master's Voice again. What's gone to pot *this* time?' She'd dropped her helmet and goggles and leather gauntlets on the bench: ripping open the jacket with its Air Transport Auxiliary 1st Officer's gold stripes on the shoulders. Jill, who was a year or two older than Suzie – Suzie being twenty-two now – had less than half her flying hours and only one stripe, as yet. Suzie asked her, moving her dark head towards the source of the Prime Ministerial broadcast, 'What's this about?'

'Hitler's invaded Russia. Could be a break for us, they're saying.'

'That what *he*'s saying?'

'In a nutshell he's saying let bygones be bygones with Uncle Joe, we'll fight the bastards together.'

'Don't have much option, do we?'

'I suppose not. But the great thing is the Germans are less likely to invade *us* now, aren't they?'

Suzie nodded. 'I suppose that *is* something.' She was

changing into a skirt instead of the slacks she'd been living in. Thinking, historic moment, probably. Sunday, 22 June 1941. Remember it, tell one's grandchildren. Three days before my wedding this was, I'll tell them. Boring them to desperation, no doubt: and may that be the least of *their* problems, the little sods ... Jill asked her, 'You were stuck out last night, were you?'

'Was indeed.' Buttoning the skirt. 'At bloody Banbury. Brought a Hurricane from there to White Waltham this afternoon. I took an Oxford up to Prestwick yesterday, then a Hudson Kirkbride to Ternhill. Still don't like Hudsons ... Spent last night at Banbury intending to take off first thing with the Hurri, but it wasn't fit to fly until well into this afternoon. Ancient specimen – Mark 1, pre-war. Then a taxi Anson from White Waltham. And here we are. How about you?'

'Oh – usual. Short hops, you know ... Listen – what I came to say – you had a telephone call—'

'*Uh?*'

'No – not your Chris. Sorry – should've warned before I spoke, shouldn't I.'

Damn right you should ... Controlling it, though: aware of how tired she was – and hungry – and that her nerves *were* jumpy ... Jill smiling at her, asking brightly 'Guess who it *was*, though?'

She waited for it. Not caring all that much: since it had not been Chris.

'Rufus Chalk?'

She'd flinched. Then thought, *Doesn't make sense* ... On the edge of the bed with her knees drawn up, her arms around them, bent forward so that her face was hidden for a moment ... Jill added – began to, looking down at her – 'He's – well, obviously, he's *Diana* Chalk's—'

'He's also Chris's commanding officer. Didn't you know?' Jill didn't, of course – hadn't, until this moment. Suzie told her – flatly, patiently – 'I first met Diana through

Rufus. At my parents' house – several years ago. They'd only just got engaged then. If it hadn't been for Diana I'd probably never have learnt to fly. And it was through Rufus that I met Chris. Getting the picture – Jill *dear*?'

Rueful smile . . . 'One lives and learns.'

'Doesn't one, just.' A new thought struck her. 'Speaking of Diana – is she around?'

'Uh-huh. She's stuck out, too. He asked for her – after I'd told him you weren't back yet, and he said he'd try again later. But he didn't ask for *her* to—'

'At Dundee, is he?' She saw the other girl's nod. 'Well, I *will* ring him.'

'He said you'd have the number, but if you had problems getting through to him – knowing what the lines are like – he'd—'

'How did he sound?'

'Well – normal – I should think. No panic, no—'

'Panic.' Suzie shrugged. Agreeing that there wouldn't be. She knew about panic. About terror. In recent years, she'd plumbed the depths. She shook her head: you learnt some lessons, but there was no immunity. She was on her feet again: petite, trim figure taut with worry. There *can't* be anything wrong.'

'Some duty thing, perhaps, he couldn't get to a 'phone so—'

'Yes. That *must* be—'

'So come on. Supper, *then* call him. If he hasn't tried again by then, eh?'

It made sense to eat first. Even though it meant putting up with the others' chatter while she was doing it: chatter about her wedding to Chris, in particular, this being scheduled for the 25th – Wednesday, three days' time – at home, Glendar-ragh, in Perthshire. She'd arranged for her leave to start on Tuesday, day after tomorrow, and she was counting on getting an airlift northward. There were ferrying flights to Prestwick all the time: but alternatively she might get herself to Donybristle, the Fleet Air Arm receipt and despatch unit, or RAF Edzell, a repair and storage depot. So, no problems *there* . . .

And if Rufus was in Dundee – well, so was Chris, for God's sake!

She'd been letting this situation get her down a bit, she knew. She did always worry, when he was at sea. Well, *God* . . . And with the wedding coming up, having to count the days, no matter how full and strenuous one's own were, each night had been another small ordeal, a further tightening of the screw. On the one hand had been the fact they were overdue – which could mean nothing more than a few days' extension of a patrol, but could also, especially at night when the mind was so much more vulnerable, carry implications that were – unacceptable. (Unacceptable if there'd been any choice. There never was, of course: the only option lay in your own reactions. As once before – that *real* nightmare, which had a tendency to hang around.) But that – the fact they'd been overdue – had been one side of the vice; it wasn't now, since Rufus was back and Chris obviously had to be too: and the other – present tense – was her own state of mind.

Not that there was any question of not going through with it. She loved him, was *in love with* him – and he was with her.

So *shut* your mind: get on with it.

They'd fixed the wedding-date between them – she, Chris and Rufus, those two deciding it was an odds-on bet that their submarine – their 'boat', as they called it – would be in Dundee by that date and for roughly a week after it. Which would allow for a few days' honeymoon, therefore. Most submarine patrols – those out of Dundee, anyway – had a reasonably predictable duration of between fourteen and eighteen days – at this time of year, when constant daylight up in the Arctic Circle prohibited long-range patrols to northern Norway – and there was normally a rest and maintenance period between patrols of about a fortnight. Less of course if there was any flap on, when all the boats had to be turned round fast and pushed out again; but in hopes of 'normal' circumstances, Rufus had agreed with them that the 25th would be as safe a bet as any.

Surely was, too. Rufus would have been making the call because Chris for some reason couldn't get up to the mess, up on that hill above the dockyard. Suzie had visited Chris there, was visualizing the town and docks while she ate her supper. There must have been some reason he'd had to stay on board the damn submarine. He was its first lieutenant, Rufus Chalk's second-in-command: he'd be coping with some technical problem or other, and Rufus would have told him, 'I'll ring her, tell her she'll hear from you tomorrow.' Something like that.

The call came just as she'd finished and had taken a few sips of coffee that was too hot to drink. The telephone, in the passage outside the mess, had rung three or four times in this past quarter of an hour; when it rang again and someone answered it then yelled 'Suzie Cameron-Green! Suzie, telephone!' she actually ran to it: thinking *Could be Chris, this time . . .*

'Hello?'

'Suzie – Rufus. I tried earlier but—'

'I know, I had the message, I was going to call you back. Just had to get a bite first, I was famished.' She paused fractionally; then asked him, 'Where's Chris?'

'Well, that's why I'm calling. Thing is – *first* thing is he's perfectly all right – nothing to worry about at all. *But* – I'm sorry, truly *very* sorry – you're going to have to postpone the wedding. Damn nuisance and disappointing, I know, but—'

'Postpone . . .?'

'I'm sorry, Suzie.'

'For how long – and *why*?'

'This is – difficult . . . Public telephone, walls having ears, all that. I can't give you much explanation. In fact as to *how long* I couldn't say anyhow – I mean I don't know . . . But you *don't* have to worry – as I said—'

'Tell me what you can?'

'Well.' The pause probably lasted only about three seconds, but it seemed much longer. Then: 'All right, Suzie. Just this. Another first lieutenant went sick, and he's taken his place. So he's – away now, and—'

'Are you saying he's gone straight back out on patrol?'

'I know how you must feel. And I *am* sorry. Frightfully disappointing – and a damn nuisance, all your arrangements . . . But – there wasn't any alternative. If there had been, I'd—'

'Surely there'd be a dozen or more other first lieutenants who might have—'

'No – the change-over didn't take place here, you see. There was no choice, no option – believe me, Suzie. I can't name – oh, location, or—'

'Which boat is he in now?'

'Have to go easy on ships' names, too. It wouldn't mean anything to you, anyway. But listen – I must explain one angle – mine, partly, but your question "how long" – you see, I'll need him back with *me* when I'm next ready to push off.'

'So when he does get back from this other—'

'Exactly. I'm sorry, but—'

'Couldn't you take someone else in his place? So he'd—'

She'd checked herself. In the short silence, she heard Rufus clear his throat. 'It'll be a few weeks before you two can get spliced, Suzie. I'm just giving you the facts of the situation, there's nothing else I can—'

'All right.' She took a long breath. 'All right. I understand. At least, I—'

'I'll telephone again if or when I have any fresh news for you. I might get word when he's on the way back. *Might* – not saying I *will*, if you don't hear from me it won't mean bad news, but—'

'I know. I understand. And – thank you, Rufus. I'm sorry to be so stupid.'

'Oh, nonsense!'

'Caught me off-balance, rather. Just got back from some delivery trips – we're working flat-out, all of us.'

'But you're well, Suzie, are you?'

'I'm – sparking on all cylinders. And you, Rufus?'

'Fine. Listen – will you tell his parents – and your own, of course – that it's postponed? *I'll* tell Patricia.'

'Oh, but she's still away. Long enough this time, I *must* say. Left before you did, didn't she?'

'Yes.' A pause . . . 'Yes. She did.'

'Well.' Suzie crossed her fingers. 'Any day now, I'm sure. Don't worry – she *will* come back to you.'

'To me?'

'She *is* my sister. We don't have all that many secrets from each other.'

'And?'

'And good luck – to you both. I only wish—'

'You've no idea how long she thought she'd be away?'

'No. Not sure she ever knows. But—'

'No . . . Well – changing the subject – slightly – I gather Diana's not on the home base at this moment?'

'Stuck out somewhere. I could find out where, if you like.'

'No – thanks. She'll telephone, when she can. She knows we were due in about this time.'

'Three days ago, I thought.'

'Some married life, eh?'

'Well – exactly . . . Your example right under my nose, and I – truly must be raving *mad*!'

'I don't think so. Not at all. It won't be like this for ever, Suzie – not for you, I mean. Light at the end of the tunnel, that's the thing to keep in mind. Chris'll be through the wringer too, remember, with your flying . . . But – well, as someone we both know tends to say – *Alles sal reg kom*. Huh?'

The quote, in Afrikaans and meaning 'All will come right in the end', was a phrase used quite often by Diana, Rufus Chalk's blonde and leggy South African-born wife. She was an ATA Flight Captain now: was also, incidentally, seeing rather a lot of a Belgian ferry pilot by the name of Jacques Vernet. Of whom Rufus had probably never heard ... The Germanic-sounding aphorism was an irritant in the back of Suzie's mind: partly because she had good reason to know that it was not by any means always to be counted on. Unlike Rufus Chalk, who always *could* be. She was seeing him in her mind's eye – tall, red-headed, stooping slightly at the 'phone, with that thoughtful, quietly determined look of his: quiet-voiced too, telling her, 'Don't worry about Chris. No reason to – honestly. A few weeks' delay isn't the end of the world, is it. Suzie dear – look after yourself?'

'Well – you too. And – thanks, for—'

He'd hung up – cutting short the thanks he didn't need, and leaving a whisper in her mind as the line went dead, *I love you too ...*

Chapter 2

JUNE 1937

For Rufus Chalk it started four years earlier, four years almost to the day – or rather evening, the evening on which he first set eyes on Suzie Cameron-Green. The calendar date wasn't in his mind, but he knew it was the day the Duke of Windsor married Mrs Simpson, which establishes it as 26 June 1937; and he had a clear visual and audial memory of Suzie's father, Sir Innes, holding a match to the bowl of a pipe and muttering between puffs, 'So they're man and wife now. Ye Gods!'

There'd been mention of the wedding on the six o'clock news, to which they'd just been listening; and in the same bulletin a report of the fall of Santander to General Franco's troops.

'Damnable. Really – damnable'. Sir Innes dropped the spent match into the cut-off end of a brass shell-case. 'But—' lowering himself into a vast and rather decrepit armchair, and gazing across the room at Chalk – 'at any rate it's over and done with, now. Water under the bridge – long live the King, eh?'

George VI had been crowned six weeks earlier. Chalk had been a brother officer's guest on board a destroyer at

Spithead for the Coronation Review of the fleet a week after that event. He raised his glass of malt whisky: 'Send him victorious.'

Sir Innes nodded. 'We *are* going to have a war, aren't we. Question is, will we be ready for it?'

'Question of the hour, sir, isn't it.' He put the heavy tumbler down. 'But it depends how long they give us, I suppose.'

Actually the Navy by and large wasn't in such bad shape, thanks to the admirals having played their cards skilfully in recent years. But the other Services – well, the Army, for instance – one had heard on ostensibly good authority that infantry battalions were still only allowed two Lewis guns, one for stripping-down drill and one for firing practice. Effectively one machine-gun to each battalion. Barely credible ... Glancing at his host, whom he knew from his brother Guy to have been a major in the Seaforths in the last war, he decided that to invite confirmation might be less than tactful. He asked him instead – *very* tactfully, considering he couldn't be far short of sixty – 'Are you on the Reserve, sir?'

'No.' Fingering his grey moustache. 'No longer – alas.' A squarish face softening somewhat into jowls, thinning but still mostly dark hair turning more white than grey at the temples ... 'But tell me now – this submarine you're building here—' the pipe-stem jabbed vaguely southward, the direction of Glasgow and the upper reaches of the Clyde – 'You did say, didn't you, that *you* are building it?'

'Standard phraseology, sir. Misleading if you took it literally. Actually one's appointed to "stand by" the ship while she takes shape – in this instance, in Barlows' yard.'

'Barlows', eh. Fellow there I know slightly – Buchanan. He's been here to shoot. Can't remember why – someone must have brought him ... Financial director, that what he calls himself?'

'I haven't met him.' Chalk added, 'The people I deal with

are the yard managers and foremen, mostly. Admiralty officials from time to time. Nothing as rarefied as directors. So far, anyway – I've only been on the job a week.'

'We inveigled you out here rather precipitately, I'm afraid.'

'Well – very kind, sir, extremely so—'

'That young brother of yours – blame *him*. And my wife – almost certainly egged on by our younger daughter . . .'

Sir Innes reached for his glass. They were in what was called the smoking-room, in this gaunt old house, Glendar-ragh, on the Perthshire–Argyll border. The room led off from the cavernous entrance hall: it was comparatively narrow for its length, with a high-ceiling, a tall sash window at the far end and smoke-stained timbers around the fireplace. It could as well have been called the rod-room, judging by the number of fly-rods and associated gear that lay around.

'So how do you spend your days at the shipyard? Does it keep you busy?'

'It does, actually. In the normal course of events I wouldn't have been appointed yet – my CO would have been first on the scene. Plus an engineer. Then someone like me, and a handful of senior ratings, others as the job progresses. I'm first lieutenant – second-in-command. So happens my skipper-to-be hasn't yet got home from the China Station, so I'm as it were holding the fort.'

'Keeping a sharp eye over the builders' shoulders, is that it?'

Chalk nodded. 'An eye on progress generally, and watch-ing points of detail. There are always options – practical things based on one's own experience in other submarines. And of course a mass of paperwork – Admiralty stuff, stores lists and so on. The engineer I have with me was here first, he's seen her taking shape on the stocks more or less from the word go. She was launched only a few weeks ago, you see.'

'And how long—'

'To completion, best part of a year.'

'As long as *that*!'

He nodded. 'Does seem slow. If war becomes really imminent I'm sure everything'll move into high gear pretty smartly, but that's how it is now. Barlows have one other submarine of the same class that was laid down about ten months ahead of mine – *Trumpeter*, my boat's name is *Threat* – and *Trumpeter*'s completion trials are scheduled for late August.'

'All start with "T", do they?'

'It's a new class, sir. In this first batch we're getting fifteen. They're being built in a number of different yards – here on the Clyde – two at Scotts – and at Birkenhead, and Chatham – oh, Vickers, at Barrow ... Mind you, we're still building the "S" class, obviously.'

'Nothing obvious about it as far as I'm concerned. Total damn mystery, to me. In fact the very notion of going under water – my boy, wild horses wouldn't—'

'It's nothing like you probably imagine sir. I'd guarantee that if you spent half a day at sea with us you'd have a completely different view.'

'I would indeed. I'd have died of fright ... All this building, though – other ships as well as submarines, presumably, I'm told all the shipyards are busy now – must amount to a major naval expansion – am I right?'

'Not as "major" as most of us think it should be. Surface ships, for instance, we're building quite a few destroyers, but nothing like enough. I could try to explain that – if I can without boring you ... Well – submarines, since that's what I know most about – under the terms of the London Treaty we were left with an available tonnage for this new "T" class of 16,500 tons. We need no fewer than fifteen of them, for a start, simply to replace old submarines that really shouldn't still be in commission. And that's what's led to fixing the "T"-class displacement at 1100 tons – 400 tons smaller than some they're replacing. Better, for sure, better in all respects, but smaller. You see, we stick to our treaty obligations, we don't cheat. Whereas the Germans, although under the Treaty of Versailles they aren't allowed any submarines – therefore don't need crews either – a few years ago they connived with the Finns to have a new German-designed U-boat built there – in Finland, ostensibly for the Finnish navy – and they've been using her for an undercover training programme. At Hango, in Finland, every year from late spring up to September when the ice sets in. So by now they've a good number of trained U-boat men ready for the "off" – by which time you can bet they'll have gone into mass-production of the same boat in their own yards.'

'And we've been aware of this going on?'

Since '35, to my certain knowledge. A man I served under – out in Aden during the Abyssinian crisis, as it happens – actually got the details – including builders' plans of the U-boat – from some contact he had in Finland, and forwarded it all to the Director of Naval Intelligence. Where it went from there, God knows, but – that much is plain fact, sir.'

'I'd say it's damned alarming!'

'Oh, Daddy.' A girl's voice. 'Don't say *you're* alarmed . . .'

The door from the hall had been opened quietly: and this had to be Suzie, Chalk realized. She was wearing jodhpurs, and a green shirt that hung outside them; dark-brown, unruly-looking hair curled around her ears. It could only be her, and he'd have recognized her anyway from his brother's ravings – Guy was mad about her – but he also thought the ravings had barely done her justice. Vividly blue eyes under the tumble of dark hair, and wide cheek-bones: mouth open at this moment, laughing – as she staggered, clutching at the door for support, an overweight black labrador almost knocking her down as it cantered in. She'd told it, 'You're supposed to be a dog, not a hippo!' Sir Innes had turned back to Chalk: 'I simply cannot understand how or why our people should have kept quiet about such a thing ...' He allowed the interruption, then: 'My younger daughter, Susan. Suzie, Lieutenant Rufus Chalk, Royal Navy.'

She came on in: stepping over the dog, which had flopped down in a heap at Sir Innes' feet. Guy's descriptive powers had failed badly, he thought: at close range she was even more strikingly attractive than he'd thought initially. About eighteen, he guessed – right for Guy, who was twenty-one. Then he remembered – she was seventeen. Certainly no child: the green shirt swung loose but not loosely enough to disguise the fact that it was very adequately filled.

'Heard lots about you.' Her voice was pleasantly low-pitched. He was on his feet, with her hand in his; she told him, 'You're Guy's hero – I suppose you know?'

They talked about Guy again later, over a quiet family supper – a salmon killed the day before by Sir Innes, followed by summer pudding. There'd been reference to the Cameron-Greens' son Alastair, who was a subaltern recently out of Sandhurst and currently stationed at Fort George – he'd followed his father into the Seaforth Highlanders – and Sir Innes told Rufus that he suspected Guy was rather wishing now that he'd 'gone for a soldier' instead of into land management.

'Never said anything to me about it. But you've seen a lot more of him recently than I have, of course.'

Guy was at the Royal Agricultural College, in Gloucestershire, with about another year to do, and last year he'd spent a period of six months on release from the course for practical experience as a trainee-assistant to the factor on this estate. He'd landed up here through the good offices of his and Rufus' sister Betty, who'd overlapped with the Cameron-Greens' elder daughter Patricia at Cambridge. Betty – who was now married, and in fact pregnant – had written to Patricia, who'd done the rest.

'We're *very* fond of him.' Eve Cameron-Green's ice-blue

eyes smiled. She was wearing blue, too: a long, rather tubular dress of some material that shimmered in the lamplight. She had a fine-boned, pretty face: the eyes looked bigger than they were, in that delicate bone-structure. Nose and forehead almost identical to Suzie's: eyes quite a different blue, though. A pretty woman, must have been *very* pretty as a girl – but nothing like as – frankly – sensational, as her younger daughter. She was saying – about Guy – 'And – did I tell you in my note that he's promised to spend most if not all of his summer holiday here? Anyway, he *has* – and as you're so near, *any* time you have free you'll be very welcome. Just telephone and say you're coming. Or don't bother to telephone, just come!'

'You're astonishingly kind, Lady Cameron-Green.'

'I don't know why it should be astonishing,' she laughed. 'We'd love it, and you two can make up for having seen so little of each other. Patricia will be here too, of course. I just *hope* she won't be a bag of nerves, worrying about her exam results.'

Patricia was twenty-two and about to graduate from Girton. Guy had described her as 'awfully nice but a bit of a blue-stocking': and Rufus hoped to goodness – alerted by the apparent bracketing of that invitation with the information that she'd be here too – that there were no ulterior motives which might explain the warmth of his own reception.

There couldn't be. Guy must surely have told them that he was engaged. He'd have told Suzie, anyway – having told her practically every other damn thing there *was* to tell. Mentioning it confidentially, perhaps – since the engagement hadn't been announced yet; this would explain why none of them had referred to it.

Sir Innes cleared his throat. 'Your brother told me when he was here that he was thinking of trying his luck in Kenya – when that college throws him out.'

'Yes, I know. That he'd thought of it, I mean. But I don't know how far he'd—'

'He was thinking of going to fight in Spain, too.' Suzie watched Rufus across the table as she interrupted. An elegant Suzie now – in a floor-length, dark-red skirt and a cream blouse, her dark hair swept back and a gold chain bracelet on her wrist. She'd seen his surprise, and nodded. 'Fact. I told him I thought it would be an *idiotic* thing to do.'

'I couldn't agree with you more!'

'Imagine it. Guy of all people – never met a Spaniard in his life, he admitted that – to go rushing out there to a war that's got nothing to do with him – and as likely as not get *killed*—'

'Suzie, please . . .'

'Mummy, boys *are* being killed – English ones included – and on both sides, too! It's a fact. Alastair was here when Guy brought up the subject, and he knows quite a lot about it – Alastair does – and he asked him which side he'd join if he did go. Well, Guy was absolutely stunned, the Loyalists – International Brigade, that crowd – was the only side that to his mind anyone might *think* of joining. Alastair asked him if he realized he'd be fighting alongside communists and Russians, the people who murdered their Tsar and his children and did filthy things to thousands of other people – all right, they aren't *all* communists, but the other side aren't all fascists either, a lot of them are just individuals who loathe communism. In fact, the main reason the Army started the rebellion in the first place was they could see a Russian-type revolution happening in Spain if they didn't. Well—' she shrugged – 'that's the gospel according to Alastair. And I think Patricia agreed with him. I don't know the first thing about it, I'm not in the least bit politically minded, but I do see the point – when each side's doing horrible things to the other, how do you choose?'

'Much better *not*, I should say!'

'Quite.' Sir Innes nodded to his wife. 'Certainly for young Guy.'

'Exactly.' Suzie looked back at Rufus. 'Shall I tell you what I think's behind it?'

He nodded. With the passing thought that as well as being decorative she had her head screwed on pretty firmly. 'Please.'

'You. He admires you tremendously, you're a man of action, authority—'

'Oh ...' He gestured ... 'Anyway, how would that mistaken view of me give him the notion of going to Spain?'

'Because as I said before, you're his hero, and he feels he's got to do something to – well, earn your respect, I suppose.'

'He wouldn't do it that way.' He added, 'He's got as much of my respect as he needs, in any case.'

Her mother said, frowning at her, 'This is the first *I*'ve heard of the Spanish idea, Suzie.'

'Well – it's Guy's business – and only *talk* ...'

'Might be part and parcel of what I was saying earlier on.' Sir Innes nodded at Rufus. 'An idea he'd rather go soldiering than farming.' He glanced at his wife. 'You haven't heard about that either. No reason you should have, either – only a suspicion I've had that he may be rather envious of Alastair.'

'All this war-talk, I suppose. It's pernicious. Every time one looks at a newspaper or turns on the wireless ...' Eve frowned at her husband: 'But if he feels like that, why doesn't he join the Territorials? He could have his cake and eat it – go soldiering, and still finish at his college. Why not suggest it to him, Innes?'

'If they'd give him the time off for it – as they well might. Might be obliged to ...' Staring at his wife: 'My dear – that's really a top-hole idea!'

'*Well.*' Her eyebrows hooped. 'Would you *believe* it. *I* have had a good idea. Heavens, whatever next?' Glancing round then, as the elderly manservant came back into the room. 'We'll have coffee in the drawing-room please, MacKenzie.'

He'd accepted a glass of brandy and a cigar. Sir Innes meanwhile talking about friends he had in Kenya who might be useful to Guy if he did decide to try his luck out there.

Guy was the king-pin in all this, obviously. It would be for Suzie's sake – she, he guessed, being the apple of her parents' eyes. Even though Guy didn't have a penny to his name or even any real sense of direction yet. Perhaps they'd decided he'd be worth waiting for?

Perhaps he would be, too. Despite certain interludes of apparent lunacy in past years – in the light of which this Spanish notion might not be out of character, come to think of it – Rufus had always known he could have done a lot worse, in the draw for a younger brother.

'On the subject of Spain, Chalk—' Sir Innes had his cigar going properly, at last – 'I was thinking, when Suzie was talking her head off – the best of all reasons for your brother to stay well clear – at any rate if it's the government side he'd join – is that the fascists look odds-on to win. Uh?'

He nodded. 'Santander yesterday, for example. And Bilbao only last week.'

'Where'd he be *then*?'

'I know. I'll talk him out of it. *If* he's serious – which I very much hope he isn't.'

'I read that Mussolini's got fifty thousand men in Spain now. Fifty thousand!'

'Quantity to make up for lack of quality. The Loyalists smashed a whole army of 'em, didn't they, two or three months ago, place called – well, begins with "B"? Saved Madrid in the process. Didn't the Italians break and run?' He shrugged. 'I'd say they were in their element using flame-throwers against half-naked Abyssinians, but that's about their limit.'

'You were in Aden in '35, you said?'

'In a Home Fleet submarine. One of half a dozen L-class boats sent out there, with a depot-ship. We were praying we'd be given our heads, but of course no such luck. You know, sir, we could have stopped that invasion in its tracks, if we'd been allowed to. The Mediterranean Fleet could have – on its own. Closed the Canal to them, to start with, and then if they wanted a fight – wiped 'em up.'

'Shame we didn't. Might've stopped the rot elsewhere.' Sir Innes brushed ash off his smoking-jacket. 'Stopped Mussolini, anyway. Might've stopped Hitler last year too, when he re-occupied the Rhineland. Eh?'

'D'you think we could have?'

'You mean you think Baldwin was right. Inadequate forces, and anyway the people wouldn't have stood for it.'

Chalk nodded. 'I'd say he judged the public mood about right, sir. More's the pity. And as you say, we were hardly in shape – especially as the French weren't going to back us up?'

Baldwin had gone now. Retired, three weeks ago, and Neville Chamberlain had taken over as head of a National ministry. Sir Innes was saying – about Baldwin – '– judged the mood right on the Abdication, too. Unlike certain others one could name.'

'Churchill.'

'First and foremost, certainly. Although – well, how much of his thinking was actually bad judgement – or romanticism – and how much a matter of trying to use the situation to oust Baldwin – the real issue between them being rearmament?'

'Wouldn't that still have been misjudgement?'

'Indeed.' Sir Innes nodded. 'In fact it must have set back his rearmament campaign. A politician's most passionate arguments tend to fall on deaf ears when he's put a foot in it once too many. As Churchill certainly has.'

Chalk shook his head. 'I can't claim to be very well informed, in those areas.'

'Well ...' A shrug. 'Blotted his copybook over India,

didn't he. Then the Gold Standard ... But we were talking about Abyssinia – stopping Mussolini. Really poisonous fellow that, you know. Streak of violence in him right from childhood – stabbed a schoolmate in the bum with his penknife, at a very early age, never looked back since. Spent some period in Switzerland sleeping in public lavatories. I was reading a magazine article about him ... And what about this Frenchwoman – actress – twenty times in one day?'

'La Fontange ...'

'Odd thing to boast about, in public. Eh?'

'Well – yes ...'

A fleeting image of Mussolini with long ears, like a buck rabbit jumping on and off ... Sir Innes was saying, 'And he has nothing to gain – according to what I've read – from meddling in that war. Except self-esteem – his own view of himself as Caesar sending forth the legions.' Sir Innes paused, expelling a cloud of smoke. 'The Germans, on the other hand, know *exactly* what they're about. A major attraction to them, I'm told, is that Spain is a source of certain minerals which are vitally important to their own war industry. *And* of course a proving-ground for new weaponry and tactics. Bombing techniques for instance, as at Guernica – getting their eye in, eh?'

'If it's not a painful subject—' Eve Cameron-Green touched his hand – 'your father was killed in 1918 – flying?'

'Yes. In the Royal Naval Air Service. Over the trenches, but—'

'Frightfully sad.' She sighed. 'Innes lost both his brothers. Within a few weeks of each other. He was in France himself too, at the time. Well, *most* of the time ... Do you remember your father?'

'Yes. And acute anxiety, I remember. My mother's – much as she tried to hide it. But I was only eight when he was killed, and obviously we hadn't seen much of him in the war years.'

'Just on his leaves. Yes ... Guy, of course, would only have been a toddler. And your sister – four or five?'

'Five. She was twenty-four the other day.'

'And starting a family, we're told?'

'So *I'm* told.'

Sir Innes broke in, stuffing a pipe as he crossed the room towards them, 'According to intelligence received, you're contemplating matrimony yourself, Chalk. Is the report correct?'

So they *did* know. He was happy to confirm it. 'In a year or so, probably. We haven't announced it yet. Time we did, I suppose.'

'The lass is a pilot, flies her own machine, Guy told us?'

'Yes. Her name's Diana Villiers. She's South African. Takes people joy-riding or on taxi trips. Business men going to conferences, or Nabobs to race-meetings. Over to France quite often – Le Touquet, that sort of thing.'

Sir Innes took the pipe out of his mouth. 'Are her people still in South Africa?'

'In the Cape. Her father has horses – which actually win races, I gather. He also has a fruit farm. Beautiful place, going by the photographs.'

'You haven't been out there – or met her family?'

'No. Met her in London – through a friend of mine who'd been on the South Atlantic station.'

'Is she very pretty?'

'*I* think so, Suzie.'

'Well – let me guess. I have second sight, you know. She's – oh, rather tall, blonde—'

'Chalk Junior *has* been gabbing, hasn't he.'

'Might she—' Eve Cameron-Green cut in – 'if it's not a silly thing to suggest – perhaps it's *much* too far for her to come – might she be persuaded to pay us a flying visit here?'

Driving south in his little car on the Sunday evening, his

thoughts were first that Guy was a very lucky young man, and second that it was going to be marvellous to see something of him – much more than he had in the past few years. And if Diana would come up too – what more could a man ask for? Incredible . . . She *would* come, he felt sure; they'd already discussed her flying up to Glasgow, if or when it fitted in with whatever other commissions she might have.

Inverherive was astern now – as much as there was of it. Crianlarich a mile or so ahead. A turn to starboard there would bring him down to the top end of Loch Lomond. On the port beam he had Ben Lawers bulking hazily against fading blue sky: ahead, Ben More, and back on the quarter Ben Lui and more distantly Ben Cruachan. Beautiful, all of it. It was some years since he'd been up here, but he knew the country reasonably well and he'd checked the map to remind himself of the landmarks. Might make some week-end tours, he thought, show Diana around – if she was ever up here for long enough.

He'd acquired this little Austin about a fortnight ago, never having owned a car before but feeling that it might be advantageous to have one up here. At that stage he'd envisaged its main use as transport for himself – and others, no doubt – between the shipyard and wherever he found digs; he'd still been dithering, tempted by the idea of a car but prudence suggesting it might be wiser to settle for a bicycle, when he'd found this vehicle on offer in a garage in Fareham for thirty pounds. Fareham because he'd been at Blockhouse then, the Gosport submarine base. He'd beaten them down to twenty-seven pounds ten shillings with a tank full of petrol thrown in: not a bad deal, he'd thought – although it was a large enough investment for a lieutenant living on his pay. The car had only done a few thousand miles, and an engineer from the flotilla had looked it over for him and found nothing wrong.

It was brown. On his way up north he'd diverted by way

of Brooklands, the field Diana was operating from in her Fox Moth, to show it to her and to say goodbye. She'd prowled round it – tall and blonde, and that pantherish walk of hers ... Every time he saw her again after yet another period of separation the sight of her really did almost take his breath away.

She'd stopped at the passenger side, smiling at him over its rain-wet roof.

'Well, d'you like it?'

'I'd better, hadn't I?'

'Huh?'

'Love me, love my dog?' She patted it. 'It's sweet, anyway. And you could always change the colour, couldn't you. Bit drab, isn't it? Where are we going for lunch?'

She was off that afternoon, to fly some motor-racing people from Croydon to Le Mans. And he hadn't been able to leave Portsmouth until that morning and was due on the job at Barlows' on the Monday. He'd said to her over the telephone from Blockhouse, the night before, 'How about flying *us* to – well, what about Biarritz?'

'One day.' She'd laughed. 'Why *not*?'

'In a way, I'm serious.'

'For "serious", read "impatient"?'

'Certainly – I admit—'

'Or "importunate". And the telephone, my pet, is hardly the ideal means of communicating that kind of—'

'You're right. We'll discuss it tomorrow.'

'See you then, anyway. It's got to be a very quick and *early* snack, mind.'

'I'll be with you by noon.'

'Bye, darling ...'

That was how it was. For various reasons an early marriage wasn't on the cards, and meanwhile if he didn't love her enough to wait ...

He did. He'd sworn to it about a hundred times.

He told her at Brooklands – answering her question about

lunch – 'Anywhere, as long as it's close. One thing about this paintwork, though, is it won't show dirt. Shower of rain occasionally, Bob's your uncle!'

Her Fox Moth – successor to the Puss Moth she'd had before – was blue and silver, and had cost her seven hundred and fifty pounds – late last year, when he'd been on his way back from Aden. The same amount of money would have bought a new Rolls-Royce, she'd told him.

This little vehicle was all right, though. Certainly no Rolls: you couldn't hear the ticking of the clock, for instance, partly because it didn't have one. But it got along all right. Suzie had said she loved it.

Suzie, he thought, picturing her in his mind: young Guy was a *very* lucky fellow ... Crianlarich coming up ahead now. A left turn would have taken him through Glen Dochart to Killin and Loch Tay. Some other time: with Diana on board, perhaps. That salmon-leap under the Dochart bridge, she'd *have* to see it ...

This afternoon, during an introductory tour of the Campbell-Green estate – Rufus driving this Austin, and Suzie in the back with two terriers named Tartar and Minx – Sir Innes had explained that although the life at Glendarragh was idyllic as far as he and his wife were concerned, they were very conscious that their daughters weren't going to find it so at all, after any length of time. In recent years they'd never been at home for longer than a school holiday – and as often as not had had friends to stay, in any case – but now – 'Take Suzie, there. Adores the place, happy as a lark to spend all day on a horse and as often as not completely on her own – eh?'

'Well, that's true, I am!'

'It won't last, you see. For one thing because despite appearances you're no simpleton—'

'Thanks!'

'—and young people need to consort with other young people. Isn't that so?'

She'd told Rufus, 'It'd break my heart to leave. Truly. I've *longed* to be home!'

'And now you are, and revelling in it. And as long as it lasts, my dear girl, nothing could delight your mother and I more. But how long will it be before you begin to feel marooned here?'

'I don't know why you're so keen to put me off the place!'

'My dear girl, you know perfectly well—'

'I'm *completely* happy – honestly!'

'You know you've got Guy coming for six or eight weeks, don't you. But what if you hadn't?' He'd glanced sideways, at Rufus. 'This is my point, you see. Eve and I are stuck here. And God knows I've no complaints. I've reached an age when – well, often enough I look around and ask myself was ever a man born luckier . . . Oh, look there now – look down there!'

'It's beautiful . . .'

He'd stopped the car. Presently, driving on, climbing a dirt hillside road, Sir Innes began again. 'What I was saying is we know we're going to lose 'em – inevitably, I suppose it happens to all parents – but we don't want to before we have to. That's what it comes down to. I know they'll always come back, after they've flown the coop – depending on circumstances, of course, and their husbands – but that's something else, nothing to do with having them here full-time, a family complete unto itself. Alastair'll always come, I'm certain – whenever he gets a leave. But there again, you see, with a war coming—'

'*That* again . . .'

'Yes, Suzie. Plain truth of it is that this summer – well, Eve's right, could be the last normal, happy one we have for a long time. So let's make the most of it, we thought – liven the place up a bit – have a few chaps like you and Guy around. As I said, with him in the offing we don't have to give another thought to *this* one—'

'Oh, *don't* you!'

'– but Patricia's rather a different case. After Cambridge and quite a bit of London this glen of ours could seem like the back of beyond almost, at first sight. In some ways I suppose it *is*. And she doesn't quite share Suzie's country interests.'

'She does – actually.'

'Nothing like to the same extent.' He looked at Rufus again: 'Anyway, we want to make this a summer to – well, to look back on.'

They'd stopped for a distant view of grazing deer – hinds, and some small calves with them. Driving on again, Suzie told him – returning to the subject of the summer's planned festivities – 'There's one special weekend – end of August – that'll be a *real* hoolie.'

'Silver wedding, Chalk. I suppose it's what's made us think this all out to the extent we have. Milestone in one's life, eh . . . But – do your best to be with us for that one, will you?'

'Thank you. I'll mark it down. Silver – twenty-five years—'

'Married in 1912. Little knowing what we had coming to us then, by George . . .'

Suzie urged him, 'Your fiancée – Diana – ought to fly up for that weekend. Do persuade her?'

'I'll try. If she could, and you had other friends coming up, she might bring them.'

'Gosh, what fun! How many can she fit into her – Fox, did you say it is?'

'Yes. Fox Moth. It has a cabin that holds four, and she drives from an open cockpit behind. But for longer trips if she does without a fourth passenger she can carry extra fuel. Technically – allow me to impress you with this – it's a De Havilland DH83.'

'I *am* impressed!'

'Me too. I'm completely ignorant about aeroplanes.'

'I'd absolutely *love* to fly . . .'

Sir Innes muttered, 'Break your damn neck. Plenty of easier ways . . . See up there – Rufus? Those high crags? There's an eyrie up there – golden eagles. One chick hatched about a month ago – Suzie and Alastair were up there soon after. There were two eggs, he'd been keeping an eye on 'em.'

'It'll be getting its feathers by now, but it was just a ball of white fluff when we saw it.' She laughed. 'Ball of fluff with this little angry face in the middle of it, glaring at us. Alastair said if it was up to him, he'd shoot it.'

'He'd do nothing of the sort.' Sir Innes shook his head. 'You're so easily taken in!'

There was an argument then, as to whether eagles did or did not take new-born lambs, and whether Alastair meant what he'd said or had only been teasing her, knowing how protective she felt towards them. In her view, having golden eagles on the place was well worth a few sickly lambs that probably wouldn't have lived in any case. Her father took up the teasing, then, pointing out that a lot of people would say *that* was a brutal attitude to take.

'Only because they're ignorant. Far more lambs are taken by foxes – which the eagles take – huh? Well, they certainly take fox *cubs* if they get half a chance . . .'

He'd been given yet another invitation – by Suzie's mother, when he'd been on the point of leaving. She'd asked him whether he had any personal friends in other ships or submarines in Clyde yards who might like to come out for a weekend.

Suzie had murmured, 'For Patricia, huh?'

'No, Suzie, that is *not*—'

'Daddy was rattling on about it this afternoon – young men so thin on the ground, keep the girls at home, Suzie's all right because she's got Guy—'

'I'm quite sure he didn't mean it that way at all. He certainly wouldn't have been as – *blatant* as you make it sound.' She turned back to Rufus. 'But we'll be having a biggish party here in August—'

'Your anniversary.'

'Oh, they told you—'

'A hoolie – whatever that—'

'It's a word Suzie favours. Actually it's of Hindu origin. Brought back here by old soldiers, I imagine. Anyway, young men *are* few and far between. Everyone we know has daughters. And Alastair may not be here to bring *his* friends – you realize, Suzie – if he's been posted by then?'

To a large extent, of course, the welcome they'd extended to him stemmed from the two existing Chalk/Cameron-Green friendships – Suzie's with Guy, and Patricia's with Betty. He'd come in on the same ticket, so to speak. He cautioned himself, negotiating the long curve of road bending gradually southward toward Ardlui, not to take too much advantage of it. He had to keep in mind that he was here to build a submarine: at this stage, in fact, he was that submarine's acting CO. Not at all a situation in which to risk falling down on the job by giving it less than his full attention.

He'd ring Diana, anyway. Have a word with Guy too. He frowned – with the loch ahead of him, its water lead-coloured in this failing light. Headlight time ... He was frowning at the recollection of Guy's threat about Spain. It might have been just talk, of course: in which case the best thing would be not to mention it, risk stirring up something which might otherwise continue to lie dormant. Better just keep an ear to the ground and be ready to quash any such notion if it was mooted.

Chalk asked me – more than half a century after the weekend he'd been describing – 'Is it going to work, d'you think? Will you be able to translate these random recollections into a lucid narrative?'

'Can't see why not. It's what I'm for.'

He smiled. Captain Rufus Chalk, DSO and bar, DSC and bar, RN (Retired). 'Comforting – I imagine – to know *that*.'

'Well – let's say it's my way of scratching a living. But answering your question – as we agreed, I'll be bridging any gaps with a touch of novelist's licence – bits you may be vague about or where events were beyond your ken anyway – and you can approve or disapprove the end-product – within reason?'

'As long as it ends where I say it ends.'

'That's agreed.'

He'd made this point before. Despite which his eyes were on mine, and insistent, as he repeated it. Blue eyes in a tanned, still well-muscled face: amazing, really. Telling me, 'No novelist's licence beyond that point. No further research elsewhere, either. Full stop.'

I touched the little tape-recorder. 'Switch off, finish.'

'Very well, then.' He moved his head, indicating the house behind us – former farmhouse, with this large stone terrace which he'd built to take advantage of the view across Glandore Bay. This is in West Cork; I'd heard he was there and written to him, and he'd replied that his wife was going to be away in England the week after next – a grandchild's birth expected, and he couldn't go with her 'on account of the dogs'. (They bred red setters, I'd since learnt.) He couldn't put me up, he'd written – he'd be 'pigging it', on his own – but there was a decent hotel in the village.

So here we were. He was saying, 'I've a snap of that Baby Austin – if you'd like to see it. Other stuff too – including snapshots. Report of the Tribunal of Inquiry – you'll want that.'

'I'd like to borrow whatever you have – after we've got an outline on tape.'

'You can take it all away with you. I was casting an eye over it last night, refreshing my outworn memory. It's the connections that link the brain-cells that wear out, I'm told.

Can't remember what they're called . . . Where was I, now?'

'Passing Crianlarich southbound for Dunbarton, where you said you'd found yourself some digs.'

'Two rooms – bed and sitting – and the use of a bathroom. Breakfast and evening meal laid on. A Mrs Blair: a strikingly – er – substantial widow.'

'Not so much wrong with the memory, I'd say.'

'No one could *possibly* forget Mrs Blair!'

'Ah . . . Anyway, when you got back you telephoned your fiancée – and your brother?'

'Yes. I must have. But thinking of it – the Cameron-Greens' generous hospitality – well, that Sunday afternoon when Sir Innes and Suzie came in my motor on a tour of the estate – not all of it, of course, a lot of it's steep hillside, forested, and the bare tops which take a bit of getting up to, I can tell you—'

'That Sunday afternoon, you said—'

'Yes. By the end of it, when Lady Cameron-Green asked me to rope in a chum to join the summer's frolics, an obvious candidate sprang to mind. Man by name of Dymock.'

He'd grimaced. I waited, and he added after a moment – his face averted, eyes resting on the ruffled water in the entrance to the bay – 'Worst mistake I ever made.'

Chapter 3

At about eight next morning he drove in between Barlows' tall iron gates and parked his car behind the shed they called the Submarine Office. It faced the fitting-out basin – on the far side of which a more or less submarine-shaped object surrounded by a platform of floating timber was eventually to become His Majesty's Submarine *Threat*. It wasn't yet: in Barlows' books it was Job No. 1793. Still an 'it', rather than a 'she'. The job number was stencilled on every sheet of steel currently being welded to a grid-like framework on top of her pressure-hull: her casing, that grid would become, a steel deck on which men could walk when she was on the surface but through which the sea would flood when she dived. Chalk lit his first cigarette of the day: inhaled deeply as he studied her. Studied *it* – bare steel glittering in the flare of oxyacetylene torches and elsewhere patched and streaked tawdry-bright with red lead, and the sparking of flame from the torches reflected in the basin's scummy water.

Festoons of electric cables leading into the embryo's hatches from shoreside powerpoints was evidence that work was in progress inside as well. And it would be oven-like in there within an hour or so, he realized. The sky was clear, there wasn't even a light breeze and the sun was already well up. As it would be over Glendarragh too by this time. One could visualize that scene – as a dreamlike contrast to this one: sun poking over the hills to flood the glen and flush the stone of the house and outbuildings, and the hills' tops clear against blue sky. Just up the road, you might say, but – another world entirely. Inhabited by different creatures? The harshness of the contrast – here – brought a line of Kipling's to his mind: *Reeking tube and iron shard* . . . Glancing to his left to where on this near side of the basin *Threat*'s sister-ship *Trumpeter* lay stern-on to him, and in a comparatively advanced state. Externally, in fact, *Trumpeter* was complete. She'd be commissioning, in two or three weeks' time, would be wearing the White Ensign when they started on the series of tests and inspections culminating in her Final Acceptance Trials.

Lucky beggars, he thought.

He dropped his cigarette-end and put his toe on it, crossed stone paving to the entrance of the Submarine Office – up two wooden steps into a central passageway which ran between cubicle-like offices – *Trumpeter*'s first, glass-topped doors marked *General Office*, *Commanding Officer*, *Engineer Officer*, *Stores* – then his own ship's similarly labelled, and in one of them *Threat*'s Commissioned Warrant Engineer, Nat Eason, was stooped over a mass of blueprints and other drawings. Chalk pushed the door open: 'Morning, Chief.'

Eason glanced round. As usual, with a cigarette jutting. 'In for a bloody scorcher, eh?'

'Looks like it. What's new?'

'What's on the desk in there.' Checking the time: the fag-end was between thumb and forefinger as he straightened, smoke drifting from thin lips and nostrils. 'Good weekend?'

'Marvellous, Chief. Yours?'

'Fair.' Eason stubbed out the cigarette in the lid of a Players tin, and nodded. 'Fair.' He was a smallish, wiry man;

Warrant Engineer meant that he'd been commissioned from the lower deck – come up the hard way. He could have been a horseman: sinewy frame, broad shoulders, flinty grey eyes deepset. He paused in the doorway: 'Yeah, one thing. Bow-cap indicators – they'll have 'em arsy-tarsy if they get *their* way.'

'How d'you mean?'

'Fit 'em same as bloody *Trumpeter*'s, won't they.' He pointed with his head at the heap of blueprints. 'I checked *Trumpeter*'s drawings too. Want to come down, I'll show you?'

'They're not fitted yet, surely?'

'In *Trumpeter*, I'm saying. Leave 'em to it, they'll fix us up the same ... Look – you got your six indicator dials – right?'

Chalk stared at him. Bow-caps were the front doors on torpedo tubes, the missiles' exits when they were fired, and the indicators inside allowed torpedomen to see at a glance whether they were open or shut. This was obviously essential, since if a rear door were to be opened when the bowcap on that tube was already open you'd have the sea gushing straight in.

He nodded, waiting for the rest of it.

'Five from top is number six. Five's at the bottom, six where five *oughter* be. Strictly as per the drawings, this is – would you believe it?'

At periscope depth, thirty-two feet say, which was where you'd be when you were exercising tube drill or firing practice torpedoes, the weight and force of that inrush of sea would be – murderous, irresistible. A nightmarish vision: not *new*, one did have to contemplate all such eventualities, the disaster scenarios, in order to guard against their occurrence and – God forbid – to be prepared to cope with them, if they happened ... Eason shrugging, muttering 'You know how they are, these fellers. Here's the drawings – all right, some bugger cocked it up, we *know* that, but it's still how we got to do it – as laid down, right? Squaring their own yardarms, that's what – they got the blueprint they can point to and they're in the clear – eh? So in *Trumpeter* it's how they're bloody *leaving* it. But look, sir – if you'd get that Hamilton geyser by the short an' curlies—'

'I will. Right away.' Hamilton was Ship Manager in this yard – a personage, one of the bowler hats. Chalk added, 'I'd better see it for myself first. Don't doubt you, Chief, but he can't bull me then, can he?'

'Want to bet?'

The engineer took a caustic view of bowler hats. Stooping over his drawings again . . . Chalk decided that his own desk-work could wait. Visiting *Trumpeter* now he'd kill two birds with one stone: check on this bow-cap problem, and have a word aside to Toby Dymock, who was *Trumpeter*'s First Lieutenant – second-in-command – as he himself was, or rather would be, in *Threat*.

Dymock wasn't hard to find: he was on the fore casing, in conversation with his CO, a lieutenant-commander by name of Pargeter. Dymock, of fairly rugged construction, looked almost willowy beside Pargeter, who was shorter and stocky with an aggressive stance to match: legs braced apart, bunched fists on his hips . . . Glancing round at Chalk as he came abreast of them on the stone-flagged quay; Dymock called 'Morning, Rufus', and Pargeter told him, 'Come aboard. Got news for you.'

About the bow-cap indicators, he guessed, as he crossed the narrow, ribbed plank that bridged the gap between the quay and *Trumpeter*'s casing. The plank's inboard end rested about midway between the submarine's gun and her fore hatch, and below him as he crossed it scummy water lapped the bulge of saddle-tank: newly-painted and already oil-stained. They'd have to paint ship again when she was out of the yard's hands, he guessed. Turning forward; a hinged flap of the casing was open and he edged round it, one hand up to the jumping-wire. Then around the fore hatch, which in harbour was effectively the submarine's front door. Lights inside shone on the gleam of new white enamel paint, and you could smell it. A sailor's voice was raised in song: *Nothing else would matter in the world today . . .*

He saluted 'Jacko' Pargeter. 'News, sir?'

'Yes. Of your skipper.'

Trumpeter's stared up at him. Brown, rather sad eyes, reminiscent of a bloodhound's, seemed to belie the man-of-action stance. 'He'll be joining on the twelfth. Means he and his wife'll be up here the weekend of tenth/eleventh. We're – ah – finding them a billet – something for a couple of months, then they can take over the place we're in. My wife and Margaret Ozzard are old friends, you see.'

'Well, that's—'

'He's been stuck at Palma – Majorca – recently. Did you know?'

'No, sir.' Chalk showed his surprise. All he'd known this far was that Ozzard was bringing an L-class boat home from the China Station.

Pargeter explained, 'Diverted there after calling in at Malta. Apparently we have a squadron based at Palma now – *Hood* included – keeping an eye on the Italians who've been throwing their weight about on the Spanish coast. Approaches to Alicante and Barcelona, for instance. It was news to me too.'

Chalk said, 'There've been rumours, of course, that they've been getting up to no good on that coast.'

'In support of Franco.' Dymock, stating the obvious. 'Blockading the Loyalists' supplies. Franco and Co having virtually no navy of their own.'

'Sinking ships without warning, is the truth of it.' Pargeter gazed sadly at his first lieutenant. He added, 'Neutrals. No warning – and no opposition, of course. Money for old rope: right up the Italians' street, eh? Call it a blockade, if you like: but they've no damn business interfering in someone else's civil war.'

'The *Mirror* was right, then – a week or so ago.'

'Not *only* the *Mirror*, Toby.'

Chalk said – indicating Dymock – 'All he reads, sir. But *we* should be giving them some opposition. If it weren't for the dead hand of the Foreign Office, I suppose – all-same Abyssinia—'

'Yes. Yes, exactly ... Anyway, that's the news, Chalk. Ozzard's been relieved now, he's on his way home by train through France and he'll be with you here by the twelfth.'

'Heady days of freedom numbered, Rufus!'

Dymock, smiling that film-starish smile of his ... Not, Chalk thought – by no means for the first time – that he could help the way he looked. Other men, one knew, tended to look askance at him, on account of those 'Flash Harry' looks and rumours of his allegedly numerous successes with women. He'd said to Chalk once, 'I can't help it if they like the look of me. I don't try harder than anyone else does. Anyway, it's not all *that* frequent ...' The plain fact was – to Chalk – that he was a good friend and a good submariner, and they'd known each other all their naval lives, from Dartmouth onward. They'd arrived there as thirteen-year-old cadets in '23, had gone to sea in the training cruiser as cadets in 1928, becoming midshipmen in the fleet in '29 and both joining the same submarine training course in '32.

He told Pargeter – in reference to 'Ozzie' Ozzard, *Threat*'s appointed CO – 'I'll be gla ' to have him here. Apart from anything else, for some fire-power when it's needed. Why I'm here now, for instance – I'm told there's a problem with bow-cap indicators?'

Dymock nodded. 'Surely is. These damned *idiots*—'

'Take him down and show him.' Pargeter turned away. 'Meanwhile, Number One, if you want me you'll find me in the office – until about mid-forenoon anyway.'

'Aye aye, sir.'

'You're fully justified in digging your heels in over this, Chalk. Dig 'em in hard, if I were you. Too late in our case, it'd mean a delay to the schedule, and that's one thing we can't afford. But in point of fact the whole system's wrong, in my view – and that you *won't* get changed.'

Chalk's fingers touched the peak of his cap, as Pargeter left them. He asked Dymock, 'What whole system's wrong?'

'The bowcap operating levers. Instead of the pointers showing either "shut" or "open", there's a neutral position. It's the new thing, Admiralty-approved. Come on down, I'll show you.' Starting towards the fore hatch, he glanced back: 'Good weekend, Rufus?'

'First class. And as it happens I've an invitation for next weekend which includes you. Or for the one after – wouldn't matter. Are you free for either – or both?'

'I – don't know, exactly. I mean thanks, but – life's a bit complicated, just at the moment. I'm thinking of buzzing down to London, in fact, this next weekend. But then again – look, let's get this inspection over, eh?'

He rattled down the upper part of the sloping steel ladder, grasped a projection overhead and swung himself down the rest of the way, landing on his toes on the corticene-covered deck below, Chalk following suit.

'Look out for wet paint.'

'Bet your life!'

'Probably for'ard too.' Nodding towards the Tube Space, where they were going. He asked a torpedoman in dungarees, 'Still wet around the tubes, is it, Harrison?'

'Shouldn't be, sir. Except in spots, you might find.'

'We'll try not to.'

This compartment – the Torpedo Stowage Compartment, more usually referred to as the Fore Ends – in which there'd be three reload torpedoes in the racks on each side, and in which the torpedomen and some others would sleep, was about 25 feet long and 16 wide – 16 feet being in fact the internal diameter of the pressure-hull. And forward of this – where Dymock led now, stepping over and around electric cables, tool-boxes, paint-pots and men at work – was the Tube Space. Heavy watertight doors, one to port and one to starboard and both latched open now, gave access to it – actually to a shelf of decking behind the upper four tubes' rear doors. Smaller, separate bulkhead doors below the level of the platform were for use when loading torpedoes into the bottom pair of tubes. The tubes were of a size to hold 21-inch-diameter torpedoes; the six of them filled most of the space even at this after end of the compartment, and just about all of it at the bow end where it narrowed. Whatever space wasn't occupied by the tubes was filled with a mass of piping and firing gear that served them: all of it, each pipe and valve, familiar, instantly identifiable to Chalk and Dymock as they wormed their way forward between the various projections, checking carefully for wet paint as they went.

'There you are.' Pointing. 'Number five at the bottom, and six where five *should* be.'

Nat Eason had been right, anyway. Chalk asked Dymock as they made their way back towards the platform, 'Did I understand your skipper correctly – that you're leaving this as it is?'

'We really haven't much option. Changing it would mean pretty well taking all this lot out again. Or so we're told. Could be a case of bullshit baffling brains, but – well, for instance it's a fact that a team's due up from Pompey this week to check the tubes' alignment, and if we put 'em off we mightn't get 'em back for a month of bloody Sundays. And—' he joined Chalk on the ledge behind the tubes – 'as the skipper mentioned, we're on a tight schedule. Final acceptance trials last week in August, for instance – and he's dead against allowing any postponement.'

'What's the rush?'

'Can't really tell you. Except they want this class at sea

and operational, and we're supposed to keep our place in the queue. Skippers may have been told to push things along at all costs, for all I know.'

'Might be more effective to tell the yards that.' Chalk added, stooping and peering forward to where they'd just been, 'You can see number five indicator from here, you know—'

'Can indeed – if you hang upside down like a bloody bat!'

'– and there's a lot more wrong than five being where six should be, isn't there?'

'You mean the positions of the pointers.'

He nodded, checking the rest of the dials. 'Vary from one to the other, don't they?'

The bowcap indicator dials were circular metal discs five or six inches in diameter, with a brass pointer on each that circled to point at 'shut' or 'open'. But the 'shut' and 'open' positions weren't by any means in the same position on all six dials. On numbers five and six, especially, they were in opposite positions.

Chalk shook his head. 'Toby, I wouldn't wear this. Delay or no delay, I'd insist they refit the whole damn lot and do it properly. Heaven's sake, man, you know as well as I do, you need to be able to run your eye over those dials and see all the arrows pointing one way – parallel to each other, right? Not have to waste time reading each one individually – which way's that pointer, which way's this . . .'

'Sorry to horn in.' The voice came from behind him, the open watertight door, and glancing round he found Mike Searle, this boat's torpedo and gunnery officer. Searle, who'd only recently put up his second stripe – promotion from Sub-Lieutenant – was smallish and dark, darkly tanned too. He played a lot of cricket, which would account for the sunburn. Telling Chalk, 'Fact of the matter is – well, skipper says leave it as it is, we *can* get used to it. And the TI's reasonably happy. Obviously, it's a major cock-up, but—'

'Too major, I'd say, to even *consider* accepting it.'

He wished immediately that he hadn't said that. It was the truth, but (a) not strictly any of his business, (b) only a reiteration of the point he'd already made to Dymock. Although in reality it more than surprised him – *shocked* him, that such an experienced submarine CO as Jacko Pargeter should be willing to put up with it. Even if *Trumpeter*'s torpedomen did get used to it: in an emergency, needing to check those dials quickly, to know for sure and *instantly* . . .

He wasn't given to flights of fancy. This wasn't one, anyway. It was a compound of knowledge, professional experience and common sense. You were taught, in training – and passed it on to junior men when training them – to think ahead and imagine the worst combinations of mishap, bad luck, equipment failure – and all those things happening at once – so as to be ready to react quickly and effectively to just about anything that might go wrong.

But – he'd made his point. So – best thing was to make sure they didn't do anything like this to *Threat*, but otherwise, leave it. The decision was reinforced by seeing the half-smile on Dymock's face, and being well aware of how some of his brother officers saw him – 'Old Rufus', who always does things by the book, etcetera. And one adjective which more than once he'd heard applied to this alleged propensity of his – and which stung – was 'pompous'.

The hell with them. He told them both, 'Your business, anyway. Or rather your skipper's. *I* wouldn't live with it – but that's neither here nor there.'

'I agree, though.' Dymock nodded. 'Just the special circumstances I mentioned . . . But have a dekko at the operating levers, now. This is the new-fangled system he's beefing about. Just look, you'll see it – and there isn't a thing anyone can do about it, it's the system we're now stuck with.'

'What's the neutral position for?'

'Right question, Rufus.' Dymock explained, 'The theory is you put the operating lever to "shut", and that's fine – bowcap shuts. As one might expect. But then shove it into "neutral", you've *locked* it shut. Even if telemotor pressure fails – say an oil pipe's cracked by depthcharging – you're safe, it'll *stay* shut.'

'Or open, if—'

'Yes. Whichever was the last position before the pointer was put to "neutral", that's how it locks.'

'Objection being that at a glance you can't tell which.' He understood how they felt about *this*, anyway, and agreed with them. 'Shut' meant shut and 'open' meant open: neutral meant damn-all. He said slowly, thinking about it as he spoke, 'The hand who's put it to "shut" and then to "neutral" knows all right – unless someone else has been at it in the interim. But otherwise?'

'Double check – on the bowcap indicator – or indicators, plural.'

'First ensuring which indicator's relevant to which tube – and which way each individual pointer—'

'Well – as we were saying – that'll be second nature. Once we've exercised tubes a few times.'

Back to that earlier disagreement. Chalk let it lie. Dymock asked him as he turned away, 'What's this weekend invitation, Rufus?'

On the casing, where it was cooler and on the whole quieter – most of the noise of hammering and drilling was coming from Job No. 1793 on the far side of the basin – Dymock listened to what Chalk had to tell him about the Cameron-Greens and Glendarragh.

'So what does one do all day?'

Chalk shrugged. 'Usual sort of country-house routine. Marvellous country, incidentally – dramatic scenery and so forth. Climb mountains, if you want to. Eagles' nests, on the tops. And they have horses – and a tennis court – oh, and very good fishing. I gather that's how Sir Innes spends most of his time in the summer months. You fish, don't you?'

'Have done, but—'

'Also they have an anniversary coming up, and they're planning various festivities – "hoolies", as Suzie calls them.'

'I can imagine. Reels and so on. Sporrans flying in all directions.'

'If you're not interested, Toby, forget it. Bugger off down to London. I agree, much more your natural habitat. And come to think of it, young Searle might fit in quite well at Glendarragh. He's more of an age for Suzie and young Guy, too. Yes, that's a thought, I'll ask him instead.'

'What's the older sister like?' Dymock broke off, as a Chief PO approached. Barrel-chested, and black-bearded . . . 'Mind signing this, sir?'

'What is it, Cox'n?'

'Stores requisition, sir.'

Dymock scribbled a signature on it. Then enquired, 'What have I now indented for – the Crown Jewels?'

'Only some of 'em, sir. Don't want to be greedy, do we?'

'How's the battle generally?'

'I'd say we're holding our own, sir. Rest of the ship's company coming next week – as you know, of course—'

'Finding digs for 'em should be easy enough?'

Chalk moved away – to the plank and over it to the quayside – with Dymock's question about Suzie's sister in his mind, and remembering a studio portrait of her, silver-framed amongst a number of others including one of Alastair looking pleased with himself in his Seaforths uniform. The portraits were displayed on top of a grand piano which both Suzie and her mother played – as Suzie had told him, 'When the spirit moves us.' She'd added, 'Quickest way to get the place to oneself. When I have *my* bash, even the mice troop out.' But in that portrait, Chalk remembered, Patricia had long, fair hair brushed down so that a curtain of it screened half her face, and Suzie had commented, 'She had a touch of the Veronica Lakes, at that stage.' Turning to her mother: 'About a year ago, was this taken?'

'About then. But you're being unfair. It was the photographer's idea, not Pat's.'

He remembered Suzie's snort of derision: 'I *bet* it was!'

'I was there with her at the time, Suzie. I am *telling* you.'

'All right. But fact remains, it *was* her Veronica Lake period. Since then she's been doing a Marlene D. Was when she was last here, anyway . . .'

Chalk told Dymock as he came over the plank to join him on the quayside, 'Going by a photograph I saw, she has a look of Marlene Dietrich.'

'Who has?'

'Patricia Cameron-Green. You asked me what she's like. But it doesn't matter, does it – since (a) she won't be there, not this next weekend anyway – and (b) you won't be either, as you've better things to do.'

'As it happens, I've been having second thoughts about the weekend in London.'

He explained, rather vaguely, that there was some person he'd be meeting in London if he did go down there at the weekend, but that it might be better – wiser – to give it a miss . . . 'And a pressing engagement elsewhere, such as the Cameron-Greens' invitation—'

'It's not pressing, in the least. As yet they don't even know of your existence. Only *I'd* like a firm decision – say by this evening, one way or the other?'

'I'll come. Definitely. Please, accept for me. And – thanks . . . Look, we'll go up there in my motor, shall we, give your old rattle-trap a rest?'

Chapter 4

It was a Riley 12, bottle-green with black mudguards, and Dymock had bought it new only a few months earlier. Before that, he'd had a Morris. Toby Dymock, Chalk reminded himself as the Riley purred its way up the eastern shore of Loch Lubnaig, certainly did not have to live on his pay.

Which one might have thought would make him even more acceptable to the Cameron-Greens. Exceptionally good looks, charm, a respectable occupation *and* private money: what more could people want, who had an unmarried 23-year-old daughter on their hands?

In point of fact, though, this had little or no relevance, in the present circumstances. From Eve Cameron-Green's point of view, Toby Dymock would be simply another presentable young male to make up numbers for the summer's jollities. Help fill the house, and make life amusing for the girls. While Dymock's reasons for accepting the invitation were somewhat questionable: or at least – Chalk thought, glancing at his friend's profile as he shifted gear to cope with the steepening incline – contrary enough to arouse a degree of curiosity. His first reaction, after all, had been to decline on the grounds of having some sort of appointment in London; then within a minute or two he'd had his second thoughts and jumped at it as an excuse – apparently – for backing out of that previous engagement.

He hadn't mentioned it again, and Chalk hadn't asked him about it. For one thing he'd been busy, hadn't had time to think about it much until now. Having a firm date for his CO's arrival, he'd had to get down to the one job he really disliked – official correspondence, clearing his desk – or rather Ozzie Ozzard's – of a backlog of Admiralty departments' demands for 'returns' of this and reports on that or the other. Mostly trifling, and some of it more or less incomprehensible, designed one guessed to occupy the civil servants' daily working hours and thus justify their employment; but some of it involved a certain amount of research before the laborious two-fingered typing on a rattly portable typewriter which was itself a valuable item on one of HM Submarine *Threat*'s lists of permanent stores.

He'd have that desk clear, anyway, before Ozzard took it over on the 12th. But he also had his own letters to write – to Guy and to Diana, to start with, putting them in touch with each other in the hope that she'd bring Guy up with her in the Fox Moth in a few weeks' time. It would save Guy the train fare, provide Diana with some company on the long flight up, and give them an opportunity to get to know each other. They'd only met once before, over a rather hurried meal at a London railway hotel.

The loch was narrowing now on their left, as they approached Strathyre itself. Forest crowding in on the right. He warned Dymock, 'Look out for deer, around here. They tend to crash out on to the road right under your front wheels. Strathyre forest, this is, and it's stiff with 'em.'

Dymock eased his foot on the accelerator. 'Right.'

'Get an antler through the windscreen, you'd know all about it.'

'You ever done that?'

'Uh-huh.' He smiled. 'I'm a *careful* driver.'

'I believe you, Rufus.'

That reputation again: old Rufus, who took no chances. He didn't remember where or why it had started, taken root. He asked Dymock, 'What was the – er – assignation in London that you've shied out of?'

'Assignation?' Glancing at him sharply. Chalk had wanted to needle him, and evidently succeeded. 'Who said anything about an assignation?'

'You did. You told me you'd arranged to meet someone. That's what an assignation is, old lad.'

'It's come to have a certain connotation though, hasn't it.' Eyes back on the narrow road; Strathyre village was behind them now. 'As you know damn well.'

'I suppose if your mind works that way – indicative of an interesting degree of sensitivity—'

'Rufus.'

'Huh?'

'Go to hell?'

Nearing Lochearnhead, Dymock slowed the car, bumped on to the grass verge and stopped. Winding the window down, he stared eastward down the loch – which wasn't much of a sight, on this late Friday afternoon. Since midday the sky had been clouding over, and the water was steel-grey, reflecting the drabness overhead.

'Won't be a minute.' He got out. Chalk, assuming that he was going to relieve himself, stayed where he was and lit a cigarette. Then he saw that Dymock was only standing at the roadside, stooping forward to rest long-armed on the drystone wall. Motionless, staring across the water.

He got out, went to join him. There was nothing else on the road; in the past hour they'd seen only two or three other vehicles.

Dymock glanced round. 'Not much to look at, is there?'

'Changes with the sky. Blue sky, blue loch. Why, what were you expecting?'

'Nothing.' A shrug. 'Anything. I was here once on a fishing trip with my father. Just the two of us. School holiday time, it must have been. I saw the name when we were looking at your map, and it rang a bell. In a snapshot album – a page or two labelled "Loch Earn, 1920".'

'You'd have been ten.' The calculation was easy enough, since they were the same age. Chalk flipped his cigarette-case open. 'Smoke? Now I know why you were so keen to come this way.'

It was a longer route than he'd have taken if it had been his own choice. He'd have taken the same road as last weekend – up the side of Loch Lomond to Crianlarich.

'Thanks.' Dymock expelled smoke. 'Anyway, there's nothing here I recognize. Thought there might have been something to trigger recollection, you know?'

'Did you catch any fish?'

'One or two. With the old man's help.' Dymock shrugged. 'Not that he'd have been exactly old, at that time. He was using a crutch, had his left leg blown off at Passchendaele.'

'In '17.'

'Yes. As I may have told you. But imagine – only three years earlier. From *that* – to this . . .' He'd gestured towards the loch. 'I think he took me along because he wasn't sure how he'd manage, first time he was doing it on one leg, and he wouldn't have wanted a lot of people fussing him or seeing him make a fool of himself.'

'Which he did not, obviously.'

'No. Mostly we were in a boat, with a gillie, but otherwise he leant on the crutch and fished right-handed.' Dymock flicked his quarter-smoked cigarette into the water, turned back towards his car. 'Nothing here that I remember, anyway. But we could have been at the other end of the loch, for all I know. Is there a fishermen's hotel there, d'you know?'

'Bound to be. And the loch must be – oh, seven or eight miles long. You might well have arrived from that direction – from Comrie, that'd be.' He opened the passenger door, and got in. 'We might make a trip that way, some time.'

'Oh. It's not important.' Dymock switched on, pressed the self-starter button, and the engine fired. Chalk, who more often than not had to start his Austin with the crank, felt envious. He asked, raising his voice over a shift of gear, 'Your father still going strong, is he?'

'Still going. Wouldn't say exactly "strong".'

'D'you see much of him?'

'Last saw him – oh, between Christmas and New Year. Spent a couple of nights down there.'

'In Devon – is it?'

'Remotest corner. He has some fishing on the Torridge.'

'Long way to go – from most places.'

'It is. And in any case—'

He didn't finish. Chalk remembered, though, that Dymock's mother had run off with some other man, and his father had later married the widowed daughter of a peer, who'd been left a large estate and ran her own pack of hounds. He'd told Chalk that 'the old man' – as he called his father, speaking of him with obvious affection – had taken to the bottle to such an extent that he was rarely sober. He'd divulged all this – and more – at the end of a guest-night at Blockhouse, the submarine headquarters at Gosport, when neither of them had been particularly sober either. Whether he remembered having unburdened himself as he had was a point in doubt: Dymock had been drunker than he had himself, and it had never been mentioned since that night.

He asked him now, 'What about your mother? Is she more conveniently – er – located?'

'Much more. They live in Suffolk, but have a rather grand flat in London. Haven't I told you all this before?'

'You may have. I've a rotten memory.'

'The flat's in a new – well, "complex", they call it – called Dolphin Square. Very ritzy. That's where I see them most often. But the place in Suffolk's beautiful. Elizabethan, with oodles of land. He farms – keeping his hands clean, you know – I think I *must* have told you?'

'Possibly. Although you've always been somewhat reticent about your family.'

'Well – divorced parents aren't anything to crow about, are they?'

'They're facts of modern life, old man. And becoming a lot more so than they used to be.'

'Not that I've anything to grouse about, personally. My father and I get along very well – when he's *compos mentis* – and he makes me an allowance. Out of his own quite small income, I might say, not his wife's considerably larger resources. And my mother and her husband are very hospitable. I can use the Dolphin Square flat whenever I like, and I do quite often – when they aren't there, mostly.'

'Any – er – issue of their own?'

'None. Oddly enough. I mean you'd think, having done a bolt and so forth – eh?'

'Yes. You would.'

'*Your* father was killed, wasn't he? At about the time mine lost his leg?'

'Later. 1918.'

'Leaving no money, I remember your saying.'

'Three of us children, too. Mama brought us up on a shoestring – with help from the paternal grandfather, but she still did a marvellous job, considering.'

'And is *she* still – "going strong"?'

'Going, but far from strong. More or less bed-ridden.'

'I remember now, you told me. Damned awful luck, on top of the rest of it.' He added, after a short silence. 'Are we about halfway to Glen Dochart, would you say?'

'Roughly. Then about twelve miles west'll bring us to Crianlarich.'

'Any chance we'd get petrol there?'

'Doubt it. But you've got the two full cans, haven't you?'

'Oh, yes. Rather keep that for real emergencies, though. Not that it matters.'

Chalk contributed – more as a gesture than help of any real significance – to his mother's fees in a nursing home in Hampshire. The real financial burden fell on his sister Betty – or rather on her husband, who luckily could well afford it. In fact Chalk suspected that there might not be all that much luck about it: that Richard Traill's attractiveness to Betty might well have been enhanced by his ability and willingness to support her mother. He was a director of a well-known brewery, and had interests in restaurants and hotels. She wouldn't have married him *only* for that; and the marriage seemed happier than most, despite his being twenty years her senior. It might be expected to become even happier now there was a child on the way.

Coming up to Glen Dochart, to the T-junction where you could turn right to Killin, or left – as they were doing – to Crianlarich and points west and north ... At this point the glen's bottom-land was a mile or so wide, with the river splitting it and the slopes on each side rising steeply to something like 3,000 feet. While northeastward, Ben Lawers on Loch Tay's northern shore bulked a thousand feet higher – backed, Chalk noticed, by cloud that was breaking up, its remnants flying on the wind to leave widening areas of blue.

'Weather's doing what they said it would, for once. We may have a fine weekend.'

Dymock glanced at him blankly. Still elsewhere, in his own thoughts. In the last quarter-hour neither of them had said a word.

A shake of the head. 'Sorry. What—'

'I said we may have good weather coming.'

'Ah.' Leaning forward to look up at it. 'Yes. Touch wood.' He checked the time. 'And we're near enough on schedule. The little bus shifts a bit, eh?'

Cattle grazed on the valley floor. Beyond them, over the river and on that side's lower slopes, those barely-moving, from this distance maggot-like objects could only be sheep.

Dymock asked him – the question perhaps arising from his recent preoccupation – 'You haven't met the Buchanans yet, have you?'

'Buchanans.' He shook his head. 'Should I have?'

'He's financial director of Barlows'. And rolling in it. Great stone pile of a house up here – well, at Helensburgh – and one in London. In Belgravia, I might add.'

'Come to think of it—' Chalk remembered where he'd heard the name – 'Sir Innes Cameron-Green mentioned him. When I said we were building at Barlows'. If it's the same man, he's been to Glendarragh to shoot.'

Dymock nodded. 'You don't surprise me. I tell you, when he feels like taking a break he charters a damn great yacht on the Riviera. What do you say to *that*?'

'Well – the obvious reflection is that Barlows' must do pretty well out of us.'

'But he has fingers in other pies as well. Goes to Johannesburg quite often, for instance. And New York. *Queen Mary*, the captain's table, all that stuff. I've only met him twice, actually. Once in the Barlows' directors' dining-room – I was there with Jacko – and more recently at their house.'

Chalk said, remembering more, 'Sir Innes doesn't know him well. Someone else brought him along to a shooting party, he told me. It was only my having mentioned Barlows' that made him think of it.' He paused, watching the Dochart which was close on their right now, swirling and tumbling over rocks. He re-focused on Dymock. 'What's Buchanan's background?'

'Oh – clearly Scottish. But I think he was at Harrow. Yes, that's it. He told me he'd had thoughts of a naval career but his eyes weren't good enough, couldn't tell red from green.'

'Must be tricky recognizing tartans.'

'I'll ask him.' Dymock chuckled as he edged over to pass a lorry. Then – still in its dust – 'Tell you one thing, Rufus. Zoe Buchanan's a stunner.'

'His wife?'

'But she's not here much. Spends most of her time in London. Actually I suppose they both do, but he's often up here on his own.'

'What should I say – bad luck?'

'For God's sake—' a glance sideways, frowning – 'Don't start *that*.'

Chalk shrugged, wondering why else Dymock should have brought up the subject; but otherwise having only very limited interest in Buchanan or even in the 'stunning' qualities of his wife. He was more consciously noticing how the hills seemed to squeeze in on either side, a couple of miles ahead where the glen abruptly narrowed. He remembered that bottleneck, and how much more strongly the river ran there, the same amount of water pouring through but confined in a narrower, rocky channel. Equally familiar – now that he saw it again – was Ben More, up to the left beyond that point where the hills closed in, set back a few miles from the glen itself and towering black against the intermittent sun. He'd been up there, in his youth. Once you got to know this country, he thought, you carried it in your mind for ever.

Crianlarich: and turning right, northward up Strath Fillan towards Tyndrum, bearing right there on to the road for Fort William. Dymock was beginning to mutter about petrol again, and sure enough the Riley's engine spluttered out just as they were approaching the Bridge of Orchy; they had to put in enough from one of his precious tins to get them to a pump.

Finally, Glendarragh: the house tall and grey, as angular and unsmiling as a maiden aunt. And the tree-covered rise over which the drive had climbed at the end of its mile-long, pot-holed track shut out the last potential warmth of the day, the rays of the lowering sun. Dymock muttered, having run his eye over the gaunt stone frontage, 'Bit of a mausoleum, isn't it?'

'Well.' Chalk was immediately defensive. 'It's certainly not – what d'you call it, Dolphin Square?'

'Say *that* again.'

'You see too many Yank films, Toby.'

'Who's this?'

Chalk glanced round. He'd been out of the car, stooped at the window for this exchange with Dymock, who was still behind the wheel as if having second thoughts about stopping here: he'd swung the car right around, pointing back the way they'd come, braking and stopping it parallel to the steps which led up to the front door.

'This' was Mackenzie, the general factotum, coming for their luggage. Chalk told Dymock, 'Butler, sort of. Name's MacKenzie.' Then in a double-take: 'And *this* is Suzie.'

Running down the steps: in jodhpurs – her usual daytime rig, he recalled – and a patterned jersey. Dark hair flopping ... Dymock, getting out on his own side of the car and watching a terrier – Tartar – peeing on his offside front wheel, probably hadn't had much of a sight of Suzie yet.

'Don't tell me you've got a *new* motor, Rufus!'

'I won't.' He waved a hand. 'It's his.' He nodded: 'Evening, MacKenzie. Mr Dymock'll show you—'

'Grand to see ye again, sir.'

'Suzie, you're looking marvellous!'

'Oh, I'm a marvel, all right. But listen, I heard from Guy, he's—'

'I know. Hoping to fly up with Diana.' He saw her eyes move, heard Dymock's tread on the gravel. This is Toby Dymock. Suzie Cameron-Green.'

He thought her eyes had widened – as in surprise. Then, that what he saw was a conscious return to the proprieties; as if some now departed Nanny had whispered in her ear 'It's *rude* to stare ...' She'd put her hand out, said in a tone of voice that precisely imitated her mother's: '*So* glad you could come.'

'Well, it's very kind of you all, to invite a total stranger.'

He let go of her hand. 'I say. Rufus did mention that you were frightfully pretty, but—'

'*Frightfully*'s about right.' She had to turn her back on him, in a move to take Chalk's arm. Her initiative, not his ... 'Rufus, listen.' Starting back towards the house. 'I doubt if Guy told you this – but he's decided *not* to go to Spain. Isn't that a huge relief?'

'Certainly is. No, he didn't tell me—'

'You weren't supposed to know he was thinking of it, were you. And the other good news is Alastair's coming home tomorrow. Only for one night, but it's a start, isn't it? I mean, with you two here—' she glanced round over her shoulder: 'Alastair's my brother. Did Rufus tell you we're planning lots of lovely parties?'

'He did mention something of that sort.'

Eve Cameron-Green met them in the hall; Mackenzie bringing up the rear with their suitcases. Eve offered Dymock her hand: 'You must be Lieutenant Dymock.'

'Well – Toby Dymock, Lady Cameron-Green.'

'How nice – and that you could come. I see my daughter's already welcomed you. Rufus – how clever of you to arrive precisely at the time we expected you!'

'Actually—' Dymock put in, smiling – 'I was driving.'

'Awfully smart car.' Suzie pointed through the front doors. 'Look. That green – er – whatever it is.'

'Whatever it is, she says.' Dymock informed her, 'That, let me tell you, is an example of one of the finest *marques* on the road today. Excluding Rolls-Royce and Bentley – and I suppose perhaps Alvis, at a pinch—'

'And Austin, Morris, Hillman, Ford—'

'Oh, *really*—'

Suzie's mother wasn't certain whether or not this was a serious disagreement. She cut in, 'Isn't it astonishing, how many different kinds there are!' She was at the door of her husband's study, rapping on it before she pushed it open a few inches ... 'Innes, our guests have arrived.'

'Well, tell them the whisky's in here!'

Chalk laughed. 'I think we heard that. With your permission—'

'Go on in. Suzie and I'll see you later. MacKenzie'll unpack for you meanwhile, and I expect Innes will show you where your rooms are. Don't let him keep you *too* long.'

Chalk, who'd been closest to it, was already in the doorway. 'Evening, sir.'

'Come on in, Chalk!'

'Yes.' Holding the door and looking back into the stone-flagged hall, he was surprised to see Suzie gazing at Dymock in a way that suggested there was some important exchange in progress between them. At the same time he had a sight of her mother's back as she retreated, and as she went out of sight he heard Dymock murmur to Suzie, 'Nothing on earth would keep me *very* long.'

He thought, while half listening to Sir Innes' account of the past week's fishing, that for Dymock that kind of thing was probably only a matter of habit. Or good manners: as if it might have been rude *not* to compliment a girl by showing personal interest in her.

He'd better be warned off, anyway. Suzie was no Mrs – what was that name – Buchanan? Suzie would think he meant it. Being young and impressionable – she could have had no experience of men like Dymock.

Possibly, he admitted to himself, he was making an unwarranted assumption and doing Mrs Buchanan an injustice. But the tone of voice in which Dymock had described her – unless one only imagined that, Dymock being the man he was . . . At this moment, watching Sir Innes, seemingly listening attentively to a story about catching thirty fair-sized mountain trout in less than two hours. That was the subject-matter at this moment, but it tended to jump, one such reminiscence giving rise to another and the stories spanning about a quarter of a century. For anyone who let his thoughts wander at all, it was a minefield: which Chalk was risking, remembering Dymock in the car this afternoon, that frown and his weary, mildly irritated 'Don't start *that* . . .'

'What about it, Chalk? Take a picnic lunch, shall we, make a day of it?'

'Marvellous idea, sir!'

'Capital! Looking at Dymock: 'The three of us, eh?'

'Well.' Dymock had reservations, evidently: Chalk saw them coming. 'Only thing is, I have a sort of compulsion about using my own gear. Can't explain it in any way that makes sense, but it could date from an occasion when I broke my father's favourite rod.'

'You won't be getting your hands on *my* favourite rod, I promise you!'

'No, sir.' He joined in the amusement. 'But I really do prefer to fish with my own stuff. Next time – I very much hope there may be a next time – I'll bring it. *If* I'm invited again.'

'Just as you please, of course.' Sir Innes, looking puzzled, turned in his chair to face Chalk. 'Just you and I, then. I'd wait for Alastair, but we'd lose half the day. And we'll show 'em, we'll catch enough fish for three – eh?'

'Well, let's *hope* . . .'

'They're like the Loch Leven trout, these little mountain fellows. Not necessarily all that little, either. But they have the orange spots in their marking that's typical of Loch Leven fish – if you've ever fished there?'

He hadn't.

'Never mind. Of course, this weather's too bright by half. But you never know up here, it can change suddenly, we may get a decent spell of cloud . . .' He asked Dymock, 'Won't mind if we leave you to your own devices, eh?'

'Not at all, sir. It's my fault, entirely. Stupid of me – I should have thought, and put a rod in.'

'You can always change your mind. Hope you will. I've plenty of tackle here. Perhaps you'll persuade him, Chalk?'

'I'll—' he nodded, looking at Dymock and thinking *I damn well will* – 'I'll try to, sir.'

'Otherwise, Dymock, Suzie'd no doubt show you round the place. And Alastair'll be turning up at some stage, of course. In time for luncheon, I imagine. Never misses a square meal if he can help it. But Suzie'll look after you.'

When he'd changed for dinner, Chalk went along to Dymock's room. Dymock, who hadn't finished dressing, was surprised to see him.

'Rufus . . . To what do I owe this honour?'

'Coming straight to the point, I think it'd be a good idea if you joined us tomorrow on this fishing expedition.'

'But I explained—'

'Codswallop. You don't give a damn whose rod you use.'

'My dear fellow – why d'you say that?'

'Because nobody's so damn precious they wouldn't fish with a borrowed rod. As Sir Innes is obviously thinking too, only he's being polite to his guest. Who's here, incidentally, at *my* behest.'

'What exactly are you saying?'

'That I think it'd be better if you came with us. Even if – in view of your alleged aversion to using borrowed tackle – you don't fish.'

'I'm not quite on the wavelength, Rufus. Your words are comprehensible, but what's behind them—'

He nodded. 'All right. It would be better that you did not hang around Suzie.'

'*Oh . . .*'

'Well?'

A smile: a small shake of the dark head. 'Rufus – my dear old chap – I'm not going to take this seriously – since that might well involve punching you on the nose—'

'I heard you promising not to deprive her of your company for too long. That was within five minutes of first setting eyes on her. She's very young, perhaps gullible – vulnerable might be the word – I'm extremely fond of her and even more so, Toby, of my brother Guy.'

'So on the strength of my having made a flattering remark – no, *two* flattering remarks, I'd already told her she was pretty, hadn't I – and that was within five *seconds* of meeting her—'

'It was, indeed.'

'Well, Rufus, I can't say I've ever noticed how *you* talk to girls—'

'Just normally. Without seeking to impress, or captivate. But the last straw, the reason I'm here now, is that damn-fool lie about not caring to fish with borrowed tackle. It's transparent, Toby—'

Someone had tapped on the door. Then a call: 'Rufus?'

Suzie ... He went to the door and opened it. She was dressed for dinner, in a narrow, turquoise dress, a double rope of pearls and the bracelet which he remembered she'd worn on the previous weekend. The dark hair pinned up ... Her glance went past him to Dymock, who was standing now, with no socks on and the ends of his tie dangling on a starched shirt-front.

'I knocked on your door, Rufus, got no answer, guessed you might be jawing in here, and then heard your voice. Hello, Toby. I only wanted to warn you both that dinner's to be sharp at eight – cook gets in a tizzie otherwise – and the parents are already down, so—'

'*I'll* be down in ten seconds flat. Thanks for the warning.' He told Dymock, 'Better get a wriggle on, Toby.' In the passage with Suzie, he pulled the door shut behind him. 'Is my tie all right?'

'Come to the light, I'll see.'

She straightened it for him. 'That'll do.'

'Thanks ... You're looking exquisite, Suzie!'

'Oh my God, you naval people ...'

'Doesn't Guy—' following her towards the gallery at the head of the stairs – 'doesn't my little brother pass any comment when you're looking especially stunning?'

Dymock's word – as used to describe Mrs Whatsit. He'd recognized it, too late, just as it slipped out. But – Dymock's manner, too? Looking back down the corridor he was relieved to see he hadn't left his room yet. Imagining the sardonic grin . . . Suzie was telling him, 'Guy does rather lay it on, at times. Runs in the family, I dare say.' She laughed, glancing back at him – at the head of the curve of stairs, looking he thought less pretty than actually beautiful; her hands flew up to cover her ears just as MacKenzie struck the dinner gong.

But there you are, he told himself, when they were sitting down to dinner – one *does* pay compliments to girls. Even though in this instance he'd been (a) telling her nothing but the truth, and (b) in intention, as it were, only keeping Guy's end up for him. Despite which he rather wished now that he hadn't said as much as he had to Dymock. Although the exchange in the hall had been rather too intense, he thought, to be passed off as just another social interchange. And on top of that, of course, the idiotic lie about not wanting to fish with any rod but his own – so blatant a move to get Suzie to himself tomorrow.

Perhaps one was too protective of one's little brother, he thought. Perhaps one should let him fight his own battles. If there was any battle to be fought, even: looking at her across the long mahogany table, recalling the expression he'd seen on her face when she'd thought herself alone with Dymock in the hall, it occurred to him that she might only have been trying to make this stranger out, or put into perspective something he'd just said.

Now, she'd said something about a cousin – one who'd had a bad fall from a horse six months ago and was still laid up – and her mother had seized on it quickly, asking Dymock whether he had many cousins: 'I mean of course first cousins. The other kinds are two a penny, aren't they?' Her light laugh was camouflage to the fact that it was a leading question aimed at getting a run-down on his family.

'Only two. Both female – my mother's sister's daughters.'

'Oh. Well, two's enough to be going on with . . . Where do your people live, Toby?'

He put down his fork. The *soufflé* had been delicious. 'My father's in deepest Devonshire, and my mother and her husband have a place in Suffolk. They – my parents – split up, years ago. When I was twelve, actually.'

'Heavens!' Suzie's blue eyes shone. 'Did they divorce?'

'Suzie—'

'It's all right.' Dymock gave his hostess one of his smiles. 'Old history, now . . . Yes, Suzie, they divorced. And both re-married. My mother immediately, and the old man a few years later.' He told Sir Innes, 'Speaking of fishing, my father's mad keen. He has a double-bank stretch of the Torridge, and he goes to Ireland most years for salmon and sea-trout. Stays with old Army friends over there and has a whale of a time.'

Chalk put in – feeling that he'd been locked in his own thoughts for too long – 'Despite having lost a leg at Passchendaele in '17.'

'Oh, really.' Sir Innes frowned, putting his mind back. 'Third battle of Ypres, that was. I was in the previous one – summer of '16. But – lost a leg, you say. Well – wait a minute . . . Dymock. *Dymock?* Why, I knew him!'

'In the war, sir?'

'No. After – as fellow members of Boodles. He *was* a member there, wasn't he?'

'I didn't know, but – I'm sure . . .' Dymock pushed the bone of one lamb chop aside and started on another. 'He isn't now though, I don't think.'

'Must be a dozen or more years since we last saw each other. But I remember him well. Coming back to me now. He was using a crutch when I first met him, then he graduated to two sticks. He was having an artificial leg of some kind fitted, as I remember.' Staring at Dymock across the table, he pointed downwards. '*This* one – the left – he'd lost. Eh?'

'Yes. He could lean on the crutch and cast right-handed.'

'He was in the club a great deal, at that time. I was only in and out, myself – had a job at the War Office, for my sins – but as I remember he was almost always there. Charming fellow, first-rate . . . But his wife had—'

He'd checked: looking at his own wife. She'd shaken her head: 'Innes, he was only just *telling* you—'

'My mother had done a bunk, with the man she's married to. I was at prep school: I suppose during term-times he did live at his club. It was a year or two at least before he met his present wife and moved to Devon.'

'And she was Mary Ellesley. Old thingummy's daughter. Ellesley was killed in about the last week of it, wasn't he?' Sir Innes slapped the table. 'This is extraordinary, you know, quite extraordinary. Haven't thought of old Charlie Dymock in years, and now out of the blue—' Sir Innes paused, gazing at Dymock. 'Old Charlie Dymock's boy. You'd have been born about – when—'

'1910, sir.' Glancing at Chalk. 'Same year as Rufus.'

'Obviously a vintage year.'

'*Thank* you, Suzie.'

'Not a patch on the '19, mind you.'

Chalk smiled. 'We won't dispute that for a moment.'

'But look here, now.' Sir Innes was frowning at Dymock. 'This nonsense about not fishing with borrowed tackle – you don't mean to stick to that, do you?'

'Afraid I do, sir.' He hesitated. 'At least – *did* . . .'

'That sounds better. Eh, Chalk?'

'Does indeed.' Dymock's eyes met his momentarily, shifted away again. He told Suzie, 'Fact is, I'd been rather hoping for a game of tennis.'

'So *that*'s it!'

Suzie's mother laughed, looking at her. Dymock protesting that he'd thought of tennis only because he hadn't expected to be going on the fishing expedition – not the other way about, for heaven's sake . . . Suzie said, 'We *must* play, anyway. The court's mown and marked out – most of it my doing, I might add!'

'Tomorrow?'

'You're on.' She switched her smile from Dymock to Chalk. 'With Alastair here, we could make it a foursome.'

He nodded. 'You and your brother versus us interlopers?'

He suppressed an urge to raise a laugh at Dymock's expense by pointing out that he'd have to play with a *borrowed* racket. Dymock's surrender, he thought, had been enough to be going on with; with any luck he might behave himself, from now on.

Chapter 5

Driving south to the Clyde on the Sunday evening, Chalk said, he and Dymock didn't talk much. He told me, on his terrace overlooking the bay at Glandore, 'I remember that there was – well, as you'd expect – a considerable gulf between us. In my own thinking, incidentally, there was a degree of ambivalence – as I saw it he'd behaved extremely badly, taken advantage of the invitation which after all *I'd* extended to him, and I wasn't trusting him an inch as far as Suzie was concerned, but at the same time I didn't want this *contretemps* between us – after all, we'd been friends for a very long time, and we were going to have to get along together in the Service for a lot longer yet. So at least some of the time I was trying to convince myself that his interest in Suzie didn't have to be any of my business. No obligation to act as my brother's keeper, I told myself. In fact if she was going to allow herself to fall for this bugger, Guy might be well out of it anyway.'

I put in, with diffidence – 'If I could ask you a rather personal question – it's important, to the story as a whole – is it conceivable that by this time you might have developed rather a soft spot for her yourself?'

'I don't know why you should imagine so. It was my

brother's relationship with her that mattered – the danger to it that Dymock might pose. Plus the fact I'd brought the fellow up there with me, introduced him—'

'Yes. I know. But at the same time it's not impossible that in the course of your first weekend there you might have come to rather more than just *like* her. It matters because if so, it could have influenced your view of things. One or two things you've said – for instance, seeing her as beautiful rather than just "pretty"—'

'Entirely objective observation. The thought behind it being "Gosh, but Guy's a lucky fellow!"'

I'd nodded. 'What I'm getting at is how much you might have been prejudiced in her favour. Whether – for instance, remembering that scene in the hall as you described it – whether you didn't have any thought that she could have been encouraging Dymock – or at least meeting him halfway.'

'At that stage—' his eyes were narrowed against the light reflected from the bay below us – 'no, I did not have any such thought. But mind you, she'd only have had to look back at a man and not actually spit in his eye, and he'd feel encouraged . . . But—' a raised forefinger wagged to and fro – 'it wouldn't have been *intentional* on her part. It was – oh, how she looked, obviously – isn't it always, at least to start with? – but not just the colour of her eyes or the shape of her nose. Her whole personality . . . Remember that song of Chevalier's, *one look that sends you crashing through the ceiling?*'

'Well – sorry to flog a dead horse, but there you go again.' I explained, shifting the emphasis slightly, 'What I'm wondering is whether the Suzie-Dymock flirtation – for want of a better word – might have been less one-sided than you thought at the time. Your sympathy for your brother could on its own have been enough to affect your view of it. Well, obviously it must have, that was the main issue . . . But – well, *now*, would you put all the blame on Dymock, as you did then?'

A long breath . . . 'Dymock was Dymock. I think he did genuinely fall for her later. Benefit of the doubt, anyway . . . But at the time, the dire effect of his self-indulgence – for which one *must* attribute blame, if words mean anything at all, and he was self-indulgent to a marked degree – there isn't any doubt at all that to start with he was simply amusing himself. And I disliked him for it – intensely.'

'You didn't come to dislike *her*, for letting your brother down?'

'No.' Staring out across the bay again – with a hand down to rub his rather heavyweight red setter behind its ears. It was the only one that roamed free, the rest were kennelled behind the house, with a big wire run. He'd said of this dog earlier – its name incidentally was Rufe – 'Fat old sod, isn't he? No shooting this time of year, that's half the trouble. Other half is he's so damn placid, nothing like the bag of nerves most of 'em are.'

It was why Chalk-bred setters were in great demand, I'd gathered. They had an unusual breadth of head, and temperaments to match.

Answering my question about Suzie, though – shaking his head, a movement so small that it was like a twitch of nerves . . . 'No, I did not. First out of sympathy for the ordeal she was put through – which we'll come to, obviously it's the main focus of your interest in all this . . . Second – she was extremely young, inexperienced.' Quiver of the head again . . . 'I knew right from the start she'd been far more a victim of circumstances than a cause of them. Another major factor, which I mentioned just now, was my own sense of responsibility for the whole thing. Responsibility to my brother, primarily. *I*'d brought Dymock to Glendarragh. I can tell you, I've lived with that ever since. But – back to your question about Suzie, attribution of blame and so forth – Dymock was by nature a seducer, he was nearly ten years older than her, had a great deal of experience, and he *was* damn good-looking. What's more, she simply did not envisage the potential damage . . . Which – all right – might not have been inevitable exactly – that's hindsight, I suppose – but it might at least have been foreseen as a possibility – by her parents, particularly. In fact they were either blind to it or saw it and did nothing about it. Took a calculated risk, perhaps.'

'Are you saying they approved of him – despite having allegedly been very fond of Guy?'

'Pragmatically they must have seen certain rather obvious differences. I mean advantages. Dymock was after all a man of some substance, with a clearly marked-out future before him. How many years might it have been before anyone could say that of Guy? Dymock was also extremely personable – *and* Sir Innes had known and liked his father . . . All in all, young Guy could be given a friendly pat on the head and told to go and play.'

'I see.'

'And Suzie wouldn't have realized how cruel she was being. Wouldn't have guessed at the depth of the wound she was inflicting. Partly because he had all but literally swept her off her feet, and in that state of mind – can't expect good judgement, can you?'

'But the same would have applied to Dymock. If he genuinely fell in love with her?'

'Yes. *If* he genuinely fell in love. Bloody great "if", that is too. Alternative is that it was just another conquest. In his time he must have pinched quite a few girls from other men; his attitude would have been "Well, bad luck . . ."' Chalk shrugged. 'Natural enough, too. Law of the jungle, may the best man win, so forth. But there and then, *I* wouldn't have made any allowances at all, I'd have hanged him.' The clear blue eyes held mine. 'Didn't have to, did I.'

There was a silence. I used it to check that the recorder was working and that the tape had some way to run.

'One other question – of a general kind.' I put the recorder down between us on the table. 'When you tell me how you felt about this or that, should I allow for the influence of hindsight? In other words, how much latitude for interpretation do I have?'

'Well, I've been giving you both aspects, as far as possible. How I felt then, and how I see it now. But if it doesn't seem to add up, use your own judgement. Just bear in mind that I'm describing it as accurately as I can recall.'

'So far, your recall's fairly staggering.'

'Probably because it's been kept fresh. I've been over it in my mind God knows how many times. But as I say, you must use your own judgement, when you're putting it together. There *could* be a touch of hindsight here or there – or even totally crossed wires. The more-or-less hundred-per-cent reliable memories relate of course to the main events, things you *couldn't* forget; but as for who said what to whom and precisely when – well, take our drive south that evening. If Dymock and I did have any exchanges of conversation, I don't remember them.'

'All right ... Actually there's a slight discrepancy here. You and Dymock hardly on speaking terms, but where we broke off – at dinner at the Cameron-Greens – you said you were hoping he might behave himself from then on. Presumably he hadn't.'

'Couldn't have, could he? You're right. I suppose he'd just gone on – well, forcing his attentions on her ... But – wait a minute, there was *some* damn thing as it were sticking in my gullet.' He passed a hand over his eyes. 'Something I sort of half remember. Give me a minute ...'

'It can be counter-productive, to concentrate too hard. Let's see if we can't as it were creep up on it. For instance, d'you remember how the fishing trip went, that Saturday?'

'I know we caught a lot of trout. And I remember chatting with Sir Innes about the more immediate concerns of that pre-war time. Spain, for instance. Including Jacko Pargeter's information about so-called "unidentified" – meaning Italian – submarines sinking neutral ships. And Austria, where the

Nazis were positioning themselves to take over. Austria was obviously at the top of Hitler's hit-list – as we'd term it now – at that juncture, and Sir Innes kept himself well informed on international affairs – what with reading all the journals of the day, and having friends at or near the centre of things. But he hadn't heard what Dymock had to tell him about the Italian submarines' murderous activities. I think it must have been kept quiet – probably to avoid pressure being exerted on the government to do something about it. Pargeter had elaborated on the subject – to Dymock – since that first mention of it, and apparently it was an open secret to those in the know that they'd sunk at least one British freighter and some French and Russians – and Anthony Eden was actually bestirring himself to call for an international conference of Mediterranean naval powers ... Apart from that – I think we may have had the overcast conditions we needed. Caught an astonishing number of orange-spotted mountain trout, anyway – and had our picnic, saw a few red deer on our way down in the early evening. The visual memories last, you know, when others fade. Like snapshots ... But I'm sure we must have talked about a lot more than Spain and Austria ...'

He snapped his fingers. 'Got it. There was talk about the ensuing weekends – when would Diana be coming up with Guy, and so forth. We were going to have to prepare a suitable landing-strip for her, incidentally. But the coming weekend was the one when I was going to have to stay down there in order to meet my new CO, who'd obviously want a progress report from me, and I mentioned this to Sir Innes, who expressed disappointment but at once asked Dymock, 'You'll be with us, I hope?'

Dymock thanked him, and accepted, and Sir Innes told him to consider it a standing invitation. Any weekend that he was at a loose end, etcetera. Well, you can imagine – can't you? Dymock like a cat that's collared all the cream: and looking at me with a gleam of triumph in his eyes ... *That* was it. Not a word said – so nothing to take him up on – but it was still to all intents and purposes a statement of his intentions. That, and then of course sticking to her like glue the rest of the weekend. May not *sound* like much – but remember *I'd* brought him up there, he was supposed to be an old chum and he knew damn well that she was my brother's girl – eh?'

Chalk had asked Suzie when they'd happened to be alone together for a minute, 'Are you still looking forward to having Guy here?'

'Of *course* I am!'

Then she'd done a double-take on the question. 'Why ask me that, Rufus?'

'Just hoped you were. He's certainly looking forward to seeing you again.'

'I know he is. I hear from him too, you know!'

'You mean he actually puts pen to paper?'

It had become a joke then, and she relaxed. 'On occasion, he does. Widely-spaced occasions, but—' shrugging – 'not so dusty. I mean I can't complain, I probably write less often than he does. But of *course* he writes, Rufus – how else would I know he's given up the idea of going to fight in Spain?'

Her brother had joined them at that moment.

'Who's off to Spain *now*, for God's sake?'

'Talk about picking up fag-ends . . .' She told him, 'Guy was thinking he might. Now he's had second thoughts.'

'Yes, I remember. We both told him what a chump he was. I'm glad he's seen sense, finally.'

Alastair Cameron-Green was about five-eight or five-nine, solidly built, with rather close-set eyes and a nose between them that gave him a hawkish look. A young hawk, only recently into feathers . . . Nodding to Chalk – 'Awfully good chap, your brother.'

'*I* like him.' Glancing at Suzie. 'I think she does too.'

'So I've heard.' Her brother laughed. 'And I *am* delighted he's changed his mind about Spain. Particularly as he was set on joining the wrong side.'

'Aren't most foreign volunteers fighting for the Loyalists?'

'Most British, apparently. But one's heard there are chaps of just about all nationalities on both sides. Germans fighting Germans here and there, and so forth.' He added, 'Any case, the fascists are going to win. They've got the fire-power, you see. And they're tightening the noose around Madrid week by week. It's really only the eastern part of the country that's held by so-called Loyalists now.'

'And the south. Some of the ports down there, anyway. Why d'you say "so-called" Loyalists, though? That's the government side, after all.'

'Certainly. And hand-in-glove with the Russians, aren't they? May have been elected, but they've already sold out to Moscow. If they won, Spain would be communist and under Moscow's rule. Even as it is they've got Russian commanders and generals – eh?'

'While the other lot have God knows how many Germans and Italians fighting for them. German tanks and guns – bombers and fighters too. What about that?' Suzie challenged him: 'What about Guernica, for that matter?'

A few months earlier, the Basque town of Guernica had been flattened, reduced to rubble allegedly by German dive-bombers – a new variety, Junkers 87s, which for some reason were being called 'Stukas'. There'd been world-wide condemnation of the slaughter and destruction, and as a direct result of it a lot more foreign volunteers had gone to join the Loyalists. It might well have been what started Guy's mind working in that direction, Chalk had guessed.

'Interesting point there, Suzie.' Alastair put a hand on her shoulder. 'We've heard quite recently that that was pure invention. The Germans *did* attack the place – it's a rail centre, or was – but then the Republicans moved in with explosives and did the rest. Terrific propaganda *coup*, d'you see. They used Asturian miners – chaps who know all about dynamite. And before this they'd done the same to Irun – or so I'm told.'

'You're *told*.' Suzie nodded. 'Question is, who by?'

'By more than one first-hand report from Spain. Primarily an Englishman who was in the town soon after the event. For the moment I forget his name – but the way he described it was quite convincing. To me, anyway.' Alastair shrugged. 'Suzie, I'm not saying the Germans are whiter than white—'

'Glad to hear that.' Dymock, joining them, smiled at her. 'Sorry – got trapped.'

'By our father which art in his smoking-room?'

'That's not a *bad* guess. You were going to take me to see some pasture that might do for a landing-field?'

'So I was.' She glanced at Chalk. 'More to the point to take Rufus though, now I've found him. It's his finacée who'll be using it, after all ... Pony-paddock behind the house here, Rufus. We've got hay on it at the moment, but it's about ready to cut and I imagine all we'd need to do after that is fill in a few holes here and there. Any idea how long a run she'll need?'

'Not off-hand. I'll ask her, and let you know. Let's go and see it, anyway.'

Dymock suggested, '*Then* tennis, Suzie?'

She looked round at the others. 'Foursome? Alastair?'

'As long as I don't have to partner *you*.' He told Chalk, 'She poaches – continually.'

'I can handle that.' Dymock gave her one of his smiles. 'You and I'll take these two on, Suzie, shall we?'

'If you like. But I warn you, I do poach.' She took Chalk's hand, pulled him after her. 'Out through the back's the quick way.'

One in the eye for bloody Dymock, he'd thought, as they left the house. Then, passing through the stable-yard, he caught himself up on that, realizing that he'd reacted as if *he* were Dymock's rival! (And little guessing that in something more than fifty years' time he'd be reminded of this momentary aberration by the question *Might you by this time have developed a soft spot for her*?)

Bloody interrogation ... But the question had struck home, even stimulated a continuing process of recollection. Of Suzie for instance on their way to look at this paddock, asking him – again – which weekend it was that Diana was hoping to fly up.

'Bringing Guy with her on the 30th. She'll fly back next day – she's a working girl, you know. Actually she has a new prospect in the offing – instead of free-lancing, a regular job in air-survey work, map-making.'

'Hope she gets it.'

'So do I.'

'D'you think she'd take me up – in her Fox Moth?'

'Sure she will, if you ask her ... This the field?'

'Yes. If we get up on that wall – get a better view ... Rufus, why are you and she not – personal question, this, very rude I know, but – well, you've known her quite a long time, Guy said, so—'

'Why don't we get married?' He clambered up, turned to put a hand down to help her but she was already there beside him. 'Why don't we name the day, you're wondering?'

'I'm sure there's some good reason.'

'Two, as it happens. One, she's going out to the Cape this autumn, staying there about four months. It's summer then, and her parents have been pressing her to come. Her mother's not too fit, apparently.' He was looking round at the field of hay. 'Certainly looks big enough. When it's cut, is the ground good and level?'

'As level as most fields. We'll be cutting it this week anyway, you'll see for yourself.'

'Weekend after next, that'll be.'

'Oh, yes. Papa did say ... Why is it you can't make this next one?'

'My skipper's arriving. Have to stay on the job, therefore. Speaking of which, the other reason for Diana and I to wait is that in two years' time I'll be getting my half-stripe – making me a lieutenant commander – and my pay'll be a bit more worth having. Should have a command of my own too, by that time – if I don't blot my copybook.'

'Better not, had you.'

'Exactly.'

'But I don't think *I'd* wait.' Her dark hair was blowing in the wind. 'Once I was sure, I mean.' She laughed, her eyes shining with the sun's reflection in them. 'After all, when one's made one's mind up?'

'Only thing is – if the lucky man's my young brother, Suzie, as I hope he may be—'

'*If* . . . Long wait. I know . . . But another thought – which I'd forgotten for the moment – is that with a war coming it mightn't be such a good idea anyway.'

'I think you could look at that either way.'

'Alastair says we'll be at war within a year.'

'He could be right, too . . . Anyway, Suzie – thinking of this as Diana's landing field – she could make her approach from either there – northwest – or the reciprocal, from the southeast over those trees. We'll have to put a wind-sock up, I suppose. Know what I mean?' She'd nodded: she'd seen them, hadn't until now known what they were called. He asked her, 'What's the prevailing wind here, in mid-summer?'

'West or northwest, mostly. Anything up to hurricane force, usually with sheets of rain. Or hail . . .' She laughed. 'It's anyone's bet, tell her.'

'She'll find that *very* useful.'

'On second thoughts though, better not say anything that might put her off. We have wonderful summers, hardly *any* wind—'

'If you were to stand here with your hair blowing out like that, Suzie, we wouldn't need to bother with a wind-sock.'

'Like me to take root, would you?'

'Wish I had my Brownie with me. Snap you as you are this minute – and with that background—'

'Title it "Wind-sock". Bound to win a prize then!'

'I'd put it in a frame and give it to Guy for Christmas.'

He took his eyes off her. 'Diana would have a run of about a hundred and fifty yards. Be enough – I'd guess.'

'Warn her not to fly low over the farmstead – cattle, etcetera. Well, I'll show you – draw you a map. But look – she could put her machine in that byre, if it has to go under cover.'

'If we get one of your midsummer hurricanes.'

'Exactly. What date did you say she's coming?'

'Bringing Guy, the 30th. Back south next day. Then she'll fly up again for the anniversary party at the end of August. The hoolie, that is.'

'But we'd better have a small-scale hoolie on the 30th. Dress-rehearsal hoolie.' She was climbing down. 'Patricia'll be here too, then – she comes about the middle of the month.' Looking up at him: 'You'll like her.'

'I'm sure I will.' He jumped, landing beside her. 'Hope Toby Dymock will too.'

'Oh—' starting back towards the house – 'of course . . . Heavens, they'll be waiting for us, won't they.' Over her shoulder: 'Sorry you won't be here next weekend.'

'So am I. But my skipper would be extremely put out if I wasn't there when he arrived.'

'Well, just make sure you're here every weekend after that. Promise?'

'Probably not every one. Most, I hope. Anyway you'll have Guy in less than a month, remember.'

'But Toby's going to be tied up after this next weekend, he says. Tests and trials – and crew arriving? Is that the truth, or just a let-out?'

'Why would he want that?'

'I don't know. Well – he might have some girl somewhere.' A quick, searching glance. Then, getting no reaction: 'Or just feel he's seen enough of us.'

Most unlikely. In any case it *is* the truth. *Trumpeter*'s due for her final acceptance trials in the last week of August, and between now and then they'll certainly be busy. All kinds of tests and trials – basin dive this week, I think – and the last batch of crew arriving, which makes the first lieutenant in particular *very* busy.'

'What's a basin dive?'

'The basin's the dock *Trumpeter* and my submarine are lying in at the moment, and the dive's for the dockyard people to satisfy themselves she's watertight and check the ballast in her keel.'

'I'd have thought *you*'d be the ones who'd want to satisfy yourselves it's watertight!'

'Well – yes. But the boat's in the builders' hands still, it's their test. Primarily to get the ballast right. The big one – ours, you might say – is in the final acceptance trials. This dip in the basin – dips plural, actually – they do in slow time – *very* slow, so if anything goes wrong they can stop and get her up again.'

'Is anything likely to go wrong?'

'Extremely *un*likely.'

'Good.' Walking long-strided beside him, through the stable-yard again. Glancing up: 'Toby's offered to show me round his submarine, some time. When the paint's dry, he said.'

'And that prospect pleases?'

'Shouldn't it?'

'I'd wait till Guy's here, if I were you. He'd love it. And then I could take you both into Glasgow for a meal.'

Nat Eason, *Threat*'s engineer officer, remarked approvingly on that Monday morning, 'You fixed the bowcap balls-up double-quick, Number One. I got the word five minutes ago.' Glancing at his watch. 'Crack of bloody dawn that is, to this shower.'

They'd met on the quayside of the fitting-out basin – in a bedlam of hammering and rivetting, and men's voices raised to penetrate that constant background roar – close to the shore end of *Threat*'s gangplank. Or rather, Job No. 1793's gangplank. It wasn't the crack of dawn to the workforce: Eason had been referring to his *bêtes noirs*, the bowler hats.

Chalk suggested, 'Indicative of a guilty conscience over the way they've buggered-up *Trumpeter*'s, probably. Hear it from Hamilton, did you?'

'No bloody fear.' The engineer snorted. 'No – Tom Fairley came by. He's the bloke gets things done, round here.'

Fairley was the yard's Foreman Engineer. Chalk said, 'It was Hamilton's arm I twisted, anyway.'

'Flipper, more likely.' Eason laughed, giving himself a coughing fit, dropping his fag-end and squashing it with his toe, still coughing. Then, recovering: 'They're amending the drawings, Fairley said.'

'But not the operating system with that neutral position in it, I imagine.'

'No mention of that.' The engineer admitted, 'And I didn't think to ask. But the skipper might try, when he gets here – new face, the bastards might show willing?'

'It'd be wasted effort, I'm afraid. No, best thing we can do, Chief, is get used to it.'

'Yeah. I suppose . . . Ah – very civil . . .' Accepting a new cigarette, from Chalk's case. 'You won't be off to the Highlands *next* weekend, I dare say?'

'No, I won't. Might be as well if you stuck around too, Chief.'

'I'm broke, any road.' Eason flipped his lighter into action. 'Costs a fair whack, this living ashore.'

'I'm sure – with a wife to keep – and a child—'

'One and a half. Bun in the oven, as they say.'

'Well, congratulations!'

'Hit or miss, I reckon. No skill in it . . . Listen, we got four ratings joining – right?'

'Including your Leading Stoker. We're going to be busier than we have been, Chief. I am, anyway – I want that desk clear, by Saturday. Some of the bumf will need *your* attention, incidentally.'

'I got a special way with bumf.' Expelling a long plume of smoke . . . 'Long as it's on thin paper, mind . . .' He'd mimed his meaning: now he pointed with his head. 'Here's the Debs' Delight paying us a visit.'

Dymock: approaching round the end of the basin, from *Trumpeter*'s berth at that end. Eason muttered, 'I'll leave *you* the pleasure', and started across the plank.

'See you in the office later, Chief.' Chalk waited, smoking his cigarette and gazing across the oily surface at *Trumpeter*. One more or less complete submarine, ready for her baptismal total immersion. It would be a year before *Threat* reached that stage. He glanced to his right: 'Morning, Toby.'

'Morning . . . Message to you from my skipper. Remember I mentioned people called Buchanan?'

He nodded. 'Barlows' finance director.'

'Correct. They're having a cocktail party at their house at Helensburgh – on Wednesday – and he's asked Jacko to bring you along. Don't ask me why. But Jacko's ordained that *I* should bring you – since I know the way, and so on. It's for Wednesday at six-thirty, I might pick you up at your digs at six – all right?'

'I wonder why he'd invite me – not having met, in fact not knowing me from a bar of soap?'

'Well – he's a Barlows' director, he'd know who's who in the yard. And after all, you're acting skipper. They tend to hobnob mostly with COs.'

'Although they've counted you in.'

'As I said – *mostly*.'

'Well – it'd be undiplomatic not to accept, I suppose.'

'It would, really. Unless you've something else on?'

'Would they expect a formal acceptance?'

'God, no. Jacko'll pass the word.'

'I'll take my own car, anyway. Sooner be independent – thanks all the same. Tell me how to get there?'

'I'll draw you a map.'

'Fine.'

'And by the way, Rufus – thanks for introducing me to the Cameron-Greens.'

'This Buchanan thing's not some kind of *quid pro quo*, by any chance?'

'Not at all. I said – comes through Jacko.'

'You're doing your basin dive that day, aren't you? Wednesday?'

Dymock nodded. 'But we'll be up and dry again by mid-afternoon, latest. You coming to watch?'

'I might.'

'*Trumpeter*'s christening. You can be a godfather, if you like.'

The Buchanans' house, set back off the road that led from Helensburgh to Crosskeys and Loch Lomond, was pretty much as he'd visualized it from Dymock's description of it the other day as 'a great stone pile'. Somewhat larger than most, but otherwise typical of the Scottish suburban villa: grey stone, sash windows, slate roof, and a semicircle of in-and-out driveway. A carriage-house too, back there. Obviously serving as a garage now, but with an upper storey like a sail-loft. Chalk backed his little Austin in between a brand-new Flying Standard – a new job, there weren't many on the roads yet – and a huge old shooting-brake, and amongst other cars between there and the door he spotted Dymock's Riley.

The one *good* thing about the Dymock-Suzie situation, of which Chalk was frequently reminding himself, was that after the coming weekend he wouldn't be able to get up there much. And Guy would be moving in only three weeks from

Friday. From then on, it could be left to him entirely.

The Buchanan front door stood open, he saw as he went up the steps. A heavy door with pseudo-baronial carving: again, par for the course ... A roar of voices from inside. He pulled the bell, heard it clang somewhere in the rear regions, and within seconds a uniformed maid appeared: as quick as a genie with a lamp, except that she was carrying a tray with glasses on it. Passing through the gloomy hall in any case, he guessed.

'Good evenin', sir. May I enquire your name?'

'Chalk. Lieutenant Chalk, Royal Navy.'

'Lieutenant Chalk – aye, they're expecting ye. If ye'd step this way, sir ...'

Her pronunciation of his name reminded him of an Edinburgh street-children's chant: *Edinburgh rock, Banana an' chalk* ... The way they said it, the words rhymed. He was in the doorway of a room on the right of the hall, and shaking his host's hand. A rather soft hand – but a firm handshake – a lightly checked suit unquestionably from Savile Row, silk shirt made to measure probably in Jermyn Street ... Chalk, having taken this superficial inventory in one glance, was conscious of being subjected to a rather more deliberate assessment by Buchanan. Then the probing light-brown eyes seemed to relax, creasing as he smiled ... 'So glad you could join us, Chalk. Sorry there wasn't time to get an invitation to you directly. I'm Andrew Buchanan – as you'll have realized. We should have met before, of course, but I'm not up here all *that* much—'

'And I've only been here a fortnight.'

'Ah – you've met.' Dymock, beside them. Looking smart in a suit of light-grey flannel. 'No introduction needed, eh?' Buchanan had turned away to beckon the maid with her tray; Chalk nodded to Dymock. 'Evening, Toby.'

'Made sense of my map, anyway. Brilliant cartography, of course.' He drifted on. Buchanan offered, 'Champagne? Sherry? Scotch? Dry Martini? Or something more esoteric?'

'Scotch, please. With water.' Glancing round: he'd already concluded that about seventy percent of the male guests might be town councillors or bank managers, plus a sprinkling of Elders of the Kirk. Some ferocious-looking women, mostly in small packs.

'Are we treating you well at Barlows'?'

He nodded downward at his host. 'So far, very well.' Buchanan was of slightly less than average height, somewhat overweight for it and probably in his middle forties. Apart from his weight he obviously took good care of himself: expensive barbering, soft hands doubtless manicured, very white teeth in a face that was lightly tanned. From the neck up, in fact, the image of the hero on a romantic novel's dustcover, Chalk thought: not all that unDymock-like ... He told him, 'As it happens there was one rather knotty-looking problem last week, I mentioned it to the Ship Manager only on Friday and by first thing on Monday I was told steps had been taken to put it right. That's not bad going.'

'Good. Good ... They tell me your captain's arriving in a few days' time, but if you or he ever have any less easily solved problems and it's anything *I* can help with—'

'You're not talking shop, are you?'

A salver with a tumbler of whisky on it was being proffered from the left, and this was obviously his hostess on the right. And she *was* – using Dymock's description of her – a stunner. Almost literally stunning – so suddenly and at such close range, in a waft of musky scent. Small, shapely: and quite a bit younger than her husband. Chalk told her – taking the whisky without looking at it – 'Definitely not, Mrs Buchanan. Not a word of shop.'

'Amazing. Andrew does tend to drone on about ships and things.'

'Well, that's true.' Buchanan nodded to her. 'But I don't to you, sweetheart, you'll admit that much.' He told Chalk, 'I honestly don't think she knows how I make our living ... Have a chat later, shall we?'

'I'd like that.'

He left them, one hand held up in farewell and his wife murmuring, 'Bye, darling . . .' Then: 'They *have* given you a drink, have they?' He showed it to her, and noticed as she glanced down at it how thick and long her eyelashes were. Eyes – as she looked up, smiling – rather narrow, greenish – perhaps hazel – in a pale face with prominent cheekbones and a wide, brightly painted mouth. 'I'd better warn you, I already know a *lot* about you. For instance, that your first name is Rufus, that you are twenty-seven years old and engaged to be married to a girl who flies aeroplanes, and that you and Toby have been friends since God was in nappies. One question he's never answered though, not at any rate to my satisfaction – so perhaps you'll try – is what kind of lunacy is it that induces otherwise apparently normal men to go in for submarines?'

'You did say *apparently* normal.'

'Is the answer that you're all peculiar, then?'

'We may be. Wouldn't know it, would we?' He sipped his drink. 'But – no kind of lunacy, as I see it. We – enjoy it, derive a great deal of satisfaction from it. Perhaps largely because we believe it's important for the Navy's future. But as I'm forbidden to talk shop I won't pursue that any further.' He put a hand to her elbow, as someone tried to squeeze behind her. 'Unless you want me to, Mrs Buchanan?'

'Definitely not. But shall we cut the formalities down to their very roots?' The greenish eyes held his as she pointed at herself. 'Me Zoe, you Rufus?'

'Fine – Zoe . . .' He thought he'd managed not to show his surprise: but first names, after only about three minutes' conversation, was – well, somewhat *avant garde* . . . He told her – with an instinct to match it, *not* to seem staid or disapproving – 'I must say, I like that name.'

'Rufus is rather fun, too.' She'd stopped the maid, who'd been passing with a silver shaker, and was having her glass refilled. It was on the large side, for a Martini glass. She sipped at it, and grimaced. 'Disgusting. Really – foul. But it seems to like *me* ... Now where were we ... Oh, I know – I was about to ask you where you come from, and do you have family still there, a Mummy and a Daddy?'

'"Mummy" is in a nursing home – permanently – and "Daddy" was killed in the war.'

'Oh, God, that *damn* war ... I'm sorry – Rufus ... Stupid of me, should know better than to ask that sort of question – of our own generation. So *many* ... And this one that's coming is going to be far worse, isn't it?'

'I don't know.' He sipped his whisky. 'A lot of people say so.'

'We'll have their bombers over us on the first day, won't we? Isn't that what they're practising for in Spain?'

'Partly. Or so one supposes. But there are two things you can set against that. One, we won't be their only target, I mean we'll have allies – like France, Belgium – and the Germans can't be everywhere at once. And two, by the time it starts we'll have built a lot more bombers and fighters of our own, please God. Same as we're building ships. Which I mustn't mention.'

'Absolutely *not*. But what about poison gas? What can anyone do about *that*? I think it's going to be total bloody hell.' She drained her glass. 'We must live for today, Rufus. Enjoy life while we have it. Don't you agree?'

'Well – up to a point, but—'

'Are you always so cautious?'

'On this particular subject—'

'There's no "up to a point" about it!' She was slightly plastered, he'd already realized. As well as – all right, sticking to that word – *stunningly* attractive. Tiny age-lines at the corners of her eyes emphasized it rather than detracted from it, and her figure in the low-cut, skimpy black dress – well, it took a lot of self-control to look anywhere else. He imagined himself glancing up and finding Diana's coolly critical gaze on him – that way she had of doing it, as if she were reading one's mind. Which God forbid … Mrs Buchanan – Zoe – was beckoning to a man in striped trousers who'd taken over the maid's duties: 'Rufus, do finish that whisky, you've been nursing it for ages …'

'So – as we were saying – your captain's arriving this weekend, Chalk.'

He nodded to Andrew Buchanan. 'His name's Ozzard. He'd have been here before me, but he was bringing a submarine home from the China Station and they've been delayed in the Med somewhere.'

'In connection with Italian naval activity, by any chance?'

'Could well be.'

Buchanan was on the ball, all right. It would no doubt be crucial to his business activities, Chalk supposed, to keep himself well informed. Then another question came in from his right, from one of the dark-grey suits. A fair number of these men were shipbuilders, directors of other Clyde yards – *not* town councillors. The answer he gave to this one's question gave rise to reminiscences about earlier types of submarine that had been built up here. Thinking how Zoe would have loved to be listening to it, he glanced round – over grey, bald, or balding heads – and saw that Dymock and Jacko Pargeter were with her. The latter had arrived late, with his wife Helen, and Chalk had guessed, seeing a table in the adjoining room set for eight, that they might well be among those staying for supper.

Buchanan drew him away from the group of men who were now discussing technical details of the old E-class – of which there were none in commission now, fortunately, although they'd played a noble part in the war. In the Dardanelles, for instance, earning VCs for men like Holbrook, Nasmith, Boyle and Saxton White. Buchanan asked him, 'What are your thoughts – strictly between ourselves –

of this new T-class? Will you be happy to go to war in them?'

'Yes, I will. Or would ... Advantages being – well, as you'll know, they have a stronger pressure-hull than earlier classes – should therefore withstand depthcharging better – and they have a wider range. And theoretically at least we'll get under faster.'

'You mean dive more quickly?'

He nodded. 'It's a fairly vital aspect of a submarine's performance.'

'Crash-dive—'

'That's a popular term for it. I've never heard it used among submariners.'

A shrug. 'I suppose we laymen pick up our terminology from the newspapers. Or it's American, perhaps. What else, though?'

'Surfaced speed's disappointing. They're trying various types of diesel in different T's, I know. But I'd say the answer's much bigger, more powerful ones. Whether that's a possibility with the current limit on displacement, I *don't* know.'

'London Treaty terms, you mean.'

'Exactly. I suppose once seconds are ordered out of the ring there could be some changes made. But it ought to be thought out in advance, oughtn't it? What better diesels might be available, what re-tooling's needed, and so forth.'

'And other design changes around the installation of heavier machinery, I'd imagine. Not that I'm technically equipped to make any judgement there. Less so than you, obviously. But what you've told me's very interesting. Anything else you can think of, straight off the bat?'

'Well – one comparatively small item. The operating gear for bowcaps. Meaning the front caps on torpedo-tubes, the doors that—'

'I know what bowcaps are.'

'There's one aspect of the system which I personally

dislike. I'm not alone in it, either, not by any means. Trouble is, it's an Admiralty-approved system, so there's not much we can do about it.'

'Rather a small point of detail anyway?'

'Yes. But design's made up of detail, isn't it. Operational efficiency – and safety – depend on it too.'

'Are you saying this system's unsafe?'

'It could be if it was used without proper care and training.'

'Wouldn't that apply to just about every piece of machinery, in a submarine?'

'To an extent, yes. But a lot more so in areas where – well, where there's potential ingress of water – in large quantities, under pressure . . .'

'Yes. I can imagine—'

'Don't worry. We'll – come to terms with it. But tell me, have you ever been to sea in a submarine?'

'D'you know, I haven't.' Buchanan seemed embarrassed to admit it. 'I'm new in this particular business. A company – amalgam of companies, actually – I work for them, in fact I'm a junior director – has a major financial interest in Barlows', and they put me in here about – oh, less than a year ago. I've retained other responsibilities, elsewhere, but this is exclusively my domain as far as finances go. Which is the key to the whole thing, of course. And with a war coming – which'll put submarine construction into high gear very quickly—' He paused, looking around at his guests and their glasses: then finished '– you see why I wanted to pick your brains.'

'I'm flattered.'

'Don't be. You aren't the first I've asked.' A shrug. 'At my end – well, the shipyard business is comparatively simple – and potentially very profitable, with the introduction of new systems aimed at saving time and money.' He dropped his voice, added after a glance round, 'Innovations which are not popular with some of these stalwarts here, of course.'

He paused again, as the woman with the drinks tray approached. 'A Scotch and water here, please, and one with soda.' Turning back to Chalk . . . 'I'd better be careful what I say, in present company.'

'I dare say.' Chalk glanced at their immediate neighbours. 'And changing the subject, if that's a good thing to do – and re your telling me you've never been to sea in a submarine – I was thinking – you may have thought of it already – *Trumpeter*'ll be going out for her final acceptance trials next month, won't she? If you want to see how a submarine works, why not include yourself in the Barlows' team for that?'

'Would they have room for a mere observer?'

'For a Barlows' director?'

'But – on principle, I'd have thought—'

'There are always a few extra hands on board. I'll be one of them myself, if I can swing it. A chance to see how one of this new class behaves – well, not to be missed.' He explained. 'She'll be commissioned by then, flying the White Ensign and her own crew handling her, but until her skipper signs for her she's still technically yours. What's more, the builders provide lunch for all hands, and by tradition it's a damn good one.'

'So I'm footing the bill anyway?'

'You are indeed. Spending some of those vast profits . . .'

He heard, while making his way across the room a few minutes later, a booming and slightly blurred Scots voice intoning, 'It's been inevitable I tell ye, since '34. August '34 – when the German army took the oath of allegiance to Adolf Hitler. Make no mistake, they pay close heed to such oaths, those square-heads!'

'Why, *hello*, Rufus!'

She was still on her feet, anyway. She'd put her glass down on the chimney-piece beside her, he noticed. Giving it a rest: not a bad idea either. He nodded to Pargeter. 'Evening, sir. Basin dives went well, I gather.'

'Found some small leaks.'

Dymock put in, 'None a few bits of chewing-gum wouldn't fix.'

His captain added, 'Got the ballast about right, that's the main thing.' After a wary glance at his hostess, he changed the subject. 'Found your way here all right, Chalk.'

'Oh, yes. Even with *this* chap's notion of a map.'

Pargeter's sad eyes smiled. Then: 'If you'd excuse me, Zoe – mustn't monopolize you, not at this stage of the evening anyway. Better see who Helen's stuck with, meanwhile.' He winked at Chalk as he moved away through the throng, jaw jutting.

Chalk said, 'I suppose it's about time *I* got back to Mrs Blair.'

'Mrs Blair?'

Dymock informed her, 'His landlady. A rare beauty. Weighs in at – what is it, Rufus, seventeen stone?'

'Something like that. Heart of gold, though, and a dab hand with the mashed potatoes.'

'Sounds like a treasure. But—' Zoe poked at him with a scarlet-tipped finger – 'don't you *dare* leave us yet! We've hardly spoken, you and I!'

'Don't you want us out of the way? You're having a supper party, aren't you?'

'Have you been snooping, Rufus?'

'Doesn't take a Sherlock Holmes, with that door standing open.'

'It's going to be sheer purgatory, anyway. Except for the Pargeters. Shop, shop, shop ... I really can't think why I bother ... Oh, I was going to ask you, Rufus – do you ever get to London?'

'On occasion.' He failed to hear whatever Dymock had muttered to her. 'Not often. Usually only passing through.' A nod towards Dymock. 'Not like this character here, for instance.'

'Toby?' She showed surprise. 'Toby's *never* in London, nowadays.' Her stare was accusing. 'If he has a weekend to spare, he rushes up to the bloody Highlands. I think he's got a girl up there, some wee Highland lassie ... You don't happen to know anything about her, do you, Rufus?'

'Zoe—' Dymock was shaking his head – 'you do talk the most awful tripe, at times!'

'Perhaps I shouldn't blame him. *I* was in London this last weekend, and bored absolutely to distraction. People tend to let one down, you know. I *hate* that. But there I was, spitting *blood* with boredom. Oh, I can see that given that choice – London on spec or a roll or two in the heather – well, obviously ... Surely you know *something* about this secret love of his, Rufus?'

'Zoe – please—'

'*Do* tell, Toby. At least, admit it. I'm agog – so's Rufus, look. Can't you see your old friend's agog?'

'I'm sure he is. But—' He made a show of checking the time. 'Heavens – *must* say goodbye ... Zoe – thank you *very* much ...'

He'd put his hand out uncertainly, she'd ignored it, and he'd gone. She reached for her glass. 'Shame. Upset him, somehow. Do you think it was my allusion to rolling in the heather?'

Chalk agreed, 'Might well have been.'

'Anyway—' she'd drained the glass – 'so much for *him*.' Glancing round, then. '*What* a boring party this is. Aren't *you* bored, Rufus?'

'Not really.' It was the truth, he hadn't been. He told her sincerely, 'No. As a matter of fact, not at all.'

'*Well*.' The greenish eyes smiled. 'If you're telling me what I *hope* you are—'

'Mrs Buchanan – sorry tae break in.' The woman had purple hair and a small husband practically in an arm-lock. 'Only a wee moment, tae thank ye for the *grandest* party—'

'*So* glad you could come, Mrs – er—'

Chalk left her to it. Feeling it definitely was time for him to be on his way too, but seeing Dymock in conversation with Buchanan – so there'd be a hold-up there ... Then a man he'd never seen before in his life waved to him, beaming; he nodded, forced a smile. Meanwhile that couple had left, and Zoe was saying with her hand on his arm, 'It's much too big for us. Except Andrew does like to entertain, on the rare occasions when he's there. Which is hardly ever, I may say. Most of the time he's in Timbuctu or up here or – God knows ... So if you do happen to be – as you put it, "passing through" – well, we're in the book—'

'*You* don't spend much time up here, then?'

'As little as I can help. I *loathe* the place.' She was silent for a moment, frowning at him. 'Are you just a tiny bit *proper*, Rufus?'

'I hope not. But—'

'I hope not, too ... Anyway, tell me about your flying financée. Where does she fly *to*?' Eyes wide, and the edge of the Martini glass pressed against her lower lip ... 'Not round and round in ever-decreasing circles like that bird – you know, the one that finally vanishes up its own—'

'Flies all over the place. Wherever the customers want to be taken. Mostly sporting events, race-meetings and so on. But anywhere – including France, Ireland—'

'Fascinating ... Although Andrew roams much more widely than that. South Africa, Sweden, America – I go *there* with him, usually. God knows what for ... I need another drink.' Glancing round ... 'Damn, they've finished dispensing them. And we can't send for one when nobody else is getting any. Tell you what – if we creep out together, just slip out like wraiths—'

'I've had more than enough, Zoe. Truly. Besides, I *must* go. Did I gather you won't be up here much longer?'

'Leaving tomorrow. Andrew's staying here, says he has

to. And – Rufus, London is definitely no place to be alone.'

'I can't believe you would be. Not for long, anyway.'

'That's the second nice thing you've said. You know, if you really *tried*—'

'I was telling those fellers there—' A heavy, dark-suited man of about fifty was talking as he lurched up to them.

Zoe ignored him, told Chalk 'You *do* improve on acquaintance, Rufus. In fact I think if I took you seriously in hand—'

'– my considered opinion, dear lady, that war became inevitable back in '34, when the German army took the oath of allegiance to Adolf Hitler. That oath's not given lightly, d'ye see—'

'I'm sure it isn't.' Chalk nodded to him, then turned back and took Zoe's free hand, squeezed it gently. 'I really *do* have to go.'

'I suppose if you *have* to—'

He'd nodded. 'Sorry.'

'Remember – in the book – Andrew Murray Buchanan. Second initial's important, because—'

'I'll write it down.'

'Same evening Hindenburg died.' The bulky man took a grip on Chalk's arm. 'August second, '34. Nazis had it set up ready for the old feller to breathe his last, and that very night every serving unit in the square-head army had to swear by God to render to Adolf Hitler – I quote from memory – render to Adolf Hitler, leader of the German nation and people, Supreme Commander – unconditional obedience. Unconditional, mark you!'

Chalk disengaged himself from the clutching hand. 'Doesn't improve the prospects, I agree. But I'm off now, so—'

'Aye. You be off.' The man turned all his attention on Zoe. 'D'ye see, Mrs Buchanan – that oath's binding on 'em. Any man as—'

'Rufus, try not to be *proper*?'

'I will.' He called back, 'I promise!'

'– any man as broke it, they'd put him up against a wall. So no matter what Hitler may want 'em to do henceforth—'

Chapter 6

'Ozzie' Ozzard was a tallish, large-boned man with bushy eyebrows and dark hair already wearing thin. He was a lieutenant-commander, in his early thirties. Chalk had met him once – in Gibraltar, years earlier, when he'd been an L-class boat's first lieutenant and Chalk a brand-new sub-lieutenant, and he remembered even from then the older man's abrupt, jerky manner of speech. Which hadn't changed. But he'd thought it unlikely that Ozzard would remember him, and sure enough he didn't. They shook hands: 'Decent of you to come out, Chalk.' He raised his voice: 'Maggie! Come down and meet Rufus Chalk!'

There was a large, cool room, originally a dairy, full of luggage and packing-cases which they weren't intending to unpack here, only when they moved into the Pargeters' cottage, about half a mile away; they'd be transferring themselves to it when *Trumpeter* left to join her flotilla, in about six weeks' time. From Barlows', this place was about halfway to Helensburgh, on high ground above a river called the Leven. And on this Sunday morning Ozzard was wearing old flannel 'bags' and a torn open-necked shirt, Chalk remembered.

'Is there anything I can help with, sir?'

'No. Thanks . . . Except I want to see *Threat* – whatever there is of her.'

'Whenever you like. I've transport outside.'

'Pargeter said you had your own. I'll have to get one too, when I can. Meanwhile we'll get lifts from them – or you . . . Ah, Maggie. Rufus Chalk, my Number One.'

'Sacrificing his weekend – or some of it.' She was about five-four, and not by any means bony. Curly light-brown hair framed a round, smiling face. Cotton frock, plimsolls and an apron; the small hand grasping his was hot and damp. 'We aren't fit to be seen, either of us. But how *very* nice of you to come out.'

'Not at all. I've been looking forward to your getting here.'

'Hah!' A bark of amusement from Ozzard. '*Bet* you have!'

'Fact, sir. For one thing your official correspondence has been – to put it mildly – voluminous, and until a few days ago I've been single-handed as far as desk-work's concerned. It's all cleared up, I'm glad to say; and *now* we have a Leading Telegraphist who can actually type, and a Leading Stoker as engineer's store-keeper. Among four hands who joined this week.'

'What about the plumber?'

'Eason. Commissioned Engineer. Knows his stuff, keeps at it, and he has the eyes of a hawk for the yard trying to put one over on us.'

'That happened?'

'It would have, but thanks to Eason – well, a stitch in time. Barlows' are very cooperative, actually, this was just one blunder that he put his finger on . . . Question of timing now, sir – seeing *Threat* – do you have any plans for lunch?'

'Sandwiches.' Maggie Ozzard told him, 'Courtesy of the Pargeters, and they're feeding us tonight too, bless them.'

'What about early afternoon, Chalk?'

'If I'm back here to pick you up at – 1400?'

'Perfect!' Glancing at his wife. 'Eh?'

'Well – do you have far to go now?'

'No.' Chalk told her, 'Dunbarton – I've digs there. It's no distance – four miles, roughly.'

'And will there be room for me, on this guided tour?'

'Lots of room.' He looked back at her husband. 'I'll give Eason a ring, sir – he's expecting it, and he'll meet us down there. Oh, and I've made some notes for you – left 'em in the car, I'll get them – Barlows' personalities, and so forth.'

'Good. Well done.'

'You were diverted to Palma, we hear.'

'*Weren't* we. Expecting thirty-six hours in Gib, and dear old Pompey a week later – then *zingo*, off to the bleeding Balearics!'

'As from the moment I heard of it—' his wife put in – 'I've been conscious of a deep hatred of Italians.'

'I can imagine.' Chalk added, 'But you've left trouble behind you in China too – according to the BBC this morning?'

'Heard some of that.' Ozzard said, 'Switched on too late. Japs on the warpath near Peking, wasn't it?'

'Battle for some bridge, and the fighting was said to be spreading.'

'There's trouble brewing in Shanghai, as well.' Maggie added, 'It won't be the Chinks who start it, either ... Like some coffee?'

'But you haven't even unpacked?'

'This lot isn't going to be unpacked. We'll live out of suitcases, for now. But vital necessities such as coffee and gin are available all right. May be just a little early for the Plymouth ... Coffee for you, Tim?'

'Please.' He pointed at a packing-case, as his wife went through to the kitchen. 'Sit down, Chalk. Smoke? About the Japs – in my opinion we're facing a bigger threat from them – in the short term – than from Germany. Not the conventional view, I know – and I'll admit I don't like what I heard two days ago in London about goings-on in Austria, for that matter. Hitler's appointed an SS officer to command the local Nazis, and this chap – Keppler – has induced Chancellor Schuschnigg to let an equally unsavoury squirt called Seyss-Inquart into his government. Trojan horse if there ever was one. All working in the same direction now, isn't it? Ah, Maggie . . . Point is, Chalk, they may need us to be out of the builders' hands a lot sooner than they think!'

The Ozzards had arrived late on the previous evening, so the Pargeters had given them a meal and put them up. Chalk, waiting for a call from Jacko Pargeter that never came, had spent the evening writing letters to various people including Guy and their sister Betty, and he'd had a long telephone call from Diana. In his letter to Guy he'd included a reference to Toby Dymock, mentioning that the other Cameron-Green daughter, Patricia, would be down from Cambridge soon and that they were all hoping she and Dymock might like each other.

He, Chalk, was hoping they might, anyway. It was wishful thinking, considering that Dymock was up at Glendarragh this weekend, with Suzie to himself. Not even Alastair was going to be there to queer his pitch for him. Easier not to think about it . . . Although another piece of wishful thinking – the odds against which he thought might be slightly shorter – was that by the end of a weekend of undiluted Dymock, Suzie might decide she'd had enough of him.

Maggie Ozzard asked him later, on their way back from the 'guided tour', 'What do you usually do with your weekends, Rufus?'

'I've friends at a place called Glendarragh. A few hours away by road – in the wilds up towards Fort William. My younger brother's known them for some time and they got in touch when he told them I was here.'

'Would you have been up there *now* if we hadn't been coming?'

'Might have.' He looked round at her and smiled. 'I knew

you *were* coming, so the question didn't arise.' He changed the subject – on that white lie – to *Trumpeter*, her near-completion and his hope of getting his own name on the passenger-list for her acceptance trials. Ozzard's gruff answer was what he'd expected: he, Ozzard, would certainly expect to go along, Chalk's chances would depend on whether or not they had room for him.

He added, 'But there'll be several T's completing at other yards before we do. You'll get your chance, Number One.'

Chalk asked me – after he'd been into the house to fetch two tankards of beer – 'for lubrication of vocal chords. Not so sure that *you're* entitled' – whether I'd known Ozzard. Which I hadn't.

'I knew *of* him, of course.'

'Earned himself a chestful of gongs, didn't he. In the Med, when he had—' the old man put a hand up to his forehead – 'damn it. Name of his boat – in the 8th Flotilla. *Can't* have forgotten!'

My memory had slipped too. So – creep up on it … Ozzard had had three stripes by then: and his boat had been a 'T', for sure …

'Got it. *Typhoon*.'

'Of course!' He shook his head. 'Frustrating business, getting old. I think something happens a split second before you're going to say whatever it is. Like a connection breaking … And – well, I can only say I *think* it was on one of the next few evenings, in the week after Dymock had been at Glendarragh solo, that Zoe Buchanan telephoned me at my lodgings. Could have been later, but – doesn't matter, it was *about* then. I asked her how on earth she'd got the number – when there must have been about a thousand Mrs Blairs in the book – and perhaps a hundred of them in Dunbarton – and she said she'd got it from Toby Dymock. Then she added – after I might have left rather a marked silence, by way of a comment on her having had *his* number

– that *she* hadn't had it, her husband had, she'd looked it up in the book he kept on his desk. Then she'd got through to Dymock and got my number from him. She wanted to know whether I'd done any thinking about taking a long weekend and spending it in London. I told her – untruthfully, I suspect – no, I hadn't. Mind you, I found it difficult to believe that it was me she was after, I thought it more likely that she was using me as a stalking-horse just to get hold of Dymock. It was obviously Zoe whom he'd been supposed to meet in London, he'd ducked out of it – for whatever reason or reasons, possibly similar to those which deterred *me* from any such involvement – at that time ... But that was why she'd been going for him at the cocktail party – to embarrass him in front of me, punish him for having let her down. I hadn't said anything about it to Dymock, incidentally – although I'd been tempted to pull his leg. What he did or did not get up to with Mrs Buchanan was hardly my business, after all.'

'But you thought she was still pursuing him.'

He put down his tankard. 'I *liked* her. Partly I dare say because she'd shown interest in yours truly – whether genuine or not, the effect was the same – isn't it always? But she was so outgoing – in a funny way, *honest*. Perhaps I mean *forthright*. She'd say what she thought, and she'd expect you to tell her what *you* thought – no half-truths or prevarication. Downright lies, certainly – but that's – well, the other side of the coin, isn't it. She was a man's woman – that sums it up. And ruthless – also an attraction. Fascination, in fact – oddly enough ... But I was *very* cautious. To start with I suppose I was by nature, and then – well, matters were tricky enough already *vis-à-vis* Dymock, and even more so there was Andrew Buchanan as a major factor in the equation. He couldn't have been unaware that his wife had a tendency to kick over the traces when she felt like it. At least, I didn't see *how* ... As things turned out – well, we'll come to that. But he was no fool, and

– well, holy smoke, last thing I'd have wanted was a run-in with a Barlows' director! Inconceivable. I'd have had to leave my job – one way or another. Might account for Dymock's having developed cold feet too, eh?'

He added, after a pause, 'I liked Buchanan, anyway.'

'Did she ring again?'

A nod. 'Can't tell you exactly when or how often, but she – kept in touch, all right.'

'With Dymock too?'

'She did tell me – later – that she hadn't. But – hardly matters, does it? She was no more than – well, a slight distraction, and barely *that*; one's thinking was dominated by the Suzie-Dymock affair.'

'Affair?'

'The Suzie-Dymock relationship, then.'

'So she hadn't had a surfeit of him, that weekend?'

'Regrettably not. But now listen. Of this period – four or five weeks it must have been – I've been working at it, but all I can remember are bits and pieces, snatches of conversation and – as I may have put it before – an occasional visual memory like a snapshot. Which one then wonders if one trusts: to what extent the mind distorts recollection over the years. And certainly rearranging the jumble in any logical sequence is beyond me. Possibly because it's overclouded by what followed? But that's the best I can give you now – pictures in the fire, as it were.'

'I'll paste them together.'

'Glad *I* don't have to. What d'you think of this beer?'

'I'd like to know where to get it. It actually tastes of hops.'

'I make it myself. Saves money, and I agree with you it compares favourably with a lot of the swill that comes in cans . . . But – nose to the grindstone, now – we were talking about the weekend of 10–11 July – when the Ozzards arrived.'

'And Dymock was at Glendarragh.'

Chalk nodded. 'There particularly of course, I can't do more than put two and two together – possibly coming up with five. Not having been present ... Dymock himself didn't mention the weekend, not a word, and I didn't question him about it. Didn't want to show that much interest, I suppose. I wasn't exactly seeking his company, anyway. There was more to be learnt – deduced – the weekend after, when I *was* up there. I've a sort of rough diary here, you see, so at least the dates are right . . . But from as much as I did see of Dymock, he was – riding high. Frenetically active – *Trumpeter* nearing completion, with all these tests and inspections in progress, and she had her full crew by this time. But he was obviously delighted with himself – radiating good humour towards all and sundry.'

'Except towards you, I suppose.'

'Well – we were keeping out of each other's way.'

'But are you saying he was in love?'

'No, I'm not.' One of those quick, almost imperceptible headshakes of his: it was a signal of impatience, or annoyance, or both. Telling me quite sharply, 'Draw that inference if you like. All I'm saying is he was cock-a-hoop.'

Arriving at Glendarragh late-ish on the Friday evening – the 16th, this was – he was met not by Suzie but by her mother – with MacKenzie in the background, as always – and from the moment he saw her he was aware of her embarrassment and efforts to hide it. How lovely to see him, etcetera, and how they'd missed him last weekend: then, spotting the loose end of a conversational link dangling from that, she'd asked him whether his captain had arrived, and did Chalk like him: oh, and his wife, he was married, was he not?' – what was *she* like? It was quite a few minutes before she told him – volunteering the information, since Chalk hadn't asked – that Suzie was exercising her pony. It had been so hot these last few days, early mornings or evenings were really the *only* times . . .

'Has she heard from Guy, d'you know?'

'I – *think* so . . .'

Momentary hesitation: the doubt in her mind being – he guessed – whether or not Suzie's correspondence with Guy was a safe subject; then she'd decided either that it was, or that she'd hardly be able to avoid it. This was, after all, Guy's brother she was talking to.

'Yes, she *did* have a letter from him. I'm not absolutely sure she's written back to him yet, though.' That bright, high laugh: 'Suzie's *terribly* lazy, when it comes to letter-writing!'

'So's Guy. They're obviously made for each other.'

The laugh again – only worse, almost a short burst of hysteria. 'I wouldn't necessarily have been told, anyway. She's *so* secretive, these days, one never knows – I mean, one simply *doesn't* . . .'

The line might as easily have been *It's her business, none of mine*.

And Sir Innes wasn't talking about Suzie, or Guy – or about Toby Dymock for that matter – any more than he could help. In his study, as usual over glasses of malt whisky, his interest was all in Ozzie Ozzard's recent diversion to Majorca and the Italian submarine activity off Barcelona. Ozzard had in fact filled in a few details on this, so Chalk was able to elaborate to some extent; but not all that much, and when their conversation flagged he tried a change of subject: 'Did Dymock bring his rod with him, last week-end?'

Sir Innes glanced at him. 'Did he – bring his rod? Oh – yes . . . But we didn't fish . . .' A moment later he was talking about Spain again. And Chalk didn't see Suzie until she came down a few minutes before the dinner gong. She apologized . . . 'Sugar and I went much too far. Stupid of me – she isn't as fit as she ought to be. And as I'd already worked her rather hard I had to let her take her time, coming back.'

'I gather you've heard from Guy?'

She glanced at her mother: a look of surprise, he thought. Or surmise: what other beans might she have spilled . . . But she confirmed it casually enough: 'Yes – a few days ago. Seems longer – not *since* last weekend.'

'You'll have him here in a fortnight, anyway.'

'We're *so* looking forward to it.' Eve Cameron-Green was wearing the blue, shimmery dress that she'd worn the first night he'd been there, and a diamond-and-sapphire bracelet on her wrist, and Suzie was in green with the gold chain she often wore. Her mother added, with that same high laugh: 'And to have him – and Diana – actually dropping in on us out of the sky—'

'We've cut the paddock, by the way.'

'And there's a bit of spade-work needed.' Sir Innes came in on *his* cue. 'If you're feeling up to it tomorrow, Chalk. Otherwise there's next weekend too, of course – and I dare say your friend Dymock may be here to lend a hand.'

'He doesn't think he will be, now.' Suzie told her father, 'Some sort of inspection that Saturday, he said.'

Chalk asked her – noticing her mother's alarm and Sir Innes' surprise – 'You've heard from him recently, have you?'

She'd coloured slightly: but shrugging, stuck with it now . . . 'Only a note – came this morning. To let us know it's unlikely he can come. Sorry, Mama, I'd forgotten, should've—'

The dinner-gong boomed. Suzie's mother was complaining as its reverberations died away, '– as long as we *eventually* get to hear such things. So Cook can be told, at least . . .' She sighed, with a glance at Chalk. 'I think I mentioned to you how secretive this girl can be!'

'Forgetful, not secretive.' Suzie asked him, 'What's a DESA inspection, anyway?'

'You probably mean DSEA. Stands for Davis Submerged Escape Apparatus. It's the escape system we're supposed to use – well, *in extremis*. Consists of a face-mask, oxygen bottle, and a breathing-bag here on one's chest. You strap it on and then float up, breathing oxygen. If that's the inspection they're due for at the weekend, it'll be because a team's coming up for it from Blockhouse – our submarine headquarters at Gosport – and they'd want to be back by first thing Monday. Makes sense, therefore – except that we could check it all ourselves and they could save the rail fares.'

Sir Innes said – easing his wife's chair in, and moving round to his own – 'But I'd guess it must be of the utmost importance – that of *all* things!'

'I'm only saying we could do it ourselves. It's a matter of counting the sets – there's one for every man on board, plus a few spares – making sure none of them's defective, and checking the mechanics of the escape chambers. Two of them, one more or less at each end of the boat. How it works is two men get in – into each chamber, or whichever you're using – you flood the chamber up until the pressure inside and out is equalized, then they open the hatch and climb out, float up to the surface. In the submarine there's gearing to wind the hatch shut again, and the chamber's drained down for the next pair to get in. And so on, until you're all out.'

'You make it sound easy.'

'D'you think so, Innes?' His wife stared at him wide-eyed. '*I* think it sounds absolutely terrifying!'

'Well – certainly would be to *us*, but—'

Suzie broke in: 'Have you ever had to do it?'

'Not in earnest. Very much hope I never do have to. But we have a practice tank at Gosport with an escape chamber in its base and fifteen feet of water above it. That's very little, compared to the sort of depths one might be at in a real-life emergency, but at least we learn how to go through the motions . . . What I was going to say just now, though – changing the subject entirely – I was hoping earlier that you might have had the paddock cut in time for Toby Dymock to do the levelling last weekend. Sir Innes mentioned that he didn't fish, and I thought perhaps my luck was in!'

'I *think*—' Sir Innes paused with a soup-spoon halfway up – 'we only cut it on Monday – or Tuesday, was it?'

'Monday.' Suzie smiled. 'Hard cheese, Rufus.'

'So what did you do – play tennis all weekend?'

He had them all startled, with that question. But Suzie told him evenly enough. 'We did play quite a bit. I wanted to *win* a set – for a change – and he wouldn't let me. I call that thoroughly unsporting, don't you?' She saw him still watching her, waiting for more, and she finished, 'Rest of the time we just – you know, wandered around. He didn't see much of the place the time before, did he.'

'Rufus?'

He leant on his spade. She had all the dogs with her – Bertie the labrador and both terriers. Saturday morning: he was filling in all the holes that he could find in the recently cut paddock, using earth which he was having to fetch by wheelbarrow from a mound behind the barn. Luckily there weren't all that many holes. He was working bare-chested, and had borrowed a pair of old khaki trousers from Sir Innes.

Suzie commented, glancing at his bare torso, 'Muscle-man himself . . .' She quoted a current advertisement: '*You too can have a body like mine* . . . Rufus, you and Toby have known each other donkey's years, haven't you?'

He agreed: 'Since we were boys. Cadets, aged thirteen.'

'So tell me what you really think of him? I mean *honestly*, in your heart of hearts?'

'I'm not sure I've got one of them.'

'Rufus – seriously?'

'Well – we've known each other all this time – thirteen, fourteen years, roughly – so wouldn't the fact I brought him here in response to your mother's invitation have already told you what I thought of him?'

Thought – not *think*.

'Didn't need to ask, really, did I?'

'But—'

He'd hesitated, jabbing one-handed at the stubble. Imagining Guy looking at him at this moment and urging him *Go on, tell her – she's asked for it, she said she wants it honestly . . .*

'But what, Rufus?'

'I'd thought of him as perhaps hitting it off with your sister. Patricia's a few years older than you and she's been away at Varsity, had more experience generally than you have. I think – frankly, Suzie – that you're too young and *in*experienced to let yourself become at all seriously involved—'

'I wasn't asking you about *me*!'

'Hang on. Seriously involved with *anyone* that much older than you are. But with Toby Dymock, of all people . . . It's him I'm talking about, not you. He's had a lot of experience, with girls.'

'So what's wrong with that?'

'Only that he has a way of – moving on to pastures new, you might say. In other words letting them down – having I suppose bolstered his own ego. You've asked me to be honest, Suzie. He and I have been friends for a long time, but if I had a young sister I'd certainly warn *her*.'

'So—' a shrug – 'I've been warned.'

'You asked for my opinion – heart of hearts, etcetera – didn't you? And as I said, I thought he and Patricia might – take to each other. It never occurred to me for a moment that he might pick on you. I'm kicking myself for that, believe me.'

She thought about it. Then: 'Rufus, I know that what you've said you mean absolutely for the best. But—'

'The truth as I see it, is what I've told you.' He corrected himself: 'The truth as I know it.'

'But you're Guy's brother, aren't you.'

'Oh, yes. And as concerned for you as he is. Knowing how he feels about you, and – Suzie, let me tell you something else. Just between you and me – please forget it after you've let it sink in. Simply that I understand, entirely, Guy's feelings for you. I didn't know he had such good taste – or luck, for that matter.'

She'd stooped to the dog again. 'Asking me to forget *that*, Rufus, is asking a bit much.' Glancing up shyly. 'Thanks.'

'So remember this too – that I'm warning you you'd be wasting yourself, on Toby Dymock. And I'd bet on it ending in tears – yours, not his, and I don't want that for you.'

'I don't happen to agree with you, that's all. I do accept that you believe what you're telling me, mean it for the best and all that, but – Rufus, no matter how he may have behaved with other girls or women in the past—'

'This is different?'

'Yes.' A few seconds' silence, staring at him ... '*Yes*, it *is*!'

'You wouldn't accept that he might have told every one of them exactly that?'

'No, I wouldn't. Or I don't care – because this time it's *true* ... I'll tell you something, Rufus – I've had *three* long letters from him this week ...'

He'd been in two minds about spending the next weekend at Glendarragh – even if he found he could make it, which was by no means certain. Dymock might or might not be there: if he was coming, there'd be two ways of looking at it – one, to be present oneself as a reminder to Suzie of Guy's existence, and to cramp Dymock's style at least to some extent; or two, to stay away, primarily because there was no pleasure in witnessing Dymock's pursuit of her, and as a by-blow making sure her parents knew how he felt.

Eve Cameron-Green pointed out that Patricia would be home – for the first time in months – Alastair would not be and Toby probably would not be: for Patricia's sake as well as Suzie's wouldn't he *please* make a point of coming?

This conversation took place over some meal: it might have been lunch on the Sunday. Chalk had explained that it would have to depend to a large extent on whether the Ozzards wanted to be away on either of the two coming weekends. He didn't want to take the next one off if it would spoil his chances of being here when Diana flew in with Guy. That was something he could *not* miss, and in anticipation of not being able to come for the 23rd–25th he'd finished the hole-filling, put up a pole for a wind-sock – which Suzie had said she'd make, sewing an old sheet into tubular shape – and whitewashed the fence-posts along the paddock's southern boundary. He was going to send Diana a sketch-map; the white posts would provide simple orientation for her, he hoped. The important thing was that it was done, would be ready for the 30th even if he couldn't get up here between now and then.

'Disappointing for Pat if you can't. Specially as Alastair won't be here.'

He nodded to Sir Innes. 'My skipper doesn't want the shop left untended, you see. And he and his wife have old friends in Edinburgh whom they've sworn to visit. I'm putting in a strong plea to be free for the 30th – which is the vital weekend, obviously – so if they do want to shoot off to Edinburgh – d'you see?'

'But you'll come if that side of it's all right, will you?'

Lady Eve put in, 'Of *course* he will!'

'Well – I can't be absolutely certain, I'm afraid.' Meeting those ice-blue eyes, he thought he saw the dawn of understanding. It was important that they should understand – how he felt about what was happening, and that he was committed to the Diana-and-Guy weekend but not necessarily beyond that. He asked her, 'Can we leave it that I'll let you know before the middle of the week?'

As it turned out, on that weekend, 23rd–25th July, the

Ozzards went to their friends in Edinburgh and Chalk stayed to 'mind the shop'. Not that there was much to 'mind' as yet; but Ozzard declared that he believed in starting as he meant to go on, and although *Threat* was still no more than a steel carcass there should be one responsible officer within call – of Barlows', or Submarine Headquarters, or the Admiralty – at all times. Chalk, as it happened, agreed with him.

Diana telephoned on that Saturday, from London. She'd had his letter with the sketch of Glendarragh and the proposed landing-ground, and she told him she thought she'd get her Fox Moth down on it, all right.

'You *think*. What happens if you can't?'

'I *will*. Don't worry. Well, if the weather closed down or something boring like that I'd put down at Glasgow, I suppose . . . But Rufus – if I fly up that valley – sorry, glen – up the middle of it from the southeast, the house'll be smack in front of me, won't it?'

'Yes. You'll come in over a small wood, *then* see it. Or you'd see it from higher up before that, I suppose. But coming over the trees – as you say, it'll be dead ahead of you. Grey, rather grim-looking. And my white fence-posts will be off to the right. I'll be there with my fingers crossed – I expect the rest of the house-party will be too. They're all tremendously interested – as well as keen to meet the intrepid birdwoman . . . Have you spoken to Guy lately?'

'Yes. I'll be picking him up at Worcester. Fairly convenient for us both. He sounded very chirpy, I thought.'

'Well, who wouldn't be?'

She laughed. It was an extremely sexy laugh, and she knew what it did to him. He asked her quietly, 'Do that again?'

'Now you be *good*, Rufus. Until the 30th, anyway . . .'

'Diana – darling—'

'No – I shouldn't have said that. I didn't *mean*—'

'But I *do*. Someone asked me the other day why didn't we get married right away, and while I was trotting out the good, sound reasons I was thinking for God's sake why *don't* we? Diana—'

'We'll talk about it, when I'm there ... Is everything all right with you, Rufus? Is the Rolls going well?'

'Never better – either of us. But I'm *longing* to – see you ... What sort of time, on the 30th?'

'Between late afternoon and sunset. Depends mostly on the weather. Wind, particularly. But we'll be there before dark, no matter what.'

'You'd better be. They're giving a party to celebrate your visit. Eightsome Reels, and all that!'

'Dressy?'

'We'll be in white ties, I imagine.'

'*Now*, the man tells me ...'

Hanging up the receiver of Mrs Blair's telephone, his smile faded. With an awareness of something wrong, some element at variance with the cheerful tone of that conversation. In *his* mind, though, not in hers, something he hadn't been able to talk to her about.

Guy. Guy at this moment being 'very chirpy'. And all the rest of this jollity over his and Diana's coming. And among those waiting – Toby bloody Dymock, who'd be there only because he, Rufus Chalk, had caused him to be.

In Barlows' yard on the Sunday afternoon he met Andrew Buchanan, wearing golfing clothes and in the company of Jacko Pargeter, who was about to show him through *Trumpeter*. A Sunday was, of course, the best day for it.

Dymock, Pargeter told Chalk, had gone up to Glendarragh yesterday – Saturday – afternoon.

'Some girl up there, I suspect.'

'You're right, sir, there is. He's in pursuit of my young brother's girlfriend.'

'*Is* he now!' Pargeter laughed. 'Want me to stop his leave? Don't think I could, on those grounds. A case of may the best man win – right, Andrew?'

Buchanan seemed to take the question seriously.

'Not entirely. Question is who decides which *is* the best man. Judgement in that area tends to be subjective, doesn't it? And the female of the species can be the worst judge of all.'

Chalk agreed. 'I think you've put your finger on it.'

'Not that it gets one anywhere . . . I had your note, by the way. But you shouldn't have bothered – just for a couple of drinks, in rather a dull crowd, at that.'

'Well, I enjoyed it. Is your wife still away?'

'Oh God, yes. She's not tired enough of London yet to consider moving back up here. But she's coming with me to Gothenburg next week – business *and* pleasure.'

'Speaking of which—' Pargeter butted in '– we'd better get a move on, if we're going to manage eighteen holes after this.' His spaniel's eyes rose to survey the lowering, dark-grey clouds. 'May not, at that . . . By the way, Chalk – it was your bright idea for this fellow to come out on our acceptance trials. Darned *good* idea, too. We'd have thought of it sooner or later, of course, but—'

'Might not have, too.' Buchanan nodded to him. 'Grateful to you. Have you heard yet whether *you*'ll be coming?'

'I'm afraid it's unlikely.'

He heard Pargeter explaining as they moved away that as a matter of routine there'd be a test-dive in the Gareloch first, but that as far as the boat's first venture to sea was concerned – the official acceptance trials – literally hundreds of people were clamouring to go out in her, and the lists had already closed. It was as good a way as any of letting him know he'd missed the bus, Chalk supposed – putting a cigarette in his mouth and lighting it as he looked after them. That was Mike Searle, *Trumpeter*'s torpedo officer, meeting them at the gangplank. Pargeter was standing aside for Buchanan to cross it first: then the civilian was teetering over it. Submarine planks took a bit of getting used to. But he'd made it, all right. Then Pargeter. Searle saluted each of them as he stepped on board.

Chalk slid his lighter back into its pocket, drew smoke deeply into his lungs. He smoked too much, he knew. Not as much as most men did, but still too much – certainly for one who prided himself on keeping fit. Those three were moving towards the fore hatch: Buchanan turning to look back at the four-inch gun mounting and upwards at the loom of the conning-tower behind it. *Trumpeter* motionless, with the scummy water lapping round her: as if – Chalk thought, breathing smoke – she was only biding her time, waiting for release. The three figures had disappeared into her fore hatch now, and he was imagining her as she'd be in just a few weeks' time – ploughing the clean, deep water under her own power, pitching rhythmically across the long, green swells . . . Then diving – the loud, pluming escape of air from ballast tanks, her long forepart nosing into foam of her own creation and the dark sea rising to embrace her. Gradual disappearance then of hull, casing, gun, conning-tower, the standards that housed her periscopes.

Just sea, then, the rolling green, unbroken.

But the list had closed. And Pargeter was the one and only man who could have overridden that, added one more name. He'd chosen not to – and probably quite rightly: for obvious reasons there did have to be a limit.

Chapter 7

***Snapshots** – from Chalk's visual recollections. Animation and dialogue added under licence.*

The paddock: with its boundary of whitened fence-posts, Suzie's wind-sock hanging vertically like washing out to dry, stables and byres and one end of the gaunt, grey house and a stack of chimneys just visible (though out of focus) in the background. Closer to the imaginary camera, a group of men and women with their eyes mostly on the treetops and the soft evening sky above them. This group comprising Rufus Chalk, Suzie, her brother Alastair and sister Patricia, Sir Innes and Lady Cameron-Green, and Toby Dymock. At a slight distance from them, butler MacKenzie has house-maid Janet Forest and stable-boy William with him. Cook, MacKenzie has told Lady Cameron-Green, has declared herself unable either to leave her kitchen or to dispense with the assistance of Lily Cross, the kitchen-maid. But at a greater distance – and in that weaker focus – a group of estate workers and a few women – their wives, presumably – with seven or eight children tumbling around.

Cigarette and pipe-smoke rise and drift in the windless

evening air. Sir Innes has left the house-party group and is on his way over to the farm-workers. He's using a stick, on account of sciatica in one knee.

Chalk mutters, putting his lighter to Patricia's cigarette and then to his own, 'Any second now. Unless of course she didn't like the look of the place.'

'Or of *us*.' Patricia smiles up at him sideways. She's blonde, with good cheekbones – not unlike Zoe Buchanan's shape of face – and really quite a bit like Dietrich – if you look for the resemblance. Or want it . . . She's quiet – has none of Suzie's ebullience – and is noticeably more intelligent than her parents. (Chalk recognizes that his estimate of her intelligence may be prejudiced by the fact that she obviously isn't impressed by Dymock: although this is something of a two-edged sword, in relation to the Dymock-Suzie business.)

'Might she have thought it was the wrong place?'

Diana, Pat means. Ten minutes ago the Fox Moth swooped down over the house – rousing most of this lot out of it and stampeding the sheep grazing on its north side – then banked away and vanished southward. Diana would be circling to get into position for her approach from the southeast, Chalk assumed; but he's thinking now that it must be a very large circle she's making. Suzie comes up with the obvious explanation, calling to her sister 'She'll be having a good dekko round – for Guy to see what the glen looks like from up there. Don't you think? Oh golly, I do *hope* she'll take me up!'

The Fox Moth comes into sight at that moment – suddenly, as out of nowhere, its undercarriage clearing the trees by what looks like only a few feet. She's throttled back, and the machine's slightly nose-up as it drops towards that end of the paddock, close to the line of the fence. Suzie still gabbling with excitement and clutching at Patricia's arm. There's cheering, too, and the estate workers are waving their caps. The 'plane bounces once – twice – as its wheels touch, then it's trundling across the field towards them with the throttle open and noisy. Suzie's rushing towards it, Dymock trotting after her: it's passed them, so they're virtually chasing it now from astern. Patricia shaking her head: 'What a jerk . . .'

Another one, Chalk notes, who says exactly what she's thinking. In Americanese, too, learnt no doubt at Girton. She's definitely attractive, with a good figure, pleasant manner and a lively sense of humour; while accepting that she's too old for Guy, he can't help thinking how splendid it would be if he did fall for her. Teach Suzie a lesson . . .

It's not on the cards, unfortunately. He's on his way to meet the Moth as Diana brakes and stops it; she's switched off, waves to him from the open pilot's cockpit, while in front of her the evening sun's flashing on the canopy over the passenger cabin as Guy slides it back. Diana's pulled off her helmet, Guy's climbing down, is on the ground – initially somewhat wobbly on his feet – as Rufus reaches him and hugs him. Smiling up at Diana . . . 'Guy, old chap, this is *marvellous*!' With a shrewd suspicion that it's going to be bloody awful before long – but with his eyes on Diana, and helping her down while Guy hurries to meet Suzie.

'Rufus – sweet of you, but actually I'm not crippled!'

'Never mind.' In close-up, as she turns in his arms. 'Even if you were you'd be the most beautiful thing on earth. Darling, you're *lovely*—'

'Put me down?'

'Yes.' Kissing her again. 'I will . . .'

'What's that?' Pointing at the lifeless wind-sock, as he releases her. 'Flag of surrender?'

'Rufus, introduce us!'

Suzie must have greeted Guy somewhat perfunctorily. He's staring after her, looking surprised and disappointed. The rest of the party's clustering round now, and Suzie's decided not to wait for an introduction. 'Diana – I'm Suzie Cameron-Green. Please, *please* will you take me up?'

'Of course. Not just *now*, mind you—'

'Diana.' Rufus takes her arm – and the leather helmet out of her other hand – turns her to face their host and hostess. 'This is Diana Villiers, my fiancée. Lady Cameron-Green, Sir Innes.' Then – 'Diana – Patricia, and this is Alastair. And – over there – Toby Dymock. Guy, you haven't met Toby—'

'Hello, Toby.'

They're together, where Guy met Suzie a moment ago and she left him. Dymock puts his hand out: 'Heard a lot about you. Known Rufus heaven knows *how* long.'

'Oh. You're the submariner he mentioned.' Guy isn't taking much interest in Dymock, though: much more in Suzie, at whom he's gazing anxiously over Eve Cameron-Green's head while exchanging greetings with her and with Sir Innes. Innes telling him 'First rate to have you back with us, Guy. First rate!' Suzie's talking to Diana again; Alastair calls 'Hey – you chaps – lend a hand here, get this contraption into the byre?'

'*Contraption?*' Diana glares at him. 'What do you mean, contraption?' Eve Cameron-Green takes her arm. 'Come on into the house, my dear. Leave it to them, they can stable your machine. You must be dying for a hot bath – and a drink first?'

'What a *brilliant* idea!'

'Petrol's in the byre too. Cans and cans of it.' Sir Innes, meeting her smile, touches his moustache. 'Came yesterday – enormous lorry.'

'That *is* a relief . . .'

'I expect you're famished, too.' Lady C-G is more or less towing her away. 'A tray in your room might be the best thing. Dinner's at eight-fifteen, you see, and our other guests have been asked for nine-thirty.' Diana's looking back at Rufus as if she doesn't want to leave him, and Guy has an arm round Suzie, telling her, 'I'll leave it to them – I'm excused, *I* brought it all the way from Worcester.' Leave it to Dymock and Alastair, he means: especially as they're being joined now by MacKenzie and young William. 'Suzie, it's been an absolute *age...*' Patricia asks Rufus, nodding towards the house, 'Coming?'

The rest of the snaps, half a dozen of them, would have been taken – with a flash, of course, that explosive equipment photographers often used – in the staircase hall, which is spacious, panelled in age-darkened oak and has been cleared of furniture for the dancing – eight or ten couples in the frame at this moment, jiggling around to *Yes, My Darling Daughter*.

The gramophone's on the half-landing, tended mostly by Alastair and his sisters, Alastair assisted some of the time by his girlfriend Midge Campbell: but they're dancing now. Midge lives near Oban in Argyll; she's tall, red-haired, pale-skinned with a lot of freckles. Suzie's looking after the gramophone at this stage, and Guy's sitting on the top stair with his long legs pointing down towards the kaleidoscopic swirl of heads, kilts, multicoloured frocks.

Diana in silver, looking radiant. Dancing this one with Toby Dymock. Dymock murmuring into her ear, 'Thank heaven the reels are over. This is what *I* call dancing.'

'Well – I suppose it is. Of a sort ... Haven't you been rather monopolizing Suzie, by the way?'

'D'you think I have?'

'She's supposed to be Guy's girl, you know.'

That smile ... 'Not doing much about it, is he?'

On the half-landing, Guy demands of Suzie, 'What's he got that I haven't – apart from a rather oily manner?'

'Who?'

'You know darned well. Chap you dance with all the time. Name's – what, Dymock?'

'His name's Toby, there's nothing oily about his manner, and I have *not* danced with him all the time.'

'Hardly with me at all.'

'One does have to mix, Guy. Being family, especially. Besides, you're going to be here how long – six weeks? Eight?'

'Nothing to do with it. As *you* know perfectly well. I've been longing for tonight, counting the damn days!'

'You ought to be down there dancing too. Look at Diana, there, she's not clutching Rufus all the time!'

'He's doing a line with Pat, if you ask me. Having told me in his last letter he was hoping she'd get off with this friend of his – the oily one . . . Well, here's what – I'll mix like mad, once I'm getting fair do's from you.'

'What d'you mean by "fair do's"?'

'Say every other dance. In between – one dance in every two – you mix too – but *really* mix!'

'That's ridiculous—'

Alastair tells them – having caught some of this while coming up the stairs – 'Take her down and give us all an eyeful, old man. I'll relieve you of that chore, Suzie.'

'About time, too.' She points at a pile of records. 'Those are the ones we've played.'

Patricia and her mother, who have been upstairs, stop on their way down to chat to Alastair. After about half an hour he's still stuck with the gramophone duty. His mother asks him, 'Couldn't someone else do that for a bit? Don't you want to dance at all?'

'Yes, I do.' He looks at Patricia. 'Any volunteers?'

'All right. I don't mind.' She leans on the balustrade. 'Not for ever, though. If I'm still here in ten minutes, say – send someone else up, will you?'

'*That* chap, perhaps.' Alastair points at the black, shiny head close to Suzie's. 'Two *oiseaux* with one *pierre* – one, keep the music going; two, give her a rest from him.'

'Suzie is perfectly capable of giving *herself* a rest.' Eve C-G shows annoyance. 'From him, or anyone else.'

'Guy, d'you mean? She's doing *that*, all right!'

'I meant no such thing, Alastair. I'm only saying let *her* decide who she dances with or doesn't.'

'You wouldn't say that, Mama—' Patricia slides an arm round her mother, squeezes her to show affection – 'if it was someone you disapproved of.'

'Someone of whom she disapproved, you mean.' Alastair shakes his head. 'Snakes alive, what's Cambridge *for*?'

'That's a more pertinent question than you realize.' Patricia asks her brother, '*You* disapprove, do you?'

'I think she's being unfair to Guy, that's all. I've nothing against Toby otherwise.' He shrugs. 'Well – nothing much.'

'He's a smooth operator, that one. And cleverer than you probably realize. Must be, to have fooled Rufus for years. Ask me, Guy doesn't have to worry, he won't be in Suzie's *sight*, by Christmas.'

'Who won't?'

'Toby, of course!'

Alastair winked at his mother. 'Got him in *your* sights, Pat?'

'Does the Army teach you always to say the most irritatingly *stupid* thing?'

'On target, was I?'

'No, you were not. In fact he's the *last*—'

'Well, I'll accept that. Some of us – the more acute observers – have been rather interested in your carryings-on with Rufus.'

Sir Innes, reappearing after taking himself off to recover from the reels when they finished an hour ago, has been listening to the late news.

'This so-called Royal Commission on Palestine – Peel's thing – they've recommended partition.' He's telling his wife this: she'd thought he was going to ask her to dance. 'They're proposing an Arab state and a Jewish one, and a continuing British mandate for Jerusalem and Bethlehem. I suppose because those are the places they'd most likely fight over. But it'll please no-one at all – especially not the Zionists. And we'd need corridors to the sea – which'd be devilish hard to police. Well, the whole thing would!'

'It's miles over my head, Innes.'

'The simple truth of it is that partition as a political solution tends to raise more problems than it solves. What time's supper?'

'Oh, about midnight. Half-past, perhaps. Only ham-and-eggs and fruit salad. Why, are you hungry?' She doesn't give him time to answer. 'Innes, Suzie's dancing practically all the time with Toby. Making it so *obvious*.'

'Have a word with her, then. If you think it matters. I'd have thought it was up to Guy.'

Guy hands Rufus one of the two glasses of whisky he's been out to fetch. 'Betty sent her love, by the way. She's about ready to foal – as you know, I suppose ... Must say I'm rather looking forward to being an uncle.'

'So am I. Here's to her and it.' He puts a hand on his brother's shoulder. 'Damn good to see you, Guy.'

'Me too. I mean – to see *you*.' The grin fades. 'Can't say I'm frightfully taken with your fellow submariner, though. Never leaves Suzie alone for a minute. And *he* could just about be *her* uncle!'

'Well – not quite. But it's my fault he's here, and I'm more sorry than I can say.' Another gulp of whisky ... 'If I'd had the least notion he'd chase after Suzie, I wouldn't have dreamt of introducing him. Lady C-G asked me if I had any chums who'd help to jolly things along, and he was a natural choice because (a) he's here and (b) he and I've been friends a long time and I've never had reason to – you know, think twice about him. I *did* think he might be about right for Patricia – whom he'll have met last weekend, when I wasn't here – but that doesn't seem to have worked.'

'She can't stand him. I like *her*, always have done.'

'Betty thinks a lot of her, too.'

Smothering a yawn ... 'Sorry. Been a long day. Is Dymock going to be around for long?'

'No. That's one mercy. His submarine's being built in the same yard as *Threat*, and she's just about completing. Final acceptance trials in not much more than three weeks.'

'Pushes off then, does he?'

'Does indeed. To join whichever flotilla *Trumpeter*'s sent to. That's the boat's name – *Trumpeter*. Portland's about the most likely, the 6th Flotilla.'

'Wouldn't be a bad distance, either ... But Rufus – Suzie's changed, you know?'

'If you say so. I've only known her a few weeks.'

'Believe me. Six months ago she wouldn't have given that fellow the time of day.'

That old Black Magic ...

Dymock's voice in Suzie's ear as they dance – this being some time after the late supper – 'Come and see over *Trumpeter* soon?'

'Is the paint dry?'

'*Bone* dry. So any time, as far as I'm concerned. Weekends are best, of course. Even if I can't get leave I could take a few hours off, come and fetch you. Or if you came down under your own steam I could meet you and drive you back.'

'Don't know, honestly. There are – complications ... But – suppose I asked Rufus to leave his car here, you could take him back in yours and Guy could bring me down to the submarine – *and* bring me back here—'

'Leaving Rufus without transport. Which he needs, for getting between his digs and the yard. He mightn't be much in favour of the idea in any case – old Rufus can be a bit of a stuffed shirt, you know. In any case I don't want a whole crowd with us – do you?'

She hums, – *has me in its spell* ...

'Better idea. We've some friends who live down in that area – a place called Milngavie, spelt M-I-L-N-G-A-V-I-E.'

'Pronounced Milngye?'

She nods: her forehead's in contact with his jaw, but not intentionally and she pulls her head back. 'If I invited myself to stay with them – I was at school with their daughter, Jean, she's been here once or twice – gosh, I could ask her for the great anniversary hoolie, couldn't I . . . Anyway – if I stayed say two nights with them, and on the day in between—'

'I'd show you over the boat, then take you out to dinner.'

'Don't know about *that*. For one thing Jean would want to come along too, and for another my parents—'

'Best of all, fix it for a Saturday night – this next weekend or the one after. I'd take you out that evening – pick you up in Milngavie and take you back there – then Sunday forenoon collect you again, show you over *Trumpeter* and deliver you back here by sundown. Huh?'

'Well, it'd be lovely, but—'

'Your parents might not approve – that it? Sweet girl, all you say is you're staying with these friends and I'm going to collect you on the Sunday to show you the boat, then whisk you home. How's that?'

'I'm already being terribly unkind to Guy. There's also what the Munroes might think – if I'm staying with them—'

'We can fix that. I'll work it out. And Guy'll get over it. He's too young for you now, Suzie. Like a big puppy, isn't he – frightfully nice, all that, but—'

'I don't want to hurt him. Really I *don't*, Toby.'

'Of course you don't. Even *I* don't, and I barely know him. But I'm not going to be here much longer, you know. I'll come back and see you when I can, when I can get leave – try and stop me! But it won't be all that often. God knows *where* I'll be, even in a month's time: and of course with this war everyone says is coming—'

'Don't *talk* about it!'

'No. All right . . . But Suzie – *please*—'

'I might ring Jean and ask her for the 28th, the anniversary. Just to see how the land lies. But meanwhile, not a word to anybody – not a whisper to *me*, even . . . And Toby, listen – after this one, I'm not going to dance with you again. Guy's looking like a sick dog already.'

Diana in his arms. Yielding, loving, cheek to cheek. Her murmur close to his ear, 'We're making an exhibition of ourselves.'

'We're allowed to. We're engaged.'

'Do wish you could come out to the Cape with me.'

'So do I. No such luck, though. Going to be a grim four months, this winter.'

'*Five* months. I'm going in September now, remember.' She's caught her breath, they're face to face and he's disbelieving, thinks he hasn't heard right or she's got it wrong. He hears her now: 'Rufus! My *God*, I didn't *tell* you!'

They've stopped dancing: even as much dancing as they were doing before the conversation took this turn. He's still holding her: they're holding each other, deaf to the music . . . Shaking his head: 'October was the dreaded month. October through to February – *all* dreaded . . . Oh, *damn* it!'

'The only thing is – does it make *so* much difference? We'd only have seen each other about once – if that, even . . . With you stuck up here and me working—'

'I'd thought of asking for a week's leave at about the end of September, beginning October – on the assumption you wouldn't work right up to the moment of departure . . .'

'I'm *sorry*—'

'What date in September? Are you going by Imperial Airways again, or by the mailboat?'

'Flying-boat. Imperial. Darling, I'm *so* sorry . . . 2nd September – a Thursday – from Southampton of course.'

'And the anniversary party here's on 28th August. It'll be our farewell party, now. Oh, damn and *blast* it . . . Any special reason, going a month early?'

'Yes. Daddy asking me to come as soon as possible, on account of Mum getting – well, not getting any better. I have to read between the lines a bit, with him . . . Might even have gone sooner, except for bookings I've accepted, people I absolutely must not let down. That must be how I forgot to tell you – so busy getting in touch with people and cancelling even later bookings and ones that aren't important. Doesn't excuse me, I know—'

'I'm sorry about your mother.'

'*I*'m sorry about – all of it. Leaving you – and not having told you – oh, if only you *could* come with me!'

'Out of the question. Couldn't get leave. Couldn't afford it—'

'I could handle that.'

'No. You couldn't.' A glance round. 'Anyway – we're supposed to be dancing.'

'I've spoilt the whole evening, haven't I?'

'No. You're here *now*. This *makes* the evening.' Pointing with his chin: '*That* spoils it.'

Suzie, clasped by Toby Dymock . . .

'Guy's been wildly looking forward to getting back here. Getting back to *her*. And it's my fault, I brought Dymock up here – never *dreaming*—'

The record's finished, scratching round, and Suzie and Dymock are separating, Dymock looking fed up as she walks away from him. Diana murmurs, 'Little tiff? Keep your fingers crossed . . .' Raising her voice as a new record starts: 'Should have done more than dreamt, my pet.' She's back in his arms and Crosby's crooning '*little charms about you . . .*' 'You might have seen it was a dead cert from the start. *I*'d have told you . . . Your brother's a love, but he's – well, young. She is too, of course, but she's what you might call *emerging* . . . Highly susceptible, meanwhile. She's sweet, too: I can understand *exactly* how she feels.'

'Meaning you find Toby attractive?'

'No. Actually, I don't, at all. I mean in *her* little slippers, at *her* age—'

'He's still behaving like a cad.'

'Don't you mean like a man?'

'No. In fact – at the risk of sounding pompous—'

'Oh, please don't.' Her arms slide up around his neck. 'Don't *want* you pompous!'

—my sweet embraceable . . .

'I want *you*, Diana. Any way I can have you. But I'm not an older man stealing you from some kid.'

Last snap: Guy, dancing with Suzie.

'There's a film I want to see. Would you come? It's on in Glasgow next week, Midge says. *Lost Horizon*. Stars Ronald Colman and—'

'I've read stuff about it. How would we get down to Glasgow and back again?'

'Might get a lift. There'd be *someone*—'

'Now you remind me – I may be going down in any case. Not to Glasgow exactly – to the Munroes, in Milngavie. Jean Munroe's asked me down for a night or two – and I haven't seen her for ages.'

'Never heard of her.'

'Well, we were at school together. Anyway it's not definite yet – she's got to ring me or I'm ringing her, I forget which. All the same I *would* like to see that film. You'd think it'd be on for longer than a week – in a town like Glasgow?'

'Midge has seen it – in London, saw it on the opening night or soon after. She says she'd see it again if she got the chance. So it *must* be good. Look, if I could get myself down there when you're with these Munroe people—'

'I don't even know if I'll be going. Or what their programme will be if I do. Guy, that was my *foot*!'

'Sorry . . .'

'Just lamed for life, that's all . . . Tell me, was the flight up here *frightfully* exciting?'

'Well – yes. Yes, it was . . .'

'Diana's promised to take me up for a flip tomorrow, before she leaves. She was telling me over supper about her 'plane – the Fox Moth. Did you know it's the first British aeroplane ever to pay its way commercially? Something to do with the load it can carry, and the petrol consumption, all that. And it won the King's Cup, five years ago. Not *this* one, I mean *a* Fox Moth did. Oh, and the Prince of Wales had one. Duke of Windsor as he is now . . . But guess what – Diana says if I'm still keen after I've been up with her, I ought to think about learning to fly myself! She'd put me in touch with a flying club where they'd give lessons. She learnt in South Africa, but there are clubs all over the country and she'll find out about Glasgow – there must *be* one . . . What are you laughing at?'

'You. Wondering how'll you fit this in with climbing Everest and winning the National.' He chuckled again as he kissed her cheek: stooping almost double to get there. 'Not to mention a few other – enthusiasms. I'm barmy about you, Suzie.'

'I'm very fond of you, too.'

'Fond . . .'

'You're like a brother to me. I was thinking about it, and that's *exactly* how you are to me.'

'Not in the least how *you* are to *me*.'

'Guy!'

Midge Campbell, dancing with Rufus: reaching to poke Guy in the ribs. 'What are you looking so *glum* about?'

End of hoolie, end of 'snapshots' – more or less . . .

The guests had all gone by three. Breakfast, Lady C-G told the house-party, would be 'any old time'. Suzie had squawked, 'But Diana's leaving before lunch and before that she's taking me up! *And* the Fox Moth's got to be pushed out – *and* fuelled!'

'Suzie.' Her mother put an arm round her shoulders. 'Any

old time means whenever anyone wants it.' She pointed towards the dining-room. 'In there – by cock-crow. MacKenzie will certainly be up, William will be mucking-out; if you need more volunteers than that you'll just have to wake some up.'

Rufus Chalk decided, washing and cleaning his teeth then returning down the fifty-odd yards of corridor to the room they'd given him this time, that he'd be up early too. He'd never had any difficulty in waking when he had to; it was probably the result of years of watchkeeping at sea, getting up to the bridge not just on time but five minutes ahead of it.

He pushed the bedroom door shut, hung his gown on the hook, went over to the bed.

Hard as boards. And when he put more weight on it, it squeaked. But – one had slept on worse ... He switched on the bedside light, went back to the door and turned off the overhead one. No lock on the door, he noticed. Crossing to the window, to let some air in: the whole house was stuffy, just as in winter he guessed it would be freezing. Trivial thoughts – he was aware of this – aimed at holding off the sadness he'd been feeling ever since she'd told him she'd be leaving in September, not October.

What with that *and* the Guy-Suzie situation ...

Diana was right, of course, that he probably wouldn't have seen her more than once in that month. But once would have been a lot better than not at all. And she'd be *gone*, that was the real sadness, if a week's leave came up he'd have no use for it ... The window had stuck; he had to hammer at the frame with the heel of his hand before it would budge at all. Then as it yielded he was conscious of the noise he'd made and that some people might already be asleep. They could be – or could *have been*: he'd had to wait some while to get into the bathroom, and those who'd been ahead of him in the queue might well be in dreamland by this time.

Behind him – having forced the window open, inhaling

cool night air and admiring the stars and a half-moon – he heard his own door being pushed shut. Hurriedly extracting head and shoulders from the musty-smelling curtains ... 'Diana!'

'Hush.' She'd tossed a towel and a macintosh bag of washing things towards an armchair, and missed – through looking at *him*, not the target ... She was in his arms, whispering with her mouth close to his, 'Lightning decision.' Slightly breathless ... 'Floors creak, doors stick then *burst* open. Waiting for snores – fatal, wake *everyone* ... So I thought now or never – vanish *en route* bathroom – also known as disappearance from human ken – uh?'

'You're brilliant – as well as—'

'Then at cock-crow – *back* from bathroom ...'

'Wring the cocks' necks so they *can't* crow. Diana, I *love* you—'

'Love *you*. Hasn't been easy – holding you off.'

'Been bloody torture.'

'Well. *Well* ...'

Her dressing-gown, which he'd pushed back over her shoulders, slid down into a heap on the board floor. '*Diana* ...' Diana naked, in the circle of his arms. Magic circle: break it, she might turn out to be unreal, a figment of his prurient imagination, long frustration, the dread of losing her for that eternity of five months. His pyjama top had been open; he shrugged it off, and she yanked at his trouser cord.

'Oh, *my* ...'

'Diana—' mouths separated for a second – 'Diana, darling—'

'No key in the door.'

'Put the light out?'

'No—'

'All right, but – no, hell, why should they ... Diana, you're so *gorgeous*—'

'I'm awful!'

'– so lovely I can't *believe*—'

'Look – moonlight out there. Open the curtains – lamp out *then*?'

Mid-morning, Sunday: most of the people who'd seen Diana arrive had straggled down to the paddock to see her leave. Not Lady C-G, who hadn't risen yet, but Sir Innes was there, telling Chalk that the Japanese had taken Peking the day before.

Diana had made a short flight with Suzie. Suzie disembarking bright-eyed and thrilled, telling Guy, 'I'm going to do it – learn to fly – I *am*, I *mean* it!'

Dymock had not been with them at that stage, but he'd arrived soon after. When he'd appeared, coming from the direction of the stable-yard, Suzie had gone to meet him – with old Bertie lumbering at her heels – and from a distance of about a hundred yards Rufus had heard her calling to him, 'I've been *up* – and you weren't here to see! Toby, I'm going to have flying lessons, Diana's promised . . .'

She'd reverted to a normal speaking tone, then, Rufus only heard about one word in five, but apparently Diana had promised to find out what flying clubs were in reach of here, and which instructors were or weren't up to scratch, in terms of experience and reputation. She'd said she'd try to have this information by the 28th.

Guy was on his own now: Dymock was with Suzie beside the Moth. Rufus drew Diana aside. 'I *thought* I loved you before. But now – oh, crikey . . .'

'Me too. I don't think I've ever felt so reluctant to take off. I love it up there, you know, always have, it's where life begins. Or *did*.'

'Guess when *my* life began?'

'I don't have to. I was there.'

'*I*'ll say . . .'

'Twenty-eighth isn't so far away, Rufus. Four weeks?'

'It's the thought of the twenty-ninth appalls me.'

'So *don't* think about it!'

'The day life stops, until – what, end of February?'

'Afraid so.'

'*February* twenty-eighth, then. And between those dates – vacuum . . . You'll have your mother to look after, of course.'

'And you'd better look after Guy.'

'Yes.' He saw that little brother had been joined by Patricia, who had her arm round his waist. Guy looking down at her, smiling as he talked, and Patricia beginning to laugh – slow beginning, as if she was trying to suppress it – at whatever he was telling her. With her head back to look up at him she really was very pretty. Rufus told *his* girl, 'Yes, I will. Damn shame Pat isn't a few years younger.'

'Then she'd be like Suzie. Where'd *that* get anyone? No, he should be a few years older.'

'H'm . . .' Looking over at Suzie, now – who still had Dymock with her. 'Except that when Toby shoves off – which I'd bet will be the end of it as far as *he*'s concerned—'

'Won't help, I'm afraid. Guy won't feel about Suzie as he did before, and vice versa. Rufus, darling – I'm going now.'

'Be careful, please. No chances – no flying in bad weather—'

'No nothing. Only you. Twenty-eighth.'

Guy came over to join him, while she was taking off. The Fox Moth lifting, then climbing to clear the treetops: from this angle of sight it seemed for a few moments she mightn't make it. He murmured, 'Phew . . .'

'Some girl, that.' Guy looked over to where Suzie was still waving, with Dymock still in close attendance. 'You're a lucky man, Rufus.'

'I know I am. *Damn* lucky. But listen, now. I don't know what's gone wrong with Suzie—'

'Don't you?'

'I mean – I suppose – that I don't know what she sees in Dymock. But Guy – it's not the end of the world. Even if it feels like it at the moment. Other fish in the sea – as they say . . . It's true, though – this sort of thing's par for the course – happens to us all, probably won't be the last time you'll go through it.'

'Plenty to look forward to, then, haven't I?' He didn't smile. 'Rufus – changing the subject – are you going back this afternoon?'

'I thought I'd leave after lunch. Why?'

'Cadge a lift down with you, can I?'

'Of course. But—'

'Could I spend tonight at your digs – on a sofa, or the floor?'

'There's an unused bed in my room. What are you up to?'

'Third request – run me into Glasgow some time on Monday, for the London train?'

'Going to Betty's, are you?'

'No. Don't break out in a rash now. I'm going to Spain. Paris first – where the Republicans have their recruiting office.' He put a hand on his brother's arm. 'No big deal, Rufe. Lots of us out there already. I'd planned it before, actually – shouldn't have changed my mind, that's all.'

Chapter 8

Chalk told me, on his terrace in County Cork, that he'd tried to talk his brother out of it. 'On the drive down to Dunbarton that afternoon, then half the night in my digs over a bottle of Scotch I happened to have in store against emergencies. But I took the wrong tack: although even if I'd done it right it'd probably have been futile. In retrospect I can see that: if he'd been thinking of it earlier on, then been treated as he had – well, at his age, and the way he felt about her, and with no other firm plans laid anyway . . .'

He hadn't finished his beer, although I'd polished mine off some time ago. I'd decided that if or when he proposed refills I'd offer to fetch them, to save him the legwork. Not that he showed any signs of decrepitude. He had nine acres here – mostly woodland which he'd planted himself, he'd told me, and looked after without any outside assistance – and he was out with his pack of setters for an hour or so in the early mornings and every evening. (No connection between red setters and his name or formerly red hair, he'd told me. It only happened to be a breed he'd always liked.)

He was filling his pipe. Glancing at me, the long, bony fingers still working at it . . . 'I had two good lines of argument with Guy. One was that it was as clear as day the

Republicans were going to lose that war, so he'd be joining the losing side, and once the thing crumbled – well, if he was still alive, conditions in a Spanish prisoner-of-war camp mightn't be all that salubrious. And in any case, what did he imagine he'd be fighting for? Fighting Fascists – German or Italian – fine, I was already of the opinion – not original, but sustainable in argument – that the only good ones were dead ones. But that was peripheral, in a sense, just as it was that the side he'd be joining was supported by international communism; the two sides were really no more than rival *colours* of totalitarianism, two different varieties of knife at the free world's throat. And remember, when the war – *our* war – did start, the Russians and the Germans were hand in glove, might well have remained so if Hitler hadn't ratted on the deal. What I'm saying though – was saying to Guy – it was a Spanish fight, being conducted in Spain, the roots of it entirely Spanish, and both sides had already committed the most foul atrocities – which wouldn't have been much of an encouragement to go there, I'd have thought – so (a) how did you choose this side or that, and (b) how could either be worth an Englishman's life?'

He'd paused, to put a match to the pipe. Then, breathing smoke: 'Another line of argument was one I'd thought of when they'd told me before that he was having thoughts of Spain. I pointed out that we had a war of our own coming damn soon: why risk life and limb in someone else's – especially as ours would be a struggle for survival, a time for all hands to the pumps.'

Attending to his pipe again . . . 'It was a pointless debate, and I knew it. Had to try, though. I'd have given a fortune – if I'd had one – to have been able to talk him out of it, but – he'd made his mind up, he was going anyway. When or if our war did start he'd come back like a shot, and by then he'd have learnt a thing or two about soldiering, so he'd be a lot more use than if he'd sat at home and waited for it.'

'He did go, did he?'

A nod, through a cloud of smoke ... 'And I drove up to Glendarragh the following Saturday not to stay but to talk to Sir Innes and explain my position. I'd spoken to him over the wire, telling him I'd like to have a heart to heart, and when I arrived the rest of the family weren't in sight. Out, or just keeping their heads down – I don't know ... We talked in his study, and I told him that Guy was in Paris by that time, signing on. It was news to him, and seemed to upset him quite genuinely. He had a lot of time for Guy, I knew for a fact he thought highly of him. And when Guy had been expressing his regrets that he couldn't stay, saying goodbye to each of them in turn – including Suzie, with no detectable hard feelings, no recriminations of any sort – which I must say impressed me, when I heard it from Sir Innes – he hadn't mentioned Spain at all, and of course the embarrassment of the Suzie-Dymock romance was a good enough reason for him to disappear for a while. None of them had suspected his intentions. Not even Patricia. He'd let her and Suzie believe that he was going to our sister Betty, to be with her when her child was born, and they were content to swallow that.'

'Rather extraordinary, that *none* of them should have guessed – Suzie particularly, who'd known of his plans earlier?'

'But what difference if they had?' He shrugged. 'They *may* have. Head in sand may have suited some of them. Lady C-G, for one ... Can't really say – memory's not all *that* clear. But I don't think so. Until I told them – told Sir Innes, that is. After which I said the rest of my piece – roughly that while I retained warm feelings for them all and blamed no-one for anything, I wasn't going to be able to spend as much time up there as I had been doing. Dymock would obviously be there whenever he could make it, and I found little pleasure in having to stand by and watch his antics with Suzie. I'd spend the anniversary weekend with them, if I was still welcome – which it seemed I *was* – Diana was coming then, and it was Sir Innes' and Eve C-G's anniversary that we'd be celebrating, after all. And *after* that – well, Dymock would be leaving pretty well at once, in *Trumpeter*. Trials scheduled for Wednesday 25th, back in the yard for any minor adjustments, but that weekend would certainly be their last on the Clyde. And with him gone – well, I didn't actually say to Sir Innes that they'd probably never see the bugger again, I only *thought* that was how it might turn out. Couldn't envisage the leopard changing its spots.'

Chalk added, 'Meanwhile Sir Innes was an understanding, thoughtful sort of man, and Patricia had disliked Dymock even before this turn of events, of course. She was fond of Guy too. Alastair I didn't think had taken to Dymock either ... Lady C-G on the other hand – I deduced this largely from Sir Innes' not including her in his comments, although he did talk about Suzie's, Patricia's and his own feelings – I think his wife took the view that Suzie might be on to a good thing with Dymock and would have been wasting her time with Guy.' He wagged his head. 'A certain shrewdness about that woman. It had occurred to me before that I'd felt less genuine warmth from her than from any of the others. An eye to the main chance, you might say ... Anyway – at least for the time being, best thing I could do was stay away. Having had this talk with Sir Innes, cleared the air between us rather than prevaricate and have to make excuses all the time.'

He'd paused. 'Am I making sense to you?'

'Very much so.'

'Amazing. You deserve some more beer. If you still like it?'

'If you'd tell me where to find it – you're doing all the work around here—'

'No – thank you, but it's easier for me.'

'All right. But one question, while it's in my mind – was Dymock at Glendarragh when you went up to see Sir Innes?'

'I don't *think* he could have been . . . It was the Saturday after the party, and in *Trumpeter*'s state of near-completion he could hardly have absented himself again so soon. He must have been making certain arrangements for the weekend *after* that – as I learnt later. But here, look . . .'

The rough diary he'd reconstructed in a notebook with all later dates stemming from the one we'd established as a fixed point of departure – 26 June, the Windsors' wedding day. On one page as he flipped them over I read *Zoe and husband in Gothenburg*, and I was surprised that he'd bothered to note it down. But he wasn't showing me that, he'd riffled on to a double page headed *Weekend 30 July–1 August. 'Dress rehearsal hoolie'*. Under that heading he'd made the notes of what he'd called snapshots, the numbered entries culminating with *Guy's decision on Spain*.

Long, knobbly-knuckled fingers flicked pages over to the heading *Saturday 7 August*, under which he'd noted *Visited Glendarragh for talk with Sir Innes*.

'So from here, the next weekend would have been—' fiddling more pages over – '14 and 15 August. I've jotted down here that I stayed in Dunbarton. And here I've noted *Dymock, Suzie, Milngavie, etc. Call from Sir Innes early hours 15th.*' He nodded, pushed himself up. 'Take a bit of telling, that bit. I'll get our beer first.'

It had turned out that the Munroes could only have Suzie for the Friday night of that weekend – Friday the 13th as it was, ominously – instead of Friday and Saturday as Dymock had suggested. He was remaining in the background, all arrangements being made by Suzie in concert with Jean Munroe. Jean was thrilled that she was coming, and even more so with the invitation to the Cameron-Greens' anniversary dinner and dance at the end of the month. She and Suzie had been friends at school, but Glendarragh was socially-speaking several cuts above Milngavie: it was an invitation in respect of which Jean's father would unquestionably finance the provision of a new frock.

Dymock had grudgingly accepted that he could *not* collect Suzie from the Munroes and take her out to dinner. At the Glendarragh hoolie he'd talked airily of doing so, but it was obviously out of the question. It was agreed, though – with Suzie's parents – that he'd collect her in Milngavie after lunch on the Saturday, show her over his submarine during the afternoon and then drive her back to Glendarragh.

'We might stop for supper somewhere along the way. If you've no objection? Then it won't matter if we're late – no need to keep food hot, or anything. It's a longish drive, after all, and she'll be hungry – so will I.'

Suzie agreed – looking at her mother – 'It *would* be rather fun.'

'Where would you stop?' Sir Innes suggested, 'Callander? Or – tell you what – Lochearnhead, the hotel there. Bang on your route!'

'That might do.' Dymock had agreed. 'Certainly convenient . . .' Then a new thought: 'Tell you what – there's a small fishing hotel at the other end of Loch Earn – village called St Fillans, isn't it?'

'May well be.' Lady C-G was amused. 'But what they'd give you to eat, heaven knows!'

'A freshly killed salmon, for sure.' Her husband cocked an eyebrow at Dymock. 'Bit off your route though, isn't it? Up to you, but I'd have thought Lochearnhead would be a great deal handier.'

'It would.' Dymock nodded. 'But as it happens I've an ulterior motive. Years ago I spent a few days there with my father – 1920, summer holidays, and it was the first time he'd fished since he lost his leg. Didn't want to do it too publicly, so he picked on what was then a rather remote place and only took me along. In fact he didn't need any help. We fished mostly from a boat, but even from the bank after a few casts he found he could manage very well. It's one of my—' he'd glanced at Suzie – 'rather special boyhood memories. All the time I've been up here I've been meaning to go and have a look at the place.'

'I've love to go there.' Suzie queried, 'Can't be so *very* far off our route – Loch Earn's less than ten miles long, surely?'

'I should think it is. Quite a bit less, possibly.'

'That's it, then.' Dymock smiled at Suzie. 'If you'll chance it. Certainly won't be ritzy!'

'Who wants the Ritz?'

'Well –' Lady C-G smiled at her husband – 'as only one small voice speaking in this wilderness—'

Sir Innes told Dymock, 'Tricked me into taking her to London two or three months ago—'

'*Six* months ago at *least*!'

'Not long enough for my bank account to have recovered, anyway.' He asked Suzie, 'You'll go down by train from Tyndrum, will you?'

'If someone'll take me that far.'

'I will. That's no effort.' He thought about it, and added 'Make it Crianlarich, if you like. I'll go on into Killin, see what's his name.'

'Well, that'll be marvellous!'

'The Munroes will meet your train, will they?'

Chalk knew nothing of Suzie's visit to Barlows' – or of the Munroes' existence, even. For all he knew Suzie would be at home with her family, as usual, and the only thought he gave it was to wonder whether Dymock might have gone up to them this weekend. It was fairly likely, because the following one would be the last before *Trumpeter*'s acceptance trials – which were scheduled for the 25th. It wasn't likely that any of them, let alone the first lieutenant, would be taking time off then.

Maybe not this weekend either. If it had been *Threat* completing, he knew for sure *he* wouldn't. Not even to spend a last night with Diana.

(Diana, and nights with her – one past and one in the near future – would have been occupying his thoughts quite a bit, at this time.)

He didn't see Suzie or Dymock in the yard that Saturday afternoon because he'd gone into Glasgow for a haircut and to find a farewell present for Diana; and if he *had* known she was coming he'd have stayed clear of the yard anyway. Nat Eason saw them though, and told him on the Monday morning, 'Your chum had one of his popsies down the boat Saturday. Didn't get a close look myself, but Wally Bristol did and he reckoned she wasn't hardly out of her rompers. "Bet she was later," I told him . . .'

Chalk had known about it by that time anyway: he'd been heavily caught up in it, in fact. He'd let Eason finish his story because he hadn't wanted to have to waste time and effort explaining the background – how he'd been woken by a telephone call in the middle of the night – well after midnight on the Saturday, therefore Sunday morning – Mrs Blair taking it down in her hall, fairly growling with anger, and having then to climb the stairs, vast in a pink wool dressing-gown and her hair in curlers, to wake him. While his own first thought at her bark of 'Telephone for ye! *This* time o'night, Lord's sake!' had been why on earth she'd be 'phoning at such an hour. It was Zoe that he was picturing – because she'd telephoned a few times in recent days – on one occasion when Diana had been trying to get through to him from Deauville – and late as this was, Zoe was not a woman to hold back, once the spirits moved her . . . Then a very different guess – which rocked him, sent his brain spinning – *Diana. Accident* . . . From halfway down the steep, narrow stairs he'd called back to Mrs Blair, 'Man, or woman?'

'Huh?'

Wouldn't mean anything anyway: doctor, nurse . . .

The telephone was fixed to the wall, its receiver dangling. 'Chalk. Who's—'

'Ah, Chalk.' Gruff *male* voice. 'Innes Cameron-Green here. Sorry to roust you out of bed.'

'What's up?'

He wanted to know whether Chalk had any idea where Suzie might be, where Dymock might have taken her. 'Should have brought her home well before midnight, you see – hours ago. It's now—' a pause – 'past two-thirty, no sign of 'em and no word. I *am* sorry to wake you, Chalk—'

'That's all right. But where would he have been bringing her home *from*?'

'Well – St Fillans.' His tone suggested that Chalk should have known this. 'That's where he told us they'd stop for a meal.'

'Small village at the eastern end of Loch Earn?'

'Fishing hotel there – they were going to have a meal on their way back here. I've telephoned – woke *them* up – but the manager chap says they've had no such people dining there tonight. *Last* night. Place is full up with fishermen, he said, people who go there year after year, any strangers would have stuck out like sore thumbs – or words to that effect. I'm trying to stay calm about this, Chalk, but—'

'Where would they have been before – I mean *en route* back to Glendarragh from where?'

'As far as I know, from Barlows' yard.'

'Barlows' – really? But why, what—'

'Early this afternoon he was supposed to have been showing her over his submarine. Yesterday afternoon, as it is now. Obviously you didn't run into them.'

'No.'

'Would you have? Might you, if they'd been there?'

'No. I was in Glasgow . . . I suppose they drove down here from Glendarragh – this morning?'

'No, *no* . . .' A pause. Then: 'I'm sorry. Keep forgetting, you didn't know.' There was a shake in his voice, Chalk realized. 'No – Suzie's been with friends – a former schoolfriend and her people – at Milngavie. Dymock was to fetch her from there after lunch – and he did, I've spoken to the girl's father, they left at about two-thirty – with the intention – well, as I said—'

'Showing her over *Trumpeter*. And then up to St Fillans . . . The obvious guess is he may have had some trouble with his car?'

'Breakdown or an accident. Yes. But I've spoken to the police, all the obvious places around that area and along the route they should have taken, and – nothing. They've all promised to keep an eye out, and to telephone me here if they have any news.'

'There are some fairly remote places he could have broken down at, aren't there.' Chalk was thinking aloud. 'Miles away from a telephone or garage. He'd have a shot at fixing it himself – but I doubt he'd be any great shakes at that . . . Still, they could be on your doorstep any moment – he'd get it mended eventually – with help from some other motorist perhaps. May be well on his way. I'd try not to worry, if I were you, sir. Meanwhile – question is what *I* can do . . . He'd have been getting to St Fillans through Comrie, wouldn't he?'

'According to my map – no other way. And I've talked to the police there. I doubt there's *anything* you can do – thanks all the same. I only wondered whether you'd any idea what his intentions might have been when he set out.'

'None at all. As I said, I didn't even know Suzie was coming down.'

But there had to be *something* he could do . . .

Fully awake now, telling himself they'd have broken down, somewhere where there was no mechanical assistance – at this time of night anyway – and no telephone. It was Suzie's welfare and comfort he was thinking about: Dymock didn't matter a damn . . .'

'Sir Innes – I can't just go back to bed on this. One possibility is – well, making for St Fillans from this direction you'd take the right fork out of Dunblane then bear left at

Braco on to the road for Comrie: that's the route you've had in mind, talking to the police?'

'Of course.'

'But he *might* have gone up through Strathyre – can't be much further that way – and turned right at Lochearnhead. Up to that point it's a better road and one he knows well by this time. Then to get from Lochearnhead to St Fillans, the road along the north side of the loch's distinctly primitive – was when I last saw it – and along the south bank it's no more than a track. So he'd have taken the upper one. Logically . . . Anyway, I'll start out as soon as I've got some clothes on. Luckily there's petrol in the tank, filled it on my way out of Glasgow this afternoon.'

'Mean you're going *now*?'

'Yes. I'll take that route, and – I suppose come on up to you then – for breakfast. But I hope they'll be with you long before that.'

'Damn good of you, Chalk.'

'If I find them along the way—'

'I'll be sitting beside this telephone.'

'But perhaps I'll bring them. Anyway bring *her*.'

Leaving Dymock to look after his wretched car . . .

Counting bloody chickens, he thought, hanging up. Picturing Suzie on that Strathyre Forest road, miles from anywhere, probably no traffic on it at all at this time of night. And his own warning to Dymock about deer on the road, colliding with one and getting an antler through the windscreen . . .

'I said something about cutting this short.' Chalk leant to tap his pipe out on the wall edging the terrace. 'Doesn't seem to work, does it? Getting long-winded in my dotage . . . But – skipping the next few fairly hellish hours – I got to Glendarragh at about ten that Sunday morning, and there was Dymock's Riley, large as life. If I hadn't been tired and hungry I might have just reversed course and headed for home: except I needed to be sure Suzie was all right. I'd come a fair distance and I'd had her image in my mind every mile of it, these awful nightmares of what *could* have happened. And drawing blank after blank. At Lochearnhead for instance – I'd woken them up in the hotel there, and it wasn't the first place I'd stopped at . . . All I remember is a succession of disgruntled, barely comprehensible Scots startled out of their slumbers by this wretched Sassenach asking about a young couple in a green saloon. It was raining, by the way, quite heavily . . . So – from Lochearnhead I took the road – if it could be called that – along the loch's north shore to St Fillans. Ten miles of narrow lane, not metalled but with those twin strips of tarmac one used to find in the Highlands. They have 'em in some parts of Africa too, as a matter of fact. If you meet another vehicle you put your offside wheels on the nearside strip and the other fellow does the same, and if you're lucky there's room to scrape past. I didn't meet any other vehicles. One thing I do remember – having thought of it a great deal, over the years – is that in my mind I was reassuring Guy, telling him not to worry, I'd find her and I'd break Dymock's damn neck for him. That would have been incidental, mind you – to find her and get her home was the imperative.'

'Since you mention it – I meant to say this before – I'm surprised Guy hadn't broken Dymock's neck at some earlier stage. Or at least punched him on the nose.'

'Not in Guy's nature. Wouldn't have helped, either, *vis-à-vis* the C-G family. What's more, Dymock would have made mincemeat of him. Guy was fairly skinny, and Dymock was – well, quite a bruiser, really . . . Where were we?'

'On the way along Loch Earn to St Fillans.'

'Yes. Drew blank there too. The people were if anything less pleased to see me than they'd been at Lochearnhead. They'd had Sir Innes on the blower, then as soon as they'd got back to sleep they'd had the Comrie police, and now with dawn in the sky here was I asking exactly the same questions. Plenty of rain still coming down too, and my car's wipers had packed up, which didn't help – especially negotiating that track along the south bank, heading westward back to Lochearnhead. Dymock might have been fool enough to have come that way – might have decided it was the side he and his father had fished, for instance, on that holiday he'd told me about. I'd remembered that and guessed it might be his reason for coming here. You'd have needed some compelling reason – my God, what a road! And roughly in the middle, between two hamlets whose names I couldn't have told you even later that same day, I spotted a set of car tracks – tyre tracks anyway – which seemed to have gone over the mud-and-grass bank into the loch. Well – you can imagine – I thought I'd found them. I was sickened. Pulled a branch off some stunted tree, waded in and poked around and thank God found nothing. A car wouldn't have gone far in from the edge. In retrospect I can only guess that someone with a tipper-truck backed up there to get rid of some load or other. Waste-products from an illicit still, for instance. They used to do a lot of that: same as they make poteen here. But I must have spent an hour groping around – soaked to the skin, and coated in mud, I wasn't exactly a sight for sore eyes when I tugged on the door-bell at Glendarragh. Set all the dogs barking, and I couldn't blame them. But Sir Innes was kindness itself. They *all* were, I suppose. I had a bath and breakfast, he leant me some clothes, and – well, Suzie was as grateful for my pointless efforts as her parents seemed to be, and thoroughly apologetic for the mix-up that had made them necessary. While Dymock, who *should* have been fairly grovelling, wasn't at all: as I recall it he was – on guard, slightly hostile.'

'Where had they been?'

'That was the question of the hour. *And* most of the day. Dymock had his story, and although Suzie was vehemently backing him up her father was far from convinced. I don't recall quite all the ins and outs, but I can give you the gist of it – of the yarn as Dymock told it. First of all, he'd changed his mind about going to St Fillans. He'd been talking to one of the Barlows' bowler-hats, mentioned that he was contemplating going there for a meal, and this fellow – foreman engineer, name of Fairley—'

'You've mentioned him before, in connection with the torpedo-tube rear doors.'

'Well done.' He nodded. 'Fairley had told Dymock the food at that pub was the worst in Scotland. No doubt in this modern age it's of *Cordon Bleu* standard, but according to Fairley it wasn't a place you'd even take your wife. Why not, he suggested, go a different way entirely, and eat at this pub or hotel in the Trossachs – which he named. He'd been there recently, and in his opinion there was nowhere to touch it. Well, Dymock didn't want to give her a rotten meal the first time he took her out, so he drove up through Aberfoyle and that forest – forget what it's called, huge area of forest just south of the mountains – or hills, rather – stopping to admire the scenery here and there – he *said* – since this place was comparatively close and they didn't want to eat too early. I'll tell you in a minute where the doubt comes into that bit about admiring the scenery. Anyway, they finally got there, and the food was every bit as good as Fairley had said it would be. I've an idea it was off the main road, somewhere on its own. Not that *that* matters two hoots ... But – they wined and dined, and incidentally Suzie admitted to her father and mother that she'd had quite a bit more to drink than she was used to. I remember this because I seemed to be the only one who found it significant in terms of her support of Dymock's story; if she'd thought of it as a detrimental factor she'd have kept her mouth shut. Follow?'

'You mean she had nothing to hide, so—'

'Exactly. And she recounted it as rather amusing – smiling at Dymock as if it was a private joke between them. I made a guess or two on *that* score, too. But it didn't make Sir Innes any happier. The rest of the story is that when they went out to the car, it wouldn't start. Dead as mutton. Water in something probably: at a later stage the magneto was mentioned. I can't even remember what a magneto was – or is – can you? Anyway – back into the hotel they went, to find out where there was a mechanic Dymock could get hold of, only to be told that (a) there was no such creature this side of Callander; (b) if there had been he'd never have come out at that time on a Saturday night, especially in such foul weather; and (c) the telephones weren't working anyway. Water in something there too – junction-boxes, was the guess. Obviously it was raining cats and dogs all over Scotland, not just where I was a few hours later. And of course Dymock couldn't contact the Cameron-Greens. He was in a hole, and knew it, and all he could think of finally was to set off on foot to a village a few miles away where the hotelier or publican told him there resided a man by name of MacDougall – or somesuch – who ran a taxi. I don't remember how far it was Dymock had to hike. But Suzie stayed in the pub – downstairs, in an armchair beside a good fire, was what I think she said. Yes – she said they'd offered her a bed, on or in which she could have rested while awaiting Dymock's return with or without the taxi, but she'd declined this. Possibly because she was aware that people's minds jumped to certain conclusions when beds were mentioned, and she wouldn't have wanted to make things worse than they were already. This was 1937, remember, and Dymock had his reputation, which she knew about – from me, if not from him. She hadn't seemed at all surprised when I'd mentioned it that morning in the paddock, and I'd wondered then whether he might have warned her that he had this unearned reputation. Undeserved, *of course*.'

'Getting in ahead of any gossip that might come her way. *And* making himself more interesting to a young girl?'

'There may have been a little more to it than met the eye,

however. I *will* try to cut it short now. Dymock found Mr MacDougall, who was willing to come out with his taxi, and it transpired that he was an amateur mechanic as well as taxi-driver. He shoved his head under the bonnet of the Riley and after about five minutes, hey presto, he had it running perfectly. This was at about 0500 – daylight, anyway.'

'Sir Innes didn't believe the story?'

'I think his line was that he wouldn't accept it without corroboration. It rang *almost* true to me and I'd guess to him too, but he would have been extremely anxious not to leave room for any innuendo against his daughter. People being prone to gossip as they are, you couldn't blame him. Not in *that* year of grace, you couldn't . . . One thing in Dymock's account of events that bothered me was his statement that they'd stopped to admire the scenery more than once: in heavy, continuous rain and the depths of rather a gloomy forest. It seemed to me unlikely. In which case there might be a conclusion to be drawn: but it was none of my business, and I promised to cut this short, so I'll give him the benefit of the doubt. I'd *certainly* give Suzie that benefit, but – well, Dymock was the organizer, *she* wasn't, and if he'd planned all this so as to get her there early enough to – to make a long evening of it, shall we say – that doesn't mean she'd have – co-operated. In fact I'm damn sure she *didn't*.

'Two reasons, by the way, for suspecting something of the sort. One, from what one knew of him he'd hardly have gone to all this trouble if he hadn't had some ulterior motive. Second, there'd been mention of the offer of a bedroom – which she'd declined – and this I thought might more typically have been Dymock's idea than the publican's. The suggestion of it might also have been mooted earlier in the evening than we were now expected to believe. And her little joke, rather at his expense I thought, about the amount of wine he'd given her: as if he'd tried it on and she'd out-manoeuvred him. Those were my private thoughts – out of a naturally suspicious mind, so far as Dymock was concerned. I was only suspecting his intentions, mark you, I didn't for a moment believe he might have had his way with her. In fact it was obvious from Suzie's general attitude that he *hadn't*. Obvious to me, anyway.

'Whether Sir Innes' view of it ran on similar lines I can't say, but he must have given Dymock to understand either that he didn't believe him or at least that he couldn't accept his story without corroboration. Dymock consequently got on his high horse – a basically *defensive* reaction, is my guess – and told Sir Innes that any such doubts were insulting both to himself and to Suzie. Whom, he added at some slightly later stage, he loved deeply and sincerely, wouldn't *dream* of compromising or harming in any way. He told *me* some of this, incidentally, a day or two later – that he was in love with her and she was with him, he'd never felt like this about any girl before, effectively this was the first time ever ... I'm ad-libbing slightly, don't recall his exact words. But that was the drift of it, and the climax came before there was any telephone connection restored: Dymock, I was told later, had asked for Suzie's hand in marriage, and while Sir Innes was pondering the question Suzie told her mother that if they didn't let her marry him she'd leave home at the first opportunity and never speak to them again. Or she'd die of a broken heart – that sort of thing. Then later in the day the telephone fault was cleared, Sir Innes spoke to the people concerned and had the story *partially* confirmed. I'd left by this time, was on my way south – so this is second hand now, plus putting two and two together from as much as Patricia told me – but as far as corroboration was concerned it seems there were a few gaps, the publican either uncertain or unwilling to swear to this or that.

'So, less than a hundred percent satisfied – *faute de mieux*, you might say – Sir Innes summoned Dymock to the study and asked him, 'Do you genuinely love my daughter and wish to marry her?' – and probably, 'Can you provide for her in the manner to which she's accustomed?' – and that was that. Engagement to be announced at the anniversary celebration on the 28th. I had nearly all of this from Patricia, incidentally, a bit later; she also told me that her mother was delighted, Sir Innes clearly much less so. But confirmation of the engagement also came to me from Suzie, in a note in which she asked me whether as a special favour I'd write and break the news to Guy.'

Chalk glanced at me and shrugged. 'Damn cheek, eh?'

He told Suzie – over the telephone, on the evening of the day he had this note from her – that it was very much up to *her* to write to Guy. She argued the point, but he made it plain that he wasn't going to haul her coals out of the fire for her: and he gave her the only address he had, the Spanish Republican recruiting office in Paris.

He told her, 'They'd forward a letter, I imagine. It may go from pillar to post a few times before he gets it – don't be surprised if there's no quick answer. He may *not* get it, even. I doubt if the mail can be in a very organized state out there. Anyway – I'll see you on the 27th or 28th, Suzie.'

'Not before?'

'I won't be up next weekend, if that's what you mean.'

'You sound – unfriendly, Rufus.'

'I'm sorry. I'll go through the motions – congratulations and so forth – but I'm not going to pretend to you personally that I think your engagement's a good thing. In fact I'd implore you – for your own sake, Suzie, if you have any doubts—'

'I haven't. None at all.'

'Well – so be it . . . The other thing of course – speaking frankly, Suzie – well, asking me to write to Guy on your behalf is really adding insult to injury. A couple of weeks ago you were telling me with delight that Guy had decided against going to fight in Spain, and since then you've treated him in a way that made it inevitable he *would* go. You didn't intend it, obviously, but it was – predictable. Perhaps you think it was worthwhile – on the basis that you can't make an omelet without breaking eggs. My own view is that the omelet's a bad mistake. Suzie, I don't mean to seem unfriendly, and I *do* wish you happiness. You, as an individual. But look, this has been a rather longer call than I'd expected . . .'

Then on the Wednesday – seven days before *Trumpeter* was due to go to sea for her acceptance trials – he ran into Dymock in the central passage of the shed they called the Submarine Office.

'Morning, Toby.'

He'd been about to pass him, on his way into *Threat*'s general office. Dymock put a hand on his arm: 'Got a minute?'

'I suppose so . . .'

'Let's get some fresh air.'

The hut did get stuffy in this warm weather. On the heels of that drenching weekend high summer had returned, producing almost tropical conditions.

Chalk offered – they'd turned along the edge of the basin, towards *Trumpeter* – 'Cigarette?'

'Just put one out. Anyway, what price fresh air?'

'You tell me. Your idea, this, not mine.'

'So it was . . . Rufus, you know of course that I'm going to marry Suzie?'

'I know your engagement's to be announced on the 28th.'

'You'll be there, will you?'

'No reason not to be. I was invited and accepted before you'd even heard of Glendarragh.' He'd lit his cigarette. 'And Diana's coming.'

'Yes. Of course . . . You – er – disapprove, I gather.'

'Since you ask me – yes.'

'Because of Guy?'

'Partly. But also because I can't see any future in it.'

'Meaning what?'

'I don't believe you're the right man for Suzie. I think it'll come to grief and she'll be hurt. As it happens, I'm very fond of her.'

'D'you think I'm *not*?'

Glancing at him, thinking, You're too fond of yourself to be worth a damn to *any* woman, for more than a week or two . . .

He said, looking at *Threat* across the basin, 'I'm sure you think you are, Toby.'

'I *love* her. That's what I want you to know. I know what people say about me – half of it's untrue, incidentally, and the other half's exaggerated – Rufus, I've never felt like this about anyone in my life. I'm *in love* – never was before, I know it now – and she is with me. Can't you accept that – accept *us*?'

'My brother's in Spain, Toby.'

'Well, of course, I'm sorry about *that*, but—'

'You're only as close as you are to Suzie because you chased her from the moment I introduced you to her. I wish to God I hadn't. You could have spent that weekend as you'd intended, couldn't you – in London. *Much* more your mark . . . Toby, you can say it's true love, etcetera, but at that stage you were only amusing yourself – as you've done a dozen or more times before – and *that* is why my brother is in Spain.'

'I'm told he planned to go months ago.'

'To the great relief of those of us who are fond of him, he'd decided against it. Your activities changed his mind back again.' He shook his head. 'I'd rather not discuss my brother with you.'

'We've been friends a long time, Rufus.'

'We *were* friends, for a long time.'

'All right. All *right* . . .'

Peering over Chalk's shoulder then, his expression changed. Chalk swung round, and saw his CO, Ozzard, looking their way as he paused near the entrance to the shed.

Chalk transferred the cigarette to his left hand, and saluted.

'Morning, sir.'

'Morning, Chalk.' He'd returned the salute. 'I want a word with you.' A jerk of one thumb towards the offices. 'In my caboosh?'

'Aye aye, sir.'

'All set for today week, are you, Dymock?'

'Just about, sir.' Dymock added, 'You'll be with us, I gather.'

'*Was* to have been. Come on, Chalk . . .'

He saw Nat Eason in his office. As always, the engineer had a cigarette in his mouth, eyes narrowed through its smoke as he glanced up from a blueprint. Removing the stub now with a nicotine-stained finger and thumb, opening his slit of a mouth – wanting a word too, evidently . . . Chalk put his head in the doorway, told him 'With you in two shakes, Chief', and followed Ozzard into the office marked COMMANDING OFFICER.

'Take a pew. Smoke?'

Chalk took one, although he'd trodden on the remains of the last only seconds ago. Flicking his lighter into action as he sat down: Ozzie was lighting his own.

'About *Trumpeter*'s trials this day week. As you'd know initial test dive's normally made in the Gareloch here. Can't be in this case, because the loch's closed to all and sundry, still will be next week. Acoustic experiments, all hush-hush. *And*, it's been decided at some dizzy height that she can't do it in Kilbrannan Sound or Inchmarnock Water or the Arran side of the Firth either. Too much traffic, is the reason given. Including some minesweeping exercise – which is fair enough . . . Oh, and destroyers using the measured mile off Arran. What it comes down to is *Trumpeter*'s first dive'll be in Irvine Bay – between Ardrossan and Lady Isle, roughly.'

'Longish way to go.'

Ozzard's deepset eyes blinked at him under the shaggy brows. 'And the outcome as far as you and I are concerned is I'm being shanghai'd into acting as trials liaison officer on board an escorting tug. So I can't go out in *Trumpeter* – and consequently you *can*. I've fixed it with Jacko Pargeter. All right?'

Chapter 9

To a submariner's eye *Trumpeter* was a lovely sight – new paint, polished brass, brand-new White Ensign whipping in the breeze. There was an air of purpose – even excitement – about her. To Chalk's slightly envious eye, anyway – envious because it was going to be such a long time before *Threat* reached this stage . . . They'd moved *Trumpeter* out of the fitting-out basin yesterday evening and secured her alongside in this entrance/exit channel, with catamarans between her bulging saddle-tanks and the sheer stone wall; she was subject to tidal movement here of course, so that hemp breasts and wire springs and the lashings on the plank would have been adjusted a few times during the night. And even in that, there was a certain return to normality: the routine of a gangway watch, and the watchkeeper or sentry having to keep his eye on the moorings.

Now – 0920, twenty minutes past the promulgated embarkation-time for passengers – the tide was well up and the plank from shore to ship was more or less horizontal. Chalk, and the group of others with him – Andrew Buchanan, Nat Eason and two commissioned engineers from T-class boats building at Scott's – were waiting to be invited to go on board.

'What's this?' Buchanan, in corduroys and a golfing-jacket over a Fair Isle pullover – nodded towards an approaching van. 'Not *more* food?'

They'd been watching two men from a catering firm carrying luncheon stores aboard: and with the Clydeside Chandlers van barely out of sight this other one was drawing up. Navy blue with an RN number-plate and – Chalk saw who it was, suddenly – Mike Searle, *Trumpeter*'s torpedo officer, slamming the passenger door shut.

'What you got there?' Eason, calling to Searle as he came over to the edge of the quay – a smallish, neat man, tanned from the cricket field. Eason asked him, 'Forgot the champagne, did they?'

Searle's glance swung from the engineer to Buchanan. 'Leg-irons for the passengers, that's all.' He called down to the submarine's casing, 'Four hands up here please, Second.'

Addressing the Second Coxswain, an outsize leading seaman who at this moment was climbing around the side of the tower, coming from the after casing. Second Cox'ns had charge of submarines' casings, ropes and wires and anchor gear. Searle, joining Chalk's group, glanced up at the mainly blue sky with its streaks and patches of high white cloud. 'Nice day for it. We're lucky.' Then to Eason, answering his question, 'Extra DSEA sets – passengers for the use of.' A nod to Buchanan. 'Morning, sir. Don't worry, we won't need 'em.'

'You're Searle – right?'

'Absolutely right, sir.' He looked round as some sailors came over the plank. 'Two boxes of DSEA in the back there. Weigh about half a ton apiece. Break 'em open if you have to.'

'Aye, sir.'

'Twenty-eight sets to the box.' Chalk narrowed his eyes, working it out. 'How many passengers?'

'Forty.' Eason corrected himself: 'Forty-five, could be.'

He'd only won himself a place on this trip at the last minute. The list was compiled and controlled by his opposite number in *Trumpeter*, Lieutenant (E) Wally Bristol, whose orders from Pargeter had been that the total number of souls on board shouldn't exceed one hundred. So as *Trumpeter*'s own officers and crew totalled fifty-three, Bristol had tried to keep the passenger list down to forty until he'd been sure there'd be no additional late-coming senior officers to be accommodated. Additional, that would have been, to the pair of four-stripe captains and one commander who were on board already. As were a large contingent from Barlows', half a dozen Admiralty officials and a few others who could claim to be directly concerned with the trials and/or the Barlows' contract. Those left in this small group waiting to be allowed on board – Chalk, Eason, Buchanan and the two commissioned engineers – were strictly joy-riders. Buchanan could of course have gone straight on board, but he'd elected to wait – admitting to Chalk, 'I must be the least useful chap in this whole shebang . . .'

The cases had been unloaded and were being dragged towards the plank; the van was leaving. Searle came back to them. 'Were to have been more observers than there are, Hennessy says. He was holding five places for chaps coming up from Birkenhead, and they cancelled, A "T" at Cammell Lairds due for trials next month, apparently, so they were told to save the rail fares and hotel bills, wait for that one. Parsimonious bastards.'

'Who? Blockhouse, or Admiralty?'

'Well – Admiralty. Bloody civil servants. Even if FOSM had to make the signal . . . Anyway – despite those drop-outs – passenger total I *think* is forty-six.'

Eason trod on a cigarette stub. 'Not countin' the ship's cat.'

Buchanan fell for it . . . 'Is there one?'

'Problem is—' Eason told him – 'in DSEA terms, I mean – you need a special set. Tricky, see, fitting a nose-clip on a cat.' Nodding seriously to Buchanan. '*And* takes some training.' Glancing at Chalk, he broke into a snigger, overcome by his own humour, and others laughed with him. This was a jaunt, a day out, there was a holiday spirit in the air: even the Barlows' bowler hats had looked quite jolly as they'd filed on board.

'Seriously, though—' Buchanan asked Chalk – 'and cat or no cat – do *we* get trained?' He tapped his own chest: 'Do *I*, I mean. But it could apply to some of our chaps as well . . . If they had to use these masks and stuff, not knowing a thing about it?'

'I'll give you a demonstration.' Chalk added, 'Not – as Searle mentioned – that you're likely to need it.'

Eason had turned away to chat to the other two engineers. Chalk meanwhile was doing some more mental arithmetic. *Trumpeter*'s complement of officers and men – 53. Regulations were that there should be DSEA sets on board for all hands plus one third of that number as spares, in case sets might be damaged or otherwise defective. 53 plus a third – 71, and sets came in boxes of 28, so the least they could have drawn from stores was three boxes – 84 sets that would already be on board, most of them in the sealed steel lockers provided for them. And now with the number of 'souls' on board increasing to about a hundred, for God's sake – but say 99, for mathematical convenience, so you'd add 33 – the figure became 132. Five boxes, therefore – 140 sets. QED . . .

It *was* going to be very crowded, though. Nearly twice as many on board as there'd normally be.

Buchanan was saying, 'Your skipper's going out on some tug, I gather.'

'Official title Trials Liaison Officer.' Chalk added, 'All he has to do in practice is make sure other shipping stays clear of us. Main problem could be trawlers – fishermen. But he's not *going* out, he's *gone*. Tug's slower than we are, it was due to shove off at about first light. My good luck that they wanted anyone of Ozzie's seniority for such a boring job.'

'We'll meet him down there in the Firth, I suppose.' Buchanan said, 'Nice fellow, Ozzard. He's lunched with us a few times.'

'Be daft not to, if your lunches are always like that one you gave *me*.'

Thursday or Friday of last week, this had been. Commanding Officers could lunch in the directors' dining-room every day if they wanted to, but Chalk had been Buchanan's guest primarily to thank him for having agreed to act as his 'minder' on this trip. Meaning, effectively, make himself available to answer any questions on technical and/or other naval subjects. Which was no imposition at all – as he'd told Zoe last night when she'd telephoned from London ostensibly to ask him whether it was true that he'd be taking care of her husband. And was it really dangerous? He'd told her yes, he'd be looking after him, and no, it wasn't dangerous at all. In fact no Royal Navy submarine had been lost on trials since the war. She'd seemed happy enough with these assurances, and shifted to her standard theme – when would he, Rufus, be coming down to London? And a new one: why didn't *he* ever telephone *her*? He'd got her number, hadn't he?

Actually he hadn't. Although she'd given it to him half a dozen times.

Eason came back to them, counting on his fingers. 'There's twenty-eight Barlows' fellers on board, plus six from London, then the Blockhouse team – that's four – plus us lot here, plus other odds and sods – it *is* a hundred, near enough! Crikey, what a bloody *scrum*—'

'Scum?'

'Yeah, that too . . . Hang on, here's Prince Charming.'

Dymock, coming over the gangway. Looking exceptionally smart. Best superfine uniform – not as a rule worn when seagoing – and a blindingly clean white cap-cover – with a cap-cane inside it too, by the look of it, not at all the crumpled piece of headgear he normally affected . . . Behind him, on *Trumpeter*'s casing, sailors were moving to stand by ropes and wires. Searle was there – chatting to the Second Cox'n – a huge man, towering over the Torpedo Officer. There was only one hand in the bridge, as yet. Probably the signalman. Dymock raised his voice: 'Would you come aboard please, gentlemen? Skipper sends his apologies for having kept you waiting. Getting things stowed and settled below. Rather cramped, I'm afraid . . .' To Buchanan, then: 'CO was asking where you were, sir. We thought you'd have boarded with your other chaps.'

'Preferred to wait with my minder.' A movement of the head in Chalk's direction. 'Thank you, all the same.'

Noticeably cool tone. Not a very friendly manner either. Dymock had noticed it too. His glance, quick and sharp, shifted from the civilian to Rufus Chalk, then back again. Chalk meanwhile aware of a twinge of discomfort: having his own view of Dymock now but thinking of recent telephone conversations and wondering – especially in Buchanan's presence – whether the pot might not be calling the kettle black.

He couldn't stop her telephoning him. Well – on the face of it, he couldn't. Admittedly he hadn't tried to . . . But that – he was able to reassure himself – was the full extent of his transgression. He'd no intention of telephoning *her* – ever . . . All he really wanted was an uncomplicated life – meaning, to avoid unnecessary complications or involvements and to concentrate on Diana. On her and on his job, and to hell with all the rest of it.

Zoe included.

'After you.' He ushered her husband towards the plank. Behind them, Dymock was apologizing to the two engineers for having kept them kicking their heels here for so long. Their names were – he racked his memory, mostly for the mental exercise – Melhuish, and Cheyney. Both were old buddies of Eason's: who was muttering as they filed along the casing to the fore hatch, 'Standin' room only below, I reckon. Fuck *this* for a bloody lark . . .'

Chalk rather agreed. He thought – while waiting for some hold-up in the vicinity of the hatch to clear so they could go on down into the submarine – that if he'd been Pargeter he wouldn't have allowed the number on board to climb anywhere near a hundred. Although the only passengers one could obviously have done without would have been himself and Eason and this pair of plumbers. And Buchanan, at a pinch. And Barlows' might have been persuaded that they didn't need as many as twenty-eight of their men on board. He'd have argued for a maximum of twenty: you'd have the total down to nearer eighty, then.

But of course – this hit him suddenly – some would be disembarking, transferring to the tug, before the dive anyway. It was what always happened: he'd forgotten it. You'd be losing those Barlows' men who were only concerned with the engine and steering trials, and of course the caterers – who were only on board to serve lunch – and perhaps a few others.

So all right: the only drastic overcrowding would be between now and the start of the diving trial. With a distinct feeling of relief, he tapped Buchanan on the shoulder . . . 'When Jacko says sorry for not having dragged you on board sooner – as he's bound to – why not tell him you'd like to be on the bridge – or gundeck – accompanied by your minder, naturally – for the trip down-river and the surface trials?'

'I suppose I could.'

'Be a lot more comfortable. *And* scenery to enjoy.'

'All right.' A nod. 'I'll ask him.' Stooping into the hatch then, turning to clamber backwards down the steel ladder. Chalk followed – frontwards, the proper way – and paused at the bottom, on the TSC's corticene-covered deck but clear enough of the ladder, looking around him at gleaming white enamel and the sparkle of brass valve-wheels here and there.

A few sailors were stowing gear – or re-stowing it, to save space – and beyond them, right up forward, watertight doors port and starboard stood open, allowing a view of the rear doors of the upper four torpedo-tubes. All of it immaculate – the new white enamel, and every piece of brightwork highly polished. Familiar odour of shale oil – shale being the fuel on which torpedoes ran, but it was also used as a cleaning and polishing fluid for the corticene. The scent of it was as familiar – and as appropriate here – as linseed oil was in a cricket pavilion.

Looking for'ard, still, he was remembering the wrongly-placed bowcap indicators, and that potentially confusing system with the operating levers.

But they'd have come to terms with it by now. As he'd have to himself, since the same gear was to be installed in *Threat*. Making way for Eason and his friends to pass on their way aft ... Buchanan, who'd been peering into the thick glass window in the forward escape chamber, turned back and pointed at the empty reload torpedo racks, 'No torpedoes yet?'

'Not in the tubes either.' Chalk told him, 'She'll get those later.'

'Will they have what-d'you-call-'ems – explosive heads?'

'Warheads. Not at *this* juncture.' He added, 'Soon enough, no doubt.'

'Well. Darned *little* doubt ... What do they have in place of warheads?'

'What we call blowing heads. There are collision heads as well, which just crumple, but it's the blowing kind we have normally. At the end of the run compressed air blows the water out so the fish will surface and float, nose up, and boats can pick 'em up. That's to say, get a line on and tow 'em to some crane. The practice heads are painted bright orange so they can be spotted easily even in a rough sea.'

'So you don't actually hit any practice target.'

'No. You set the depth mechanism so they'll run under. Running right under counts as a hit.'

'I see. But – sorry, one more question?'

'Many as you like.'

'Well – the absence of them – of all that weight – must affect the submarine's trim quite considerably?'

At least the man asked reasonably sensible questions. Chalk told him, 'It's allowed for. Apart from the fact we've got a lot more bodies on board than usual – extra weight – the trim's adjusted by the amount of water that's either put into or taken out of the auxiliary and compensating tanks. Did Jacko explain the trimming system to you?'

'I didn't quite take it all in, I'm afraid.'

'I'll explain it, presently. Let's go aft now?'

By ten o'clock *Trumpeter* had the Tail o' the Bank ahead of her, Greenock abaft the beam to port and Helensburgh – a smear of whitish seafront with the hills enclosing it on all sides except the sea frontage – on the starboard bow. Diesels rumbling steadily and the sea washing over her tanks, swirling white and noisy below this gun-platform and the bridge. She was making about fifteen knots, Chalk guessed. He was on the gun-platform with Buchanan, also a Lieutenant-Commander Quarry and Harry Calshot, a lieutenant whom he knew well. They were both visiting from the Gosport submarine headquarters. And now, just arrived, Nat Eason and his two pals – arriving as the rest of them had via the bridge, the conning-tower hatch and the iron rungs down the tower's sides. There were two hatches giving direct access to the gun for its crew, but they were kept shut and clamped, partly as a routine safety precaution but also because the wardroom, at the bottom end of this guntower, was far too crowded for the access ladders to be rigged. Down below there, Eason had confided to Chalk, there was barely room to fart.

Buchanan lowered a pair of glasses which Pargeter had

lent him. 'No good. Might have seen it if I'd looked sooner. Hills in the way, now.' His house, he'd been looking for. He and Chalk were up front in the oval-shaped gun platform, up where the gun's barrel projected over the shoulder-high protective screen, so their view was directly ahead and out on both bows. Virtually an all-round view, except that it was blanked off astern by the looming bulk of the conning-tower. Buchanan gestured towards Helensburgh: 'How far would you say that is?'

'About four miles. Sea miles – eight thousand yards.'

'I'd have thought more than that. But I'm sure you're right.' He glanced round, and lowered his voice, leaning closer. 'Tell me something else. Changing the subject rather drastically ... In confidence, what's your frank opinion of Dymock?'

The last person who'd asked him that had been Suzie – who'd been hoping for a different kind of answer than he suspected Buchanan might be fishing for. Entirely instinctive suspicion: but the thought was immediately of Zoe, and that if ever there'd been a time for caution, this was it ... He told him – looking at him under the gun's grey-painted barrel – frowning, letting his surprise show – 'Haven't thought about it, in any – you know, analytical way ... He's a fellow submariner I've known all through my Service career, that's about all.'

'About all. Is it, really.' Cocking an eyebrow; but it was a comment – with a touch of irony in it – not a question.

Chalk added – on the defensive, but hardly knowing why – 'I've simply accepted him, not made a study of him ... Yes, that *is* all.' Instinct again warned him not to make more of this than he had to; he changed the subject. Pointing: 'Entrance to the Gareloch there. Right by your front door, you might say.'

'Would I be right in thinking he's a womanizer?'

That guess had been right. He temporized: 'Awkward question, rather.'

'You mean giving it a straight answer's embarrassing for you?'

'Slightly. Yes . . . But incidentally, in the Navy it's not called womanizing, it's called poodlefaking.'

Buchanan smiled rather grimly. 'Interesting that you'd need a special word for it.'

'Possibly Nelsonian origins?'

'Faked *his* poodle all right, didn't he. But I think I can take it from these evasions that – *without* hedging – the answer's an affirmative?'

He shook his head. There was no reason on earth to defend the bastard. But no reason to tell tales out of school, either – that was yet another instinct.

'Until quite recently it's true that he's had a certain reputation. Gossip, about half of it exaggerated and the other half probably invented. A lot of it sour grapes, because girls tend to run after him, for some reason. They like his looks, I gather. But things have changed rather suddenly now, as it happens. Do I gather you haven't heard about his engagement?'

'Engagement?'

'I thought it might have prompted these questions. Or this question. I think you know the girl's father – man by name of Cameron-Green?'

'*Those* people . . . Yes, I—'

'You shot there once, he told me. Anyway – she's much younger than Dymock, and my own young brother is – was – very keen on her. He's taken it rather hard, and in consequence Dymock and I aren't on the best of terms. What makes it rather worse – for me – is that I introduced him to them. But there it is – spilt milk . . . This *is* in confidence, by the way.'

'Of course.' Watching a tug with a string of lighters: *Trumpeter* had altered to starboard to get by. He shook his head: 'I don't remember that I met the daughter.'

'Two of them, actually. Both very nice and very pretty. It's the younger one – Susan – he's picked on. Seventeen.'

He changed the subject again. 'That's Gourock coming up on your side now. Kempock Point . . . Then to starboard here, Kilcreggan, and to the left of it – just about *there*, when we open the view of it a bit – is the entrance to Loch Long. Top end of Loch Long's a torpedo range, incidentally – for torpedo-firing trials – and there's a pub at the village – Arrochar – which'd be a perfect place to take your wife for a quiet weekend. If you wanted one – and enjoy walking, not doing much else. Wonderful scenery. Steepish walks, mind you – for instance there's a hill up behind Arrochar village called the Cobbler that's about 3,000 feet.'

'Sounds as if you've climbed it.'

'I have. More a steep walk than a climb, though. I just about ran down it once, in heavy rain. I'd gone up thinking I'd beat the weather, and I didn't.'

'You're a fitter man than I, Gunga Din.' Buchanan was peering ahead, towards Strone Point and Holy Loch. 'You mentioned torpedo-firing trials in Loch Long. Might *Trumpeter* be doing that?'

'Doubt it. There are torpedo-ranges in the south too, you see.'

'Ah. I'd been rather assuming they'd go straight down to – Portland, is it?'

'Yes. Sixth flotilla. The four-stripe captain you met before we came up here – McAllister – commands it. He's up to see how this boat's officers and crew look like shaping.'

'Indicating that they *will* be going down there right away?'

'I'd imagine so.'

'Well.' Buchanan had the glasses at his eyes again. 'Well, *well.*' He hadn't reverted to the subject of Dymock, but it was obviously still in his mind. For whatever reason . . . Sweeping the glasses slowly across the entrance to Loch Long as *Trumpeter* plugged on westward and it opened up to view. He murmured after an interval of silence – broken only by *Trumpeter* herself, her pounding diesels and the sea's rushing and thumping through the casing under their feet – 'Must be beautiful up there. In autumn, I should think – those wooded hillsides?'

'Beautiful at any time. In decent weather, mind you. Can be fairly bloody when it's bad . . .'

It was eleven-thirty before they were out of the narrows between Bute and Little Cumbrae. There'd been quite a bit of traffic and still was, freighters inbound and outbound. Trawlers were visible now off the Arran coast. No sight of the minelayer that was supposed to be exercising: but the exercise might not have started yet, and there was plenty of other enclosed water they could have been using: Inchmarnock Water for instance – north of Arran, east of Kintyre – or Kilbrannan Sound to the south of Inchmarnock.

Trumpeter began to swing, under starboard helm. Steering trials commencing – her long forepart lifting to the swell, carving white water out of green.

'Where's our tug with your skipper on it, I wonder.' Buchanan was using the binoculars again. 'One of those, could it be?'

'Those are trawlers. Wrong place, anyway. No, he'll be plugging on down towards the Ayrshire coast. We don't rendezvous with him until early afternoon – just before the dive.'

'Does one feel it – diving?'

'Not really. Deck might tilt a little. Probably won't this afternoon, because we'll be doing it in slow time. The light trim I mentioned – your people will have put it on her, as I said, and it's really to be expected – trial dive, they always prefer to flood her down slowly, rather than dive fast and then have to pump out ballast.'

'I'm in favour of that, I think.'

'But there'd be no danger in it anyway. We'll be in – oh, twenty fathoms or more, I imagine, she'd have to be *very* heavy to go down so fast she'd hit the bottom.' A smile – to show he was joking, that there'd be no question of it . . . He'd given him a rough explanation of the trimming system, during the run south past Rothesay, and mentioned that he knew for a fact she was trimmed very light. One of the Barlows' men had landed to check the draft-marks for'ard and aft while they'd been waiting on the quayside, Chalk had gone over to talk to him and elicited that she was floating three or more inches higher in the water than she might have been.

'The diving procedure, now.' Buchanan had lowered his binoculars, nodded forward towards the submarine's long, plunging forepart. 'Those circular brass things are the vents which are opened – in pairs, you said – to let the air out?'

'Right.'

'The water then floods in through open holes in the bottoms of the tanks.' He saw Chalk's nod, asked, 'All of them at once?'

'When you're diving in a hurry, yes. Not today, though. Incidentally, number one main ballast is a single tank, up for'ard there. It's two, three, four, five and six that are each two tanks, one port and one starboard – in those bulges. Called saddle-tanks. And yes, those round things are the vents. Operated like almost everything else by the telemotor system – basically oil under pressure operating on a ram, forcing it this way or that. Do you *want* this much technical description?'

'That much is more or less comprehensible. The telemotor system you say operates not only the main vents but other things as well?'

'Periscopes, hydroplanes, steering, bowcaps on the tubes—'

'The system you said you don't favour.'

'Only the neutral position, we don't like. Not just me – any of us. In fact we aren't going to use it – no need to, we'll put the levers to either "shut" or "open" and ignore "neutral".'

'So then you'll see at a glance what's open and what's shut.'

'Exactly. Mind you, I've no idea what your own people will be doing.' He thought again, and shook his head. 'Doesn't matter. There's no reason they'd be opening or shutting bowcaps.'

'That's a question I was going to ask. Our people in co-operation with the Admiralty overseer, you said, have put on the trim. But will they still be running things when we dive?'

'No. The boat's crew will. Jacko Pargeter, in fact. Although your lot and the Admiralty chaps'll still have their fingers on the pulse, so to speak.'

'Sounds to me like too many cooks.'

'It's the established process of hand-over, that's all. And to date it's worked all right.'

Resting with his forearms on the steel bulkhead, the four-inch barrel against his shoulder, his eyes on the submarine's long, grey-painted fore-casing and the sea cleaving away brilliant-white, seething away aft over the fat curves of her tanks . . . Glancing at Buchanan: 'Isn't it beautiful?'

'Well – I suppose . . .' It hadn't occurred to him, evidently, until this moment. He nodded – faintly. 'Yes. It *is* . . .'

'Would you satisfy my curiosity on one thing, please?'

A quick sideways glance . . . 'Dymock?'

'Yes. What's behind those questions?'

The light-brown eyes held his: the flickering in them was the reflection of light from the sea's bright surface. 'Strictly between ourselves?'

'Of course.' Looking past him, Chalk spotted what might well be the Admiralty-chartered tug with Ozzard on board. He'd borrow the glasses in a minute . . .

'What's behind it—' Buchanan spoke quietly, after a precautionary glance round – 'is that he's been chasing my wife. I should say, he *was* chasing her. You've astonished me, with the information that he's engaged to one of the Cameron-Green girls. Considering that only two or three weeks ago he was pestering Zoe with telephone calls – to such an extent that that's why she went down to London, to get away from his – well, harassment.'

'She tell you this?'

'Night before last. I telephoned to suggest she might come back up here for a week or two, and she said if Toby Dymock had left, or when he did, she'd happily come back. I had to worm the rest out of her. She'd kept it to herself because she didn't want to make a fuss. Thought I'd make a song and dance about it – with embarrassment to all concerned, placed as I am here. D'you understand me?'

'Yes. Of course ...' Wondering: perhaps Dymock *had* been pursuing her? He shook his head. 'I'm awfully sorry.'

'Hardly for *you* to be sorry.'

'Well – my friend, or he was. Brother officer, all that ... Are you going to do anything about it now?'

'I honestly don't know. The obvious thing's to confront him with it, tell him a few home truths and scare him off. But if he's engaged now ...' Thinking about it, watching the sea part and cream away to port and starboard, the long forepart lifting to a swell and then smashing down, the submarine's bow buried for a moment in a boil of sea: then lifting, tossing it away in streamers on the wind. The swell had been gathering strength as they moved south, and she was pitching quite hard. Buchanan glanced back at Chalk. 'A word to Sir Innes, perhaps. If he's the sort I think he is – and the girl's as young as you say – what d'you think?'

'I doubt it'd change the odds. She's set on it absolutely. I know her quite well – I think ... Less through length of time than through my brother – who was *very* close to her – and a sister who's a friend of the other daughter – but I got nowhere, talking to her. And Sir Innes wasn't exactly enthusiastic, but that made no difference either. Despite the fact that they're a very close, united family. Or have been, up to now. She's adamant. You could prove Dymock was the greatest libertine alive and she'd say that may be how he *was*, he's a new man now.'

'Think he could be?'

'*Can* a man change that much?'

'So – what would you do, in my shoes?'

'I think I'd let sleeping dogs lie. Unless you feel compelled to have it out with him. In which case, I'd say go ahead. But his engagement to the Cameron-Green girl's hardly your province, is it?'

'None of my business. No, I suppose it isn't. Although for the girl's sake – in the long run – and your brother's—'

'Too late to salve anything there, I'm afraid.'

'Oh. Well, I'm sorry. But you see, if I do nothing, he goes down south leaving his fiancée up here presumably – and Zoe's on her own in London—'

'She could tell him to go to hell, couldn't she?'

'She *would.*' They were watching an oiler ploughing northward. Red Ensign: and a group of men on her stern watching the submarine. Waving, now. 'I just don't like leaving her in that situation ... In fact I'd better have it out with him – *and* bring her up here. Much as she dislikes the place. Happens to be where I have to spend most of my time – especially now, with certain plans for expansion at Barlows'. Trouble is I'm too damn busy, she's on her own too much and she has no real friends up here. You may have noticed at that dull party you came to, she was knocking it back a bit?'

'I did, yes. Not that she's alone in that.' He put a hand out: 'Borrow the glasses, a minute?'

She'd been 'knocking it back a bit' largely because Dymock had let her down by not showing up in London ... But – trying to make sense of it: Buchanan had heard this from Zoe, he'd said, two nights ago. And last night she'd been on the line to *him* and said nothing about it. Suppose

– pure supposition, but it might hold water – suppose she'd heard about the engagement, it had touched her on the raw – as it well might have – and she was acting out of spite, getting her own back on Dymock for having ratted on her. It might be in character, he thought – and fit the circumstances. Remembering her sarcastic *If Toby has a weekend to spare he rushes up to the bloody Highlands! I think he's got a girl up there . . .*

But *how* she'd have heard . . . Well, Dymock might have written – or more likely telephoned, he'd hardly have been so rash as to have committed himself to paper . . . But that wasn't at all improbable. He, Chalk, certainly hadn't told her about it. Hadn't even mentioned Dymock recently. He'd realized she'd have to hear about it some time, that she'd want to know why he hadn't told her, and he'd have to trot out some spurious explanation – like having thought it might upset her. That would do, in fact . . . The true reason – it also accounted for his not having said anything about Guy going to Spain, which was very much more on his mind, infinitely more so than the engagement *per se* – was that he was wary of letting her know anything that she could only have heard from him.

Back to earth. Or rather, to this brightly-coloured, jumpy seascape, in which he had the glasses focused on a small ship with a single funnel and a low, open stern; she was six or seven miles to the east of *Trumpeter* and steering south. Lifting swells obscured her hull several times a minute, and intermittently the white of broken water as she butted through it was like a distant flare. He told Buchanan, 'I've found our tug. *A* tug anyway – and she's pointing the right way. Throwing herself about a bit. Not that that'll worry Ozzie.' He handed the glasses back. 'Doesn't worry you, this motion?'

'Not as yet. Touch wood.'

'Good. Be a shame to miss the lunch you're paying for.'

'Have to go down inside for it, I suppose.'

'Afraid so. Pity we can't dive first.'

'Would there be less motion – *will* there be, dived?'

'None at all. She'll be as steady as a rock.' He paused … 'Getting back to what matters, though – I really don't know how to advise you, about Dymock …'

The lunch wasn't all that marvellous, and it was spoilt by lack of elbow-room. In the wardroom especially, since all the Admiralty officials and the Barlows' bowler hats considered it vital to their dignity to cram in there. It was a small enough space even for the submarine's officers on their own, but there were also these shipyard dignitaries and the civil servants, and the Portland flotilla captain – who was twice the standard size – and Engineer Captain 'Baldy' Gleeson from Flag officer (Submarines)'s staff, with a Commander Random as well as Lieutenant-Commander Quarry in his entourage. And Buchanan of course – as a Barlows' director, whether he liked it or not he had to be squeezed in between Jacko Pargeter and the Admiralty's Principal Ship Overseer, a man called Hughes who at least had the decency to be thin. Scrawny, in fact – with thin hair too, combed from the side to camouflage a bald crown. There'd been numerous introductions, and Chalk was doing his best to memorize the names of the key men.

The food on offer, after soup had been served in mugs, was cold chicken, tongue and roast beef with salads and potato mayonnaise, followed by a choice of puddings. Reaching that stage, Chalk selected chocolate éclairs and took them back to the chart table, of which he and a few others including Eason and Harry Calshot – the old friend who was the junior member of the Blockhouse party – had claimed temporary possession. Also with them was John Hervey, the boat's navigating officer – tall, fair-headed, trying not to show concern at having his pristine, beautifully polished chart table used as a food-bar. You could only eat standing, jammed against the outside bulkhead of the wardroom for support against the boat's movement, but at least the éclairs could be handled without tools.

Dymock had the watch when luncheon started, and Searle went up to relieve him when he'd finished his. Dymock came down then, filled a plate for himself in the galley and came to join the group at the chart table. Calshot was a friend and contemporary of his too, of course.

'Beef's overcooked.'

'Ours wasn't.' Chalk told him, 'You've got the scrag end, there.'

'Thought there'd be plenty. With this much movement on her.' He'd begun to eat. 'No signs of *mal de mer* that I've seen, though.'

'You haven't been for'ard.' Eason pointed that way with his jaw. 'Fellers with their heads in buckets up there, all right. *And* a Barlows' bigwig spewed all over the bloody motor-room. Christ, you wouldn't *believe*—'

'Spare us the grisly details, Chief?'

Eason sucked his teeth, glancing at Chalk. 'Don't know why I came, tell you the truth. Be happy as a fucking lark, when we get back alongside . . .'

Dymock was asking Calshot about recent comings and goings of submarines and individuals at Fort Blockhouse. Chalk, having had enough to eat and finished his bottle of Worthington E, wandered forward, looking at this and that – mainly for any detail in which the finished job differed from the plans and might be worth emulating in *Threat*.

The general layout was of course identical. Forward of the wardroom he was passing the ERAs' – engineroom artificers' – mess, then the Chief and Petty Officers', and forward of that was the seamen's mess. Less crowded than the wardroom, but still nowhere you'd have swung that mythical cat round. Passing the forward escape chamber, then – its door was shut and clamped, as it should have been, but it struck him that there'd have been room for one man to eat his lunch in there – and another in the escape chamber aft, come to that . . . Now, passing through the open circular door in number 2 watertight bulkhead, he was in the Fore Ends, where the deck-space was taken up by men sitting with plates of food in their laps. Submariners, and Barlows' men too. One of the former – a leading torpedoman, the insignia on his right arm comprising crossed torpedoes surmounted by a star – asked him as he pulled his legs in, making way – 'Jimmy of *Threat*, sir, aren't you?'

'How d'you know?'

'From when our Jimmy was showing you the tubes, sir. Bowcap indicators – the way these fellers cocked it up?'

He nodded, remembering him too: and that the name had to be somewhere in his memory . . . 'Get used to it, will you?'

'Don't know about that, sir.' He sniffed. 'Five an' six being arsy-tarsy's one thing, but the pointers going every which way, that's another.'

'Yes, I remember. So you'll have to check each one instead of just seeing 'em all parallel with each other.'

'That's the *real* bugger, sir.'

He'd remembered the torpedoman's name now – Eddington. He nodded to him, and moved on, into the Tube Space. Which was even more dazzlingly smart, at close quarters, than it had been from a distance. The brass test-cocks in the rear doors, for instance, shone like gold: so did the rimers which hung on short chains beside them. Test cocks were for checking that a tube was empty: when the lever was pushed over, it aligned two holes so that if there was water in the tube it would jet out. While the rimers' use was to ensure that the test-cock holes weren't blocked by silt, dirt or seaweed. Having opened the cock it was standard procedure to poke the rimer through: if no water squirted out after that, you could be certain the tube was empty.

Back into the Fore Ends . . .

There *were* several greenish faces. Several buckets, too, and they'd been used. The odour of vomit – stronger here than that of shale – wouldn't be helping the poor bastards much. It was bad luck: yesterday there'd been a flat calm under the summer heat, and not a breath of wind, but this swell rolling in from the Atlantic today could only be the result of recent heavy weather out there. He'd seen no forecast. Being shorebound, still a job number rather than a ship, *Threat* wasn't getting any.

He'd have gone on aft through the Control Room, continuing this look-see and also to have a chat with the boat's engineer, Lieutenant (E) Wally Bristol – whom he hadn't had a chance of talking to yet and who'd surely be with his beloved engines – but Pargeter, with Buchanan in tow, was pushing his way out of the wardroom, the group at the chart table moving into the Control Room to let them pass. Chalk put a hand on Buchanan's shoulder: 'Thanks for the lunch.'

'Huh?' Turning ... 'Oh, it's you. Wasn't such a feast, though, was it.' Dymock was a couple of feet away, still eating, and Pargeter was looking back to see who Buchanan was talking to. 'Come up with us if you like, Chalk.'

'Thank you, sir.' He followed Buchanan – to the first ladder, which led up to the conning-tower's lower hatch, through that and up the next, longer one which led vertically through the tubular steel tower to the upper hatch and the bridge. Above his head, Pargeter was giving Buchanan a hand out: Buchanan being on the tubby side, not all that agile.

The scene up here, he found, was as it had been an hour earlier. Sea brilliant green under bright sunshine, the swells heaving in from the west, wind carrying the spray away to port as *Trumpeter* broke through ridge after ridge with drumbeat regularity, tossing the shreds away, salt crystals glittering in the sun ... She was steering east, he realized. That was Lady Isle on the bow – and a crescent of the Ayrshire coast beyond, white-edged all the way from Saltcoats down to Troon.

Closer – less than a mile away, about four thousand yards northwest of the island – the tug *Clansman* was rolling hard. Pargeter, putting his glasses on her, murmured, 'Poor old Ozzie. He'll be wishing he'd lumbered you with that job, Chalk!'

'Surprised he didn't, sir.'

Pargeter was in the bridge's forefront, starboard side. Searle, as officer of the watch, was up front to port. Pargeter bawled, 'Signalman!'

'Sir.' He came forward, squeezing between Chalk and the periscope standards. Pargeter told him, 'Make to *Clansman*, Stuart: *While you prepare your boat for lowering I will close and provide a lee.*'

'Aye aye, sir.' He already had the Aldis lamp out of its stowage and was sighting on the tug: beginning to call it, flashing the letter 'A' until a light answered with a single flash from the tug's bridge. It could be Ozzard himself handling that lamp, Chalk guessed. It was a Clydeside Lighterage Company tug, chartered by the Admiralty for this job with its own skipper and crew, and he didn't think Ozzard could have had a signalman with him.

This signalman – leading signalman, in fact – was clicking out the message and getting an answering flash at the completion of each word. Finishing now, with the end-of-message group 'AR'; there was an acknowledging 'K' from the tug.

'Message passed, sir.'

'Very good.' Pargeter stooped to the voicepipe's copper rim. 'First lieutenant to speak on this pipe, please.'

'Aye aye, sir!'

Hollow tube, hollow voice ... Dymock's, then: 'First lieutenant here, sir.'

'Men transferring to the tug – have them stand by, and I want to know how many.'

'Aye aye, sir ...'

Clansman flashing. Stuart, who'd been watching for it,

sent an answering flash, which produced a stream of rapid Morse. Ozzie showing off his signalling skills, Chalk thought. Probably enjoying himself, at that. He – Chalk – had read the message before the signalman reported it to Pargeter: 'From *Clansman*, sir – *Boat is ready for lowering. Passenger capacity 8. How many to be brought over?*'

'Tell him *Wait*.' Pargeter added, '*Please*.' Then to Searle, 'Bring her round to 040.'

'040, sir.' Into the pipe: 'Port ten.'

Dymock then, from below. 'Captain, sir?'

'Yes, Number One?'

'No transferees at all, sir. They all want to stay on board.'

'*All?*'

'Ten o' port wheel on, sir!'

'Steer 040.'

'Number One: you said *all*. Even the caterers?'

'Yes, sir. And the pilot. Can't get one volunteer to leave us. The Barlows' chaps aren't keen on the idea of transferring by small boat in this swell, I think.'

Pargeter muttered – to himself – 'Don't blame 'em, really . . .' Then, to Dymock, 'All right. Say twenty men heavier than the trim allowed for. Discuss it with Mr Hughes, have them lighten her by that much.' He straightened from the pipe: spaniel's eyes blinking thoughtfully at Searle: 'Bloody hell . . .'

'Course 040, sir!'

With the swell driving up from *Trumpeter*'s starboard quarter now she was rolling as well as pitching, and there was a reek of diesel in the wind from astern. Searle proposed, 'Couldn't they be told they've *got* to transfer, sir?'

'Not really. They're not subject to naval discipline, for one thing. And God knows what sort of boat the tug has, or how good they are at handling it. Suppose it turned over and we drowned some . . .'

Chalk called, 'I could transfer, sir. And Eason. And the

two plumbers from the boats at Greenock?'

'Me too.' Buchanan offered, 'If it'd help.'

'It wouldn't. Thanks all the same. Five or six bodies – not worth the trouble. The boatwork wouldn't have been easy, anyway.' He looked round: 'Signalman – make to him, *Sorry, no customers for you, all personnel remaining on board for the dive*.'

Chapter 10

She was still on the surface.

With all her tanks full. Or damn near all. Running through Chalk's head was a well-known line from a gunnery drill-book: *This should not be possible*. The submarine was driving through the sea at half-ahead on her electric motors, with hydroplanes at hard a-dive: this alone applied a considerable force to drive her under, yet with all six main ballast tanks flooded, and by this time most of the auxiliary and compensating tanks as well, she was still ploughing along the surface with ten feet showing on the depthgauges. In other words, half awash. He could picture it – as Pargeter was seeing it through the periscope, and as she'd be looking to Ozzard on the tug: her casing submerged up to the guardrails that lined it fore and aft – they'd still be in sight – jumping-wire cutting through the water like an outsize cheese-wire, the gun awash, conning-tower still two thirds above wave-level. Ozzard, on the tug's bridge half a mile away, would be wondering what the hell was going on.

By no means the *only* one asking himself that question.

Beside Chalk, Buchanan murmured, 'Must be some logical explanation. If all you experts put your heads together . . .'

'You'd think so, wouldn't you.'

Asking himself what logical explanation there *could* be ... Buchanan adding, 'At least it's the surface we're stuck on.'

'Aye.' The Clyde pilot, a man of about sixty with a blunt face and thick grey hair – he'd brought *Trumpeter* down the river into the Firth and then elected to remain on board – smiled agreement. He'd joined Chalk and Buchanan before the dive, introducing himself as James Ballantyne and asking, 'Mind if I sit here wi' ye? Never was on one o' these craft before ...' Now he growled reassurance at Buchanan: 'They'll sort it oot, ye may be sure.'

Chalk thought, returning the old fellow's smile, *Blind advising the blind* ... They were close to the door of the wireless office, which was immediately aft of the Control Room. From here by only leaning forward you had a view into the Control Room – of Pargeter at the raised for'ard periscope, Dymock at the flooding and pumping telegraph – it was above his head, on the deckhead close to the hatch – and a group of puzzled-looking men around them. Hughes, the Admiralty overseer, Barlows' man Joe Fairley shorter and thicker-bodied beside him, and beyond them Captains McAllister from Portland and Gleeson from Blockhouse. In terms of weight, Chalk guessed, two Gleesons would make one McAllister. Other Barlows' men, including Hamilton the Ship Manager, were hanging around in the background. The rest of the passengers were distributed throughout the boat, with the main contingent in the wardroom. They'd been asked to settle down and stay put. Even one man moving from forward to aft could make a difference to the trim.

What trim, though?

That, more or less, was the question – or worry – showing in every face. The ERA at the diving panel, Coxswain and Second Coxswain at the hydroplane controls, a leading hand at the wheel – with an AB keeping the log and manning the telephone beside him – and a very young-looking, pale-faced Ordinary Seaman at the motor-room telegraphs. The signalman was there too, standing by to open the lower hatch if the order to surface should be passed. It might come to that – abandonment of the diving trial – if no answer was forthcoming pretty soon.

Buchanan reasoned again, in a near-whisper, 'If the tanks are full and she won't go down – despite our extra weight – well, there has to be something *structurally* wrong. Wouldn't you say?'

'But the basin dives went perfectly, I'm told. The day of the party I came to at your house.'

'Might have been changes made since then?'

'Only whatever the basin tests showed up as necessary. Keel-weight may have been adjusted one way or the other. But to put it *right* – and it wouldn't have been by much.'

'What if they made a bloomer? Took weight out, for instance, instead of adding some?' He lowered his voice still further. 'Shouldn't mention it, but they did join the bowcap indicators up wrongly – didn't they?'

'You're talking about your own firm, Andrew. D'you want to get lynched?'

Ballantyne was staring at Buchanan, his round eyes blinking rather fast . . .

'I wonder—' Dymock's voice, the tone sharp as if some bright idea had hit him: Chalk leaning forward, seeing him with his hand up to the electric telegraph which told men at various stations to open or shut the suctions on this internal tank or that, and to pump or flood via the main trim-line in one direction or the other – keeping his hand on it while turning to ask Fairley, 'Are numbers five and six tubes full?'

About three-quarters of an hour ago *Trumpeter*'s telegraphists had tapped out a diving signal addressed to Admiralty and to the Flag Officer (Submarines), telling them *Diving in position 55 degrees 33 North, 4 degrees 46 West, probable duration of dive 3 hours*. Pargeter had then waited for the acknowledgement, which had come about a quarter of an hour later from the naval signal station at Rosyth. The fifteen-minute delay had been spent testing the hydroplanes – turning out the forward ones, which when diving wasn't contemplated were kept folded upwards to save them from being damaged by the buffeting of heavy seas – then moving both sets of 'planes through their maximum travel from horizontal to hard a-dive, hard a-rise, back to horizontal. Having done this in the normal way – with telemotor power – he'd ordered 'Planes in local control' – which meant by-passing the telemotor system and fitting heavy iron bars to bosses inside the pressure-hull, two men sweating on each bar to turn the 'planes to angles of 'dive' or 'rise' as ordered by telephone from the Control Room.

Then he'd ordered, 'Open up for diving'. The boat's own crew had carried out this procedure, with Barlows' men breathing over their shoulders. 'Opening up' involved – primarily – removing cotter-pins from main and auxiliary vents, opening the high-pressure inlet valves to the tanks – valves known as HP blows – and other valves on that airline, also opening the Kingston valves which were fitted to the bottoms of some tanks. There were some minor items too, such as depthgauges. When Dymock had received reports from all compartments, he'd told Pargeter by voicepipe, 'Boat's opened up for diving, sir.'

'Very good.' Pargeter had had his navigator, Hervey, in the bridge with him, constantly checking the boat's position by shore bearings while she more or less stemmed wind and tide. Waiting, marking time, also with an eye on the tug, which was keeping station about a thousand yards on the port quarter. He'd passed one more signal to her, by light: *My mean course dived will be 330*.

Chalk, down below, had by that time taken up his vantage point outside the W/T office, and was joined there for a few minutes by Wally Bristol, *Trumpeter*'s engineer lieutenant.

Bristol, whom Chalk had known for some years, always looked as if he was about to burst into laughter. It was only the way his features were arranged – with a reddish complexion, very bright blue eyes, and a mouth with its corners permanently upturned. Chalk had introduced him to Buchanan, and the engineer had remarked with a jerk of his head towards the wireless office, 'Wireless telegraphy, they call it. Do better with bloody pigeons, don't you think?' He'd also talked about DSEA, for some reason, and when they were alone again – if it was possible to be alone, in a 270-foot steel tube with ninety-eight other men in it – Buchanan had reminded Chalk of the demonstration he'd promised to give him.

'When we're dived – that do? Bags of time, then, and damn-all happening. You'll hardly need it *before* that . . .'

The acknowledgement had come in at last from Rosyth, and on the bridge Pargeter had told Hervey, 'All right – down you go', and the signalman, 'Make to the tug, *Diving now.*' He was in a hurry, wanting to get on with it. Ducking to the voicepipe: 'Stop both engines. Out engine clutches. Group down, half ahead together.' The diesels' thunder died away: you heard the weather then, wind and sea and its impact on her steel. She was moving ahead on main motors now, the helmsman reporting up the tube, 'Main motors half ahead grouped down, sir!' And that message had meanwhile been flashed to *Clansman*. Pargeter told the signalman, 'All right.' Nodding towards the hatch. He vanished into it, taking the Aldis with him. Pargeter shut both voicepipe cocks, and took a final, quick look all round before he dropped into the hatch and dragged it down over his head, the heavy lid thudding down on to its rubber seating. He groped for a clip, and jammed it on: then the other, before he clambered down through the tower into the Control Room's artificial lighting.

Not as light as it had been up top. He blinked, adjusting to it.

'All right, Number One?'

'Aye, sir.'

'Mr Hughes?' The Principle Ship Overseer nodded his bald head, and Pargeter glanced interrogatively at Joe Fairley.

Fairley had smiled: 'Nothing we'd be waiting for, sir.'

'Here we go, then.' He told the Outside ERA – the artificer on the diving panel – 'Open one, three and five main vents.'

You heard a succession of thuds as the vents crashed open. On the tug, a thousand yards away, Ozzard would be hearing the rush of escaping air. Pargeter's soft brown eyes were on the nearer depthgauge – there was one in front of each 'planesman – watching for the beginnings of the dive. Then, moving towards the forward periscope, a gesture of the hands: 'Up . . .'

Fairley looked surprised at Dymock's question about those tubes.

'Five and six . . . Reckon they would be?'

'*Should* be.' Dymock's expression and tone reflected his irritation. As if he thought the Barlows' man should have known: even that by *not* knowing he might be in some way responsible for this absurd situation. It was several minutes since Pargeter had ordered, 'Open 2, 4 and 6 main vents' and the ERA had pulled out those three steel levers on the panel. He'd pushed home the levers on 1, 3 and 6, then. Those tanks being full, it was standard procedure to shut the vents so that when you needed to you could blow the water out again.

Dymock told Fairley in a clipped, slightly hostile tone, 'They're shown as full, on the trimming plan.'

'They'll *be* full, then.' Hughes, the man ultimately responsible for the trim, intervened. 'But even if they weren't—'

'Exactly.' Pargeter pulled his head back from the eyepieces of the periscope. 'With every other damn tank filled, for heaven's sake . . .'

'But—' Dymock switched the trimming order telegraph to STOP FLOODING and then SHUT 'A' SUCTION AND INBOARD VENT, and lowered his arm from it. His other hand was gripping the ladder for support. Roll and pitch were perhaps less noticeable than they had been, but there was a buffeting element in it as she slammed through the swells. Dymock suggested, 'Might as well check the tubes, sir?'

Pargeter's brown eyes rested on him for a long moment. Hesitating while he struggled with the inexplicable. In the background McAllister, Captain (S) of the Portland flotilla, muttered, 'I'm inclined to agree.'

'Get Searle in here.'

Glancing at the depthgauges again: then he was back at the periscope. The man beside the helmsman cranking his telephone . . . 'Torpedo officer in the Control Room, please.'

Buchanan touched Chalk's arm: 'A wild suggestion – out of total ignorance . . . Suppose after the basin dive our people made her far too light. As I was suggesting – *another* cock-up. So now with all these tanks filled she's still not getting down. Wouldn't a bit more weight in the torpedo tubes make all the difference?'

'It would make *a* difference.'

He hadn't really grasped whatever Buchanan was driving at. In any case he wanted to keep listening to what was going on, not waste time theorizing. And the concept of the basic trim – keel-weight – being wrong seemed *highly* improbable. Barlows' had built submarines before, they weren't novices: and her trim had been near enough right in the basin dive, no major changes had been contemplated. He remembered at the Buchanans' party asking Pargeter how the dive had gone, and his answer, 'They've got the ballast about right.' Meaning, the weight of pig-iron in her keel. Then again, the Admiralty Principle Ship Overseer – probably in collaboration with the Admiralty Constructor, another of the specialists in that team – had worked out their own trim either last night or this morning, and only shortly before

Trumpeter had cast off a Barlows' man had checked the draught-marks.

That was the clincher, really. She'd have been *slightly* light – as was customary, deliberately erring on the safe side – but not drastically so.

'Searle. Numbers five and six tubes – full or empty?'

'According to the trimming diagram, sir, full.'

'We know about the diagram. What I'm asking is, *Were they filled?*'

McAllister's voice from the background again: 'The lightness is for'ard, isn't it. As indicated by the fact you can't get the bubble aft. I'd say you're barking up the right tree, now.'

The bubble he was talking about was the one in the spirit-level in front of the hydroplane operators on the port side. Normally the coxswain would use his after 'planes to keep it half a degree aft of the centreline mark, thus ensuring that the boat had a slight bow-down angle on her. Captain McAllister seemed to have been stating the obvious – that if this couldn't be achieved, she was unquestionably light for'ard.

Searle, meanwhile, faced with that question about the two lower tubes, had glanced round in search of Fairley's assistant, Alec Rose. The trim had been worked out by the Admiralty man, but the trim diagram or 'statement' would then have been passed to Rose for implementation. He – Rose – wouldn't have gone round personally operating the flooding and pumping gear, he'd have detailed one of the Barlows' fitters.

'Alec.' Fairley had located Rose in the wardroom, where he and others were keeping out of the way. 'Was there two tubes filled – five and six?'

A mumble . . . To Chalk's ears – the full length of Control Room away, with its hushed but still accumulative sound as well as the hum of the motors still at half ahead – Rose's answer had sounded like 'I'd say they might not have been.'

'Christ.' Pargeter shook his head. 'Go for'ard, Searle, check those tubes.'

'Aye aye, sir . . .'

Chalk was thinking again about Captain McAllister's assertion that she had a small bow-up angle – so small that you wouldn't have known it except from the position of the bubble. And this being the first of the new class one knew nothing in practice about her hull-configuration's effect on performance in differing circumstances. Her designers would claim to know, but this now was the proof of the pudding, and he thought it was conceivable that although she'd now be heavy overall the combination of a small bow-up angle and the motors driving her at half-ahead was enough to stop her getting her snout in. She'd be acting like a surfboard – despite hydroplanes at hard a-dive – her hull at this angle in the water holding her up simply by virtue of her forward motion.

In which case, if you stopped the motors she might sink on an even keel?

Or, if you took enough additional weight in, right up in the bow, she'd go down like a plummeting whale?

It seemed far-fetched. He wouldn't even have considered it, if the situation hadn't been so extraordinary. The constructors clearly *should* know all about her hull-shape and behaviour under way, and you could hardly think of it as *speed* through the water: half ahead grouped down, still virtually on the surface as she was, might be giving her three knots. Not much more. If you couldn't get her under at that sort of speed – except by having her trimmed so heavy for'ard that she'd be bloody dangerous . . .

'Right, TI.' The log-keeper beside the helmsman put his 'phone down. 'Torpedo Officer reports numbers five and six tubes empty, sir.'

'Hear that, Number One?'

'Certainly did, sir.' Dymock glanced round at Joe Fairley again. 'Wouldn't you know . . .'

Meaning something like *You bloody Barlows' people* ...

'Captain.' Hughes, the Admiralty emissary, moved closer. 'Before you have those tubes filled, Captain – as no doubt you will, now—'

'Better late than never, eh?'

A nod of the bald, inadequately camouflaged head. 'Wouldn't you agree that one possible explanation of the error might be that two *other* tubes were filled?'

Pargeter thought about it. Lifting his hands from the periscope's handles, as if in surrender. 'Then we would *not* have the answer.'

McAllister – Captain (S) 6 – growled, 'Not unlikely some bloody fool filled the wrong tubes, I'd say.'

Ballantyne, the pilot, chuckled. Catching Buchanan's eye, then, he muttered, 'Rum do – uh?'

Buchanan agreed politely, '*Very* rum.'

'But they're gettin' somewhere, uh?'

'Seem to be – yes.'

'Aye.' The happy smile creased his face again. 'Aye – we'll be home to our tea *after* all!'

Chalk heard Buchanan murmuring softly to the old Glaswegian – if that was what he was – that he didn't think there'd ever been any doubt of *that*. Except that with this continuing delay they'd be an hour late for it, at least. Tea, *or* supper. Pargeter, breaking off his exchange of views with Hughes, told the man at the telephone, 'Call the Fore Ends, tell the Torpedo Officer check all six tubes.'

'Aye aye, sir.' He'd stuck his log-entry pencil behind his ear and was winding the handle on the box. 'TI?'

The letters stood for Torpedo Instructor. In fact he – a Chief Petty Officer and the senior torpedo rating, responsible to Searle for that department and all its works – would more correctly have been referred to as the TGM, standing for Torpedo Gunner's Mate. But the old designation had stuck, for some reason. What seemed odd to Chalk was that a man of his seniority and experience should have been manning the Fore Ends telephone. Unless he'd just happened to be the nearest to it when it jangled . . .

At this end, the 'phone clicked down. 'Message passed, sir.'

Buchanan murmured more or less into Chalk's left ear, 'Couldn't be anything to do with the faulty positioning of those indicators – could it?'

'No. Nobody's talking about bow-caps.'

When Pargeter discovered that all six tubes were empty, Chalk was thinking, he wouldn't simply have that pair flooded, he'd start by having some ballast pumped out of the midships compensating tank. Might take a few gallons out of 'A' auxiliary, too. Lighten her bodily, anyway, before adding that weight right for'ard . . . He was looking round for some wood to touch, hoping the tubes *would* prove to be empty. Otherwise, as Pargeter had said a minute ago, you'd be back to square one, to the problem with no solution.

'All right, TI. You hang on there, I'll see to it.'

Leaving him – CPO Frank Osborne – to guard the telephone. You did need a responsible character there to field and pass messages correctly, in a situation that was already somewhat confusing, and you did *not* need his expertise and experience just to check a few tubes. As it was, Searle had Leading Torpedoman Eddington with him on the platform in the Tube Space, and another torpedoman – Clark – right for'ard between the two tiers of tubes. Clark was there to open and/or shut the vents and suctions on certain tanks, in compliance with orders which came mainly from the Control Room.

Eddington offered, 'Sight bowcap indicators again, sir, shall I?'

'Better do that myself.' A grin at the killick torpedoman. 'Not that I wouldn't trust you a hundred and fifty percent, Eddington.'

Eddington made way for him. 'What's called having a

dog and doing your own barking, sir.'

'Actually it's called doing it according to the book.' He climbed for'ard between the gleamingly white-enamelled tubes, and Clark shifted sideways so that after a few physical contortions Searle would have a view of the indicators. It was hellishly cramped, up here in the submarine's narrowing snout. It would have been the narrowness which had caused the bowcap indicator dials to be arranged vertically – number 1 at the top, number 5 below, number 6 at the bottom – although the tubes themselves were numbered 1, 3 and 5 to starboard, 2, 4 and 6 to port. It was the invariable naval system, with anything at all – cabins, guns, whatever – to have odd numbers to starboard and evens to port.

By practically standing on his head, he'd sighted the bottom ones.

'All right . . .'

'Should be, sir.' Clark was growing a beard, but this far it only looked as if he hadn't bothered to shave for a day or two. He added, making way again for Searle to get by, 'Untouched by 'uman 'and since you last checked 'em.'

'Got a few damn monkeys around here though, haven't we?'

Laughter came loud and echoey, as in a tin drum. Which this *was* . . . Back on the platform behind the tubes Searle moved over to starboard, changing places with Eddington, to get to the test-cock on number one tube.

'Here we go, then . . .'

CPO Osborne had asked him something. The telephone was the other side of the watertight bulkhead, in the Fore Ends, and the TI was in that open port-side doorway. Searle had paused, looking round at him. 'Say again, TI?'

Louder: 'Only asked will you use the drains, sir?'

'Don't think I will. If there's any leakage in some of 'em I'd sooner it stayed where it is.'

Rather than drain down to the WRT, the water-round-torpedo tank. When torpedoes were in the tubes dry, if you needed to prepare to fire them you'd open a few valves to send high-pressure air into the WRT, blowing water from it up into the tube to fill the space all round the fish. The same effect could of course be achieved much more quickly by opening bowcaps, but this would affect the trim, making her suddenly bow-heavy, whereas transferring ballast into the tubes from a tank immediately below them wouldn't change it at all. (*Then* you'd open bowcaps – with the tubes already filled.) But similarly, the tubes could be drained-down into the WRT, when you wanted to empty them prior to unloading a torpedo; and here and now the drains could be used to check whether tubes were full or empty. When you opened the valve below each one you'd hear either nothing – tube empty – or water gushing down the pipe – tube full – or – a remote possibility – hear it *blasting* down, under sea pressure plus that of the boat's forward motion, if a bowcap happened to be open. In that case you'd wrench the valve shut double-quick.

Searle wasn't bothering with the drains, though. It would have been the TI's way of doing things, but as Searle saw it the test-cocks were fitted for precisely this purpose and were perfectly reliable.

He reached to the cock on number one tube. It was a brass lever about three inches long, could be turned from its normal position – lying flat to the tube's rear door – to stand out at right-angles to it. In this position the holes were aligned: water would have spurted out, if there'd been any.

There wasn't. He fingered it shut again and called to CPO Osborne, 'Number one tube checked and empty.'

Moving over to port, to number two. 'May as well stick to numerical order. Gets the buggers confused, otherwise.' Eddington laughed, shifting to let him get over to that side. Through the open port-side bulkhead door meanwhile they heard Osborne laconically passing that information to the Control Room.

*

Harry Calshot had joined them outside the W/T office. He'd sneaked into the Control Room from the wardroom, he said, to get a better notion of what was happening – this business about the tubes – and then having spotted Chalk he'd filtered through behind McAllister, Barlows' bigwigs and the Blockhouse three-striper, Random.

Chalk asked him, 'What's Random's job? What's he here for?'

'Haven't you met him?'

'Shook hands, that's all.'

'Oh. Well, he's running the perisher course. As from the one that starts next month. Wants to give his candidates a few tips on the T-class, I suppose. A man you and I should cultivate, Rufus, wouldn't you say?'

The 'perisher' was slang for the periscope course, more properly known as the COQC, Commanding Officers' Qualifying Course. Senior submarine first lieutenants, selected as candidates for command, were put through an intensive course of instruction primarily in the arts of submerged torpedo attack.

Chalk said, 'Be a few years before I'm in line for that, I fear.'

'If there's a war, Rufus, you *and* I – and Toby Dymock, and—'

'If – or *when*...'

Buchanan agreed. 'All the yards'll be turning out submarines like sausages, once the balloon goes up. They'll need skippers, won't they?'

'There'll be a lot of new building, all right. And recruiting – training ...' Calshot cocked an ear towards the Control Room. 'Number one tube checked empty. Five to go. Bet your boots, this *will* prove to be the answer. Flood those two tubes, and down she'll go ... Rufus, old horse, you didn't tell me – I only just heard it from your engineer – Eason, is it? – that you're engaged?'

'Am indeed.' He heard the report of number two tube

having been checked empty, and wondered what was taking Searle so long. He murmured, 'Making a meal of it, isn't he?', and continued – 'Harry, I didn't mention it because we were discussing Service matters mostly, weren't we? Anyway shan't be getting spliced for quite a while yet. Half-stripe first, I think. Better still, half-stripe *and* a command.'

'Expensive girl, is she?'

'*Rich* girl.'

'Why, you old bastard—'

'Terrific girl, actually. Flies her own 'plane – a Fox Moth—'

'I bet she's ugly.'

The Clyde pilot chuckled. Buchanan too. Chalk told Calshot, 'You'll eat those words, when you set your bloodshot eyes on her.'

'Sounds a bit too good to be true.' Glancing at Buchanan. 'Eh?'

'Well.' Chalk shook his head. 'Another way of putting it is I don't know what I've done to deserve such luck . . . She's flying up here this weekend, as it happens.'

'No wonder he's going round grinning like a Cheshire cat!'

Buchanan asked him, 'Up *here*?'

'To Glendarragh. The Cameron-Greens.'

'Oh. Dymock's—'

'No – nothing to do with him. The C-Gs' silver wedding anniversary – big hoolie, Suzie calls it . . . What was that?'

'Number four tube checked.' Calshot raised crossed fingers. 'Two to go.'

This was only a matter of 'going through the motions' – because he'd checked the bottom pair of tubes only ten minutes earlier. Eddington reminded him as he crouched behind the rear door of number five, 'We just done five and six, sir.'

'True. I'm not *that* absent-minded. We've been told to do

it again, that's all.' He moved the test-cock through the central position and over to the right, then brought it back to the centre where the holes were in line.

Nothing. Not a drip. He pushed the lever back to where it had been, and crabbed over to the last one.

'That was number five checked, TI.'

'Save me breath for five and six together, sir.'

'Right. Waste of bloody time, I know. But – that's life, isn't it.' He centred number six's test-cock and added, 'On the ocean wave, anyway. No doubt about this one either.' He turned it back. 'Tell 'em five and six are dry, TI.'

'Control Room . . . All tubes checked and dry.'

'And while we know they are, let's have a look inside 'em.' He edged back past Eddington, to get to the starboard side and number one again. Not bothering with the test-cock, he took hold of the rear-door operating lever, pushed it over and then hauled on it so that the heavy, circular door swung open. Glancing round: 'Torch?'

'Here, sir.'

He shone it into the dark and empty tube, holding the torch as far inside as he could reach but pulling his head back out of the smell of recently-applied bitumastic paint. There was no sign of any leakage at all. The torch's beam glinted along the steel runners on each side of the tube on which a torpedo's side-lugs would rest, when one was loaded. But there wasn't even an eggcup-full of water, in this first one.

He swung its rear door shut, and pushed the locking lever over. 'Number two, now . . .'

Same procedure, same result. And the same again with number three. Eddington queried as Searle moved over to number four, 'What they hanging about for, sir, d'you reckon?'

'Uh?' There was a small amount of water in number four. Just a few pints. 'Slight leakage in number four tube. *Very* slight. As well to know, though. Little leaks get to be big ones, if you leave 'em.' The discovery justified this internal check: over which he'd been taking a chance, since it had not been ordered or authorized from the Control Room. He added, 'Same as rabbits.' Glancing round at Eddington. 'Who's hanging about?'

'Well – thought we'd 've been filling the tubes as *should*'ve been full, like.'

'We will be, too.' The voice – from the port-side doorway, behind Searle – was that of Lieutenant (E) Wally Bristol. 'Excuse us, TI?'

'You're welcome, sir.'

Bristol stepped over the door's sill into the Tube Space. He had two Barlows' men with him – Alec Rose, assistant foreman engineer; and Mr Hamilton, the Ship Manager. Rose was pale with curly brown hair, in his early thirties; Hamilton middle-aged and overweight, with glasses and a yellowish complexion. Whether or not this was his normal skin-colour was a matter for speculation: *Trumpeter* was still roller-coastering, and the slamming motion was more pronounced here in the bow than elsewhere. All three were holding on – to an overhead pipe, Hamilton to the edge of the watertight door, Bristol with one arm draped affectionately over the rear end of number two tube. He was crowding Searle, rather. But evidently he'd heard the leading torpedoman's query about filling tubes: explaining to him, 'They're taking some out of "O" and "W" first – before filling a couple of these, see.'

Those were trimming or 'compensating' tanks. 'O' was amidships port and starboard, could be used also for correcting any small list, and 'W' was further aft.

'You'll hear from 'em soon enough, don't worry. What's the internal inspection for, Mike?'

'While we know they're empty, checking for any bowcap leaks. They tend to show up when she's bashing around like this, don't they? This one, for a start, needs attention.' He leant back to give himself room to swing that rear door shut.

'Seems to me it's as well to know now rather than later.' Throwing a glance over Rose and the pot-bellied Catchpole. 'So our friends here can fix it before we leave 'em?'

Bristol turned his rubicund, smiley face to the Barlows' men. 'Can do?'

'If that's what it is.' Rose nodded. 'But we'd make sure first it didn't come up from under.'

'Couldn't have. Drain's shut tight.'

Clark's murmur reached them from his position between the tubes: 'Tight as a monkey's arsehole.'

'And that's *very* tight.' Searle had got himself into position to open the rear door of number five. Taking hold of the operating lever . . . 'Bit stiff, this one.' He shifted back a little, braced himself to exert more strength.

It was beginning to shift. Taking *all* his strength, though. Bristol, listening to something Hamilton was saying, wasn't watching this. If he had been, he might have guessed at the cause of the resistance. Searle might have too – if he hadn't been so certain the tube was empty. Grunting with the effort as he forced the bar over. The locking arrangement was of geared steel lugs which had to be turned to their full extent before the door could be swung back on its massive hinges.

Last inch or two to go . . .

The sea flung it open. Clanging back – that and the implosion of sea as deafening as gunfire – flinging Searle back against the shut-and-clamped bulkhead door behind him, sea irrupting in tons per second, Searle semi-stunned but hearing a bedlam of shouts and screams over the roaring inrush – and the TI's yell into his telephone: 'Blow main ballast! *Blow!*' There were men – or men's limbs – in the port-side doorway, jamming it so it couldn't be shut, then it was clear but being *held* open for others to come through. Searle had disappeared, gone floundering to get Clark out of the maze of piping where he'd been shouting that he was trapped. It was Rose holding the door open – for Hamilton, Bristol and Eddington: Hamilton who'd been knocked down and with whose dead-weight Bristol had been struggling, and Eddington who'd gone back in to help. Then before the TI could get to the door to drag it shut, its own weight took over – would need half a dozen strong men to shut it then against the force of gravity and in the rush of rising water. The submarine's bow had tilted steeply down; she was going deeper – fast, nose-down – and incoming sea under rapidly increasing pressure was already slopping over the sill into the next compartment while four or five men struggled with that door. Eddington was dragging Hamilton's bulk over the sill, and some of those at the door shifted to make way for him and lost their hold on it: it got away from them, swung back again, all the way back so that its latch engaged – *locking* it open, now. Water waist-high and pouring over, down into the Fore Ends bilges, at this stage. Crushing pressure . . . Wally Bristol the engineer, clawing his way out of the Tube Space where he'd tried to find Searle and Clark and failed – he'd have been drowned in there too if the door hadn't resisted efforts to shut it – heard the TI's scream of 'Latch! Bloody *latch*!' Addressed not to him but to others blocking the TI's own efforts to get past them and into the Tube Space to free the door. Bristol shouted 'All right!' and turned back, dragged himself down into the rising black flood. The lights went out about then, a few seconds before she hit the bottom.

Chapter 11

Chalk had heard the violent clang of that tube's rear door crashing open and the first rush of air and sound as the sea burst in: then shouts, pressure rising in his eardrums and the telephone man's urgent 'TI says blow main ballast, sir!' – and 'Flooding through number five tube, bowcap's open. Evacuating Tube Space—' Pargeter's orders came in a fairly normal tone: 'Blow all main ballast. Group up, full ahead. Hard a-rise, fore 'planes. Get her bow up, Cox'n.' She'd already been steeply bow-down, though, the slope of the deck steepening all the time: the last thing you'd want was speed through the water, Chalk had thought – until you *had* got her bow up, for God's sake . . .

Buchanan had been behind him in the open doorway of the wireless office, and he'd had his own left arm hooked in there to stop himself sliding away for'ard. Things *had* been sliding . . . And the old Clyde pilot clinging to some fitting on the other side of the companionway: eyes wide and round, mouth slightly agape . . .

Guessing he might *not* be getting home to his tea? Or even tomorrow's?

'All main ballast blowing, sir.'

That was another thing: one's own instinct would have

been to blow only numbers one and two main ballast. To get her bow up. *Then* group up, full ahead, and blow the other tanks . . . Dymock and the outsize Portland flotilla captain had gone for'ard – Hughes then following them – slithering for'ard, grasping at solid fittings along the way.

He'd controlled his own inclination to follow them. But he had a fair idea of it, anyway: and as Buchanan had said, *too many cooks* . . . Rising pressure in the ears had been evidence enough that the sea was still pouring in. So none of them had managed to get to the bowcap operating lever. They'd have stood no chance at all of shutting a tube's rear door against sea pressure, but the bowcap, operated by telemotor pressure, would have been another matter. Much too late now. Maybe they *had* tried.

Spilt milk, anyway, he'd told himself. Isolating the Tube Space was the best bet. *Only* bet. Spilt milk, for sure, and best to ignore the lingering mental close-up of those bowcap indicators with their pointers all aimed in different directions but number five's on 'Open'.

'Depth here, pilot?'

Hervey had been ready for that question. He'd answered immediately: 'Between twenty-three and twenty-five fathoms, sir.'

Hundred and forty, hundred and fifty feet . . .

'Stop blowing five and six, Crowley.'

'Stop blowing five and six.' Going by the Outside ERA's tone of voice this could have been a routine exercise, no danger or emergency at all. He was a Geordie, by the sound of him; Chalk had seen him in the Barlows' yard a few times. 'Five and six main ballast stopped blowing, sir.'

'Stop both motors. Full astern together.'

'Full astern together, sir!' Jangle of the telegraph. There'd been a note of sharp alarm in *that* voice. Perhaps with some reason: it was at that moment that the lights had flickered and gone out, and a Scottish voice had grated, 'My word, *isn'a* this a great day oot!' Several men laughed, and the emergency lights came on. They were on localized circuits, Chalk had recalled from his studies of the plans, so the Tube Space and possibly the Fore Ends as well were probably still blacked-out. Thoughts in and out of his mind at this stage had been (a) who that might have been, with the sardonic humour – because he deserved a medal of some kind; (b) that unless the motors running astern now stopped her so that she'd virtually be hanging on her screws, she'd be hitting the bottom pretty soon; (c) that the depth of say 150 feet might make DSEA escapes difficult, but on the other hand – (d) – never mind DSEA, blowing and pumping would surely get her up, since there was such a lot of ballast in pretty well all her internal tanks – which could if necessary be pumped dry, to counter the weight of one or possibly two flooded compartments. And – last but by no means least – that if they hadn't succeeded in isolating the Tube Space they'd better make damn sure of shutting off the Fore Ends. If the water came any further aft than that second watertight bulkhead it would flood down into the forward battery, and salt water mixed with electrolyte made chlorine gas.

Which killed. But then, so did deep water, if you gave it half a chance.

He'd glanced back over his shoulder at Buchanan, conscious of having rather neglected him in the last few minutes. Beginning to tell him – the staring eyes, clamped jaw, forehead glistening with sweat – 'Don't worry. Not as bad as—'

The jolt as she hit the bottom sent men and loose objects flying, and a tremor through her steel that lasted about half a minute. Cork chips rained from the deckhead: they were in the paint, supposed to absorb condensation. The weak emergency lighting had stayed on – miraculously . . . Depths – he'd craned round to focus on the nearer gauge, at the same time hearing Pargeter's 'Stop both. Stop blowing' – the gauges showed 155 feet. 157. Slightly greater depth of water here than Hervey had reckoned, then. He looked at Buchanan again – aware that the angle was steepening, that if it got much worse you'd need ropes to get from one compartment to another – 'I was saying, – *nil desperandum*. Lots of ballast in her that can be pumped out. Jacko'll get her up all right.

'Levelling?'

Buchanan was right: the stern-up angle was decreasing. Had been doing so for some while, in fact. Chalk nodded. 'Step in the right direction.

It wasn't, necessarily. As Buchanan could probably guess. His pale-brown eyes were on Chalk's, probing for the truth.

Whatever that might be. Chalk thought, *Spin a coin. Heads we do, tails we don't*. He smiled, adding mentally, *As the actress said to the bishop*. Being a passenger had its own problems, he was finding. If he'd been in Dymock's place or Pargeter's he'd have been telling himself that it was only a matter of time, that sooner or later you'd either get her up there, or get everyone out by DSEA, or there'd be some kind of rescue operation from the surface. If they could get a salvage ship and divers here fast enough. It would need to be fast, whatever you did, because the air with only her ship's company on board would only last about thirty-six hours, whereas *Trumpeter* was carrying almost twice that number.

Anyway – he was *not* in Pargeter's or Dymock's shoes. He was a passenger. All the decisions had to be theirs. Rescue from the surface was the least likely eventuality, in point of fact.

Trumpeter had been on the bottom, anchored to it by her flooded and abandoned forepart, for about an hour. Main ballast had all been blown, the pumps were running on internal tanks, and so far this levelling was the only outcome.

Depthgauges showed 159 feet. The additional few feet would be accounted for by the fact that the stern and midships sections were deeper than they had been, through this levelling process. He didn't see how pumping could be the cause of it. Unless his brain was *already* affected in some way. It would be later: carbon dioxide poisoning would do *that* ... But sticking to the point – pumping couldn't make her heavier: and her forepart wasn't lifting, it was her afterpart sinking. So what the hell ...

Tidal movement?

Might be. Might well. For tidal information, refer to Hervey.

Pargeter had expressed the intention of having another shot at pulling her out stern-first, once all the internal tanks were empty. He and the two four-stripers, and the commander from Portsmouth, also Hughes the Principle Overseer and Barlows' man Joe Fairley were meanwhile in conclave in the ward-room. There'd been talk of trying to get a man out through the for'ard escape chamber into the flooded TSC and thence into the Tube Space, to shut the rear door of number five tube and then open the mainline suction valves so those compartments could be pumped out. Obviously you couldn't pump them out without that rear door being shut. Nothing had been done about it yet. In theory it might be a realistic proposition. The escape chamber could be entered through hatches from either the companionway immediately abaft number two watertight bulkhead or from the TSC, the Fore Ends; normal egress would be upward, through the hatch which, when the pressure in the chamber had been equalized with the outside sea pressure, could be opened from inside, but now with the for'ard compartments open to the sea it should be possible to exit horizontally in exactly the same way.

The snag, of course, was the pressure, which potentially would be killing. And there was no-one on board with experience of deep-diving, or working at any depth. The DSEA sets weren't designed for it. They were provided as short-term oxygen-breathing equipment for men who'd be in the escape chamber for only a few minutes before they'd have the hatch open and float up to the surface.

Even then, they'd have to do it *right*: and be able to withstand the pressure for those few minutes. In the training tank at Blockhouse you learnt how to use the gear, and the escape chamber was identical to those in *Trumpeter*, but with only fifteen feet of water in the tower above it you had no pressure to contend with as a major factor.

Soon after she'd hit the bottom a smoke candle had been fired from the underwater gun – in the After Ends, the stokers' mess and steering-gear compartment – and an indicator-buoy had been released from its stowage in the casing. The release gear was internal, but the forward lot was inaccessible in the flooded TSC. One should be enough, anyway, to mark the submarine's position for the guidance of surface rescuers. And the smoke-float would have alerted Ozzard to the fact that *Trumpeter* was in trouble. Otherwise, he'd have seen her finally get under at about 3 pm, and since Pargeter had signalled that he'd be diving for three hours it would be at least 6 pm before he'd begin to guess that something might have gone wrong.

It was human nature not to anticipate disaster: not to cry 'Wolf!' before it had you by a leg . . .

One worrying – puzzling – feature of all this was that no propeller sounds had been heard. If *Clansman* had passed overhead or even close, the churning screw would have been audible. The answer might be that Ozzard was keeping clear, realizing that they were in some kind of trouble but still thinking or hoping that they might surface at any moment. If he thought it was even a possibility, he'd keep clear.

It *was* a possibility, too. Damn well *had* to be.

Although if he'd seen the smoke-float and the marker – the marker particularly – he'd see it was static, not being towed, and know she was on the bottom – you'd think he *might* have come in close.

Smoke candle failed to ignite? One *had* had duds . . . And the marker-buoy: with the height of the swell up there, it might take a very sharp eye to spot it, from any distance? If the smoke-float had worked, of course, they'd have been purposefully looking for it: but otherwise?

Mike Searle, Wally Bristol and a torpedoman by name of Clark had drowned in the Tube Space. Hamilton, Barlows' Ship Manager, was dead too, probably of a heart attack. Eddington – leading torpedoman – had dragged him out of the Tube Space, and he'd died on the deck in the Fore Ends. Chalk's knowledge of what had happened in those crucial minutes was mostly second- and third-hand, but according to the TI's account Wally Bristol had gone back in to release the catch on the watertight door, had succeeded in doing so but then failed to reappear. They'd given him as much time as they could, but that door had had to be shut, and quickly. Or rather, they'd had to *try* to shut it. One didn't question this: but the TI, CPO Osborne, had told Pargeter, 'Should've been me, in there . . .'

In fact the door had not been shut. They'd just about won the battle but with inches to go one of the securing clamps had come out of its securing clip – dud clip, no spring in it even brand-new – fallen across the diminishing gap between the door and the bulkhead. The door had had to be eased back open again while the obstruction was located and removed – under water, and in pitch darkness, the lights having just gone out, and a few seconds later *Trumpeter* had hit the bottom. They'd all been knocked off their feet, the door had swung free again – latching itself again, probably – and by this time the order had come from Pargeter to evacuate the Fore Ends.

In the passage outside the wardroom Dymock was making small adjustments to the straps and belt of his DSEA set. He had both hands free for it, thanks to the bow-down angle having eased to only a few degrees now. Chalk and Buchanan had come through to the wardroom a few minutes ago, picking their way through the Control Room where men sat or sprawled over every square inch of deck-space. They were Barlows' men, mostly, fitters and so forth. There'd been an exodus, at the time of the flooding, from the TSC and subsequently overcrowded adjoining messes; they'd moved like refugees, filing through to wherever they could find room to settle. Sitting or lying in silence, in the main, each isolated in his own thoughts or fears, but some desultorily chatting. A game of cards was in progress in the helmsman's corner when Chalk and Buchanan passed through.

'Anythin' doin', sir?'

A pale young Scot of about his own age: in glasses, and with pens and/or pencils clipped in his top pocket. Chalk told him, 'Will be soon, I'm sure. Don't worry . . .'

The one thing that was *definitely* 'doing' was that the air was being used up, with every passing minute. CO_2 content growing steadily. At this stage the poison wasn't noticeable, but it soon would be.

Pargeter had asked them to join him and his VIP guests in the wardroom – the messenger being Nat Eason, who'd interrupted Chalk's lecture and demonstration of escape procedures. Wanting to finish it, he'd told Eason, 'All right, Chief – in just a minute', but Buchanan had pushed the gear back at him – mask, belt, oxygen bottle, breathing-bag, mouthpiece and nose-clip. 'Thanks, but I'd never make anything of it.'

'Any luck, you won't need to.' Eason jerked a thumb for'ard. 'They got plans for getting us up.' Eyes on Chalk's then: 'Going to be a busy night, I reckon.'

They'd gone through to the wardroom, where Pargeter had welcomed Buchanan and made room for him. Captain McAllister's wide, strong-boned face, running with sweat, creased into a smile as he greeted them; beside him, the diminutive Gleeson was deep in a highly technical discussion with the Admiralty overseer, Hughes, whose face was creased with anxiety. Joe Fairley was listening in, scowling now and then as if there were bits he didn't like the sound of. While Random, the 'perisher' man, was sketching out some other theory on a signal-pad and explaining it to Quarry – who was

CO of a 'T' currently building at Chatham. Random glanced up at Chalk and nodded, with the glimmer of a smile.

Pargeter brought them up to date. 'Dymock and Leading Seaman Billingstone are going to have a shot at getting for'ard to shut that rear door and open the compartment suctions. I say "have a shot" at it because the pressure's going to be a bastard. But if they can stand it – for long enough – well ...'

'Solve our problems.'

'Most of them. Yes. When it's done, we'll start pumping. Daren't blow – the fore hatch mightn't stand up to it, anyway we've used too much air already. That's also the reason I've decided against trying to get her off the putty as we are now.'

Random agreed. 'Makes sense.'

'Very much so.' McAllister, mopping at his face with a handkerchief like a sodden rag.

'If it'd help – share the work out –' Chalk glanced round at Dymock – 'I could go in there with them. Easily get three in the chamber.'

'You obviously haven't seen Billingstone.' Dymock was hanging a wheelspanner on his DSEA belt. 'Big Billy, they call him for'ard.'

'We'll hold you in reserve, Rufus.' Pargeter glanced at him. 'Thanks all the same.' Turning to Buchanan then ... 'The rest of it is—' glancing at his watch – 'well, it's past six now, and we've heard nothing from up top. As you may know, we've streamed a marker-buoy – so they should know where we are – but – frankly, we don't know *what* the situation is.'

Calshot was in the companionway, listening. Eason and the other two commissioned engineers were there too. And John Hervey, now.

'What it comes down to is that sending anyone out by DSEA – when we don't know for sure that there's anyone up there—'

'Pointless.'

'Yes. But at first light, perhaps—'

'But, Captain.' Hughes the Principal Overseer ... '*Can* there be no-one up there? After your flare and the marker-buoy – *and* the fact we've now been down longer than the three hours you announced as your intention?'

'Yes. I know ... I mean I've no idea. Except – look, better not let this get round – I happen to know that the tug has no wireless other than a radio-telephone with a range of twenty-five miles – in good conditions. Can't say how R/T conditions are, mind you, but that's about the range they'd need – every yard of it.'

'Christ ...'

'They *may* have need to close the land – Ardrossan, say – to get a message over. It's only a possibility – dare say I'm wrong, *hope* I am. It might account for the tug's temporary absence, though. And with the marker up there, Ozzard would know he can find us again – and what *else* could he do, in the circumstances? Then again – it'll be dark in a few hours, won't it? No point at all, then, sending chaps out. Obvious thing is, therefore – barring sounds from the surface within the next hour or two – wait for daylight, *then* think about escapes by DSEA.'

'Leading Seaman Billingstone's dressed and standing by, sir.' The coxswain, CPO West. Burly, bearded ... 'When you're ready, sir?'

'Coming now, Cox'n.' Dymock asked Pargeter. 'All right, sir?'

'Good luck.' Joe Fairley, leaning across the table with a hand out to shake Dymock's ... 'Very best o' luck, Lieutenant.'

Billingstone, Chalk saw, was the second coxswain, the big man he'd seen on *Trumpeter*'s casing. Just this morning, but it could have been a year ago. *Ten* years ... He put a hand on Dymock's arm: 'Good luck, Toby.'

Eye to eye, for one long moment. Then a nod. 'See you.'

He added in a lower tone, 'If by chance I don't—'

'Don't be damn silly.'

'Give her my love. Please.' He raised his voice: 'All right, Second. Get cracking, shall we?'

'I'll give you the rest of it, Rufus.' Pargeter was edging out around the table. 'Captain Gleeson's idea primarily, but we've all put in our penn'orth. Come daylight, however well or badly the pumping-out process may have gone, we'll send a couple of men out through the after chamber with a message for whoever's up top by then, suggesting they send a diver down and connect an air-hose to our whistle connection. Fitters can prepare for it during the night – quite a job of work, there'll be some new pipes to run, but—'

'Air for breathing, or air for blowing?'

'Blowing. With the object of getting her up there while we *can* still breathe.'

He thought, pausing in the companionway, *Fat chance . . .* Then put the same thought in a different way to Pargeter: 'Bit of a tight schedule – isn't it. We may last out as long as – midday, or thereabouts?'

'Mid-afternoon, we reckon. But if this job goes as we hope, we might get her off the bottom by – oh, during the forenoon. And in the meantime – before that, after what I might call the first eleven's gone out with our message, we'll continue sending men out, in batches of three or even four. If we were to start that at say 0500, and it goes smoothly—'

'Lighten her aft, get the stern up so the chamber's closer to the surface?'

'Well done.' When Engineer Captain Gleeson grinned like that he had the look of a little monkey. 'We did think of it, as it happens. Your bright idea, Random, wasn't it?'

'One other – which you'll also have thought of, I'm sure. Alternative to using the whistle connection—'

'The gun recuperator?'

He nodded. 'You're a jump ahead of me.'

He thought the plan might stand a snowball's chance in

hell, but not much more than that. These others must have known it too. The only way it could succeed would be if they were standing by up there with divers and a suitable air-hose and connections, and a compressor ready to start delivering air within minutes of receiving this proposal. If they had to spend more than about an hour in preparation, all there'd be to salvage would be a slightly shop-soiled 'T'-class submarine with about a hundred dead men inside her.

There'd been plenty of volunteers to go into the forward compartments with Dymock. He'd made his own choice of Billingstone presumably because he was a powerfully-built man with lungs about the size of a horse's.

They'd agreed that when they got into the TSC, Dymock would make his way through to the Tube Space, shut number five tube's rear door and then rejoin Billingstone who'd have been waiting beside the hatch of the escape chamber. Dymock would wait then while Billingstone went to open the mainline suctions. This would split the physical work between them, and more importantly, if either came to grief and failed to reappear the other would be in a position to re-enter the chamber and shut its hatch so that it could be drained down. This was vitally important because if it was left open the chamber would be unusable for any future escapes.

They climbed in, the door was clamped, flood-valve opened. The Geordie ERA – Crowley – was in charge on the outside, with the TI and the Coxswain backing him up. Onlookers were Pargeter, McAllister and Random, with others in the background including Chalk, Nat Eason, Hughes, Fairley and Buchanan.

Both men in there were now breathing from their DSEA sets. Outsiders' eyes on them through the thick glass port, as the water rose. Chalk knew exactly how it would be sounding to them in the chamber: the roar of the steadily rising water – frightening, if you let it be – and the harsh, regular huff-and-puff of their own breathing inside the masks. The flood-valve and draining-down valve here on the outside, and hatch-operating gear, were duplicated on the inside so that sole survivors or the last to leave could operate the chamber on their own. But here and now it was being done for them, so they could save their energies. All Dymock would have to do was open a vent when the water reached a certain height, and then, when the chamber was completely flooded and the pressure equalized, open the hatch into the TSC.

The rising water seethed around Dymock's mask: at the same level, Billingstone's shoulders. Dymock reaching to the vent, and Billingstone's head turning that way, watching it. The top of Dymock's head would be visible to him above water, nothing else: the water was up to his own chin . . . Chalk beginning to think they *might* pull this off: and hearing Buchanan's mutter, 'I could *never* do that.'

'Touch wood, you won't have to. As Nat Eason said. But if you did, you'd do it with me or someone else who knows the drill, so—'

Billingstone, facing the glass port, was pointing at his ears, shaking his head: waving both hands frantically close-up against the glass, then clapping them back over his ears . . .

'Stop flooding.' Pargeter said it, but Crowley was already screwing the flood-valve shut. Pargeter added, 'Drain 'em down.' Glancing round: the sad eyes seeking Chalk's. 'You still volunteering?'

'Oh, yes . . .'

Not out of any interest in heroics, but because he thought he had at least as good a chance of making it as anyone else on board. Probably a better one. It was also in his own interests as well as everyone else's to make this work. Put at its simplest, it might be a way to stay alive.

Dymock's head and shoulders were out of water now, he'd shut the cock on his breathing-tube and was pulling off his mask. Billingstone was hunched against the side of the chamber, looking utterly dejected. Chalk turned back to Pargeter. 'Toby and I together, perhaps, if he's fit for another shot at it.'

'Beg pardon, sir.' CPO Osborne, the TI, speaking urgently – emotionally even . . . 'It's my job, sir – where I *should*'ve been.'

'I've heard you were saying something of that sort, TI.' Pargeter smiled at him, and shook his head. 'It's nonsense, though. You did your level best in there – and surviving's not a crime, you know.'

'My job here though, sir. My part of ship, that, isn't it?' To Chalk: 'No offence, sir, but you're not – well, not your boat, is she?'

'All right.' Pargeter was watching the last of the water drain away. It was around their knees but still above the sill of the entry hatch, so it couldn't be opened yet. 'That *is* a point. But – TI, if the first lieutenant's unfit to try again, you'll do it with Lieutenant Chalk.'

'Aye aye, sir —'

Dymock, emerging from the chamber, was emphatic that he was in perfectly good shape and wanted to try again. Billingstone was shame-faced, stammering as he tried to explain the degree of pain he'd had in his ears, how he'd stood it for several minutes then couldn't any longer. Pargeter assured him that he had nothing to be ashamed of: the first lieutenant happened to have cast-iron eardrums, that was all . . . 'Better flake out for a while, Second. We'll need you again before long. Have someone find him some dry clothes, Cox'n.'

'What – *his* size, sir?'

Buchanan told Chalk, 'I meant what I said. I *couldn't* go through that.'

'Not even with help, and to save your life?'

'Wouldn't. I've a weak heart, I know beyond any shadow of doubt I simply couldn't stand it.'

Nobody would have thought of asking him whether he was fit or not. Or expected it to matter . . . Chalk told him, 'So you'll have to stick around until we get her up. I'm afraid you'll find the air a bit thin, by morning.'

Before that, too. By morning, you'll be breathing poison.

Another civilian – pale-faced, heavily-moustached – stopped them as they made their way aft. 'No good, then?'

One of the caterers. Chalk had heard him enthusing to Eason about this being a great experience, what a good yarn he'd have to tell his wife and bairns.

Perhaps ignorance *was* bliss. Most of the Barlows' workmen still looked remarkably untroubled. He told the caterer, 'No good that time. Having another shot, presently. We'll get there in the end.'

Get *where*?

A favoured Afrikaans saying of Diana's echoed in his mind: *Alles sal reg kom*. Literally translated – 'All will come right'. A happy thought, if you could believe it. Things sometimes did *not* go right: it was possible that Diana had yet to learn this.

Her voice over the wire then: 'Who on earth have you been gassing with, this last twenty minutes?'

He felt bad about those conversations with Zoe. Having wondered sometimes whether they might not – in her intention – be a prelude to something else. Hadn't this been the underlying reason he'd enjoyed them?

Her intention – his acquiescence?

McAllister was already in the wardroom, briefing those who'd stayed behind on what had happened. Hughes had come back too. Eason arriving then, looking as he often had when he was longing for a cigarette. Chalk told Zoe's husband, 'I'll be back . . .'

The TI had to call it off at about the same stage that Billingstone had reached. And Dymock, who'd seemed perfectly all right up to that moment, threw his hand in too.

If the TI had been able to go through with it, he'd quite possibly have kept going, but he was seen to more or less collapse while the chamber was draining down, and both men were pulled out semi-conscious.

Pargeter decided that there'd be no more attempts. Chalk offered to make one more – alone – but he turned him down.

'Lucky they *didn't* get much further. That near the end of their tether, and not knowing it – might have got in there, *then* passed out . . .'

The hatch would then have been left open – one of the submarine's two escape chambers thus put out of action. Chalk had read Pargeter's thinking: only a few hours in which to get everyone out tomorrow, even with two chambers in operation – that slow procedure of flooding up, then draining down, time after time . . .

By then, you'd be suffocating.

Pargeter told him, low-voiced outside the chamber, 'We've two rather formidable handicaps here. One's obvious – far too many men on board. The other – keep this under your hat – is that about half the DSEA sets we embarked are in *there*.' A jerk of his head indicated the flooded TSC.

A silence, while that sank in. And of course, a lot of the sets *would* have been in there. Pargeter muttered, 'Best to keep it to ourselves. Cox'n knows, of course, and the TI.'

'If you'd let me get in there, sir – shut the rear door, then—'

'No. Definitely *not*.'

He was probably right, at that. But it left practically no alternatives.

Following him aft . . . 'Try the idea of getting air in through the whistle, will you?'

A grunt: 'Nothing else for it, is there.'

Meaning – effectively – *Last straw*. . .

The whistle – operated by high-pressure air and used for

sound-signals when manoeuvring in harbour – was above the bridge, fixed to the for'ard periscope standard. The air would only go one way, normally – upward – and modifying it, turning it into an inlet for HP air supplied from the surface, would have to be the engineers' task tonight.

Pargeter said quietly, turning back to him. 'Have to face it, could take 'em hours to set it up, up there. Getting the gear together and so on.' Peering into the Chiefs' and PO's mess: 'All right, Cox'n?'

Meaning, was the TI going to be all right. CPO West nodded towards a blanket-covered shape: 'Be back on his feet soon, sir.'

'Good. But let him have as much rest as he needs.'

'Sir – I'd have a go meself, if—'

'No, we're not trying that again. Thanks all the same, Cox'n.'

Moving on: and back to the subject of getting air from the surface ... 'On the other hand, you see, by first light they may have a salvage ship up there – divers, compressors, hoses, all we need. If that was the case and we weren't ready for them, didn't at least *try* this – uh?'

'Yes.' It was a chance – of sorts. He suggested – following Pargeter towards the wardroom – 'No chance of getting her up under her own power, I suppose?'

'Hardly. With about enough air in the bottles to blow out the candles on a birthday cake?'

'I hadn't realized ...' They'd both stopped, short of the wardroom – opposite the ERAs' mess. 'So – with surfacing a doubtful prospect, sir – and nothing like enough DSEA sets—'

'Free ascents. Best men we've got – volunteers, obviously – hold 'em to the last, get all the untrained men out first. Assisted, of course.'

Christ...

'Free ascent' meant getting out through the chamber without a DSEA set. Holding your breath – as far as that was possible. In each group you'd include one man whom you'd pick as likely to be able to hold it longer than most.

Like Rufus Chalk, for instance. He nodded. 'Count me in, sir.'

'Thank you. Must say, I'd rather expected . . .'

They were back at the wardroom, then.

'What we have to think about now—' his tone was brighter and more purposeful, addressing the men around the table – 'since as you'll have heard we've had to give up *that* notion—'

'Rotten luck.' McAllister, frowning. 'Rotten.' Watching Dymock being helped into Pargeter's cupboard-sized cabin by Eason and Hervey. 'Are you sure you're right not to have one more go?'

'Yes, sir.' Pargeter sat down. 'I am. Incidence of failure's too high. Two – three – just in the chamber. Imagine how much chance they'd have when they got out of it, burning up energy . . . Anyone – including Chalk here, who's been volunteering every few minutes—'

'Good for you, Chalk.'

Quarry, that had been. Adding: 'Look here – Jacko – if Chalk and I were to have a shot at it together—'

'No.' Head back against the edge of the bunk behind him, with his eyes shut for a moment . . . 'No, forget all that. Better to concentrate on getting an air supply via the whistle – so we can then blow and keep blowing until we shift her. Rig new air-lines during the night—' he glanced at Fairley – 'put your fitters to work? – and pump out every tank we've got, including fuel and fresh water. Then – we thought three men, didn't we?' He was looking at Random, the commander from Blockhouse. Adding, 'With our proposals in writing, attached to them.'

So that a body could surface dead, Chalk realized, and the message would still be delivered.

Random was saying, '– make three copies – to be enclosed in French letters and worn—' using a forefinger to draw the outlines of a necklace – 'as decoratively as only an FL can be.'

McAllister observed, staring at him, 'You've been giving it a great deal of thought, Random.'

Nodding slowly, straight-faced: 'A certain amount, sir.'

'We were thinking earlier on—' Pargeter explained, mostly to Buchanan – 'that Commander Random should take charge of this. He's as fit as any of us, more experienced than most, and his rank should carry weight—' a forefinger pointed at the deckhead – 'up there.' He glanced at McAllister. 'You agree, sir?'

'Oh, yes.' The flotilla captain's large hands, clasped together on the table, separated and then closed again. 'Mind you, if I was a few years younger and a stone or two lighter – *and* hadn't left my FLs at home—'

Laughter. Not from Hughes, frowning at his own clasped hands, or from Joe Fairley, who forced a smile but looked embarrassed. Pargeter began – talking to Random – 'Next thing to decide is who goes with you. Essential qualifications – you'll all agree, I'm sure – fitness, and proficiency in DSEA. Object of the exercise—' He glanced up to his left, into the companionway: 'What is it, Cox'n?'

'Serve supper, sir? Leftovers from the lunch – caterers say not a lot, but—'

'Go ahead.' He turned back to the group around the table, his sad eyes drifting particularly to Hughes and Fairley . . . 'I was saying – object of the exercise being much less to send three individuals out than to get this submarine up there, save *all* our lives.'

Chapter 12

Awake again: or he thought he was. Yes – definitely: physical discomfort was evidence of it. Straightening from the flopped position he'd been in – at the end of the padded bench, leaning sideways against the tier of bunks, each of which had two men on it lying head to toe like sardines – aware of a cricked neck as well as difficulty in drawing breath. Other men's short, hard breathing – more gasps, than breaths – and sporadic snoring, occasionally a whimper or a mutter from a dream.

Trumpeter was standing on her nose again. It was why one had a problem sitting upright, and why the bodies in the bunks rested either against bulkheads or the lee-boards.

He checked the time. Five-ten. 0510. It would be light, up there. On shore, cocks crowing.

Zero hour was to be 0700. Unless there were identifiable sounds – better still, signals – from the surface before that. Pargeter's salvage vessel, for instance. Probably about as many of them within steaming-distance as there were Flying Dutchmen. But – try *anything*. At some point Chalk himself had come up with an alternative – in which nobody had shown much interest, for some reason. As for timing – originally the assumption had been that they'd make a start at first light, but Pargeter had revised this, decided that to make absolutely sure there was someone up there to receive them, and that it was fully light so they'd be spotted – one knew nothing of weather conditions, there might be a rough sea and a heavy overcast for instance – he'd wait until 0700.

Thinking about that – trying to. It wasn't easy to stay awake, at least to keep the brain properly awake. Tendency to drift off-course ... Head sideways on his hands on the table-top. Gleeson, the little engineer captain, was leaning against him on the high side. Beyond him, two Admiralty civilians. He was supporting most of their weight too. Surprising that Gleeson hadn't been squashed flat by this time. McAllister was in Pargeter's cubby-hole just abaft the wardroom heads: he'd been invited to move in there – when Dymock had emerged from it looking like death itself – by virtue less of his rank than the fact he took up so much room. He was on the bunk and Bellamy, the Admiralty Constructor, was on the deck. They'd all been told – everyone on board had – to rest, lie still, sleep if they could, expend no energy that would make them use up more air.

Except for the Barlows' workmen, of course, who'd been at it half the night. The air hadn't been as bad then as it was now, of course.

Gleeson croaked, opening an eye, 'A canary would drop dead in this putrid atmosphere.' Then he went back to sleep.

Now *concentrate*, he told himself...

About the proposal for supply of air from the surface. Odds against it achieving its purpose being – well, not favourable.

You'd get up there, all right. From the after escape chamber, with the boat's 270-foot length slanted at this angle, there wouldn't be more than twenty or thirty feet of water to float up through. Depending on the state of the tide, might be even less. Although one didn't much like this angle on the boat as it might affect the operation of the chamber, which was designed to be used when she was on an even keel.

Random had decided to have Chalk and the Outside ERA – Crowley – with him. He'd given as his reasons that they were both strong, fit men who'd been through DSEA training, had long submarine experience and were probably as level-headed as you'd find. Near enough the same qualifications that Pargeter would be looking for in the men who'd be asked to volunteer to try free ascents. Chalk's relief at Random's having rescued him from that had been hard to disguise. Shamingly so, as he and Pargeter had exchanged glances.

At some stage – memory stirring, as he worked at it – Buchanan had broken a period of silence to ask Pargeter, 'Jacko – didn't someone say the escape chamber would take four men at a time?'

There'd been some discussion, then. The conclusion being affirmative, that four should be perfectly all right. (Limiting it to three in this instance had been because the primary objective was to get *some* men out with the HP air proposal, and giving them a bit of elbow-room in the chamber might improve their chances.)

'But after this first one—' Buchanan again – 'I think you said you'd send the rest out in fours. Are you implying now that it's more dangerous than in threes?'

Pargeter's eyes resting on him with the sad look which anyone who didn't know him might have taken for regret that a former golfing opponent – or partner – should have thought it appropriate to raise such an issue.

He'd told him no, four was as safe as three.

'So why not send four *this* time?'

Pargeter had glanced interrogatively at Random, who'd asked Buchanan, 'You want to join us?'

'Oh, no. For one thing. I've a dicky heart.' A glance at Chalk. 'Told you, didn't I?'

'Yes.' He'd nodded to Pargeter. 'He did.'

'Andrew – I'm sorry to hear this, but we won't accept it as an impediment to—'

'Certainly won't.' Random had interrupted, at the same time looking round at the others. 'Someone nominate a fourth man, please?'

'Ballantyne. The pilot.'

It was John Hervey's suggestion, and nobody had raised any objection until it was put to Ballantyne himself, who'd been clearly astonished that they should have picked on him.

'Grateful, for the offer. But – sooner take m' chances – that ye'll get her up, that is . . . Wouldn't ye do better havin' one o' the youngsters go along?'

They'd settled on a Barlows' electrician, name of Cox, whom Chalk had recognized as the one who'd stopped him in the Control Room with the question, 'Anything doin', sir?'

Checking the time again. 0526.

Either he'd dreamt it, or Buchanan had told Dymock he was a four-letter man. Putting the mind to *this* now. Dream?

No. No dream – fact. He *had*. Chalk remembered also that his own inclination had been to laugh, ask him, 'Aren't we all, a lot of the time?'

Dymock more so than most, certainly. Nothing funny about it, either. When one thought of Guy.

As one did . . .

The confrontation between Buchanan and Dymock must have been fairly recent. The air had already been thin, both of them getting their words out in the spasmodic manner of speech which came from needing to take a breath between every few words. Another piece of evidence was that moment of light-headedness which had affected *him* . . . Recalling now, though, that Buchanan had opened with 'Got to hand it to you. You've got guts, all right.'

'Oh.' Weak smile. 'Come off it, Andrew . . .'

'Don't you agree, Rufus? Got guts?'

'One might certainly hope he had.'

'Going in that chamber twice. *Twice*.'

'Oh, that . . .'

'Still a swine, but – going in there *twice*. To me – defies the imagination.'

'I'm trained for it. All my adult life—'

'When not chasing other men's wives?'

'All our training – not guts, second nature.' As if he hadn't heard that. And at a lower level now: he'd been standing, then leaning, and now he'd knelt or crouched so that only his head and eyes were visible above the level of the table. Nobody had any excess of energy. Also the angle on the boat – so this *had* been fairly recent, they'd already got her stern well up . . . He explained to Buchanan, 'You train yourself to be ready for it. If it does happen – anything like this.'

'And it *has*.'

'Well – yes, but—'

'Aren't I lucky? Eh? First time out?'

Chuckling: at the same time struggling for breath . . . Chalk put in, 'Hard to believe, isn't it. Wake up properly by and by, find it hasn't?'

Hasn't happened, he'd meant. Even to oneself one had to make it clear, avoid confusion as far as possible. Dymock's voice intruding again at about this point: 'You'll be all right anyway, Rufus. Last in, first out – how it goes, eh?'

'Want to take my place?'

'Christ, no! Bloody hell, man, I'm knackered!'

'Dymock.' Buchanan's face swam back into focus. 'I still say you're a four-letter man.'

'Why?'

'Why d'you think?'

'Haven't the *least*—'

'Zoe told me. You going to deny it? Call her a liar – insult to damned injury?'

'Deny *what*, old man?'

The work had been finished by then – the hours of hammering, filing, sawing in the Control Room which they'd been using as a workshop, removing piping that wasn't needed and adapting and fitting it elsewhere. While Dymock had been in charge of getting all the oil and fresh water out of her – aided and abetted by Nat Eason whom Pargeter had asked to substitute for Wally Bristol.

The thought of Bristol raised again the question of who'd opened that bowcap. Mike Searle had opened the rear door, but only because he'd been certain the bowcap was shut like all the others. Both the TI and Leading Torpedoman Eddington had been positive on this. Although the TI had agreed that Searle should have made his prior check by opening the drains, not just the test-cocks, and Eddington had admitted that he hadn't seen him use the rimers either. There'd been a debate about this last night, but neither the Barlows' people nor the Admiralty team, who jointly had been responsible for putting the trim on, would admit the possibility of the bowcap having been opened by one of their men. But if one of *Trumpeter*'s torpedomen had been misled by those indicators pointing in different directions and opened it under the impression that he'd been shutting it – well, in the first place he wouldn't have touched it without prior reference to the TI, and in the second, if for some reason he'd thought it necessary to go ahead and do it off his own bat, so to speak, he'd most certainly have reported it right away.

The discussion had ended when it had become dangerously overheated and McAllister had called a halt to it.

'Go into it later. *Much* later. There'll be a Court of Inquiry into this balls-up, it'll come out then.' A grin at Hughes. 'See you in Court, eh?'

Buchanan leant forward so he could see him past the intervening bodies. 'Rufus?'

He opened his eyes. 'Huh?'

'*Has* got guts, hasn't he?'

Talking about Dymock again. Dymock meanwhile having vanished. Probably only below the level of the table, but it would have been a waste of effort to have looked. He agreed with Buchanan: 'Yes. He has.'

'I ask you – why would she have made up a thing like that?'

He shut his eyes again. 'God knows.'

'Zoe never did make things up. She's so – *straight*, there's no question . . . I'd trust her till kingdom come. That's why I'm not in the least put out when she wants to go down to London, for instance. I miss her, of course, miss her terribly, but—'

'You're a lucky man.'

'Yes, I am.' He paused. Then: 'And Dymock's a four-letter man.'

'As you told him.'

'I did, didn't I? And he asked *why*!'

'Yes. I heard.'

'I'm well aware that her manner can be – flirtatious, sometimes.' Peering at Chalk, querying whether he might ever have noticed this. Chalk didn't react, and he went on, 'It's a game to her, doesn't mean a thing. Play-acting . . . God's sake, Dymock didn't get far, did he!'

'Obviously not.'

'She rang me about him . . . Well, I told you. But there's your proof – if you needed any . . . Rufus, listen. If I don't get out of this—'

'You *will*.'

'If I don't – tell her for me that I love her, that she's been the greatest thing ever in my life?'

'All right.'

'Thanks. If she's still in London, go and see her? Address is in the book – in Belgravia. Andrew *Murray* Buchanan.'

'All right.' Now the whole family had invited him. 'But it won't come to that, Andrew.'

'Really believe Jacko'll get us up, do you?'

Not the way he was planning, he wouldn't, with so little time to do it in. Unless that miracle did come to pass – a salvage ship up there, everything on the top line and ready to go. It *could* happen . . .

At least those who didn't get out wouldn't know much about it. It was getting harder all the time to breathe, but also to stay awake. Bloody awful headache, too.

But not *those* who didn't get out. *Any* who didn't.

His own suggestion last night had been that they should ask for not one air-hose but two, one to be connected to the whistle as they'd been planning, to supply air for blowing tanks, and the other to the gun recuperator connection to provide air for breathing, staying alive. Pargeter had objected that this wouldn't solve the problem: you'd need a vent as well as an intake, to get rid of the carbon dioxide *and* keep the pressure down. Chalk had agreed with him, and had had the answer ready too. 'Get air in through the recuperator, and run the LP blower to suck out the CO_2. A few minutes at a time, guided by the barometer.'

'Theory's fine.' A smile around the spaniel-eyes . . . 'Full marks. But in the long run it'd slow us down. Don't *want* that. Whole point is to get her up there fast – *before* the air runs out.'

He thought Pargeter wasn't thinking straight. But perhaps it didn't matter much. They wouldn't have the gear up there, and by the time they got it there'd be no use for it.

Snoozing. Partly, anyway – in and out of sleep and dreams. In the dream-state, seeing Guy with a rifle and some kind of uniform that was familiar – except for the red band on his arm. His expression – that lop-sided grin – came straight out of an enlarged snapshot which Chalk had in a frame. There was a cricket pavilion and some flannelled fools, and girls with parasols in the background. Guy wasn't flannelled, he was in RNAS uniform, vintage 1914–18 – boots, military tunic and breeches, naval cap – derived from a portrait of their father which was beside their mother's bed in the nursing home. She'd asked him once, holding it up and frowning at it, 'Who's this man?' With Guy still in his mind, though, he was recognizing the blunder he'd made. To have argued with him – against his going to Spain – on pragmatic and even political grounds. Water off a duck's back – might have known it would be. In fact *had* known, but lacked the clarity of vision – which he had now, extraordinarily enough – to realize that he should have put it as a personal, brotherly plea not to go because he and Betty needed him – alive, intact and *here*. Should have hit that note and gone on hitting it. Guy was soft-hearted, naturally kind – which was why one had felt so defensive of him against Dymock's ruthlessness. He'd quite likely have given in to that approach – which might have been followed with a reminder of Betty being on the point of giving birth and how Guy had said he was looking forward to being an uncle. What use was a *distant* uncle – let alone a dead or maimed one? And – can't we keep it together now? – what between us we've *put* together?

Meaning the loss of their father. Having weathered *that* . . .

Awake, he found he had tears in his eyes. But it was all right: watering eyes were a symptom of the CO_2 poisoning. Camouflage . . .

'Time?'

Gleeson. Presumably the little engineer's watch had stopped. Chalk could see one on his bony wrist. From his other side one of the civilians informed him, 'Five-thirty, near enough.'

'So what time's breakfast?'

Someone – it might have been Alec Rose – muttered, 'Two eggs, bacon, sausage and tomato. *If* you please.'

'Tea or coffee?'

Gleeson again. Odd senses of humour, both of them. Unless they were off their rockers. Chalk turned his head enough to see him. Little man in his fifties, could have been eighty. Seamed face like a small, exhausted monkey's, tired little eyes on Chalk's, and telling him now – in a thinner tone, almost a whisper – 'Brekker up top, eh?'

He'd no apt answer for it. Drowsing again: hoping that Betty wouldn't have heard about this mishap. Anyway, not that *he* was in it. It was odds-on to be in the newspapers this morning; the Admiralty and Messrs Barlows' would have issued statements probably coupled with reassurance so that the headlines might read RESCUE OPERATIONS UNDER WAY. Even if they weren't. But she didn't have to know he was among the passengers. She'd never have heard of *Trumpeter*, or of Barlows'; the only address he'd given her was his lodgings, Mrs Blair's address and telephone number, so they could reach him with the news of the baby's birth . . . And then they *would* know. Her husband, Dick Traill, would make the call and Mrs Blair would pour it all out to him. He'd told her that he was going out on these trials.

The Cameron-Greens would know, he guessed. Suzie – or Patricia, but more likely Suzie – would quite likely have heard rumours first, and have 'phoned Barlows' – probably Mrs Blair as well. And Diana would know, if she was in touch with them – as she would be, because (a) she was in the habit of telephoning him at his digs every few days, when she was in a position to do so; and (b), since she was expected to arrive at Glendarragh on Friday she'd surely have contacted the C-Gs directly too. Or would soon.

She'd still fly up. Perhaps sooner. With news for Suzie of some flying course, no doubt. When Diana said she'd do a thing, she did it.

Poor Suzie . . .

Patricia would look after her, though. Dry *her* tears.

Better at it than their mother would be. Pat was practical and warm-hearted as well as bright. In fact she was really rather special. As Betty had told him: and he'd nodded, shown polite interest: 'Is she really?'

He'd wondered at times – like that one – whether Betty might be none too keen on having Diana for a sister-in-law. She hadn't been so clumsy as to say it, but knowing her as he did –

Diana . . .

His door opening, shutting again as silently as ancient, unoiled hinges would allow. Her whispered 'Hush . . .'

Patricia? *Not* Diana?

'Pat?'

'Lightning decision . . .'

'You're brilliant. As well as—'

As well as *not* Pat.

Dreaming . . . And a change of scene – Glendarragh still, but downstairs, in the drawing-room. On-stage had been Suzie and her mother and Patricia, while he'd been a silent presence, as it were, in the wings. Dymock elsewhere, doubtless being hauled over the coals by Sir Innes. Patricia had been teasing Suzie about the night's goings-on at that Trossachs place, telling her she really *might* have waited to lose it at the Astor – their mother snapping, 'That's enough, Patricia!' Pat putting an arm around her little sister and humming *There's a small hotel. . .*

Singing softly, putting her own words to it: 'I *wish* that I'd been there . . .' Beginning to giggle then, Lady C-G failing to comprehend, Chalk stifling his own amusement until Suzie herself gave way in a shout of laughter, breaking free and aiming a wild swing at her sister . . .

Thump of an explosion: then another. His chuckle as he woke, cut off by reality – excitement – and a roar from McAllister in Pargeter's cabin: 'Random!'

A third grenade exploded – telling them *Come on up. . .*

Farewells all finished in a rush, were already half-forgotten – except for Buchanan's and Nat Eason's. Eason's 'Mine's a double Johnny Walker – and no water in it, right?' A glance upward then: '*Hate* fucking water . . .' He was a part of that shifting pattern now – faces on the dry side of the glass port, a blur of them close together crowding for a view. The chamber was flooding quickly, the influx of water a churning, deafening ordeal of sound and pressure. All four of them were masked and breathing pure oxygen from their sets. The stern-up angle, he'd realized, wasn't likely to make for any problems: the problem it *had* made had been that of getting aft, uphill, hauling oneself up with handholds on engines, overhead piping, gear in the motor-room, etcetera. It had kept some potential onlookers away too, though. As well as a bunch of stokers – 'locals', the After Ends was their mess – but Pargeter was out there, and Dymock, Harry Calshot and John Hervey; Nat Eason and the Chief ERA, Hennessy, were operating the chamber – the flood-valve, at this stage. They had it fully open: you could flood the chamber fast or slowly – like turning on a tap – and Random had told them the faster the better.

Chalk was acting as nursemaid to Cox, the young electrician. He was all right, so far. No signs of any tendency to panic. You never knew, until you tried: anyone in the least claustrophobic could go crazy. The noise didn't help. He put a hand on Cox's shoulder, raised the other with a thumbs-up sign close in front of his mask, and got a nod by way of reply. Any reassurance thankfully received ... The water was seething up to chest-level – chin-high to the ERA and to Random, neither of whom was particularly tall. Random putting his hand up to the vent, ready to open it: the influx had begun to slow, as the air trapped in the top of the chamber resisted the sea's efforts to rise higher. He'd forced it open – adding a new dimension of sound – then ducked his head under the frothing surface, in accordance with the drill as taught in the tank at Blockhouse. Emerging then – momentarily, since the level was rising fast again now that the air was venting – and raising a hand to Cox – *See, how easy*? The water was over his head then, over Crowley's too and bubbling up around Chalk's mask, Cox submerged also, with Chalk's hand still on his shoulder.

Random would be first out. It was up to him to get the hatch open, then climb out and stay there – outside, holding on to the casing – to see the others emerge, render assistance if any of them was in trouble.

There was no reason why they should be. You had only to take it calmly and steadily and stick to the drill – having ignored the initial urge to spit your mouthpiece out, take a *real* breath . . . You *were* breathing – and at that, more easily than in recent hours. Breathing through the mouth – inhaling oxygen, and exhaling CO_2 to be absorbed by soda-lime crystals in the bag.

The noise had stopped, and Random was opening the hatch. With some difficulty, judging by the time it was taking . . . A dark figure in the slight radiance penetrating from that window: a surreal quality about it. 'The noble order of the French letter,' he'd called it, conducting a kind of mock investiture when he'd put the string loops over Chalk's and Crowley's head . . .

But *that* – incredibly – was daylight!

A narrow slit of it, then oblong, expanding into the full rounded shape of the hatch itself as Random forced the lid right back. Daylight filtering through about thirty feet of water – blanked off then by Random's body as he climbed up and out. Now again, that flickering light. Chalk found the exhaust-valve at the bottom of Cox's breathing-bag, and opened it for him. He'd told him he'd be doing this, not trusting a complete beginner to remember. Crowley was on his way out, and Cox would go next. Opening the exhaust-valve before leaving the chamber was a necessary piece of the drill because as you rose towards the surface the pressure lessened and the bag might have burst if it had had no vent.

The hatch was clear again. He pushed Cox up into it. Random would be there to help him out and show him the jumping-wire, which would be only about six feet above the hatch and a hazard to be avoided. He'd also release the roll of rubber apron which was attached to the bottom of the breathing-bag and served as a parachute-in-reverse: Cox had been shown how to hold it out to slow his ascent – rather than shooting up like a cork. Taking it more slowly – well, from only thirty feet the change in pressure wouldn't do him any harm, but if there was a boat up there and he surfaced under it at high speed he might crack his skull.

The hatch was still filled – by Cox ... Chalk opened his own exhaust-valve, glanced back for a second at the glass port, that yellowish glow of artificial light behind the vague dark shapes of men's heads – faces close to the glass, hands cupped against it to shut out reflections ... Then he was at the hatch as it cleared again, passing through it and out, with daylight and the surface a shimmer like bright silk overhead. Sounds of his own breath a harsh, regular huff, puff, huff, puff ... Hanging on in the aperture in the casing, Random close to him banging twice on the hull with his wheel-spanner, then dropping it through the open hatch to clatter down inside the chamber. The signal they'd have been waiting for – to shut the hatch, which had to be wound shut from inside the submarine – and then drain down, send out the next four men.

He'd freed his apron. Random, clinging to free-flood holes in the casing, was waiting for him to go up first. You could easily see the jumping-wire, a black diagonal slanting overhead. He got over to the starboard side, as clear of it as possible, and then kicked off as he let go. The wire came at him and passed by in a flash, seemingly very close. Holding the apron out, and arching his body – head back, chest out, the silver surface brightening fast then blinding as he broke out through it.

Into sunlight, patchy blue sky, the swell lifting him, swinging him around, letting him slide down its slope then lifting him again while he pulled his mask off and breathed air – *real* air. The breathing-bag was a buoyancy aid now: he'd shut its exhaust valve. Down again – swallowing a certain amount of salt while the sea rose like a wall around him; in his mind at that moment and as he was to retain it all his life – it was one of the moments that took hold and stuck, presumably would have hit him at this of all times in the realization – surprise, even – at being alive, at having been singled out to live – Buchanan's handshake and urgent plea: 'You won't forget to tell her, Rufus?' Then it was *out* of mind . . . His impression was, as he soared up on another swell, that he'd come up in the middle of an assortment of about half a dozen small ships deployed more or less in a circle with boats here and there inside the perimeter, mostly under oars. In a trough again then, seeing only sky and the heavy, threatening sea, he heard the drone of some low-flying aircraft, then from surprisingly close by a shout of 'Oars!' – which was a naval coxswain's order to his crew to stop rowing. A line splashed down close to him and he grabbed it, held on with it bar-taut until he had a close-up of a whaler's dark-blue planking and hands reaching for him. The boat's bowman was telling him, 'You'll be all right now, chum. Here – easy does it . . .'

Chalk had got up from the table, gone to the terrace wall. Leaning there with his hands flat on the stone, gazing across Glandore Bay as if that blue water lightly rippled by an onshore breeze connected somehow with a very different picture – roughish, greener water, and that scratch assembly of ships and boats.

'It was bloody awful.' Still staring out, southwestward. A course on which if you managed to avoid piling up on the Azores you'd have a straight run of about 5,000 miles to the coast of Brazil. Not much pollution in that wind, by the time it got here. Chalk told me, 'Really was. Excruciating . . . Watching for 'em to come up – deluding oneself – knowing damn few had any real chance.' He shook his head: 'Correction – knowing that at least *some* of them had no chance at all.'

'Seven more came out?'

He turned to face me. 'Yes. The first four surprisingly quickly. I was on board the destroyer *Hoste*. Her quack was badgering me to go down to his sickbay for a check-up or treatment of some kind, and I was telling him to go to hell, there was nothing wrong with me. I don't want to – well, exaggerate this, but I wasn't far off hell, in those hours. Why I should be up there when the rest of them – I knew that Pargeter, for one, wouldn't be coming up. Since it wasn't possible that they all could, and he'd have been the last out anyway. As for Buchanan – I remember saying a prayer, to bring him out.' A shrug. 'Even in those days I wasn't exactly making a habit of it. Praying, I mean.'

He'd turned away again, eyes back on the sea. 'Self-interest. Strong aversion to the prospect of carrying his message to Zoe.'

'Empathy too, surely.'

'That was what I thought it was. I've had time to think, since then.'

'But time can distort memory.'

'Can, yes. Not in this case, though.' He went on, 'Dymock, now. I didn't care if he came out or didn't. Not even for Suzie's sake – rather the opposite. But – how's this for pragmatism – it had occurred to me that it might be the ill wind that blows some good – from Guy's point of view – or mine, ours, getting him to come back from Spain perhaps. Then I'd seen it was a pipe-dream – nothing was going to change Guy's mind. Even if he'd been in England with a clear field he probably wouldn't have wanted to try again with Suzie. As for Dymock and the great love affair, my guess was she'd have found out pretty damn soon he wasn't the man she thought he was. So whether he came out of it or didn't was – frankly, six of one, half a dozen of the other. Don't misunderstand me – I wanted them *all* out, but whether the next was Dymock or Joe Soap—'

'Yes.'

'Different entirely with Nat Eason. I'd have sold my soul to the devil to have him pop up.'

'But he didn't.'

'One of those two pals of his did – Melhuish, commissioned

engineer standing by a boat building at Scotts. He was in the second team of four, came quicker than I'd expected, gave one hope that if they kept coming at that rate – at least, as many as there were DSEA sets for ... Even the free ascent prospects looked less bleak than they had, while the mood of optimism lasted. But in fact, you'd only need to start holding your breath when the vent was opened, that last foot or so of flooding up. If the front-runner got the hatch open damn fast and nobody got in anyone else's way – well, with such a short trip to the surface – letting one's breath out very slowly then on the way up ...'

Silent, staring seaward. Then: 'Optimism or not, *I* could have done it. Should have offered to – to Pargeter, when he talked about it.' Chalk shook his head. 'Anyway – the four that came up after us were that friend of Eason's and a leading stoker – name of Franklyn – who were shepherding one of the caterers and one of Hughes' assistants, a civil servant. Forget his name ... The minesweepers' boats picked them up, I think. They weren't brought on board *Hoste*, anyway. The other ships, incidentally, were two *Halcyon*-class sweepers and a boom-defence vessel – *Dabchick* – which had come down from the Gareloch. She had lifting gear for'ard – projecting bow with a large sheave in it – you know the sort of thing – and a steam winch. The tug *Clansman* was still there too, I dare say one of the boats was hers. Also a minelayer was said to be racing down to us with a team of artisans and cutting-gear – from Barlows', I suppose – and – for as much as this was worth – a salvage vessel was *en route* from the Orkneys. Imagine *that*. Not the slightest possibility she could arrive in time. And meanwhile, whether George Random was getting any response to the request for air-hoses and compressors I didn't know. He was up in *Hoste*'s W/T office most of the time, and I dare say the air was turning blue. He was in charge of all rescue operations, with Ozzard as his number two. I'd seen Ozzard, of course – for about five minutes. If anyone could have got things moving, he and Random would have. But we weren't geared to submarine disasters at that time. We didn't have the equipment or the expertise – even the *will*, really. Admiralty thinking for some while had been that getting men out was up to the submarine herself, outside assistance wasn't really practical. You won't find this anywhere in black and white, I'm sure, but it was the attitude, all right – quite evident too, from the lack of both readiness and gear.

'Ozzard had given me a brief rundown of the part he'd played, this far. He described how he'd watched *Trumpeter* every second of the hour or so when she'd been trying to dive and couldn't, then he'd seen the sudden bow-down disappearance – *very* sudden, it had worried him a bit but then he'd thought hell, Jacko'd been having problems getting under, might have opened bowcaps by way of a solution, or flooded some bow tank they'd forgotten until then. But – he'd know what he was doing. Ozzie took a fix anyway, by shore bearings, and marked it on the chart as the spot where *Trumpeter* had dived, but apart from that he just carried on, keeping clear of the submarine's planned course and watching for signals – smoke-floats . . . When she'd been down more than three hours, of course, he started worrying and passed a signal over his R/T via the local signal station to all the responsible authorities – Admiralty, C-in-C, Blockhouse. *Trumpeter*'s smoke-float hadn't ignited, by the way, and when divers finally got down to her they found the marker-buoy's line snagged round her periscope standards. *Hoste* had located *Trumpeter* by searching around Ozzie's charted position with her rather primitive A/S equipment, shortly after dawn.

'So much for the view from the surface. Ozzie's anyway. From my own – grandstand view from *Hoste*'s quarterdeck – they'd lent me dry clothes and never ceased offering me coffee, brandy, etcetera – well, I saw the next three come up. Three alive, one dead. Another of the Admiralty team, that was. Apparently he'd died of heart failure. Making two –

that Barlows' chap had passed out in the Tube Space, you'll remember. Incidentally, if they hadn't kept the door open while Eddington dragged him out – the TI should have ordered it shut – then only the Tube Space would have been flooded and more than ninety lives saved. I think you'll find that in the Inquiry's findings. But – the three who came out alive were Harry Calshot, a telegraphist by name of Carter and one of the Barlows' fitters. Name, if I remember rightly, Campbell.'

Chalk was stuffing tobacco into his pipe – perching on the terrace wall, his back to the sea. This by the way was the afternoon of our third day of interviews. Two days to go . . . He told me – jerkily, getting the pipe going – 'We waited, expecting the next batch to break surface after something like the same interval. I was thinking it was about time they made use of the for'ard chamber too. Deeper – the pressure bugbear and a longer ascent – but perfectly usable, anyway by trained men. But after a while – well, nothing at all was happening: which suggested that something of another kind must *have* happened. I kept telling myself "Any minute now" – but less and less convincingly, knowing how little time they had. And remembering what the air had been like an hour or two earlier.' He flicked a second match away. 'Then we got word – Calshot's. When they'd pulled him out of the drink he hadn't been making much sense, apparently, but he'd told Random now that they'd tried to use the for'ard chamber soon after our own escape – while the after chamber was still draining down, in fact. Pargeter had sent out only two trained men with one reasonably fit passenger in their care – because of the greater depth and pressure – and they'd found they couldn't open the hatch. They'd made two or three attempts, with a change of personnel for the third, and then given up. We heard – a couple of months later, after they'd raised her – that the hatch had been jammed by distortion of the hull, obviously when she'd hit the bottom.'

Puffing smoke . . .

'So – for'ard escape chamber u/s, and nobody coming out of the after one. Some of them – possibly all – would be dead by this time. One knew it – and still waited. Saying prayers in one's head – you know . . . I was – they told me, afterwards – more or less gibbering by then. Late forenoon. I do remember demanding to be told why the *hell* no air-hoses or divers had come. Why not by flying-boat, for God's sake? The minelayer with the cutting gear had arrived and anchored – and a lot of use *that* seemed to be, at this juncture . . . So – *Hoste*'s quack got his way, finally, gave me a shot of something or other – needle in the arm – that laid me out. And it was while I was out cold that – you know all this, you were only a schoolboy but you'd have seen photos of it on all the papers' front pages, *Trumpeter*'s stern end sticking up out of water?'

I did remember, very well. Also the impression given by the news reports that all would now be well, having 'got her stern up' all they'd have to do was cut a hole and pull them out.

Chalk was saying, 'A shift of the tide had caused it. Coupled with the extent to which they'd lightened her during the night. Anyway, Random got the boom-defence vessel to up-anchor and move in – not easy, mind you, with the swell still running, and it must have taken quite a long time – but eventually they managed to pass the bight of a wire over *Trumpeter*'s tail, taking up the slack for'ard of the after hydroplanes so it couldn't slide off. Put a bit of tension on it, I suppose, then made it fast. Meanwhile there were more aircraft making low passes than ever. Word had got out, and the Press were airborne with their cameras. And the cutting gear had arrived – did I mention that? Right . . . There was hope, you see – if they weren't all dead by then. Even if some of them were only half-dead, they might have been brought out and resuscitated. But before those fellows could get on to her tail with their acetylene burners – it was getting near sunset, but they'd have worked with ships' searchlights on them – at that crucial moment she shifted again, pirouetting on her nose very suddenly as the tide swung her, and putting an enormous strain on the wire, which snapped. And she slid under. Finish, gone. When I heard about it, I was glad I hadn't been up there to see it.'

He'd paused. Then: 'As to why there'd been no more escapes – perhaps you heard about it?'

'Not that I remember.'

'No. Well ... For obvious reasons none of this was published. We didn't bruit it about, either. But – when the divers went down, prior to raising her, they found the hatch jammed half-open with two bodies in it and two more in the chamber. One in the hatch had no mask on, and the other's mask was full of vomit. I'm not going to tell you who they were. It's not in the Tribunal's report either.'

Chapter 13

The survivors came back to Greenock that Thursday night, arriving in the early hours of Friday. The Admiralty had put out a communiqué earlier regretting that no hope remained for the 90 men still on board HM Submarine *Trumpeter*, and that rescue attempts had consequently been abandoned. There'd been 101 men on board apparently, and 11 had come out of her.

Ozzard travelled back in the minesweeper with them. Random stayed down there in *Hoste*, anchored close to the wreck, awaiting the arrival of the salvage vessel from Scapa some time next day.

Chalk's memories of the arrival at Greenock were that they'd landed at some quay, from which the Press had been successfully locked out, at about two or three in the morning. There was a crowd of wives and families there, and volunteers with cars. Helen Pargeter had been one of these – in a state of private misery but preoccupied with comforting and helping others. Maggie Ozzard was there too, of course. Chalk's car was where he'd left it, at Barlows'; he and Ozzard had arranged to meet in the submarine office at noon – he'd get there by tram – and by that time Ozzard would have conferred on the telephone with their superiors at Submarine Headquarters, should know what the future held for them. The probability was that they'd be wanted down there, at Blockhouse. There'd be a Court of Inquiry of some kind, obviously, and Chalk would be a key witness: if it looked like being a lengthy affair they might well relieve him of his job in *Threat*.

Ozzard asked him as they were driving off, 'Sure you'll be all right to get in under your own power in the morning?'

'Well – I would be, but—'

'Hang on.' Stopping at locked gates, putting his head out and calling for them to be opened. His wife was beside him in the front: she'd expected to drive, but he'd told her 'You look more whacked than I am. Go on, move over . . .' She did look exhausted: she and Helen Pargeter had been running a round-the-clock transport service, this past day and the night before it, for distraught wives and families desperately seeking news at the Barlows' offices.

'Sorry Chalk – you were saying?'

'Cheek to ask you this, sir, but – second thoughts – could you drop me at Barlows' so I could pick up my car?'

'Wouldn't the forenoon be soon enough?'

'I need to see Mrs Eason. I know it's hardly the time for a visit – and I could get a taxi, anyway—'

'Of *course* we'll take you to Barlows'.' Maggie, glancing back at him. Then: '*Poor* Mrs Eason. God, one feels so *helpless*.'

Press cameras had flashed as the gates were opened and they drove through. Ozzard muttered, 'I should go along too, I suppose. We could do that on our way – if you know where the Easons live?'

Lived . . . Chalk told him diffidently, 'I knew Eason quite well, sir, and he was the last man I spoke to before I – baled out. If you came too, it might seem to her more official than personal.'

'All right.' He asked his wife: 'Have you seen her?'

'Yes. She's – no weakling, that's for sure. Rather a fine

character, actually. Going to her parents, she said – London, somewhere . . . But she'll be asleep now, Rufus.'

'Have to wake her, that's all. Especially if she's about to disappear. *Then*, I've got to get in touch with Andrew Buchanan's wife. Messages for her too.'

Maggie reached back to him: he took her hand. 'On top of what you've been through—'

'I'm all right. I slept all afternoon. Quack stuck a needle in me.'

She'd taken her hand back, and found a handkerchief.

'It's unbelievably *awful*.' She'd taken her hand back and found a handkerchief. Her husband put his left arm round her; steering one-handed through the grey, empty streets, headlamps washing along the dull glint of tramlines. Chalk thinking – to get it straight, *keep* it straight – Mrs Eason – Zoe Buchanan – Suzie. And Diana – probably there by now . . . He leant forward again. 'If I'm to go down to Gosport, I'd suggest I might take the night train on Monday. My fiancée's flying herself up to Glendarragh – and this is the Cameron-Green family, the girl Toby Dymock was engaged to marry?'

Ozzard was silent while he thought about it. Then: 'All right. I'll say you'll be there about mid-week.' They were already almost at Barlows'. 'If you're to stay down there – which isn't unlikely, is it? – I imagine you'd take your car down?'

It had taken a lot of starting – with the crank, as was usual in the mornings. And the nightwatchman who'd opened the gates for them wanted to know whether various men of whom Chalk had never heard had survived.

It wasn't going to be easy – answering questions, delivering messages from men who'd known they were going to drown or suffocate. Even in one's own mind it wasn't likely to be easy for quite a long time, he guessed. An oppressive sense of guilt at being alive oneself didn't help much, either.

The Easons' landlord was grumpy at being woken, then caught on to the fact that this tall, red-headed and unshaven man had been in the lost submarine and escaped from it, and it had then been necessary to fend off *his* questions.

A spectator's questions. *He* had no-one to cry for.

He'd knocked. 'Mrs Eason?'

'Yes?'

Immediate answer: she couldn't have been asleep.

'It's Rufus Chalk. Mrs Eason, I'm very sorry to disturb you – middle of the night—'

The door opened. 'Lieutenant Chalk?'

'Could I come in for a moment?'

'Of course.' Her composure was impressive. She'd been crying but she was completely in control now. Dark eyes, medium-blonde hair tied back, strong jawline. A good-looking woman who must have been a very pretty girl. Her eyes raw, bruised-looking, though. She'd turned away, leaving him to shut the door in her landlord's face.

The small sitting-room was sparsely furnished but now cluttered in the disorder of packing. Two suitcases – green canvas with EASON stencilled on them – and a box half-filled with groceries. Clothes lay around; some had been Nat's. He wondered how she'd manage that box of bottles and cans if she was leaving by train.

'My husband—' turning, facing him – 'There's no hope, is there?'

'I'm afraid not.' He tried to explain, 'I came because – well, to say how sorry I am, how *very* sorry . . . I *liked* him – very much indeed. Hadn't known him all that long, but – I felt I *had* – and – well, I was looking forward to serving with him—'

'He thought you were all right, too.' Suddenly, surprisingly, she was in his arms and he was hugging her. A scent of lavender . . . 'It's a bloody nightmare. I can't get it out of my head he won't come walking in that door. Every step I hear – yours, just then—'

'I'm sorry—'

'I'll never – well, no, that's not right, I've *got* to – get used to it, *believe* it . . .'

'Mrs Ozzard tells me you're going to your parents – in London?'

'Yeah.' Separating . . . '*Bloody* submarines.' She sat down: but more a collapse than sitting. Shaking her head: '*Filthy* bloody things!'

'I know – how you must feel—'

'You do?' A touch of bitterness: and he didn't blame her. But what *was* there to say? He went on, 'Thing is, I'll most likely be going down there myself – in my rattly old baby Austin. Probably about Tuesday. If you'd like a lift south, and company of sorts . . .'

She'd said thanks, but no. The offer had pleased her, he thought, but she wanted to get away at once. Understandable enough . . . He explained briefly, then, how he'd come to escape – being picked for a team to get a message out, a vain attempt at saving the boat and all hands. Aware that she hadn't asked for any such explanation, that it was his own need he was dealing with now, his guilt at being here when her husband wasn't. Their roles – fates – could easily have been reversed – he could have been down there in the black water, Nat Eason here . . . Then they were talking about Nat again: and after some hesitation but then deciding that she could take it, that it was so typical of him she'd want to add it to her memories – he'd told her the last words he'd heard from him: double Johnny Walker, and no water . . .

She'd laughed, cried, recovered, apologized for being 'silly' and commented that that was Nat, all right. Nat to a 'T', that was!

'Tell you what – I'll drink it for him. Not whisky, though – double gin, straight.'

'There's one thing I ought to tell you. I don't want to upset you more than I may have already, but – sooner or later you'll be wondering, so—'

'So go on?'

'I'm pretty sure they'd have just gone off to sleep. I was getting close to it myself. I had a headache – I think a lot of others did too – and we were all short of breath. But apart from that, if I'd been left to myself I think I'd have just – well, flaked out. Come to think of it, a lot of them had already.'

'Just gone to sleep . . .'

He nodded. 'And when he made his joke about the Johnny Walker, I believe he meant it – taking it for granted we'd soon be knocking a few back together.'

'Might've passed on happy, then.'

'Yes. Without ever really *knowing*—'

'Didn't say nothing about me? Didn't ask you to come and see me – like you are now?'

'No. And that's another reason to believe he expected to get back.'

'Just got his old nut down, then . . .'

He was glad he'd been to see her. Although there was no real help that one could give. Only palliatives, at best – tiding them over, as it were. Driving out to Dunbarton with the first streaks of dawn in the eastern sky he'd found himself thinking about the war that was surely coming: how much better *not* to be married, risk inflicting that depth of grief. Because that was where it really hit, where the full price was paid.

At Mrs Blair's – having overcome first her bad temper at being woken, then her astonishment and jumbled questions – he tried to get Zoe's telephone number from Enquiries, but failed to raise them. He wished he'd been less pig-headed, made a note of the number which she'd given him about half a dozen times.

He'd got the number and was through to the house in Belgravia at about eight-thirty, but the maidservant who answered told him that Mrs Buchanan had taken the night train to Glasgow.

'May I ask who's calling, sir?'

He gave her his name, which she recognized immediately. Mrs Buchanan had been on the telephone to Barlows' most of yesterday, she told him, and before she'd left the house she'd heard from them that he, Chalk, had escaped by DSEA. 'She said you'd have been with poor Mr Buchanan, sir. Half out of her mind, she was. Shouldn't be going all that way on her own, I told her!'

Hanging up, he lit a cigarette – the third since getting out of bed – wondering whether she'd be at Helensburgh by now. If she'd had a cab directly from the station . . .

The Cameron-Greens first, he decided. Might try Diana's London flat, but she'd almost certainly have been making an early start, be on her way by now. Try it, anyway. Then the C-Gs, and then Zoe – having given her a bit more time to get there.

The 'phone startled him by beginning to ring just as he was about to put his hand on it.

'Hello?'

'*Rufus?*'

'Diana . . .'

'Are you all right? Darling, when did you get back – home, wherever you—'

'About four. I'm at my digs. And I *am* all right . . . You?'

'Well, I'm dancing with joy *now*! Oh, *Rufus*. . . Are you going up to Glendarragh, or—'

'Yes – this afternoon. Be there about five-thirty, six-thirty . . . Where are you?'

'Carlisle. On my way up. I'll be there ahead of you, touch wood. Have you spoken to the C-Gs yet?'

'I was just about to – partly to find out where *you* might be. You'll have been in touch with them, I imagine?'

'Of course. Several times, in the last day or so. And Suzie – Rufus, she's quite ill, poor darling – I mean from anxiety, stress and strain and—'

'As one might expect. But they were in touch with

Barlows' – the C-Gs – were they?'

'Hardly a minute off the 'phone, I gather. They've cancelled the party, of course, Pat and Alastair've been contacting everyone. Rufus, you've been through *hell* . . .'

'I'm damn glad *you'll* be there.'

'Are you?'

'Think I wouldn't be?'

'You sound a bit flat. And anyway it's – like a huge bomb's gone off, everyone at sixes and sevens. I'm having to pinch myself now – to believe it's really *you* . . . The last day and a half's been – I can't *tell* you!'

'When did you hear I was out of it?'

'Yesterday afternoon, at Manchester. The Cameron-Greens had just heard, I tried to ring Barlows' for confirmation but their lines seemed to be engaged most of the time, then when I got here I tried again – and tried *you*, but of course your Mrs Blair didn't know anything at all except she'd heard that frightful 'no more hope' announcement from the Admiralty – when earlier on they'd been saying it was going to be all right, one end was out of water and they'd only to cut a hole . . . Anyway, I tried again when I got here, and there was no answer. Darling, you're *absolutely* all right, are you?'

'Absolutely. Except it feels all wrong that I should be.'

'Well, forget *that* nonsense – you're all right, let's make the most of it! Anything to tell Suzie – if I do get there before you?'

'I don't think so.' He drew another lungful of nicotine. 'Toby gave me a message for her, but only – what you'd expect. In any case I'm going to 'phone Glendarragh now, let 'em know I'm coming.'

As if a huge bomb had gone off . . .

Meaning the upheaval might have changed how he and she felt about each other?

Or perhaps she had telepathic powers, had tuned in to his

doubt of the wisdom or even morality of marrying at this time.

The doubt was still there, too. It had been in his mind when he'd woken. Perhaps linked to his first thought of Diana: of waking with her in his arms . . .

Dialling the Buchanan house at Helensburgh, now.

Ringing. Then a clatter, and a male voice: 'Mr and Mrs Buchanan's residence. Who's calling, please?'

'Lieutenant Rufus Chalk. Has Mrs Buchanan arrived yet?'

'Not yet, sir.' Chalk had him in his mind's eye as the one in striped trousers with a tray of drinks. 'As I understand it, sir, the chairman of Barlows' Shipbuilders was sending a car to meet the train and bring Mrs Buchanan to his house. It was Madam's expressed intention to be wi' us later, but I couldna say just when.'

'Well – when you speak to her, tell her I called – and that I'll be moving around a bit but I'll try again later.'

Funking it. 'Try again later' rather than ask for the number at the chairman's house and call her there.

At Glendarragh, his call was answered by Alastair, who was effusive in his expressions of relief at Chalk's survival, and delighted to hear he'd be arriving that evening. He'd tell them: they'd be tickled pink. Diana should be there by late afternoon, too – had he known? Well, yes, poor Suzie *was* taking it a bit hard: more exhausted than anything else, in his view, she'd had a rotten thirty-six hours of it, poor kid . . . Chalk ended with 'Give her my love. Tell her I'm *very* much looking forward to seeing her.'

Finally, he rang his sister. Betty's husband fielded the call and told him before he could get a word of his own in, 'Nothing to tell you yet, Rufus. She's bearing up well, but it's very much overdue now. We're all ready for it, of course. standing by – like fielders in the slips, eh?' He'd laughed. 'Look, I'll call *you*—'

'I'll be on the move, rather. I'll ring tomorrow morning – all right? Tell Betty I'd better get good news by then, or else

. . . But listen, Dick – if you hear anything about me having been in the submarine that's been lost on trials—'

'HMS *Trumpeter*? My God, you weren't – *were* you?'

'I and ten others got out. That's why I'm 'phoning. Don't want Betty alarmed at this stage, do we?'

'No, my God . . . But I'd better tell her – since you *are* out of it – My dear fellow, thank God you are – but what an experience!'

'Start by giving her my love and say I rang to ask whether my nephew or niece had arrived yet. *Then* tell her this other thing – so she's forewarned, forearmed . . . All right, Dick?'

'Yes. Very sound. Good man . . .'

He was in the Submarine shed, sifting through two days' accumulation of official correspondence, when he heard Ozzard clump over the board floor into his own office, and went to join him. Ozzard had already made his telephone call, and had been told they were to present themselves at Blockhouse by noon on Thursday 2nd September – the day Diana would be taking off for the Cape. And while Ozzard would be returning here, retaining his command of *Threat*, Chalk was to be found a shore appointment from which he'd be readily available to attend the Tribunal of Inquiry that was to open in about three weeks' time in London. Ozzard would have to attend as a witness too, but only for a day or two.

Presumably they'd give him some job at the Admiralty. Frightful thought. An office wallah, pen-pusher . . . He'd have liked to have seen *Threat* completed, too, and taken her to sea. *And* – first thought of all, when Ozzard had told him this – London had become synonymous with Zoe. The only Andrew *Murray* in Belgravia. Zoe husbandless and Diana at the Cape, for God's sake.

Buchanan's face then, in close-up and extraordinary detail. Light-brown eyes slightly bloodshot, sheen of sweat around them, short, gasping breaths as he'd pleaded, 'You won't forget . . .'

Ozzard's voice broke in: 'Go down by road, won't you. Better meet me in the wardroom on Thursday at – say – eleven-thirty. All right?'

Driving up through Perthshire he hardly noticed anything along the way. Driving like some automaton – as if the car was finding its own way while his thoughts circled, spiralled, side-slipped ... Diana's influence in that ... But the only time he was for a while conscious of his surroundings was when he was passing Loch Earn, which under a clear blue sky and blazing sun was quite beautiful, so utterly different from when he'd last driven up this way – pitch darkness, rain coming down in bathfulls – that you wouldn't have thought it was the same place.

In a sense, it wasn't. *No* place was.

Glendarragh, though, was familiar enough, except for a car which he hadn't seen here before, a grey Morris parked close to the steps up to the front door. He braked beside it, switched off, was climbing out when MacKenzie appeared.

'A mercy you're safe and sound, sir.'

'Be more of a mercy if the rest of them were.' Glancing at the rather battered Morris. 'Whose is this?'

'Dr Graham, sir attending on Miss Susan.'

'Rufus!'

Diana, then, leaping down the steps. Or rather, loping. Panther-like – beautiful ... 'Oh, Rufus, *Rufus* ...'

They were in each other's arms. MacKenzie lurching up the steps with Chalk's suitcase, grimly blind to such unseemly goings on. Diana told him, 'The family are waiting for you inside. Very kindly left the field clear for me. Darling, it's been such *agony* ...'

'Still is, for most of them. There's some doctor here, MacKenzie said – seeing Suzie?'

The doctor was in the hall, on his way out. Fifty-ish, weathered face, grey hair. Telling Lady C-G, 'Since she refuses medication—'

'Refuses?' She'd seen Chalk coming in behind Diana. 'Rufus!'

'Doesn'ae care to take pills, she said.'

'Well, that's true, she never has. Not even an aspirin if she could help it. But—'

'It's no bad thing, Lady Cameron. If she can get back on her feet through her own efforts – her own courage, I'd say—'

'But it means we've dragged you out here for no purpose, Doctor. I'm sorry ...' Taking Chalk's hand in both of hers. 'Dr Graham – Lieutenant Chalk. Rufus dear – it must have been dreadful, but thank *God*—'

'Great heavens – you're one of the fellers that—'

'One of the lucky ones ... Over the worst, is she?'

'Ah, well. A little early to say *that*.' A smile at Lady C-G ... 'I wouldn'ae say *no* purpose, my lady. The shock of seeing me and my bag of tricks may well have triggered a recovery.' The smile faded. 'Mind you, she'll need all your support still. She's a brave wee lass, but like the rest of us she'd have her limits.' Glancing at Chalk, he frowned, peered more closely: 'You don't look too grand yourself, Lieutenant.'

'Tired, that's all.'

'Indeed ... I'd prescribe a week's complete rest—' his eyes went from Lady C-G to Diana – 'in caring hands. If I were asked, that is.'

'Very *much* what the doctor ordered.' He put his arm round Diana and asked Lady C-G, 'Can I see Suzie now?'

'I'll take you up in a minute. Diana, be a dear, tell MacKenzie we need more tea? And cake – you must be hungry, Rufus—'

'Rufus!'

Alastair, smiling broadly: 'Absolutely spiffing!' His mother was seeing the doctor out, and Diana had rung for MacKenzie. Alastair rattling on, 'Awful about Toby, of course. Suzie *is* taking it frightfully hard ... When you feel up to it, old man—'

He was slightly dizzy, he'd just realized. Doctors – they made you aware of ailments you didn't know you had. Alastair's last words trailed through his consciousness – 'Tell us all about it ...' He didn't want to *think* about it, let alone give lectures. They'd somehow transferred to the drawing-room, he found; and Sir Innes was joining them. 'My dear fellow, what a great pleasure – as well as relief ...'

Tea would go down quite well, he thought. That or a double Johnny Walker. Or – in this house – a large single malt. Bit early for that, though. Mrs Eason's voice: *Double gin – straight.* Poor Mrs Eason. And such a waste of a splendid man: like dropping something of great value down a drain, just as senseless ... Lady C-G had rejoined them, while Sir Innes and Alastair were competing for different ways of saying what a frightful experience it must have been. 'Eleven out of *how* many, was it? Knocked Suzie for six, of course – but you'll help there, make *all* the difference—'

'As well as Diana's help with this flying business. That'll help to get her mind off—'

'I'll just nip up and see her.' Diana, to Lady C-G. 'I'll tell her Rufus is here. Hello, Pat.'

Patricia – smiling at Chalk as she and Diana passed each other in the doorway. Double doors, old dark oak, same as the room's panelling. Chalk echoed Diana's words, but with more emphasis: '*Hello*, Pat.'

'Rufus. How *marvellous*.'

Narrowing those blue-grey eyes, though – up close, gazing up at him with the same sort of questioning look he'd seen on the doctor's face. Her hand closed firmly on his arm: 'Better sit down. Here—' steering him towards a sofa – 'Sit, put your feet up. Come on – before you *fall* down ... Get him a brandy, Alastair, for Pete's sake ...'

*

Suzie came to see *him*.

He'd passed out, apparently, slept on that sofa for a couple of hours, woken to find they'd taken his shoes off and covered him with a rug. Since then he'd come up to his room and had a lukewarm bath. The plumbing system wasn't all that efficient.

Barefooted, in his dressing-gown, opening the door to Suzie. He'd forgotten what a stunner she was. That dark hair and blue eyes: even pale as she was, and with dark bruises under the eyes. Her face looked thinner too – the cheekbones more prominent, eyes deeper-sunk.

Guy's girl. But more grown up than *that* one had been.

'How are you, Rufus?'

'Wrong question.' He kissed her cheek. 'How are *you*?'

'I'll – survive. In fact – I'm really quite all right. Really. *You* must have been absolutely played out.'

'Hadn't noticed it until your Doctor Graham told me I was. That's doctors for you – like witch-doctors casting the evil eye . . . Suzie—' he shut the door – 'I am dreadfully and most sincerely sorry.'

'Tell me how it was?'

He nodded. From Suzie, it was an acceptable request. 'Quite a lot to tell. I don't know how much of the technicalities you'd want. But I'll give you as much as I can – if you can stand it, Suzie.'

'I can. *Must*.'

'I think you're probably quite right. And the first thing is he asked me to give you his love. Not – as you might guess – near the end – much earlier. He was about to try something very dangerous, getting into a flooded compartment to shut the rear door of a torpedo-tube so we could then pump it out.'

'Did he manage it?'

'No. Made two attempts, but both times the men with him couldn't stand the pressure and he had to give up. And by that time *he* was played out. He was a brave man, Suzie.'

Holding her, while she cried against his shoulder . . .

Both invalids went down for dinner. Chalk was still shaky, but he thought that having told her the whole story as far as it was comprehensible had probably been good for her. In the long run he felt sure it would be: there'd be no room for *imaginary* demons to torment her.

Dinner – it was the standard Glendarragh-type menu – wasn't as relaxed as family meals in this house had been usually, but it wasn't bad in all the circumstances – which could be summarized as (1) Toby Dymock's death, (2) the effects of the 36-hour ordeal on Suzie, and (3) she and the rest of them knowing that he, Chalk, had been dead against her involvement with Dymock.

Guy was there too, in the background – and not only in *his* mind. The fact nobody asked for news of him was proof of it. Guy who'd been so warmly welcomed here, and was now God only knew where.

(Franco's rebel forces had all the Basque provinces and the Asturian mines in their control now – all the mineral resources which the Germans wanted to get their hands on – while Republican offensives near Madrid and in Aragon had ground to a halt. If the writing had been on the wall before, it was in capital letters now.)

He had an urge to break a silence with 'I haven't heard anything from Guy, yet.'

Just to have them acknowledge his existence . . .

But it would have been churlish to have rubbed salt in Suzie's wounds. She'd told him, in their long talk upstairs, that when she'd heard the Admiralty's announcement of rescue attempts being abandoned, she'd thought of killing herself, and had known how she'd do it. Her father's guns were in a locked cupboard in the smoking-room, but she knew where he kept the keys.

MacKenzie, re-entering the dining-room, was coming

round to this side of the table with his eye on Chalk and a slip of paper in his fingers. They'd heard the telephone a minute ago, and he'd padded out to the hall to answer it.

'If you'd kindly telephone to this number, sir, when convenient.' Low-voiced, stooping to put his grey head close to Chalk's red one. 'The lady said it was urgent.'

Zoe – at Helensburgh . . .

Folding the page of notepad and pushing it into his top pocket, meeting Diana's querying look and cursing himself for not having called her as soon as he'd got here. He explained, 'Wife of Barlows' financial director – man called Buchanan.' To Sir Innes: 'You had him here to shoot once.'

'Oh, *that* chap . . .'

'He was a passenger in *Trumpeter* – first time out in a submarine, wanted to see for himself what it's like. I was explaining things to him as we went along. And—' he took a deep breath – 'he gave me a message for his wife.'

Scrape of Suzie's chair, as she pushed it back. She'd put down her napkin: for whiteness, her complexion matched it. Chalk began, half up, 'Suzie – I'm sorry, *stupid* of me—'

She was at the door – MacKenzie moving that way, but she beat him to it. Patricia had jumped up, was hurrying after her. Chalk muttered, subsiding, '*My* stupid fault. Never thought – blurting all that—'

'Don't blame yourself.' Sir Innes, scowling . . . 'Perfectly natural – you felt called upon to explain—'

'Of *course* you aren't to blame, Rufus!'

The endorsement had come from Lady C-G, but Diana cut in with 'Go and call the poor woman, Rufus, don't leave her waiting.' Looking round at the others: 'Sorry – interrupting you. But if she's in the same state as Suzie . . .'

The poor woman, she'd called her. Visualizing her as some old bag, no doubt . . .

'Zoe. Rufus.'

'At last!'

'I should have tried again sooner, I know. Did try three times. Actually I passed out when I got here – nothing to do with drink, either. Zoe, I'm *so* sorry. There aren't words for it. I know there aren't, I've—'

'I'm still stunned. It *is* real, is it?'

'I'm afraid so. You aren't alone in that feeling, though.'

'Why couldn't he have escaped as you did?'

'That'll need a fairly lengthy explanation. Difficult over the 'phone – if you don't mind . . . I've a personal message for you, too.'

'From Andrew? So he did know he wouldn't be getting out.'

Flat tone. Implication being – you *were* getting out, he was *not* . . . Chalk told her, 'One reason he didn't escape – or try to – with me – is he told us he had a weak heart and couldn't face going through the escape chamber. The main problem's pressure, mostly on the eardrums. But that was his answer to a man called Random – a commander, who was organizing the first batch to go out – mine – and asked your husband if he'd like to be one of the four.'

'If he did have a weak heart, he never told *me* about it.'

'He'd mentioned it to me earlier on, though. Toby Dymock was having a shot at getting into the flooded section—'

'He's dead too.'

'Yes.' The four-letter man . . . Was she going to pretend a deep affection for him too, now? Grief – genuine grief – was hard enough to cope with. Susan's, Mrs Eason's. But *this* . . . He told her, 'In a reference to what Toby was trying to do – it involved standing up to *very* high pressure – Andrew said something to the effect that he wouldn't dream of going through it, and couldn't anyway because of his heart. If you're in doubt of it, why not ask his doctor?'

'You sound – hostile, Rufus.'

'I thought *you* did. As far as I'm concerned, for "hostile" read "defensive".'

'You say you called *three* times?'

'Tried to. First time—' he remembered that he'd been supposed to have her London number, shouldn't have needed to call Enquiries – 'was at about three in the morning. No answer. I got through at breakfast time, and your maid told me you'd taken the night train. Then I rang your Helensburgh number and was told you'd been met at the station – or *were being* met – by the Barlows' chairman. So I knew you were in good hands. Meanwhile I've had other people to see, Zoe. Our engineer's wife, for instance – that was between two and three in the morning, before I'd even got back to my digs and tried to call you in London. It hasn't been exactly a rollicking day.'

A few seconds' silence . . . Then: 'I'm sorry, Rufus, if—'

'Object of the calls was to say how sorry *I* am. I liked Andrew very much. We had some long talks, and – I am truly *very* sorry. If I *could* have got him out, brought him out with me—'

'When will I see you? If you can't give me his message over the telephone—'

'Sunday? I'll be driving down to Dunbarton – afternoon or early evening. I could divert slightly to Helensburgh.'

'Can we set a time?'

'Say six?'

Diana would be taking to the air no later than midday, he guessed, for her flight south. So he'd leave soon after lunch . . .

'Will you stay to supper?'

'Kind of you, Zoe, but—'

'Not "kind" at all. Only civilized. When you're breaking quite a long car trip—'

'The thing is I have to get packed that night and make a pre-dawn start for Portsmouth in the morning. I'll explain it all when I see you . . . Could have an *early* supper, I suppose – if the invitation still stands?'

He thought, hanging up, *Not on your life. . .*

*

This would have been the eve of the great celebration hoolie, he thought, looking round through eyes which had a tendency to close. He had a suspicion that he might have dozed off for a minute, but if he had no-one seemed to have noticed it.

But – imagining how it might have been. The excitement, and the rush of preparation, Toby Dymock in the middle of it nerving himself to the announcement of his engagement.

Then, visualizing him as he might be *now* . . . And quickly shutting the picture out. He'd definitely been dropping off then. And Patricia had come down, he realized. She was talking about Suzie, telling Alastair he was too thick to understand how hard-hit she'd been. She would *not* be 'back to her old self in a day or two'. A tone of contempt – obviously quoting him – and Alastair shrugging: 'Week or two, then. Can't mope for *ever*!'

'She's been through purgatory, Alastair. Absolute purgatory. Still *is* . . . Up there now she's frightened of going to sleep because of the nightmare she knows she'll have. Whenever she's dropped off he's screaming to her to help him, and she's reaching to him and can't make it. And she wakes *wishing she'd drowned with him*. How d'you like *that* – for a slight indisposition? Believe me, your little sister's going to need a lot of support for a long time to come. I agree the flying thing could help – once she can face it—'

Diana had told Chalk during dinner – had told the others earlier – that she'd discovered there was a flying club near Glasgow with an instructor of very high repute. She'd landed there on her way up and stayed on the ground long enough to meet him, had seen that the set-up looked pretty good, and mentioned Suzie to him. When she was ready, all she'd have to do was give this man a ring.

When Diana said she'd do something, Chalk thought sleepily, she damn well *did* it. And she really *was* a sight for sore eyes. Really startlingly attractive. Everything about her

. . . Seemed to become more so every time he saw her again, after even a brief separation like this last one. His mind boggled at the thought of how stunning she might be by the time she got back from the Cape. Rather a good line that, he thought: try to remember it and tell her, it'll curl her toes . . . She was saying, as he tuned in again, 'I'll talk to her again tomorrow. Might lure her down to the Moth, if she's up and about. One wouldn't want her to feel she's being pressured, of course – the great thing about it is that it was *her* idea, that wild enthusiasm . . .' Turning to Lady C-G: 'Am I being frightfully interfering? If I am, I'm sorry. But I said I'd find out for her, and as I'm off so soon I thought I'd better do something about it *prontissimo*.'

'Very good of you. Not in the least interfering. In fact, as Innes was saying, it could be – what was the word he used?'

Alastair supplied it: 'Providential?'

'*Aren't* we bright.' Patricia passing behind him, ruffled his hair. She added, 'Like a parrot's bright.' Looking at her mother then: 'Papa will have to buy Suzie a car, of course, for getting to the airfield and back – and have her taught to drive it.'

'He knows that, Patricia.'

'Thinks *she* knows everything.' Alastair jerked a thumb towards his sister. 'Laying down the law – God help us. Just because the FO's made the monumental blunder of accepting her. Heard about that yet, Rufus?'

'FO meaning Foreign Office?'

Patricia told him, 'They're taking me on. Had word – unofficially, a friend of Papa's – day before yesterday. Eclipsed by more recent events, but it *is* rather thrilling.'

'I bet it is. Congratulations. But taking you on for what?'

'Primarily, languages. But I've been having interviews, writing exams, Papa pulling every string in sight . . .'

'Rather a change to have some *good* news.' Lady C-G looked over at Diana: 'Exactly when *do* you leave us?'

'Leave *you*, Sunday morning – if you can put up with me

that long. Leave Southampton in the flying boat, Thursday.'

Chalk said, 'That's the day I have to report at Blockhouse.'

'But what's poor Rufus going to do—' Alastair asked Diana – 'for however long you said you're going?'

'Poor Rufus is going to be up to his ears in honest toil – I hope. And I'll be away until the Spring.' Looking round at him: 'Shouldn't poor Rufus be getting an early night?'

'Yes, he should.' He met her glance, let her see the question in his own: she lowered her eyelids, slightly, shook her head – infinitesimally, but clearly a negative. He'd caught it only because he'd been looking for it – and accepted it philosophically, having wondered anyway whether with so few people in the house, night-sounds more audible and identifiable, discretion shouldn't outweigh inclination. *And* – perhaps more importantly – whether in any case he'd be up to scratch.

He pushed himself up out of his chair. 'Should, indeed . . .'

In the morning he tried to get Mrs Eason on the telephone, but her landlord told him she'd left. He'd expected this, but if she'd still been there would have repeated his offer of a lift down to London – knowing now that he'd be going down on Monday.

He'd be going to Diana's flat. *Her* suggestion: and he'd have the use of it while she was away. Which, if they were giving him some job at the Admiralty, would be amazingly convenient. He'd suggested, 'Better by far if you stayed too. For instance, I could have splendid meals waiting for you when you came back from your trips.'

She'd trilled, 'What *would* the neighbours say?'

'Bugger the neighbours!'

'I'd much rather not . . . Anyway—' whispering – 'we'll have Monday, Tuesday, Wednesday . . .'

He'd go down to see Betty though, sometime. Possibly on

Wednesday and stay the night, *en route* to Blockhouse.

Diana had persuaded Sir Innes to come up for a flight, a bird's-eye view of the estate and its surroundings. She'd offered it as a silver anniversary present, and Sir Innes was taking it as a great adventure. Almost, Patricia had murmured during breakfast, updating his last will and testament before take-off.

Suzie had had a good night, Patricia said. No dreams, or none that she remembered. Lady C-G had ordered coffee and scrambled egg to be sent up to her room, and they were hoping she'd make an appearance downstairs before long.

Alastair asked Chalk – outside, smoking their first cigarettes of the morning – 'Any ideas what you'd like to do today? After our winged wonders return to earth?'

He had his answer ready. 'Walk.' Pointing at the tops, mist-green against a sky that had been a milky blue but already had less milk in it. 'Climb. With you as guide. Might take a picnic – sandwiches and beer, or something?'

'Damn good idea. I'll sound out Pat. Diana'll come, won't she? Only snag is Suzie – Pat may want to hang around. Although Mama'll be here . . .'

'How about Suzie coming too?' He saw doubt in Alastair's expression. 'Well, why not? Do her a world of good.'

A shrug: 'I'll see what Pat says.'

Patricia was enthusiastic, and ran upstairs at once to suggest it to Suzie. Her brother called after her, 'Tell her the rest of us won't go if she *doesn't* come.' He looked round at Chalk. 'That might fetch her. She's a solitary in some ways, but she's very family-minded.'

Patricia called from the head of the stairs, 'She's *gone*!'

A moment's silence . . . Then: 'Try the bathroom?'

'I have, stupid – Diana's in there. Suzie's *vanished* – eaten her breakfast, dressed . . .'

Chalk thought of the gun cupboard. He hadn't had a chance to mention it to Sir Innes. But – reassuring himself – it wasn't easy to think of Suzie as a potential suicide.

Besides – in that frame of mind, would she have eaten breakfast?

The possibility still existed.

'Excuse me, sir.' MacKenzie. 'Mr Alastair—'

'Huh?' Stopping, looking down from halfway up the stairs. 'Miss Susan's disappeared, MacKenzie.'

'No, sir. Not entirely.' A faint smile. 'Miss Susan is in the paddock. We were pulling the flying-machine out – William and myself – as Miss Villiers requested, d'ye see—'

Alastair called up to Patricia, 'Suzie's in the paddock!'

Running . . . MacKenzie called after them, 'She's right as rain, sir – right as rain!'

Chalk slowed to a walk, and Alastair caught up with him. 'Never understood that expression. What's right about rain? Unless one lived in the Sahara, of course . . . Here comes Pat.'

She caught them up as they went out into the stable yard. Telling them, 'MacKenzie says she's perfectly all right. Don't go dashing up as if she's some sort of escaped lunatic.'

'You're the loony. Who raised the roof screaming "She's gone, she's gone"?'

'There she is.'

On the semi-derelict stone wall from which she and Chalk had surveyed the paddock before it had been cut. The blue-and-silver Fox Moth was out there in profile to her, bright and shiny in the early sun, and she was just sitting gazing at it.

Chapter 14

He came out of the house and across the terrace towards me with a smile on his face and the old setter at his heels. He told me, 'Wasn't a man about a dog, for once. My wife about a grandson.'

'Well, congratulations!'

'Nothing but female grandchildren up till now. Poor little brat, don't envy him the world he's been born into . . .' He sat down, and the dog leant against his knees. He glanced at the tape-recorder. 'She'll be here tomorrow – so we've the rest of today and tomorrow forenoon, and that's it. Where was I?' Fingering the notes he'd made during the night – having difficulty in reading them, by the looks of it. He woke up several times a night, he'd told me, found his mind and memory clearer then than at any other time. I reminded him, 'Arriving at the Buchanans' house at Helensburgh, for what you described as a brief and bloodless interview with Zoe.'

'Oh, yes. And it was, indeed. I'll admit I wasn't particularly well disposed towards her, by that time – and such feelings tend to be mutual – but her coldness, considering that in recent weeks she'd given every sign of being in hot pursuit of yours truly – eh?'

'Right.' I had the recorder running again now.

'Anyway – the major-domo in his striped pantaloons showed me in – into the room in which on my last visit, incidentally, I'd suggested to Buchanan that he might go out in *Trumpeter* for her acceptance trials: and there she was – the wife he'd have trusted "till kingdom come" . . .'

'Lieutenant Chalk, madam.'

'Rufus – how *good* of you . . .'

The effusive manner was, he'd assumed, for the benefit of the manservant – Henderson – whom she then sent to bring a whisky and water and a Dry Martini. Still the same Zoe in *that* respect. She was in black – a very smart, expensive-looking suit of lightweight barathea, with a cream silk blouse and what looked like small rubies in a gold heart-shaped brooch.

She really *was* a stunner. No getting away from it. He held both her hands: 'Zoe – there really is no way of—'

'I know. Don't try.' The manservant left them, and her manner became more abrupt. Gesturing towards an arm-chair: 'Sit down, Rufus. You must be exhausted.'

'Oh, I've recovered.' He dropped into the chair. 'But you, Zoe—'

'It must have been hellish . . . Was it?'

'Pretty bad.'

'I'm sorry if I sounded – tense, on Friday night.'

'In the circumstances, who wouldn't?'

She was silent, watching him . . . Then: 'Did you say you're going down to Portsmouth?'

He nodded. 'Gosport – other side of Portsmouth harbour, our submarine headquarters. I expect I'll have to write a report and answer questions. Then there'll be a public inquiry of some kind. Zoe, I told you some of it – about Andrew saying he had a dicky heart – which obviously he didn't want you worrying about—'

'I've come to the same conclusion, since you told me. But you said he sent a message?'

'Yes. He asked me to tell you that he loved you, and that you're the best thing that ever happened to him.'

Staring at him: as if waiting for more ... Then her eyes closed, the thick lashes falling like a veil. A murmur: 'Thank you ...'

'Excuse me, madam.' Henderson, bringing drinks, transferring them from a silver tray to chair-side tables. Chalk waited until the door was shut again, then told her, 'He also mentioned that you'd complained about Toby Dymock chasing you.'

'I'd *what*?'

'That you'd told him you'd gone down to London to get away from Toby's pestering. And you'd promised you'd come back here when he left.' He went on, not giving her time to comment on it, 'The point he was making was that he trusted you completely. He also – in my presence – confronted Dymock with what you'd told him, and called him a "four-letter man". Dymock pretended not to know what he was talking about.'

'Well.' Looking down at her interlocked, twisting fingers. Then a sigh, and curtain-up, greenish eyes glittering at him: 'I suppose he *would* ... Is that all, Rufus?'

'Unless you want to hear the technical details – what went wrong, what Jacko Pargeter was trying to do to get the boat up – that was the big hope, you see—'

'I wouldn't understand it. But – by the time he gave you his message to me, that hope had faded, had it?'

'No. I'm glad you asked. He gave me the message just *in case* he didn't make it. When I went up – four of us – we were taking proposals to the chaps up top as to how they might help us get the boat up. It didn't come off, unfortunately.'

'Unfortunately ...' She half-smiled: then shook her head. 'I can't cry any more, Rufus. If tears are what you're looking for. I've dried up. All last night in the train – and this morning—'

'I *am* so sorry . . . If there was anything one could do – which there isn't, of course . . . But Zoe – sorry to ask this – about your very kind invitation for supper—'

'Supper . . .' Expressionless: he guessed she was only now remembering that she'd asked him. 'Are you saying you can't?'

'Would you mind awfully?'

'Well – I suppose – no, all right. I can see you're just about on your knees.'

'I was at this time yesterday. No, it's not that. But I have packing to do, and I want to clean my car's plugs before the long trip south, and – one or two other things, then get a few hours' sleep—'

'I quite understand.' Her smile was understanding, too. She could have been talking to the vicar – thanking God *he* was on his way. 'Thank you for bringing me Andrew's message, Rufus.'

He'd finished his whisky. Looking at her as he put the glass down, wondering what might be in that glossy head of hers. Having decided on the way here that he'd keep his mouth shut about the likelihood of being given a job in London: anticipating that if she got to know of it he'd have trouble – knocks on the door instead of rings on the telephone . . . He was on his feet, with her hand in his – answering her polite enquiry about his fiancée, confirming that she was very well, had been up at Glendarragh with him these last two days. Then hearing the manservant coming across the hall, his heels loud on the bare boards. 'If I can be of help at any time, Zoe—'

'Madam rang?'

'Lieutenant Chalk unfortunately won't be staying for supper, Henderson.'

'Very well, madam.' Holding the door . . .

She murmured – she was coming out to see him on his way – 'Perhaps you'll give me a ring one of these days. Let's not lose touch, Rufus . . .'

*

'She'd made no attempt to explain the Dymock business.' Chalk, on the terrace, spread his large hands. 'Not a word about all those telephone calls to me, either. It was as if one had dreamt it all – it hadn't happened . . . The last time I'd been in that house had been for their cocktail party, and if I'd had no contact with her since then we might have been on terms of this kind. Entirely contrary to expectations – having behaved like that when she'd had a husband, now she hadn't – well, I'd thought, look out!'

'Relief, or disappointment?'

'I think my nose might have been put slightly out of joint. Ridiculous – seeing I'd had no intention of having any more to do with her than was absolutely necessary. But listen to *this* . . . When I was getting into my car – I'd parked it beside an Alvis Speed Twenty, which must have been her husband's and would now presumably be hers – I looked back and she'd already disappeared, gone in and shut the door!'

'Any reason for the brush-off that you could guess at?'

'Not at the time. Felt I'd been made a fool of, that was all.' He touched his page of headings. 'I got the beginnings of an explanation a couple of months later – at Glendarragh, oddly enough, at Christmas. But we'll come to that. Leave it now that I didn't understand but didn't really give a damn either. She'd intrigued me for a while – we're all susceptible to that kind of flattery, aren't we, being chased by a very pretty woman? But there'd been something phoney somewhere, right from the start. Dymock for instance had been pretty keen to disengage: I don't believe for a moment that he'd been chasing *her*. Might have done to start with, but – anyway, her tale-telling to her husband had put the lid on it, as far as I was concerned.' He nodded, as if confirming this to himself. 'I'd been ready to cut and run.'

'And next morning you went down to London . . .'

(*Verbatim transcription from the tape now follows*)

'Yes. Then Blockhouse – I was there – can't say exactly,

but about three weeks. Had to write a blow-by-blow account of the disaster: then I suppose I was given some job to keep me busy. I went to my sister's for one weekend, I do remember. She'd had a son, so Guy and I were uncles – I'd written to let him know, adding my usual plea to come back home, no doubt. Then – well, I was appointed to the Operations Division in the Admiralty, just a day or two ahead of the opening of the Tribunal of Inquiry – for which I can give you a date, 4 October. Because it's on the report, you see. But also – to my astonishment – I found I was being jacked up to Acting Lieutenant Commander. Gratifying – until one realized it hadn't anything to do with merit. It was simply because in the Ops Division the three or four of us doing my sort of work had to take turns at being Duty Commander at weekends, and while a mere lieutenant wouldn't fit that designation a two-and-a-half could, at a pinch. So there I was with an additional half-stripe, just to push bits of paper to and fro. Although in point of fact I had to spend most of my first month there attending the Tribunal of Inquiry's hearings. In the Law Courts, easy strolling-distance from the Admiralty. And I had Diana's Chelsea flat to live in rent-free – in other words, to put it vulgarly, I'd landed with my arse in butter, so far as creature comforts were concerned. *And* there'd been one thrilling development – I'd been told at Blockhouse that I was on the list for the next Commanding Officers' Qualifying Course. George Random wasn't running the one that was going through then – couldn't, like me he had to be available to the Tribunal's barristers – but he might have had something to do with my good fortune. Selecting candidates wasn't in his brief, but I think he might have put in a word for me. Anyway, it was great news, as you can imagine. The timing had to work out right, of course, otherwise I'd be put off to the next course after that one – losing the best part of a year. The Admiralty would have released me at the drop of a hat, in the normal course of events, but the Tribunal of Inquiry had no set time-limits on it. There was this opening session which lasted about three weeks or a month, then a six-week break while the salvage people raised *Trumpeter* and did a post-mortem on her, as it were – then in about the middle of November we were back in Court again.

'I'd better get this out of the way first – the Inquiry. You've got the report of its findings there, and you'll see – well, I've told you all about it, and the same facts are there on paper, more or less, with alternative conclusions and so forth. The big question – who opened that bowcap or left it open – wasn't answered. Certainly not conclusively. But one thing did emerge from the inspection of the boat when they'd raised her: the vent-hole in the test-cock on that tube was solidly bunged up with bitumastic paint. You'll remember that Mike Searle didn't use the rimer: if he had, he'd have known immediately that he was on unsafe ground, and checked with the drain – as he should have done anyway. One can assume – as the Court did – that he didn't bother with the rimer because with a brand-new boat he'd have taken it for granted there'd be no accumulation of muck such as might have blocked the hole; he hadn't considered the possibility that the painter might have omitted to plug the hole with oily cotton-waste before he started work.'

Some time in late October he got together with Patricia. She'd started – or so Lady Cameron-Green had indicated – as a trainee in the Foreign Office, and was living in some cousins' house in Kensington. Chalk had a note from her giving him their name and the address, he telephoned that same evening and the following week took her to see *The Drum* – which was showing at the Odeon in Leicester Square, and she'd said she'd like to see it – and then to supper in a restaurant in Wardour Street.

Lady C-G's eye to the main chance again, he'd thought. It really had been an odd thing to have done – knowing perfectly well that he was engaged to Diana, who was out of the country. All right, she might have had no ulterior motive at all, might simply have thought they were good friends and perhaps both lonesome in the big city ... But Lady C-G wasn't all that naive, and Patricia hadn't been in the least bit lonely. Chalk had been slightly embarrassed, didn't tell Patricia that her mother had initiated the contact, instead allowed her to assume that he'd gone to the trouble of finding out where she was.

She was going to France in a fortnight's time, she told him, and she'd be away about six weeks. Ten days in Paris first, then in the southwest; she'd be accompanying some old aunt.

'But I thought you'd started work at the FO.'

'Oh, no. Only sort of hanging around. Keeping out of people's way, mostly, they've nowhere to put me. I start properly, full-time, on the third of January.'

'So you aren't being paid yet, even?'

'Lord no. It's just that the person who fixed it up thought I'd better get down here quickly and sort of clinch it. And I've done so.'

'I see ... Tell me, where exactly in the southwest – where you're going after Paris?'

'Saint Jean de Luz. Near Biarritz. Old friends of my great-aunt are lending us a house there. Lending *her*, I should have said. And Biarritz used to be one of her old stamping grounds – about a century ago.'

While only a few weeks ago, he remembered, he'd proposed to Diana – half-jokingly – that they might fly to Biarritz together, and she'd put him smartly into what she'd then seen as his place. For a while, after the hoolie night, he'd flattered himself with the thought that she hadn't been able to hold out any longer against his irresistible masculine charm, but more recently he'd wondered whether she might not, as it were, have been putting her brand on him. He *had* rather flirted with Patricia in the early stages of that party: and Diana had been about to leave him to his own devices for several months. She might have decided to make sure of him.

He glanced up as Patricia offered, 'Penny for the deep thoughts, Rufus?'

'You want the truth?'

'That means you're giving yourself time to think up a lie. Come on, time's up!'

'And no worthwhile lie at hand, so I'm stuck with the truth. I was thinking you're by far the best-looking girl in this room.'

'Oh, la la!'

'The astonishing thing is that you're clever too.'

'You *are* going it a bit!'

'Is the aunt you're going to France with anything to do with the cousins you're staying with now?'

A nod: 'Their grandmother.'

'*Grandmother?*'

'She's my great-aunt, actually. Mummy's aunt. Aged ninety – how d'you like that? Actually, from my point of view it's a chance to brush up my French, but in any case she's fun, I adore her.'

'I thought your French was fluent already.'

'It is, really. But there's always room for improvement. It's my German I *should* be brushing up. But—' she grimaced – 'who'd want to go *there*?'

'Could be interesting.'

'Could be horrible, too. Talking of Germans, incidentally – not looking too good, is it? These Sudetenland riots, and our house-painter friend rattling his sabre again?'

'What's the Foreign Office view?'

She smiled, shaking her blonde head. 'Anthony hasn't actually got round to chewing the fat with me – yet... Rufus, what about spending Christmas at Glendarragh?'

'Lovely idea – but I've more or less promised Betty – the mother of my nephew—'

'*What* a proud uncle! But please – make that promise less

rather than more? Oh, *do*, Rufus?'

'Will you be back from France by then?'

'For Christmas, you bet I will!'

'Well . . . Can I let you know? It's *very* kind of you—'

'Talk to Betty. I really must go down and see her – see *it* – one of these weekends . . . But Rufus, the parents and Suzie'd love it too. You can see your nephew any old time, surely?'

'It's a point. Tell you in a few days, can I?'

'Shall I be seeing you again in a few days?'

'If you don't leave for France too soon, you will – I hope . . . But changing the subject, I'm glad Suzie's enjoying her flying so much.' He glanced at the waiter: 'Thank you . . . You said she's going straight for a "B" licence – which means commercial – but does she get the private pilot's "A" licence on the way to it?'

'I don't know. But apparently she really is what they call a "natural". Her instructor told Mama so over the telephone. He's the one Diana found – and it's on her advice Suzie's aiming for the full commercial licence. It's been enormously good for her, you know, and we've Diana to thank for it.'

'Getting her over the other business, is it?'

'She still has her nightmares, Mama tells me. Screams in the night sometimes – scares her half to death – Mama, I mean. God knows what it does to poor Suzie . . . You've suffered no lasting ill effects, have you?'

'Not so you'd notice.'

Except when he let himself think back to it. When he did, he felt like a deserter. That down there, with *them*, was where he should have been.

Although *down there* might not apply now, in the present tense. The Tribunal was in recess at this time, and *Trumpeter* was being raised, might well have been brought to the surface by now. He didn't envy them the task that would follow. The stuff of which a *thousand* nightmares might be made. The detritus: and evidence of how men had died. To know about the bodies in the escape-hatch was bad enough.

Patricia had broken a silence with 'I *do* wish she'd stuck to Guy.'

He agreed: 'Not only for her own sake, either.'

'Oh, he'll come through it all right.' She'd put her hand on his. 'You'll have him back here before much longer. You *will*, Rufus.'

'I might tell him to whiz up to the Pyrenees, hop over them and meet you in Saint Jean de Luz?'

'What a lovely idea.' Smiling, and her hand tightening . . . '*Do* come for Christmas?'

Diana wrote, early in November – *This place would be heaven if only you were here too – and of course if Mummy wasn't so ill. I'm glad I came out, because it's giving her such pleasure. But she hasn't long to go – the doctor says it's a miracle she's hung on even this long – and while I don't want to seem callous I really think it might be for the best if she passed on – peacefully, in her sleep, please God – while I'm still here. Because otherwise she's going to be miserable when I go and I'll feel absolutely dreadful to be leaving her.*

Good idea to spend Christmas at Glendarragh. Was it their idea, or yours? If I had to bet, I'd say it might have been Patricia's. Be a good boy now, Rufie. I often think – and dream – of those two days we had in London. Only wish I hadn't been so rushed, but it was still heaven, a heaven I'm longing to get back to – but you know that, don't you? And I was thinking too – if, touch wood, that wretched Inquiry ends in time for you to join the next course, you'll have your own command by about this time next year – won't you? If so, why not make an honest woman of me then?

Give my love to Guy when you write. Tell him I think it's plain stupid to be hanging on out there, risking life and limb to absolutely no purpose. Now the Spanish government's had to move out of Madrid, down to Barcelona – and Franco took yet another town last week, some place called Gijon? – the Republicans don't have a vestige of a hope, do they?

I must run. Doctor's arriving to see Mummy. Darling – keep the lovely letters coming, I love you . . .

He saw Patricia twice more before she left for France. She had a busy social life anyway, and he had as much party-going and so forth as he'd have wanted, mostly through brother-officers at the Admiralty. Weekends were as often as not spent at his sister's house in Kent. Betty had taken his defection over the Christmas holiday without too much grousing, and he'd had a note from Lady Cameron-Green confirming Patricia's invitation.

Suzie had put a note in with her mother's.

Very much looking forward to seeing you at Christmas. Or before – why not? Any news of Guy? When you next write to him, please give him my love. Flying is heaven – an escape to another world – and I might never have done it if Diana hadn't come along!

He'd written back with the news of Guy, which amounted only to the fact that at any rate a fortnight ago he'd been alive and kicking and had described himself as having become 'a reasonably competent soldier'. But after this enquiry from Suzie, he'd written to him again – second letter in a week – saying he'd heard from her and that she'd asked after him and sent her love. He added that he knew from Patricia she was still having nightmares, and if he – Guy – could find it in his heart to write to her – *just a friendly couple of lines, old chap*? – he'd be doing her a great kindness. He'd added, *Then, to do us all an even greater one, come on back to England*!

Whether or not Guy received that letter, he didn't know. None of his letters from Spain had mentioned Suzie. His last – scribbled in pencil on smudgy paper torn from some notebook – had ended with *Don't write us off yet, Rufus. Great things are in the wind.*

Nearer home, a new policy called 'Appeasement' was in the wind. The first outward and visible sign of it came when Halifax, Lord President of the Council, visited Hitler in an attempt to arrange a peaceful settlement of German claims to Sudetenland. He'd gone with Chamberlain's backing but without the knowledge of Anthony Eden, Foreign Secretary, and had offered Hitler settlement of this and other points at issue – including Austria and Danzig, the so-called Polish Corridor – in the Germans' favour as long as they refrained from war.

Most people were pretty sure by this time that war was one of many things Hitler was *not* going to refrain from. While German newspapers – Patricia had told him this – were full of articles and editorials claiming that war was being forced inexorably on the peace-loving German people by the pernicious influence of international Jewry in Britain, France, Poland and elsewhere.

The Tribunal of Inquiry was still in session, with a lot of ground to cover yet. Chalk heard from Random meanwhile that *Trumpeter* was going to be stripped of all her fittings and then rebuilt. She'd be hauled back on to the stocks at Barlows' and eventually relaunched. Random was even able to tell him that her new name was to be *Tracker*.

'Not a bad name.' He'd been lunching with him at his club, the 'Senior'. He'd added, 'Horrible idea, though.'

'I don't see why. There *is* a certain amount of sensitivity on the subject, in certain quarters – and initially it won't be made any more public than we can help. Ideally there'd be no known link between the two, *Tracker* would simply be another new "T". But it'd be bound to leak out. The shipyard workers, for instance – you can't swear 'em to secrecy, and they *have* to know. Then some local paper'll get hold of it, and next day it'll be all over the *Mirror*. Probably better – in my opinion – to bring it out in the open, make no bones about it. Be much worse if we tried to keep it secret and it then got out. Anyway, what the hell – there'll be nothing of *Trumpeter* except the hull.'

'The hull in which a hundred men died.'

Random pointed towards a window. 'Men have died in that street out there. Over the centuries, probably at least a hundred. Nobody says dig it up, throw it away.'

'No, sir, but a street's a street, a ship's a ship. Closer analogy might be a house in which there's been some tragedy.'

'We're not talking about haunted houses, Chalk!'

'The problem's how people feel, though, isn't it? As we all know, sir, sailors tend to be superstitious. In fact *most* people—'

'D'you know what a T-class submarine costs to build?'

He'd nodded, opened his mouth to give him the figure, but Random was driving on: 'Not that it's by any means the only consideration. Time's a major factor. We've got to catch up – fast. Well – as you know, as well as I do. And here we have a hull ready-made and as sound as any other, why on earth not use it?'

In December there was news of a Loyalist offensive having opened near Teruel – which Chalk looked up in an atlas and found to be about a hundred and fifty miles east of Madrid. He guessed this might be the 'great things in the wind' – or one of them – to which Guy had alluded in that letter. The offensive had opened on 5 December, apparently, and the following weekend – 11th–12th, which he spent with the Traills, Betty and her husband – it was reported that fierce fighting was still in progress and it was going well for the Loyalists.

They drank a toast to Guy that evening, Betty adding, 'And may he then come home to us. Laurels and all.'

Chalk murmured, 'Happily do without the laurels.'

'Taking the long view—' Traill put down his glass – 'it won't have done him any lasting harm, you know. With that experience under his belt – well, I'm sure he'd be given an immediate commission in the TA, for instance – if he wanted it, which one might *hope*—'

'*I* should hope he'll have had more than enough of playing soldiers!'

Betty had glanced rather contemptuously at her husband, who was a keen Territorial Army man and spent a lot of weekends 'playing soldiers', as she called it. He told Chalk, 'Give your sister her way, she'd have us all bloody pacifists!'

'Oh, don't be *idiotic*, Dick . . .'

A week later – on the 19th, the following Sunday – the news was of a Loyalist victory, the seizure of Teruel from Franco's forces. Chalk telephoned Betty: 'Did you hear about Teruel?'

'Yes, I did. What I *want* is a word from Guy.'

It was Christmas, then. He went up on the Thursday night train and arrived on Christmas Eve. Alastair met him at Tyndrum in the shooting brake. The snow was quite deep and he'd put chains on its tyres, but there was a clearing sky, no sign of any more to come in the immediate future. Leaning in the train corridor after an excellent breakfast, gazing out at the whitened landscape while smoking the first cigarette of that day, he'd thought of Diana under her blue African sky and blazing sun, and wondered whether that long and lissom body might not have been cooling off in her parents' swimming-pool at that very moment.

Those two days and nights in London had been thrilling, but the first one – at Glendarragh – had been the best of all.

Best *ever*.

He glanced at Alastair: 'How's the Army?'

'Hard work, rather.' He took a hand off the wheel, to remove a fag-end from his mouth and flick it out of the window. Winding it up again, then . . . 'Training like mad. Actually they may be sending us to Ireland shortly. We'd heard Palestine, but Ireland's the latest . . . How's your Tribunal?'

'Grinding on. Exceedingly slow. Should finish before the end of January, touch wood.'

'Then a Command course? In one of her letters to Suzie, Diana said something about your having hopes.'

'COQC – Commanding Officers' Qualifying Course. It's predominantly periscope-attack training, thus known more familiarly as the "perisher".' He flipped his cigarette-case open: 'Want one?'

'No, thanks. You'll be on it, will you?'

'Seems so.' He lit his own, in the shelter of cupped hands. Straightening then, expelling smoke . . . 'One thing Diana may not have grasped is that by no means all starters get home. Some fall at fences along the way.'

'What happens to them then?'

'Back to sea as first lieutenants until someone thinks they're ready for another crack at it. Alternatively, some revert to General Service. Surface ships. From a submariner's viewpoint, that's a come-down.'

'I'm sure you'll make the grade.'

He held up crossed fingers, and changed the subject. 'All of your clan all right?'

'Right enough. The *ambience chez nous* seems to have turned a bit serious, mind you. Patricia spends most of her time reading foreign newspapers – someone at her designated place of employment sends them in batches, one lot before she arrived and another this morning. You'd think she'd want to be out and about a bit, wouldn't you, when she's home for the first time in months?'

'And Suzie?'

'Hardly ever on the ground. Even when she is she isn't, if you know what I mean. She has homework too – navigation. Might as well bark like a dog as speak to her.'

'Still doing well with her flying, is she?'

'Brilliantly, so one's told. An embryo Amy Mollison in

the family. Only thing is, with this war coming – as we're promised – opportunities for round-the-world solo flights may be rather limited. And there'll be no joy-riding, will there. Might fly a fighter, I suppose – if she could pass herself off as a man.'

'Can't quite envisage that.'

'No. Nor me.' He glanced sideways: 'What news of Guy?'

'None very recently. But he wrote a few weeks ago that he considered himself quite competent as a soldier. Hinted at something big coming soon, too.'

'He's probably in the thick of it. I envy him, in a way.'

Those old stone steps, then: and Suzie herself descending them at some rate of knots, old MacKenzie shuffling down after her: a scene evocatively *déja vu.* And she looked terrific, he thought. She had the family good looks – meaning Patricia's, there were striking similarities between them, when one had come to know them well – but on top of it in Suzie's case that marvellous colouring – the light-blue eyes, dark hair, a *vivid* look.

Some figure, too . . .

'You're a sight for sore eyes, Suzie. Flying obviously suits you.'

'So does having you here for Christmas. Hope you don't mind going to church, by the way. We get frightfully keen on it, this time of year. Well, we could leave you on your own, of course . . . Hello, Alastair.'

'I'll be jiggered! The bird-woman has actually acknowledged the presence of an earthbound mortal!'

'*Two* earthbound mortals, dimwit. If you'd been on your own I wouldn't have bothered. Good trip up, Rufus?'

'Slept like a hog. You sleeping well, these days?'

'Oh – mostly.' She'd hesitated before she'd answered, though, and he thought he'd blundered, been stupid to have asked . . . She was smiling at him though as he exchanged greetings with MacKenzie. Then: 'Nearly forgot – congratulations. You're a commander or something now, aren't you?'

'I'm an uncle, I'll tell you *that*. But – acting lieutenant-commander, that's all. And as soon as I leave my desk-job I'll be reverting to lieutenant.'

'Not for long, I bet. Have you heard any more from Guy?'

'No more. He doesn't write all that often. And the Spanish posts don't exactly run like clockwork, either.'

'I suppose not. Would have been nice to hear from him before Christmas, all the same. I sent him a card. Will your letters be forwarded to you here, in the next few days?'

He shook his head. 'Be hardly worth it, would it?'

'Perhaps not. Is the flat nice?'

'It's all right. As flats go ... You really are looking marvellous, you know.'

'Not too bad yourself. And – Rufus, you can enjoy Christmas knowing there *will* be a letter from him on the doormat when you get home. Will you ring me at once, tell me what he says?'

'Of course.'

Patricia was on a stepladder in the staircase hall, decorating an outsize Christmas tree.

'*Rufus!*'

'Careful—'

'Oh, Rufus, it *is* you.' Lady C-G, emerging from the drawing-room: 'How *very* nice ...' She raised her voice: 'Innes! Innes, Rufus Chalk is here!'

Other guests staying over the Christmas weekend were Alastair's tall, red-headed girlfriend Midge Campbell; a wild-eyed fellow subaltern from his regiment by name of Forbes; and the ninety-year-old aunt of Lady C-G's who'd taken Patricia to France with her. She'd come up from Yorkshire, was a widow, lived on her own and knew about aeroplanes, apparently. Over sherry before dinner that evening Chalk heard her telling Suzie about the fighters her brother had flown in the Great War; Sopwith Camels and SE5s were mentioned, with a surprising amount of technical detail and graphic accounts of her brother's exploits over the Flanders fields.

Patricia told him, 'She was a prodigious horsewoman in her day. Rode to hounds regularly until she was darned near eighty.'

He tuned in again: the great-aunt was telling Suzie, 'It's all in the hands. Horses and 'planes – same thing exactly, Jack used to say. And *you* were never off that pony of yours, were you, until this new bug bit you?'

He turned back to Patricia. 'Hope *I'm* as bright when I'm ninety.'

'Me too. Actually I don't think there's much point staying alive that long if one isn't. But she *is* exceptional. How's your Inquiry going, Rufus?'

'Not far to go. Should finish in another two or three weeks, touch wood.'

'Is it awful, having to relive it all again?'

'Not really. I mean, one doesn't. If one let one's imagination run riot I suppose it could get to be.'

It *was*, though. Some of the time. But it was his own cross to be borne, no-one else's business. The price one paid for being alive, he'd thought more than once.

She asked him, 'I suppose the wreck's been raised? Must have – last time we saw each other, I remember you told me—'

'Sustenance.' Alastair, with the sherry decanter poised. 'Cook's dragging her feet a bit, and Mama's getting distinctly pink around the gills. Here, Pat—'

'Not for me. Any more, I'd turn *puce* around the gills.' She smiled at Chalk: 'Excuse me. Must have a natter with the old girl . . .'

'Got *Trumpeter* up, I heard her asking.' Alastair poured

sherry into Chalk's glass, then reached to put the decanter down. 'I gather they have. What's more, it's being bruited about that they're going to patch her up and push her out again with some other name. Is it true, d'you know?'

'Where did you hear it?'

'From the old man, actually. He knows all the bigwigs, picks up the gossip. Perhaps that's all it is – gossip?'

'No. It's true.' He glanced round; then lowered his voice. 'I had no idea it was already general knowledge. You wouldn't talk about it in Suzie's hearing, I imagine.'

'I suppose not. Haven't given it much thought, tell you the truth. The old man did tell me in strict confidence – but that usually means only pass it on to your friends, doesn't it?' He nodded his close-cropped head. 'Good thinking, anyway. Might have a word in the paternal earhole, too.'

'You might, or I might?'

'Well, easier for me—'

'Yes, I agree. But – Alastair – it's not just a matter of "patching her up". They'll put her back on the stocks, strip her down to a bare hull and start from scratch. Creepy thought, I know – struck me that way when I first heard it – but it makes sense, actually.' He was giving him George Random's argument, he realized. 'All *Trumpeter* and her new incarnation will have in common is the steel hull – which it would be crazy not to make use of – when we're building ships hand-over-fist, *and* have to stick within the Naval Estimates?'

'Sense, of a sort.' Reaching for the decanter, to resume his rounds. 'Rather a *grisly* sort . . . Tell me this – how would you feel if you finished this course you're going on and they gave you command of what you called the new incarnation?'

He'd asked himself the same hypothetical question after that lunch with Random, and the answer was dead simple – as well as very much to the point he'd just been making. He told Alastair, 'I'd be CO of a brand-new submarine – called

Tracker – and I'd feel damn proud, that's what. As well as flabbergasted – as a first command, a new "T"?'

He told me, fifty years later – departing from his notes at this point – 'As it happened, my first command was one of the old "H" boats. In the Portland flotilla, November of '38. I'd joined the perisher course in April – by which time Diana'd got back to England. She'd stayed an extra month on account of her mother, who'd died at about the time she'd originally intended to come back. Anyway – there I was at Portland, Lieutenant-in-Command of this old "H", and I still had her when the balloon went up – September '39. I was a two-and-a-half by then – a real one, promotion had come through in February. We spent most of our time patrolling off the Dutch coast, in those first months of the war. Pretty foul winter that was, too, as I remember it. There were six – no seven – boats in the flotilla—'

I'd switched off the recorder.

'What are you doing?'

'You've skipped two years. Christmas '37 at Glendarragh: next breath you're on patrol off the Dutch coast, Christmas '39.'

He spread his hands, sighed. 'Sorry.'

'Back to Glendarragh, then?'

'Well – hang on a minute. Re my first command – and so forth, *all* that period really – I don't think we'll need to go into it – do you?'

'Perhaps not. But—'

'I certainly don't want to go on about *my* war. No inclination to, for one thing, and for another it seems to me irrelevant – isn't it?'

'Largely, I suppose . . . But *some*, we'll need.'

'Just bare bones, then. Bare facts. Cover them in a line or two. In fact you probably know as much as you'll need about that side of it.'

I nodded. 'I dare say. Save us time, anyway, that *is* a point.

But let's get back to Glendarragh now? Guy hadn't written, you and Suzie were worried about him, and the news was getting out about *Trumpeter* being rebuilt.' I switched the tape on. Chalk was thinking about it: his eyes were on the sea, the streaks and whorls of colour that changed with tidal streams and depths, and the ceaseless advance and retreat of blue water breaking white and melting back to blue again around the headland and the island out there in the middle.

Hypnotic – if you let it be.

He'd turned back.

'At lunch – Christmas Day – the great-aunt made an announcement that staggered everyone. Suzie in particular. Well – for "staggered", read "delighted" . . . But she was an original, that old bird. She'd said, to start with, why did we have to have damn turkey? She could get that at home in Yorkshire. This was Scotland – why not haggis, for God's sake?'

'And the announcement?'

A nod, and a slight frown. But we *had* been wasting time . . .

'She started by asking Suzie whether she'd noticed that she hadn't brought her a Christmas present. Suzie did a good job of looking surprised, and said no, she *hadn't* noticed.'

'"You're fibbing, Suzie." The old girl wagged a finger at her. "And I'll tell you why you didn't have anything from me under the damn tree. It's because I couldn't easily have dragged a red-and-white striped Puss Moth into this house. It's at Buxton – Derbyshire, that is. Not quite new but it's been very thoroughly checked over. Better arrange for your instructor to fly down there with you. And when you're safe with it you can take *me* up for a flight. In the Spring, perhaps, you could fetch me and bring me up here for a day or two – bore you all stiff again, then you could fly me home. You need to get in all the hours you can, you said—"'

'She hadn't given Suzie or anyone else any chance of getting a word in, but Suzie jumped up, dashed round the table and hugged her – tears streaming, she could hardly speak. And so *lovely* – I can see her now – I suppose not as she was just at that moment, all floppy dark hair and tears, but soon after – absolutely radiant. Like another of those snapshots printed on what's left of a brain: because I also remember what came into my thoughts then – recollection of the sharp reminder I'd had to give myself a few weeks earlier, to the effect that *I* wasn't Dymock's rival, Guy was.'

He was stuffing his pipe again. 'Had a long talk with her, at some stage. During that weekend, I mean. The other thought had been simply – an aberration. I was committed to Diana – totally. Even if she had *not* put her brand on me. Incidentally, if that had been her intention she'd certainly known what she was doing. Known *me*, you see. And I had this dream of Guy and Suzie patching it up and making a new start. I told her so – probably rather indirectly, Dymock must still have been very much in her mind, Guy more like an absent brother of whom she was extremely fond. That's the word for it – *fond*. I asked her – effectively – to give it time, give him a chance. After what she'd been through – and what he was most likely going through – in due course, not to forget how they *had* felt about each other – and so forth.'

'How did she react?'

'Well, he hadn't answered the two letters she'd sent him. Not even after *Trumpeter* had gone down and she'd managed to get herself into a state where she could hold a pen and make legible marks on paper. All I could say was – that same thing, give him time: and try to make allowances. If he hadn't been nuts about her he wouldn't have taken it so hard – etcetera. I was quite deeply concerned for them both: hard to explain, but as if they were two halves of one person – even if *they* didn't know it. I personally didn't come into the equation at all – I want to have that made clear.'

'It will be.'

A nod. 'But she had news for me too. Diana had told her

– they'd exchanged several letters – that she'd had expressions of firm interest from the Air Survey company with whom she'd been hoping to get a full-time job. And if Suzie could get her "B" licence and put in the required number of flying hours, she might be able to get her into it too. The exciting thing for Suzie now, you see, was that having her own 'plane would make it much easier to clock up the hours. I'm not sure of the figure, but I think it may have been 2,500 she had to have in her logbook. Or perhaps that was what she needed for the "B" licence. Don't remember. But thanks to the old girl it was all within her reach, and she was – you might say, treading on air. I could see her mind going back to the other thing from time to time – or to worrying about Guy perhaps – she'd have her quiet, reclusive periods . . .'

He'd fallen silent, gazing at the sea again . . . Then – abruptly – 'This business about Zoe now. Odd, really. I'd effectively put her out of mind – four months back, roughly, barely given her a thought since – and it was Sir Innes and his wife who as it were dug her up again . . .'

Before lunch on Boxing Day, this was. It was a Sunday and they'd all been to church. Suzie had been right in that forecast – midnight service on Christmas Eve – to which Chalk had not gone – then a Christmas morning service, and today back on their knees yet again. Chalk telling himself *When in Rome* . . . He was looking forward to a long walk through the snow that afternoon, in company with Patricia, Suzie, Midge, Alastair and the other young soldier, Forbes, and of course all the dogs.

Sir Innes began it. 'That Mrs – er – Buchanan . . . Last time you left us you were going to pay her a visit, weren't you. Some messages from her husband—' glancing round, seeing that Suzie was not in earshot, not even in the room – 'who'd drowned in *Trumpeter*?' Chalk had nodded: Sir Innes asked him, 'Painful interview, was it?'

'Not too bad. I was only there about ten minutes. At

Helensburgh, their house is – or was, I imagine she'll have got rid of it by now.'

'Pretty woman, eh?'

'Who are we talking about?'

'Lady C-G . . .' Sir Innes put down an empty glass. 'That fellow Buchanan – came here to shoot, once – with a rather striking-looking wife in tow?'

'*You* were struck, I remember . . . But didn't Spynie's boy bring them?'

'That was what I was about to tell Rufus. You mentioned him before, Rufus – no, *I* did. Couldn't think why we'd had him here. And that's the answer – it came to me when I was talking to old Spynie the other day.'

'Spynie?'

'George Lindsay's father. *Lord* Spynie. Vast place in the Borders. Rich as Croesus – put a lot of money into various industrial concerns, doesn't know the first thing about it himself so he employs various hard-headed business chaps – such as Buchanan – to keep the wheels turning as they should. And that's the answer. Spynie was a close friend of my oldest brother, who was about ten years my senior and younger than him by as much as another ten. Telling you that just to give you an idea of his vintage. But I saw him in Edinburgh – as I say, about a week ago – in a club we belong to. Lives in a wheelchair now, and looks as if he could be Aunt Mary's uncle.'

'Heavens.' The great-aunt had joined them. 'Are you talking about Methuselah?'

'No. Spynie.'

'Oh, *that* old codger. What about him?'

'Telling Rufus here about a man who worked for him. Where'd I got to . . . Oh, yes. He mentioned him – Spynie did – in connection with the *Trumpeter* disaster. He more or less owns Barlows', you see, put Buchanan in to lick its finances into shape. That's why we had him here – Spynie asked me if I'd introduce him to a few mutual friends, we had this shooting party coming up and Lindsay was coming that weekend anyway. So he brought 'em along. And that's your answer, Rufus. Pleasant-enough chap, wasn't he?'

'Very.'

'Couldn't shoot for toffee, I remember.'

'Who couldn't?' Patricia had drifted in. Her great-aunt told her, 'Somebody called Buchanan.'

'Oh, the one with the tarty wife?'

'You, my dear—' Sir Innes reminded his wife – 'were scheming to throw Patricia at George Lindsay – or vice versa?'

'*What* a good idea.' The great-aunt held out an empty glass. 'This seems to have evaporated . . . If you could put up with him, Patricia – heavens, you'd be Lady Spynie before long, and quite *disgustingly* rich!'

'*Couldn't* put up with him.' Patricia shuddered. 'And I *hate* that name.'

'One of the oldest baronies in Scotland.' Sir Innes turned back to Chalk. 'I was going to say, George Lindsay's been in America for several years now. His father packed him off to look after interests they have there. He must have been over here on a visit to the old boy – and Eve saw her chance.' He winked. 'Speed of a striking cobra, eh?'

'I may have considered it as a remote possibility. Why shouldn't I? But as it turned out, he and Mrs Buchanan took a *great* shine to each other. D'you remember that, Innes?'

He sighed. 'You're getting it wrong again. They'd known each other long, *long* before that weekend. They arrived together, in one car. Remember that? Look – Buchanan had worked for George's father – that company of his – for quite a few years, George was also in the business—'

'He looks like a pig.' Patricia told her great-aunt, 'Mrs Buchanan is *more* than welcome to him.'

'It seemed to me,' Chalk told me – with his back to the sea now, pipe filled but unlit in his hand – 'that this provided the key to understanding Zoe's strange behaviour. She and this Lindsay had known each other for years and were on terms of – well, enough for it to have been obvious to all and sundry that there was something going on between them. I asked Sir Innes later, when we were on our own, what about her husband, didn't he object at all, and Sir Innes said no, either didn't notice or acted as if he didn't. I'd give him the benefit of the doubt, say he *didn't* know what was going on. And to become the wife of one of the richest men in the land – I could well see Zoe going for *that*. But old Spynie rode George on a tight rein – Sir Innes told me – and he was very straight-laced indeed, wouldn't for a moment have tolerated his son's involvement in a messy divorce case. Could he have disinherited him, I asked, and the answer was probably not, but he *might* have been able to isolate him from the business – which is where all the money comes from. It was what we'd call a group, nowadays, a conglomerate controlled by the holding company, and he might perhaps have seen to it that George didn't get a foot in that door. Fired him from whatever his job was, and appointed other relations – or employees, Buchanan types – to control it. Something like that. So they'd have been waiting for the old boy to drop off the perch, you see. Meanwhile George was in the States – except for occasional visits, presumably – and we've no reason to believe that Zoe was actually in love with him, have we? She had her own tastes and proclivities, though, and she'd no doubt want to keep her hand in – didn't for some reason hit it off with her husband – and that's where chaps like Dymock and I might have come in – fairly rootless, unencumbered, tending to be here one day and gone the next – d'you see?'

'Why the recent brush-off?'

'If you'd had time to think it out, you wouldn't have to ask. Her husband was dead, she'd become a widow, so the door would be open – no divorce case necessary. Might wait for the old boy to expire, might not, but either way she'd have to go straight at least until she had Lindsay in the bag. So she wouldn't have wanted the likes of me around. Get it?'

I nodded. The recorder humming faintly to itself . . .

'Anything later to confirm this theory? Or have we finished with her now?'

'Not *quite* finished.' He smiled. 'But – for the time being . . .'

It was necessary to press on, anyway.

'So – you'd have gone back to London, to the Tribunal of Inquiry and your Admiralty desk-job. Oh, New Year first, I suppose . . . Was there a letter on the mat from Guy?'

'No.' He stooped to rub the setter's ears. 'No, there was not.'

Chapter 15

He telephoned Glendarragh to tell Suzie that no letter had arrived – she'd asked him to let her know either way – but Lady C-G told him she'd flown down to Buxton to collect her Puss Moth, and Patricia had gone with her. He left the message for her – no letter *yet* . . .

There still wasn't one when he came back from Betty's on the Sunday after New Year's Day. It had been a sombre opening to 1938: fairly acute concern for Guy, by this time, and the start of a year in which war with Germany looked like an odds-on bet.

The Tribunal of Inquiry ended in the third week of January. In that period he had several calls from Suzie – worrying about Guy and raving about her aeroplane – and he took Patricia out several times, in and around London. He was thinking at first that he wouldn't mention this at all to Diana, who'd seemed to have unjustified sensitivities in that area, but he decided it would be better to tell her – casually, as something to be taken for granted – because otherwise Suzie might let it slip out in one of her letters, and then there *would* be problems. As it was, Diana wrote: *I'm glad you see Patricia now and then – at least she's the devil one knows! Very nice too – as devils go – and most attractive. Do you get any fascinating Foreign Office gossip from her? I'm sure there's a lot going on behind the scenes that we never hear about. Give her my love when you see her next – and while you're at it, ask her if she'd like to be Matron of Honour at our wedding in the summer?*

Early in February, Hitler appointed himself Minister for War; on the 15th, Franco's forces reoccupied Teruel; and on the 20th, Anthony Eden resigned as Foreign Minister. Lord Halifax took over from him. In the Commons, Winston Churchill was leading an outcry against Chamberlain and his Appeasement policy; Eden's resignation had been partly in protest against it, too, but – Patricia told Chalk over a Sunday lunch at Skindles – more because policy decisions had been taken behind his back. Halifax's visit to Hitler, for instance, when Eden had been advocating closer liaison with President Roosevelt – to deter Hitler rather than grovel to him. Whether American support would have been forthcoming was a matter of opinion; Chamberlain thought not, that a recent proposal by Roosevelt to stage a world conference to solve all current problems didn't indicate any readiness to line up against the dictators. So in his view playing the American card would have amounted to playing a busted flush. Despite Flanagan and Allen singing – in their Crazy Gang show *The Little Dog Laughed*, at the Palladium – *How can he be a dud, Or a stick-in-the-mud, When he's Franklin D. Roosevelt Jones?*

Chalk took Patricia to see it. That morning he'd received official confirmation of his appointment to the COQC starting in April; so their date turned out to be a celebration. He was to be relieved in the Operations Division in mid-March, and would be on leave then until the course started.

She asked him at supper after the show, 'Diana'll be back by then, won't she?'

'Depends on her mother's state of health. Calling a spade a spade, whether she's still alive or not.'

'If she's *not* back, what d'you think you'll do?'

'Don't know. Haven't had time to think about it.'

'Well – do bear in mind that the parents would love to have you at Glendarragh.'

'What good taste they show.'

'*Don't* they. Suzie and I have brought them up quite well, I admit.'

'Would you be there?'

'Might get a few days off, I suppose.'

'Not worth it, just for that. Make it a week. Better still, a fortnight.'

Perhaps, he wondered, kissing her goodnight, Diana's instincts were sharper than his own?

He was shaving next morning when he heard the post pushed through the door. Riffling through it – soap on his face, still – he found the letter he'd been waiting for. Dreading, but in his heart of hearts knowing it would be on its way.

A creased, rather dirty envelope, with the only legible cyphers in the postmark – across a Spanish stamp – showing the year of despatch as 1937. Minimally two months in transit, therefore – the period during which one had not heard from Guy. He was hollow with certainty now, with dread.

Dear Commander Chalk,

My name is Gerald Oakes, and I have been fighting alongside your brother Guy for the past six or seven months. I cannot tell you how much it pains me to have to tell you that Guy was killed yesterday in the fighting for a place called Teruel. He was shot in the head, so died instantly, I'm sure couldn't have known a thing about it.

Kneeling, the letter crumpled in his hands, picturing Guy as he'd seen him last – in Glasgow, boarding the London train, looking back over his shoulder – that lop-sided, boyish grin . . .

Trying to read more: smoothing out the cheap, rough paper, seeing it through tears now.

I would like to tell you how bad I feel about him getting killed, how I and others as well in this platoon will miss him and his comradeship and what a lot we all thought of him. He was like my *brother – if this had not happened I guess we would have stayed friends all our lives. Maybe that says it. It can be no real help, I know, I am writing partly because we had an understanding that we would do this for each other if such a thing did happen, but also because I sincerely want to tell you that you are not alone in—*

He'd never been so alone in his life. Hadn't guessed what total loneliness could be like, what grief was like. If Mrs Eason had felt anything like this, he thought, he hadn't offered her one hundredth of the sympathy and comfort he should have. Probably no-one could. You tried to make it not true – it hadn't happened, none of this existed – but it did, and he'd sooner have been dead himself. Fleeting recollection of an earlier thought – that it was those left behind who suffered most. Not that one had sympathy to spare for oneself: only awareness of the hitherto unsuspected depths of sorrow. He couldn't see properly, barely recognized the noises he was making as emanating from himself, but he was fumbling through the telephone book looking for the name Eason. Somewhere in south London, she'd been going. Might not be there now, obviously, but – Christ, hundreds of them. Whole columns. And as likely as not she'd have been going to her own family, not his. Telephone-book paper was absorbent, the pages of names starting with the letters EA were blotched with his tears, soaked right through. He had to get dressed. Or ring, tell them he was sick? They wouldn't be there yet, though.

Told you not to go. Argued all bloody night, but you're so damned obstinate . . .

Dressing, it felt wrong to be performing tasks as he'd performed them before he'd read that letter – which was dated – going back to it and smoothing the damp, smudged paper out again – 23 December. He'd travelled to Scotland that night. Guy had been dead and he hadn't known it: had at times lost sleep over the uncertainty but hadn't really, deep-down, accepted that it could happen – could *have happened* ... He'd slept well on the train, he remembered: while Guy had been lying dead. Rhythm of the train's wheels – if he'd had ears to hear – *Guy's lying dead, Guy's lying dead, Guy's lying dead...*

Actually, he wasn't. The bullet had, as it were, created a corpse – probably one of hundreds – but Guy himself was here – everywhere.

Always would be, he thought. Always will be.

He went to work. Having thought of telephoning to tell Suzie but deciding to leave it until this evening: partly from a dread of finding himself incapable of coherent speech when she came on the line. He'd looked at the letter yet again – to make sure of that date, as it seemed unlikely that it could have taken so long to come through. But there it was, 23 December. He took it with him in his pocket: deadly as it was, it was a link to Guy. He wondered if it might have been in Gerald Oakes' pocket or pack and retrieved by some other companion when *he'd* been killed. But Oakes wouldn't have been carrying it with him all that time. Unless he'd been killed very soon after he'd written it and they hadn't searched him there and then. Or if only much later someone else thought of putting a stamp on it and posting it. But that didn't make sense either – the postmark, it had been posted before the end of the year. Oakes had supplied his home address anyway – in Toronto, Canada – so he could write to him or to the Oakes family – some time ... Taking the letter with him to his pointless, time-filling work at the Admiralty it occurred to him that if he'd fallen – or dived – under a bus it might have been found on yet *another* corpse: and the coroner might have accepted it as explanation, proof of intent. Traditionally it would have been a tram one dived under, but trams were being replaced by trolley-buses in

London at this time. He travelled on one, and got off in Trafalgar Square. Had he been in uniform this would have been a breach of King's Regulations and Admiralty Instructions: an officer in uniform was not permitted to travel on a bus or tram, or for that matter to carry a brown-paper parcel. But it was all right in a dark suit and bowler hat; and carrying the tightly-rolled umbrella was more or less *de rigueur*. Alighting in Trafalgar Square – in a cold northerly wind, litter scudding along the gutters – he had it hooked over his left arm, fingers of the right hand in his pocket in contact with the letter as if to guard it against pickpockets: a tall, spare man, red-haired, grim-faced, stepping on to the pavement after crossing Cockspur Street, telling himself again that it was true, inescapable, had to be faced up to *and lived with* – Guy had been shot dead, before Christmas.

And was now – presumably – under Spanish earth.

Having died for *what*, for Christ's sake?

Don't start on that. Didn't get you anywhere last time, and it was no more than academic now.

'Morning, sir!'

A uniformed pensioner, saluting. Genial, old-sailor's grin. Chalk put the handle of his umbrella to the rim of his bowler hat, murmured, 'Morning.'

Inaudible, probably. He cleared his throat loudly – by way of explanation, or apology – as he strode into the gloomy building, passing on his left the waiting-room in which Nelson had met the Duke of Wellington and signally failed to impress him. Error of judgement by his Grace, no reflection at all on Nelson.

Ring Suzie . . .

Tonight. Inflict it on her tonight.

She wasn't there, her mother told him. She was in Leicester. The Puss Moth had been overdue for an overhaul which was best done at some aircraft engineering establishment at Shoreham in Sussex. Of all places, she'd added: couldn't they have made it Land's End?

But they'd left yesterday, at about midday.

'They?'

'She took another girl with her, from the flying club. Well – we'd hardly have let her go alone. She telephoned from Leicester – oh, an hour and a half ago. To my great relief, as you can imagine. At least she'd had the *nous* to stop well before dark. But Rufus – they'll be flying on to this Shoreham place in the morning, and Suzie's planning to take the train up and spend a day or two with Patricia. Perhaps the weekend – depending on how long the overhaul's going to take, of course. If I were you I'd telephone Patricia tomorrow – no point *now*, I spoke to her an hour ago and she didn't even know Suzie was coming! That girl is *so* impetuous. Up and off – she said it was because the weather was right for it and might not be next week, but if you ask me getting the "A" licence has gone to her head!'

'She's got the "A" already?'

'Oh, yes! Just the other day – I'm amazed she hasn't told you! She did it in record time, apparently. And on this trip now you can be sure she'll be doing *all* the flying!'

'Is the other girl a pilot?'

'Far more experienced than Suzie is. But Suzie won't give her a look in – for one thing that machine's her pride and joy, she's obsessed with it, and for another – according to her – she needs to spend some vast number of hours flying it before she can qualify for her *next* licence, for heaven's sake!'

'The commercial one.'

'In even more record time, no doubt. The theory is that she'll then be paying her own way – doing what, don't ask me – and this makes it all a sound investment – less than it would cost Innes to put her through Varsity, is the reasoning. *Her* reasoning – and he seems to agree with it. Even though there was never any question of sending her to Varsity. He always *has* spoilt that child . . . Rufus, I should have asked

– have you had news – I mean, heard from—'

'Yes.' He let her hear it in his tone. 'Yes, I have.'

'Oh . . . Rufus, what—'

'The worst kind of news. Letter from a Canadian who's been with him all the time . . . I've got to break it to Suzie—'

'Oh. Oh, my *God* . . .' Her breathing was short, suddenly. 'And I've been – rattling on . . .'

She'd begun to cry.

'How – did this person say—'

'It was in the fighting for a place called Teruel, and he was shot in the head. In December. The letter was written two months ago, God knows where it's been since.'

'Would you like to come here, Rufus? They'd give you leave, wouldn't they?'

'Well – no. Thank you, but—'

'Are you all right? Are you – eating, sleeping?'

'I only had the letter this morning. Yes, I'm – eating. After a fashion. Look, I'll ring Patricia in the morning, and try to see Suzie when she arrives. Easier – to see her, I mean – rather than over the telephone.'

'Rufus, dear – my heart *aches* for you.' She was gasping again. 'Really – only just sinking in. Can't *believe* it. That lovely, *lovely* boy—'

'Yes.' Swallowing, holding himself together – just. 'Yes. I'll—' He'd been going to say he'd be in touch, but he couldn't manage it. He murmured something like 'Goodbye', and hung up – with a flare of anger in his brain: what did *you* ever do to warn her off Dymock, or to discourage him?

24 February, this was. A Thursday. He'd marked it in his diary with the name 'GUY'. Pen-rings round it then, filling the page . . . He thought of leaving the 'phone off in case Lady C-G should think of calling back – or, more likely, Sir Innes embarrassedly 'offering condolences'. Or even Patricia, still

not knowing how the world had changed, ringing for a chat or to thank him for last night. But he had to chance it, because Suzie might ring. Being comparatively close – Leicester a lot nearer than Glendarragh – it wasn't unlikely that she would, to ask yet again – routinely, it had become by this time – whether there'd been any news.

He wished there hadn't been.

His own doing, though, no-one else's. *He'd* taken Dymock up there. That was the root of it. If he hadn't, Guy wouldn't have gone to Spain. *And* he'd failed him by not using the right arguments: arguing about politics instead of begging him, 'Please, *please* don't go . . .' But introducing Dymock, of whose reputation as a womanizer he'd been aware, was what had culminated in Guy's death.

He made himself ring Betty. Luckily Dick Traill answered the 'phone and he was able to warn him that there'd been dreadful news, so Betty had that much time to steel herself, had opened her end of the conversation with a terse 'About Guy, is it?'

He promised to go down there at the weekend and bring the Canadian's letter with him. And they agreed that their mother didn't have to be told. When they'd visited her together a week ago she hadn't known who they were, but her mental condition fluctuated and she sometimes did remember things for short periods. There was simply no point.

He didn't expect to sleep. In Diana's bed with the bedside lamp on and Guy's snapshot-portrait turned so he could see it, thoughts and memories milling around non-stop. Clutching at memories rather as when you were drowning you were supposed to clutch at straws.

There was a lot of the drowning sensation. Shortness of breath, and a racing heartbeat.

He'd told Betty yes, he'd go to church with her on Sunday. She was devout, believed in all of it: he was not and *could* not, only went through the motions when he had to. Which in the Royal Navy was – routine . . . Guy had been like him in that too, though. He wondered whether if they'd shared Betty's faith – 'faith' was the key word with her, she'd argued on occasion, 'You don't need logic. Logic's only the best the human mind can come up with, it doesn't come into this' – whether if they'd been able to share that faith Guy might still have been alive, the letter on the doormat this morning from him instead of from his Canadian friend, its message 'I'm coming home, I'm on my way!'

Dreams came and went. Waking, having dropped off for a while, it felt as if he'd turned his back on his brother – let go of him, let him slip away . . .

He heard Big Ben strike midnight. He'd have thought it was more like two or three. He'd probably been sleeping for only a few minutes at a time. And he'd turned in soon after making his call to Betty, which must have been before ten – he wouldn't have called later, risked waking them all up.

He double-checked the time by his wristwatch, which was on the bedside table beside Guy's portrait. Guy in his cricket gear, grinning rather goofily at the camera. Happy.

How had he been feeling when the bullet hit him, he wondered. On the point of success – taking Teruel after weeks of fighting – he might have been in *that* state of mind, more or less – grinning, as he looked round at Oakes?

He'd dozed off again, and the doorbell rang.

Like an electric shock, startling him out of half-sleep into reacting with – for a split second, his pulses racing – *Guy*?

Confusion stemming from some dream. It was *all* dream-like, disorientating, and he was still only half awake – enough to begin to feel sick again as the long day's misery closed in around him – crushing, suffocating: the bell's second peal came as a lifeline to be snatched at.

Hurrying, climbing out of the bed: he lurched barefoot out into the hall and fumbled at the door.

'Rufus – I'm sorry if—'

'Suzie?'

This *had* to be a dream. He'd pulled the door wide open, though. '*Suzie?*'

White face, dark-rimmed eyes, that bruised look he'd seen once before. 'Mummy 'phoned me. I got on the last train. Then when I finally did get a cab he couldn't find this place.' She glanced round the landing behind her, then back to him: exhausted, almost swaying. 'May I come in – please?'

'Suzie, of *course*!'

Bewildering. Guy's girl – here, in his arms.

Holding her: holding each other. She in her slip, he in his pyjamas, the lamp still on. Clinging together, dozing intermittently – sometimes one of them asleep, sometimes both, murmuring together in the waking times between.

The other girl would be flying the Puss Moth down to Shoreham in the morning, she'd told him. Suzie wanted to spend the day here, with him.

'If you don't mind?'

'D'you *think* I'd mind?'

He'd telephone the Operations Division in the morning and tell them he was sick. They wouldn't doubt it – his boss had asked him yesterday if he was feeling as lousy as he looked. And Suzie would telephone Patricia, some time tomorrow – later *today* – telephone her mother too – and go round to Patricia's in the evening.

'As from Shoreham, you see.'

'What about the girl who's flying the 'plane down?'

'She'll be going to her brother, near Maidstone, and we'll rendezvous at Shoreham when the Moth's ready. It's a routine overhaul, nothing special, but all the servicing's been done there before, so—'

'How did you work this all out, so – instantly?'

'All I knew *instantly* was I had to get to you. Just sort of – instinct.'

'Thank God for it. You've saved my life.'

'I cost Guy his, though.'

'No. *Not* true.' He used one finger to lift a swathe of soft, dark hair back from her face. 'He would have gone out there in any case. He'd been dithering a bit, I know – and he told you he'd decided against it – but only for peace and quiet, stop us all from going on at him about it. By the end of the summer he'd have been back to it, I'm certain.'

'It's kind of you to say so, anyway.'

'Listen to me, now. He and I spent a whole night talking about it, with a bottle of Scotch between us, in my digs at Dunbarton. I was trying to persuade him not to go – used all the wrong arguments, incidentally – I've realized since that if I'd had a bit more gumption I might have got somewhere ...'

He told her about the wrong arguments he'd used: and Guy's fixed determination to go, reasons he'd given which had nothing at all to do with anything *she*'d done. He reminded her too, choosing his words carefully, that it had been Toby Dymock who'd swept her off her feet, not the other way about, and that it had been his own rashness that had brought Dymock to Glendarragh in the first place.

She thought about it.

Then: 'This may sound callous, or selfish, but – in a lot of ways I can't regret anything – to do with Toby, I mean. Only the hurt to Guy and this ghastly end to it now. *Now*, if I could I'd undo *everything*, but—'

'But let me say this, Suzie. Said it before, some of it – I remember warning you, ages ago – seems ages, anyway – that Toby made a habit of chasing girls. I knew it, and still took him up to Glendarragh with me. Makes me very much to blame – much more than you. You didn't know anything about it, it just – hit you. However you felt about him eventually, he went for you bull-headed – and he was older, far more experienced – when you had *no* experience—'

'Still haven't.'

'I mean emotionally. *Emotionally*, you hadn't.'

'Well, that's true, I hadn't. *Now* I have – quite a lot, really. And whatever you say, Rufus, I hurt Guy appallingly – unforgivably. And we'd been so *close*. Rufus, what I said just now, that I can't regret having known Toby and loved him – that's absolutely true. But I didn't know what I was doing to Guy – didn't have the least idea. If I *had* had – or if I could put the clock back and start again, I wouldn't let myself *look* at Toby. I'd hang on to Guy, wouldn't think about Toby or let him talk to me or – I'm gabbling, I'm sorry—'

'Gabble all you like. I was gabbling to myself, before you came. Thank *God* you did. You're a very sweet, kind person, Suzie. It's true you hurt him, no point denying it, but you didn't *mean* to, in a way you were as much a victim as he was. That's how I see it – and I've thought about it a lot, believe me.'

'If I were you, I'd hate me.'

'Hate? Hate *you*?'

'Fine one to talk about being kind . . .'

He craned down, to kiss her wet eyes. 'You *have* saved my life. Sanity, anyway. I've been – maudlin . . . Really. And I'm supposed to be stern, self-contained—'

'You?'

'– pompous, even. Didn't you ever hear that?' She shook her head, the dark hair soft and scented. 'Thought Toby might have mentioned it. But I don't hate you, Suzie – I *love* you.'

'I love *you*. In the way I loved Guy, to start with – because you're so alike, I think inside you're probably identical – but the way I loved Toby too. *And*—'

'All that, and there's still an "and"?'

'Saying I love you. If you want me—'

'Suzie, wait. I was thinking about this when you were sleeping. For fairly obvious reasons. Any man *would*. It's not a question of *wanting*. Well – it *is*. I'm male, you're an exceptionally attractive female, of *course* I'd "want". But first – well, to me you're Guy's girl. And – here's another thing I was thinking about earlier in the night – my feelings for Guy were to some extent paternal, not just brotherly. We lost our father when I was a small boy and Guy was a babe in arms, he never knew a father and there I was – big brother, in Daddy's shoes. I'm talking about when he was little, of course. But it rubbed off on both of us and it's probably what makes me see things – well, from an *older* viewpoint. Hence that reputation I have, probably. And when I look at you – as Guy's girl – I suppose a good part of my resentment of Toby Dymock sprang from the feeling he'd no damn business stealing girls from kids.'

'I am *not* a kid!'

'Did I say you were?'

'By implication, yes. And I'd have you know I was eighteen in December – the fourteenth – which incidentally you ignored—'

'I didn't *know*!'

'I realized that. I'd only thought Patricia might have told you. You see rather a lot of her, don't you?'

'Now you sound like Diana.'

'*Really?* Is she jealous of Pat?'

He shook his head. 'Just suspicious. For no reason whatsoever.'

'No smoke without fire, is there? I suppose I *am* too young for you ... Rufus, listen. What you said about Toby chasing girls and so forth – I knew about it, he admitted it. But with us it wasn't like that – he was in love with me, and I was with him, and that's the truth.'

'All right.'

'You don't believe it, do you.'

'I believe *you* believe it.'

'You still don't.'

'I know it didn't start that way. You fell for him while he was just amusing himself. But if that's how it was by the time – by the end of it – all right, I take your word for it . . . How about we try to get some sleep now?'

They were awake in the dawn again: still in each other's arms, Suzie warm and limp with sleep. Delicious, as well as frustrating – by his own resolve, which he suspected he might one day look back on and regret. Guy being dead was the same, the darkness he woke up into, but there was Suzie's *still* slightly astonishing presence as a counter-weight. She murmured – as if there hadn't been a couple of hours' interval, and surprising him because he hadn't realized she was awake – 'There's another side to this, isn't there. Diana.'

'I was on the point of mentioning her, once or twice.'

'She *is* another reason, isn't she?'

'Of *course* she is, my darling.'

'Call me that again?'

'Darling?'

She moved against him.

'I wouldn't make any claims on you. I promise. Apart from the fact you're going to marry her, she's been absolutely wonderful to me, over this flying business.'

'I know. Typical of her. She's a very practical sort of girl – doesn't just say things, she does them . . . Has she told you we're getting married in the summer?'

'No—'

'According to her, we are. Which probably clinches it. But it's those other things as well, Suzie darling. The whole situation – you, me, her, Guy, Toby, and the emotional state we're both . . . I'd be taking advantage – this is what it comes down to, frankly – of Guy being dead.'

'But if I tell you *I* want—'

'I said – the state we're both in. But also, Suzie, it'd be what's known crudely as a one-night stand. In case you don't know, that's an Americanism meaning a sexual encounter sort of off the bat, leading nowhere. I don't want that with you, Suzie. I'd wish I hadn't, and you'd wish *you* hadn't. There's a bond between us, isn't there – let's not make it something we'd be ashamed of later? Suzie, I'll love you all my life: I do honestly adore you. But I'll be married to Diana – I'm committed to her – and you'll be married to someone else – someone who'll sweep you off your feet like Toby did – and to me you'll still be Guy's girl. Can I be godfather to your children?'

'I can think of something a lot better.'

'So can I. Easily. And technically speaking I'd make a rotten godfather, I admit. But – practicalities, now. To start with, what shopping I'll need to do. We're all right for breakfast – eggs, coffee, bread – but there's lunch to think of. What about tinned ravioli?'

'I must say we were fairly duplicitous.' Chalk told me, on his Glandore terrace, 'With Patricia, for instance. Suzie telephoned the cousins' house and invited herself to stay for the weekend, leaving a message for Patricia that she'd be coming up from Shoreham later, and Patricia 'phoned me at about six, having had that message but also having heard from her mother about Guy. She was as stricken as I'd been. But I was over the real depths of it by then – thanks to Suzie – and so was she. Suzie, I mean. That was all right – as far as Pat was concerned, she knew Suzie had known about it since the previous afternoon, and the sharp edges do wear off. One thing I had in mind was that if anyone had found reason to suspect we'd been together in the flat all that time, they'd *never* have believed the truth of it.'

'Did you spend that leave at Glendarragh?'

'Most of it. Patricia was there for a week. And Suzie, of course – when she wasn't flying. I remember it as a quiet, pleasant-enough interlude, despite the lingering sadness. Suzie took me up in her Puss Moth, one day. She was showing off to me, so it was *fairly* frightening. She was going hell for leather for her "B" licence – navigator's licence too, I think – but she got the "B" anyway before the end of the year and became a flying instructor in the Civil Air Guard. Would you believe it?'

'Civil Air Guard?'

'Started towards the end of '38. The government saw the value of flying clubs, and at that time they were in danger of wasting away. The RAF was expanding, and that plus the RAFVR and the Auxiliary Squadrons was siphoning off virtually all the potential pilots. Government therefore set up this scheme to subsidize pilot-training through the clubs. And of course they needed instructors. By the middle of '39, I remember Suzie telling me, there were 10,000 civilian pilots in training, and 4,000 had got their "A" licences. And – cutting this short, there was a lot of shilly-shallying *en route* – in 1939 the ATA, Air Transport Auxiliary, came into being. Providing pools of mostly male but some female ferry pilots, to deliver aircraft from factories to storage depots or even to operational squadrons, and the women's section was recruited initially from Civil Air Guard instructors. Of whom Suzie was one – with an enormous number of flying hours to her credit, I might tell you. They took her on in 1940.' He'd paused . . . 'Yes?'

'You've skipped two years again.'

'Well.' A shrug. Blue seascape behind him, mug of beer in the right hand, pipe in the other. 'We do need to get on with it, don't we?'

'Within reason, yes. But what's happened to everyone in the meantime? All right, so you're at sea – but I think we need to know where, and roughly what you're up to. And Suzie's flying – but Diana, Patricia, Alastair – Zoe, even?'

'Needn't waste time on Zoe.'

'All right. But the others?'

'I did mention Patricia just now. And Diana, like Suzie, was in the ATA. I didn't see as much of her as I'd have liked, one way and another. Alastair – well, by about the end of '40 he'd have been either in the Western Desert or on his way out to it. Italy had come in against us in June, you'll remember . . . Look, I'll stick to Suzie for the moment, if I may. Early 1940, she was a Second Officer in the ATA – absolutely rotten pay, I think it was about £240 a year, out of which they had to pay for their own lodgings – but the great thing was that she was flying – was therefore happy. As well as doing an essential job. Those girls flew everything – Spitfires, Seafires, Hurricanes, Beaufighters, Wellingtons – even four-engined bombers – Lancasters, Stirlings, Liberators – when they'd qualified. Most of them started with such things as Tiger Moths, and gradually upgraded, were sent on "conversion" courses – at White Waltham, I think. I don't think more than about a dozen out of perhaps a couple of hundred women pilots got as far as the four-engined jobs. But they had their own flight engineers, too, all-girl crews.

'I went to an ATA party at White Waltham once. It was in a cottage which three or four girls including Suzie were renting, close to the airfield. The guests were mostly ATA personnel, male and female, and most of us brought bottles of this or that. In my own case, of course, duty free. I was actually Diana's guest – she was a First Officer, at that time. *And* the most beautiful girl present, let me tell you.'

'More so than Suzie?'

He frowned, thinking about it. Perhaps summoning up images of them, from those distant times and scenes. Then he told me, 'They were opposites, Suzie *petite* and dark, Diana tall and blonde. Well – in the beholder's eye, isn't it? Mine sort of took 'em all in, in those days. And I wasn't quite as saintly as your impression might be, from that Suzie interlude. Those were very special circumstances: I'd have been a shit, frankly, if I'd taken any other line. Or at any rate weak – stupid . . . But this party, now. I happened to be on leave – in London, intentionally a very brief visit – Gieves, and my bank – because the all-night bombing raids had started and I didn't see much point in hanging around. Diana came up, we had a meal and she took me down to White Waltham in her car. It was a Vauxhall Ten Four, I remember, silver-grey with black mudguards. Several of them had their own cars, for getting to and fro. Air Force petrol, I suppose. This must have been – oh, late '40. It was several months after Dunkirk, anyway. I *think* . . . Yes, it was: Patricia had recently done her first disappearing act – she'd joined SIS, you see, Secret Intelligence Service. The Battle of Britain had been fought – and won – and the Germans had given up trying to flatten the fighter bases, turned all the heat on London. *Didn't* they, just. September had been bad, but October was worse. Later we bombed *their* cities, and they seem to think we shouldn't have, but by God they'd taught us how to set about it, hadn't they? The Luftwaffe were out to kill and terrorize civilians, too, the idea was to demoralize us, frighten us into surrendering. There was a particularly frightful week of all-night raids just at that time. I left Diana down in Surrey after the party, went back up to London by train, and I got out of the place again damn quick, believe me. Spent a few days with Betty – she was heavily pregnant again at that time, old Dick had done his bit and flown the coop again – he was a Gunner – then I collected *Tumult* and took her out on patrol – from Blockhouse, but we wound up back in Dundee. I was no stranger to the place, having been based there all through the Norwegian *fracas*. Commanding *Slayer* then, not *Tumult*.' He held up a finger, seeing me on the point of interrupting: 'This sets the date, you see – late October of 1940. Incidentally, Betty had her second child – a girl – early in December.'

'I take it you were married to Diana by then?'

'Of course I was!'

'All right. But the last mention of it was you were planning to marry in the summer of '38. We're now in the autumn of '40.'

He nodded. 'I'll go back in a minute. Although there isn't a lot that's particularly relevant. Anyway, I'll tell you about this ATA party first – which is *highly* relevant . . . As I said, I went down with Diana, who'd told me Suzie had asked her to bring me if she possibly could. It was sheer luck – as I've said, I wasn't seeing much of Diana by that time. Never did, in fact, once the war started. Not a lot of leave – a hell of a lot of sea-time – and for her, almost constant flying. They really were kept at it. The excuse for this party, for instance, was that two of Suzie's house-mates shared a birthday, but the arrangements must have been very hit-or-miss, none of 'em could be certain where they'd be from one day to another. As often as not they'd be what they called "stuck out" – in other words stuck for the night at some way-out place, having delivered a Spitfire to this airfield or a Mosquito to that . . . I think Suzie was starting a leave-period that day, so she'd known *she*'d be there. As for me, I was driving *Tumult* and I'd parked her in the dockyard at Chatham to have an Oerlikon platform built on. She was a Chatham-built boat; and of course all the new T's were getting Oerlikon platforms as standard by that time. None too soon either. Anyway – there was Suzie, and there as her special guest was my own third hand and navigating officer, Chris Van Sommeren. I'd introduced them. We'd been at Blockhouse earlier in the summer when Suzie'd been based in the ATA ferry pool at Hamble, and she and another girl came over to see us. I'd only had *Tumult* a few weeks and it rather piqued me that Suzie hadn't wanted to see over her. Her chum did, I showed *her* round while Suzie waited on the jetty. With Chris, probably. But we showed them Blockhouse – for as much as *that* was worth – and had an evening out in Southsea, and I drove them home. Still had my car, kept it at Betty's mostly . . . Anyway – the relevance of all this is that young Van Sommeren was there. Suzie had wanted to surprise me, so she'd told him not to let me know he would be.'

'You say he was your navigator then?'

'This is the point, really. My Number One was Billy Davenport, but he was going for his COQC – I'd only just heard this – and I'd decided to give his job to Chris Van

Sommeren and take on a new pilot. Chris was about due for a first-lieutenancy, and he was a very competent young submariner as well as an extremely nice chap. I didn't want to lose him – would have, he'd have been pinched for a first lieutenant's job elsewhere if I hadn't hung on to him. So – they'd surprised me, but I was able to surprise *him*, too – made his evening for him in fact, by breaking this news to him there at the party.'

Chalk lit his pipe. Sitting on the wall still, scratching the setter's ribs with the toe of the kind of boot we used to call brothel-creepers.

'Before I leave this – at your behest – a word about Suzie and Chris. You're going to have to rearrange all this anyway, aren't you? – put it into some kind of sequence . . . Anyway, she told me – that night – that the last thing she'd have contemplated was ever to have become involved with another submariner. I'd hardly have expected it, either. The Dymock and *Trumpeter* business wasn't the sort of experience you'd shrug off, exactly – not in a lifetime. And for a seventeen-year-old girl in the trauma of her first love affair . . .'

He'd paused again, shaking his head. Then continued, 'The flying had provided some sort of anodyne to it. And I dare say the further hiatus of Guy's death had pushed it further into the background. In any case, she'd seen Chris a few times since that first meeting. It was obvious they'd both got it badly, the lengths they'd gone to just to spend an hour or two together here or there. I'd noticed that at sea he was interminably writing letters, and now I knew who to . . . And there it was – I'd done it again, and here she was with questions that had a strangely familiar ring to them – what did I think of him, etcetera. Did I think she was mad, or what?'

'You gave him a good reference, I imagine.'

'The best. He was twenty-two then – or just twenty-three – a couple of years older than her. He certainly wasn't any kind of Dymock either, he was as sound as a bell, and – well, she couldn't have fallen for a better man. Fallen for him, she admitted, against her will and "better judgement" – whatever that means. Submarines, she told us – me and Diana – gave her "the heeby-jeebies". She was putting it lightly, but she wasn't joking. The *Trumpeter* affair, plus her imagination – and by this time of course we'd lost a few boats, some of which must have been mentioned in the papers. In the past few months, losses I'd known of personally just here in home waters included *Spearfish*, *Shark*, *Salmon*, *Narwhal* and *Thames*. Three others in the brief Norwegian campaign. With all hands, incidentally. She couldn't have heard of more than one or two – I hoped – but she had this vision of men trapped and drowning, and an impression that the odds were stacked against us. I tried to convince her to the contrary: all right, in wartime submarines were lost, on occasion, but so were surface ships – and tanks – and aircraft fell out of the sky too, sometimes – what about *that*?

'She'd answered, "Don't worry – *mine* won't", and Diana had put a long arm around her: "Damn *right*, yours won't!"

'Before I leave this – here's another of those snapshots. Suzie and Van Sommeren dancing. He, if you remember, was fairish – brown eyes, though, light-brown hair, I suppose – and only about five-eight, five-nine. He was in uniform, of course – an RNVR lieutenant, two wavy stripes – and she was in a red dress that fitted her – in my perhaps somewhat prurient recall – like a second skin. She looked absolutely marvellous – the rich red of that dress, with her dark hair and summer-tanned complexion. And they looked darned good together – I can't tell you . . . We were dancing to gramophone records, of course, another of those old wind-up machines, and the song I remember clearly from that evening – as clearly as if I was hearing it now – was *Room Five Hundred and Four*. It was meaning something to them, too: you could see it. Well – she and I had had *our* room 504, hadn't we; and she'd left it in the same state as when she'd arrived – thanks to my damn principles. But it certainly wouldn't be like that with *those* two – anyone could see it wouldn't, and I thought my *God*, what a lucky bastard!'

Chapter 16

(The narration recorded in the following pages is a verbatim transcription from the tape. Chalk was speaking mostly from memory but from time to time consulting his own notes, especially on background historical events.)

'All right. The fill-in, now, *Recueillir pour mieux sauter*, as the Frogs say. My wedding, all that . . . But one more word about Suzie first, a point I don't think I've made effectively enough. Basically, why I'd behaved as I had, that night and day in London.

'The thing was, I knew it was vital to get it into her head that she was *not* responsible for Guy's death. You could argue the other way, obviously, but *my* argument was first the point I'd already made that it was Dymock, not her, who'd made the running and carried her along with him, and second that *nobody* – neither her nor anyone else – made Guy go to Spain. You can lose a girl or two without rushing off and putting yourself in the firing-line – eh? So for her to take the blame would have been crazy – also very damaging, when she was already having nightmares over her *Trumpeter* ordeal.'

'*Still* having them?'

'That leave I spent at Glendarragh in March – March of '38, right? – Patricia told me then that there were still – outcries and sobbing in the night. Not every night, but – often enough. In the flat in London she'd whimpered, asleep in my arms, and I'd put that down to the news of Guy having been killed. It may have been, may not. But to have allowed her to think she'd sent Guy to his death would have been callous in the extreme. And you see, she'd come to me full of this sense of guilt, and whether she knew it or not she might well have been offering herself to me in expiation. D'you see? That was how it felt – at the time, *and* since . . . And if I'd accepted it on that basis – even a suspicion of that as the basis – well, my God, what a mess. I doubt we'd ever have been able to look each other in the eye again. I didn't think it all through like that at the time. I wasn't in a state, myself, to think so analytically. I merely followed my instinct – as she had, in coming to me.'

'So – that covers *that*. Pressing on, now – Diana had originally been due back at the beginning of March, but she didn't make it until well into April, by which time I was on the perisher course. Her mother had died, and she'd stayed out there to – help her father, keep him company for the first few weeks, I suppose. They wanted her to start right away in the air survey job – which she did – and it turned out to be a lot better than the freelance flying had been. She worked more or less regular hours, and had her weekends free. I didn't – the COQC included some sea-time – but we got together whenever we could, weekends in London or down in Hampshire, two or three at Betty's. Oh, Dick Traill took rather a shine to her, that was it – and Betty wasn't too pleased, so – London or Hampshire, after that. Mostly at a pub in Fareham or the Queens Hotel in Southsea. Meanwhile the Germans had marched into Austria, and we had the first Czech crisis. It was only a matter of time, by then: and thank God we did have a little time; when it eventually came we were at least *half* ready for it.

'Diana and I were married at Caxton Hall – to Betty's disgust, in her view a registry office wedding didn't count – on 28 July, and honeymooned at Biarritz. That old daydream – but legitimate, not the dirty weekend I'd had in mind when I'd first suggested it... The wedding, though – guests included Suzie and Patricia – and Alastair, on leave from his regiment which was then in Ireland – and Betty, oddly enough, I think under pressure from her husband – and a bunch of submarine friends including the entire perisher course and George Random, our chief instructor. Suzie recognized the name, unfortunately, and froze solid for a while; Patricia saw it and got her over it. Patricia was bloody marvellous, one way and another. Always . . . But Suzie had every published detail of the *Trumpeter* disaster, including all the survivors' names, as it were stamped on her brain, and it wasn't possible not to introduce Random to her. Anyway – we had a reception at the Lansdowne Club, where Diana was a member, and she'd invited Amy Mollison – better known to the public as Amy Johnson. Her husband – Mollison – was a flyer too. In fact – no, never mind that. She was a chum of Diana's anyway – and Suzie was thrilled, of course. There was a lot of flying talk, because a Yank by the name of Howard Hughes, up till then unknown to any of us, had just flown round the world in some impressively short time. Under four days, I think, and it had taken Amy nineteen days to fly from England to Australia in 1930 – although she'd done London to Cape Town in six days more recently.

'Biarritz, then. We had a week or ten days, stayed at a very grand hotel, hired a car and drove up into the Pyrenees. I was aware of being only a couple of hundred miles north of where Guy's grave must have been, but that war was still going on, of course.

'Back in England, I watched Len Hutton knocking-up 364 runs against Australia at the Oval. And Germany mobilized that month, the French called up their reservists and

Chamberlain flew to see Hitler at Berchtesgaden. De-fusing the situation – temporarily – by giving Sudetenland to the bastards. It was the Nazis' toe in the door, of course, as far as the wretched Czechs were concerned: a few months later they marched into Bohemia and Moravia as well. At about the same time Madrid surrendered to Franco, ending the Spanish war. I know I've skipped again – but these are only cardinal points I'm filling in – all right?

'I'd finished the course, then, and taken command of an H-class submarine at Portland. Diana was working in her air survey job, Suzie was instructing in the Civil Air Guard, and Patricia had got a flat of her own, in Chelsea, not far from Diana's. Those cousins were kind but dreary people – I'd met them once or twice, just briefly – and in any case you can't live in someone else's house for ever. She'd have wanted her independence, too. I saw her now and then.

'What else – or next . . . Well, I'd heard that *Threat* had completed her trials and Ozzie Ozzard was taking her down to Portsmouth. Also that *Tracker*, formerly *Trumpeter*, had been launched – back in March, March of '38 – so *she*'d be just about on her acceptance trials by this time. I wasn't sorry that *I* wouldn't be on board, second time round.

'I was promoted, by the way, in March '39. I'd reverted to lieutenant when I'd left the job in London. But here I was now, a fully-fledged lieutenant-commander with my own command, a beautiful wife – beautiful *rich* wife – and a war coming at any minute. Chamberlain had bought a little time, that was all. It was at the end of March that we pledged support for Poland – and it was Poland we went to war over, of course, five months later.

'I got a new command at about this time. *Slayer*. A big step-up from the old H-class training boat. I had her just in time to take her down to Gib for that Spring's joint Home Fleet/Mediterranean Fleet exercises, so by the time we were back at Portland I'd shaken down pretty well and we were ready for the "off". In September, when it came, we were sent to Harwich – half a dozen of us, all "S" class, patrolling mostly around the Heligoland Bight and into the Skaggerak and its approaches. We had our successes. The French 10th Flotilla was working with us too, patrolling the Dutch coast while we worked further afield. As we've agreed, I'm not going into details of my own experiences, but *Slayer*'s score during this Harwich period was one U-boat, a minesweeper and two or three merchant ships – and in those months we'd barely heard a depthcharge.

'To keep all this in context, a few historical and other notes . . . A U-boat sank the carrier *Royal Oak* inside Scapa Flow in October, and the first magnetic mines were doing us a lot of damage – until our boffins got the hang of them . . . And the Russians invaded Finland. Hitler and Stalin had a non-aggression pact, of course. Then in December the *Graf Spee* scuttled herself off Montevideo after the Battle of the River Plate. I had a weekend leave at that time, and Diana persuaded me to take her to see *Gone With the Wind*. This was the heyday of such songs as *Roll Out the Barrel*, and *Hang Out the Washing on the Siegfried Line*. Remember? And that dance – so-called – the Lambeth Walk?

'April, the Germans invaded Norway and that campaign began, on shore and at sea. Fairly well bungled, on shore; but we weren't ready for it, were we, weren't equipped as we should have been. Ashore, that is, the Army. At sea – well, we – *Slayer* and the rest of our flotilla – were kept busy for a month or so. By the time the pongoes pulled out we'd lost *Thistle*, *Tarpon* and *Sterlet* in return for the cruiser *Karlsruhe* sunk, a couple of other warships and about twenty transports. Oh, and *Lutzow*, pocket-battleship so called, *Spearfish* blew her screws off and put her out of action for a year.

'So then – well, Norway was finished, and so was Chamberlain. Churchill took over. Early May, this was. The "blood and toil" speech. "Fight them on the beaches", etcetera – and the Dunkirk evacuation at the end of that month. Fighting on the beaches – invasion – did seem to be on the cards. Of more immediate importance to me, however, was that by this time *Slayer* had a defect list as long as your arm. She'd been worked hard for a long time before I got her, and she was clearly overdue for refit. This came to a head just at the time that *Tumult*'s CO went sick with tuberculosis, and having put *Slayer* into dockyard hands I was moved over to her. Early summer, then. Billy Davenport was *Tumult*'s first lieutenant – as I've already mentioned – and Chris Van Sommeren was our pilot. Weapons Officer was Don Sutherland, plumber Engineer Lieutenant "Stew" Tulloch. Dare say you'd have known Sutherland. No? I'd have thought you were contemporaries . . . Is this the right stuff I'm giving you?'

'It's fine. But the shoreside scene, in that summer of '40 – Suzie and Diana both in the ATA – obviously they were, the party you've described was only two or three months later, wasn't it? Was Alastair still in Ireland?'

'No, he was back, about then.'

'Patricia?'

'She was sometimes there – London – sometimes wasn't. I told you, I think, she was in SIS. I didn't know quite what that involved, at first. But she'd told me once – she'd been leaving London next morning and insisting on having an early night – told me she had a car coming early in the morning to take her to some place called Tempsford. It's near Sandy in Bedfordshire – I looked it up on the map, never having heard of it before, and when I mentioned it to Suzie – don't ask me when, but it was before that party, we knew more about such things by then – she was what's sometimes described as "visibly shaken", and told me under an oath of secrecy that something called the Special Duties Squadron operated from there, flying agents in and out of German-occupied France, in Lysanders. Which was – hair-raising. Patricia, of all people – who was so gentle, so entrancingly feminine. And with whom by that time I was in love. May not have known it – or I was suppressing it, I don't know . . . It made me feel ill, to think of her in that kind of situation – the hideously imaginable possibility of her falling into those revolting creatures' hands – feel small, too, knowing it'd take a cooler nerve than *I*'ve got, to take on that kind of work. But that's another thought, when one looks back – how everyone we knew, every real friend one had, was in it up to the neck one way or another . . . For instance – Alastair, you asked about. Well, I went for a weekend at Glendarragh – from Dundee, between patrols – and he was there, back from Ireland and soon off to North Africa. He took me stalking – something I'd never done before. Sir Innes had got himself a job connected with Army recruiting, by the way, and Lady C-G was running the estate – full-time job too, their factor had joined up. This can't have been long after I'd brought *Tumult* up to Dundee, which was shortly after the party I was telling you about. Reminds me – within hours of our arrival at Dundee, Chris had Suzie on the telephone, then rang her parents, and finally came to me with the formal request for permission to get married. I'd spoken to Suzie too, on the blower, and a couple of days later had a letter from her:

Chris tells me that he had to ask your permission! Could you have refused it, and stopped us? Rufus – seriously – I do *love him. We've decided, since you and I last spoke, that we'll try to have the wedding next spring or summer, summer probably – and if we can possibly manage it, at Glendarragh. We including you, Rufus – that's the purpose of this note, your presence will be absolutely essential . . .*

'Oh, and Chris told me that when he'd introduced himself to her father over the telephone and asked him for his younger daughter's hand in marriage, Sir Innes' response – after an explosive coughing-fit – was a wheezy "Good *God*!" Chris paid a quick visit to Glendarragh not long afterwards, though, and Suzie managed to be there too. She'd just been promoted to First Officer, incidentally.

Accelerated promotion: she'd done less than the time she should have as a Second Officer. Bucked as anything – you can imagine!

'Winter, then, with north Norway patrols back in vogue – despite rough seas and gale-force winds straight off the ice. Enough successes to make it worthwhile, I suppose. In the summer, of course, we couldn't operate very far north – around midsummer there was no darkness at all. We needed at least a few hours of darkness every night for charging batteries on the surface, and without the cover of darkness it would have been near enough suicidal. So in the summer months we concentrated on southern Norway, and the Skaggerak, the German Bight, etcetera. *Tumult*'s Jolly Roger was quite full by this time, in fact we seemed to be acquiring something of a reputation. I think we were the top scorers in the flotilla – which incidentally had by this time been joined by *Tracker* – and *Threat* too. *Threat* wasn't Ozzie Ozzard's any more, he'd taken a brand-new boat, *Tigress*, to the Mediterranean. But *Tracker*'s CO was an old friend, Johnny Mottram, and I went aboard her several times, lured partly by invitations to partake of gin – which was what we all drank, in those days – but also because – well, I had to, that's all. Everyone in the flotilla, let alone in *Tracker* herself, knew of her previous existence as *Trumpeter* and took it in their stride, so to speak, but on my visits I still got curious looks from chaps who knew I'd been sunk in her, perhaps wondered if I'd break out in a muck-sweat. To be honest, I wouldn't have been keen to take her on patrol. I still saw it all – Andrew Buchanan, for instance, and Nat Eason. And others. Dymock. Lots of them, when one opened one's mind to memory and let them in. I could look round – in *Tracker*'s wardroom, for instance, which although I knew she'd been totally rebuilt was still the same – and see them, hear them, expect *them* to hear me when I spoke. I'd be conscious of the fact I was sitting there, sipping gin-and-water, with their eyes on every gulp . . . Sounds fanciful, doesn't it? But in retrospect it *had* been a fairly gut-twisting experience.

'Anyway – I took *Tumult* out of Dundee for patrol on 31 May. Which of course was almost summer, and having made the point that we called a halt to Norwegian patrols at that time of year I have to contradict myself now. I'd been surprised, the day before, at being briefed for yet another trip up that way. Not in fact to the more distant north, only to latitude 61 degrees, not very far north of Bergen but right on the bulge, which made it something of a strategic area. Potential targets would be iron-ore carriers coming south from Narvik and having to emerge from cover – higher up, they used the inshore waters inside those chains of islands. Coming around that bulge they were often met by destroyer and/or air escorts, of course... But possibly the odd blockade-runner too, or even an ocean raider sneaking home to Krautland. And U-boats travelling on the surface between their German and Norwegian bases. In other words a potentially productive patrol area.'

'What about the daylight problem?'

'Wouldn't be all that bothersome, at that latitude and this early in the summer. There'd be no patrols any further north, we *were* stretching it a bit – but with that, mind you, came a hope that the enemy might think we'd finished for the season, feel safe and consequently get careless. There was a *bit* of a daylight problem, of course. I knew we'd have nights that would be only a few hours long; I'd surface into twilight, stay up only as long as was absolutely necessary, and while we were up there I'd stay in the bridge myself and the officer of the watch could concentrate on keeping her under constant helm. We'd also have to watch the sky – I'd have an extra lookout up for that alone. Anyway – we sailed from Dundee that last day of May, stopping *en route* at Lerwick in the Shetlands to top up with fresh water and provisions, and spent about a fortnight on the billet without seeing a bloody thing. Very disappointing. I'd been lucky,

I'd had very few blank patrols either in *Tumult* or in *Slayer* before her. I suppose I'd had more than my share of luck. It *was* frustrating, though – so much hard work for nothing. But our recall came – about the 17th or 18th, by which time the nights were getting noticeably shorter – and I wasn't sorry to be heading south. West-sou'-west actually – via Lerwick again, a couple of hundred miles away, then about 300 miles from there south to Dundee, on the surface all the way. Actually we couldn't have arranged it better. We were two or three days behind schedule – so Suzie'd be worrying, and Chris who'd been biting his nails was still *mildly* worrying, for her sake – but not only would we be in good time to get to Glendarragh for the 25th, being a few days late and having a stand-off period of at least fourteen days that we could count on, he could now reckon on getting as long as ten days for his honeymoon. Pretty good – considering there was a war on.'

(Unedited transcript ends at this point)

Tumult left her patrol area in twilight, and by dawn Chalk reckoned they were far enough off the coast to stay up. Progress on diesels, on the surface, was a lot quicker than running dived on electric motors – even with a westerly Force 7 whipping up enough of a sea to slow her down. She was rolling hard as well as pitching, with green seas crashing over every minute or so: watchkeepers were more in the sea than on it. Not that there was anything very unusual in this, but Chalk had ordered a zigzag too, to foil U-boat attack, so the boat's speed-made-good was only about eight or nine knots.

They reached Lerwick in the second dawn.

'Pendant numbers passed, sir!'

The signalman pushed his Aldis lamp back into its bracket: Lerwick's signal station had demanded identification, and he'd supplied it. *Tumult* rolling like a drunk and pitching savagely as Van Sommeren conned her towards the little harbour's entrance – sea pounding white all along the harbour wall, and the little town, mostly grey granite, seemingly crouched with its coat collar turned up, windows like eyes slitted against the spray.

'Easing a bit, sir, isn't it?'

Van Sommeren had his glasses up. *Tumult* flinging herself heavily to starboard . . . Still going over, her saddle-tanks on that side buried in the rushing boil of sea, and a huge, curling roller rushing in from ahead, the submarine already over on her ear and with her long forepart buried, that racing mound engulfing the gun-mounting, thundering against the front of the bridge then sheeting up, most of it dropping green on to the watchkeepers' heads, the rest bursting over, brilliant white. And the next one already gathering itself . . . Van Sommeren, spitting out salt water, answered his own question: 'No – isn't really, is it', and the signalman laughed. She was rolling back, swinging through the vertical to lunge over the other way while her forepart soared, shedding a torrent of white foam.

'Probably get worse before it does ease.' Chalk was mopping the front lenses of his binoculars with a wad of periscope paper. You kept a supply of it in a flapped and buttoned theoretically waterproof pocket. Glasses up again now – he'd have them dry for about two seconds – and jamming himself back against the forward periscope standard, for stability.

'There's a submarine in there already. Alongside.'

Lowering the wet glasses, and glancing round at Van Sommeren. 'Don't understand it.'

Because no submarine should be heading north now, and there'd been none on patrol up there that might now have been coming south. *Tumult*'s forepart smashing down again, jolting as hard as if it were splitting rocks, not water.

'Signalman—'

But he was on to it already, had seen the first wink of the light calling them from the Port War Signal Station. Lifting the Aldis and sending an answering flash, then they were all reading the dots and dashes as they came like bright pinpricks through the grey, salt-tasting dawn: *From Senior Submarine Officer Lerwick, to Tumult: Berth on Tracker, port side to.*

Even inside the harbour there was quite a lot of movement, and Chalk decided to berth not alongside *Tracker* but in the only other suitable space, on the quayside just ahead of her. There were catamarans there to keep her off the granite wall; but still enough of a surge for the ropes and wires to need watching. Alongside *Tracker*, even with fenders down, the bumping would have endangered their saddle-tanks' thin plating.

He began to explain his decision to the base's CO who'd supposedly have originated that signal, but the commander – a distinguished submariner now in this shore job perhaps for some health reason – knew nothing of it and didn't give a damn. A short, thickset man, brass-hatted, wearing an unbuttoned oilskin. He waved aside Chalk's explanation – this was on *Tumult*'s casing, he'd come aboard over the swaying plank as soon as it had been slid over – and told him, 'Just as well. You'd have had to have moved, anyway, to let *Tracker* out. Who's your first lieutenant?'

Chalk saw Johnny Mottram coming briskly along the quay from *Tracker*. Tallish, narrow-shouldered, neatly trimmed black beard ... He turned back to the commander and answered that rather odd question: 'Lieutenant Van Sommeren, sir.'

'Well, you'll have to go down to Dundee without him, I'm afraid.' Pausing, looking round as Mottram came over the plank, arms out for balance. Don Sutherland, Chalk's torpedo officer who was also responsible for the casing, had paused nearby with an ear tuned to whatever was being said. The commander turned to Johnny Mottram. 'Breaking the sad news to him.'

'Morning, Rufus.' A glance upwards at *Tumult*'s periscope standards, where there was no Jolly Roger flying. 'No luck this time?'

You flew the black flag with its skull-and-crossbones and symbols sewn on for ships sunk whenever you got in from a successful patrol; after a blank one, you didn't.

Chalk asked them both, 'What's the interest in my first lieutenant?'

'You tell him, Mottram.'

'Fact is, Rufus, *my* number one – Pete Shoesmith, you know him – poor sod's been landed to hospital. Appendix, the quack says. I'm going north – special op. with canoeists – sailing *now*, if not sooner – and I can't go without a first lieutenant, obviously.'

'Going *north*?'

A nod . . . 'Tricky time for it, you're right. I've got three Norwegians on board with folboats, have to put 'em ashore – well, just north of Trondheim—'

'Christ!'

'—to collect some other chap before the Gestapo get him.'

'Sixty-four, sixty-five north, roughly? Right inshore, and no dark hours at all?'

'Oh, there'll be *some*—'

'Want me, sir?' Chris Van Sommeren had appeared from the fore hatch. Chalk guessed that Sutherland had been down and told him what he'd heard. He introduced him to the base commander: 'Lieutenant Van Sommeren, sir.' A glance at Mottram: he and Chris knew each other, of course. Back to the commander: 'Van Sommeren's getting married on the 25th, sir.'

'Not *this* month, he isn't.' The commander told him, 'You're being lent to *Tracker*, Van Sommeren. Her first lieutenant's been landed sick.'

'Pete Shoesmith?'

'Only appendix.' Mottram assured him, 'He'll be all

right.' The commander broke in again, 'Sorry about your wedding. But take it philosophically – what's a few weeks' delay when it's going to last a lifetime?'

Chalk admired his first lieutenant for not pretending to be even faintly amused. As well as not showing his true feelings – except to anyone who knew him and recognized the anger in those brown, wide-set eyes. Mottram was saying, 'I'm sorry too. Glad to have you, though. If one had to pinch *any* first lieutenant . . .' Flattery, aimed at softening the blow: and glancing at his watch. 'But this is a pierhead jump, I'm afraid. I'm ready to cast off *now*.'

'In half an hour, let's say.'

'Hell, Rufus—'

Mottram's mouth shut again as he realized that he was being told, not asked. Chalk glanced at the commander: 'Excuse us, sir? Lot of ground to cover.' He put a hand on Van Sommeren's arm, turning him with him towards the hatch. 'Better hand over to Sutherland – and to me – I'll sit in on it.' He added, 'I want a word, in any case.'

Half an hour later, he watched *Tracker* cast off. The hemp breasts went first, then the wire back-spring, and Mottram swung her stern out on the other one before he backed her off the quay on her motors, pointed her at the exit then but held her where she was until the casing had been secured and cleared – Van Sommeren leaning over the side of the bridge to hurry it all up. Mottram would have had in mind, Chalk realized, that recently an 'S'-class boat's third hand had been washed off her fore-casing and drowned, just outside there.

On her way now. The diesels' rumble, and a haze of exhaust that vanished quickly on the wind . . . Chalk put his hand up in farewell, Westwood lifted his cap and waved it, but Chris must have gone below – to start sorting out his new responsibilities, no doubt. Poor bastard . . .

There hadn't been much to be said between them: only that as soon as possible after he got to Dundee he'd telephone Suzie and explain the situation, try to convince her that there was no need to worry, that it was merely a postponement – and that neither of them could have done anything to prevent it. Also that he would *not* mention the name *Tracker*. Whether she could ever have heard of *Trumpeter*'s rebuilding neither of them knew. Chalk had wondered, once or twice – especially as Alastair had heard about it – but the subject had never come up in her presence, as far as he knew. Chris had been uncertain as to whether or not he'd ever mentioned it – in any conversation connected with the flotilla, for instance. If he had and she'd known of it already, of course, her reaction might have been minimal, one might not have noticed. He'd never talked much 'shop' to her, though. No reason to: he thought *her* 'shop', the flying stuff, was far more interesting. And then again, even if she'd known of *Tracker*'s existence and provenance, she could hardly have known she was in the Dundee flotilla – if neither he nor Chalk had told her. Chalk most definitely would not have: but Chris had admitted, 'I wouldn't have seen it as having any special importance. But I realize – damn silly of me . . .'

No special importance, for God's sake. And *Tracker* going north – in June – on a canoeing trip . . .

She was stern-to now, about to pass out through that narrow opening. Diesel exhaust visible again, and her ensign fluttering wildly above it.

When Suzie had confirmed to him that she was definitely going to marry Chris, in that telephone conversation from Dundee after Chris had finished all *his* calls – to Suzie, then to the Cameron-Greens and to his own family – she'd repeated what she'd said at the party at White Waltham, that she thought perhaps she should have her head examined for loose screws, even to *think* of marrying a submariner. Chalk had pointed out that it wouldn't have mattered if he'd been a lion-tamer or a fishmonger, all she had to think about was that this was the man she loved and who loved her, who happened also to be one of the nicest men alive and in his – Chalk's – opinion, tailor-made for her.

'Don't hold his occupation against him, Suzie.'

'No. I won't. That's good advice . . . But – promise you'll always bring him safely back to me?'

'I'll do my best to, believe me.'

'*Promise?*'

'All right.' In some ways she was still quite child-like. He'd told her, smiling into the telephone, 'I promise.'

'Otherwise I *won't* – don't *want*—'

'You won't go through that again, Suzie. I swear it.'

Chapter 17

He secured *Tumult* alongside in Dundee on the 22nd at about 1930, and was in the Mess half an hour later, fending off offers of drinks and questions about his own patrol and *Tracker* until he'd telephoned to Patricia in London – no answer, which was disturbing – and then to Suzie at the ATA women's pool at Hatfield, to which they'd transferred her from White Waltham at the time she'd had her promotion to 1st Officer, for some reason. But no luck with her either. Another girl pilot told him she was on her way back from a ferrying job; it might be worth trying in about an hour, say. Or two hours, even. If she was flying back – in one of the taxi Ansons, as she might well be – she'd be on the ground by sunset, but if she was on her way by car . . .

'I'll ring later, anyway.' He felt dirty, was looking forward to a long, hot bath. Shaven – one always smartened up as far as possible before entering harbour – but slightly foul. And tired. And Pat's not being there – yet – had put a knot in his gut: she'd left on one of her SIS 'jaunts' a day or two before he'd set out on this last patrol. He asked the ATA girl, 'Is my wife – Diana Chalk – anywhere around?'

'Oh. Commander Chalk.' (Tone of surprise: and of

course, he should have asked for Diana first.) 'I'm afraid not, Diana 'phoned to say she's stuck out. I'm not sure where, but if you'd hold on I'll—'

'Don't worry. She'll be 'phoning *me*, I expect. I'm at Dundee, by the way, you might tell Suzie. Anyway I'll call her later.'

Lying in the bath, he thought about Diana. If she was 'stuck out', as they called it, and aware of his having been three days overdue, one might have expected that she'd have called to ask whether there was any news of him – of *Tumult* – and left a message telling him where he could find her. But there'd been nothing in his pigeon-hole or on the board – only one for Chris Van Sommeren, emanating no doubt from Suzie.

Chris would find it there, plus a letter or two probably, in a couple of weeks' time. Touch wood: the floating nailbrush, its wooden back. Diana, though: perhaps they all got 'stuck out' as often as she did. Suzie had mentioned once that the ATA discipline was strict, in that area, all movements and stop-overs having to be accounted for, papers or logbooks signed whenever a 'plane landed or took off, and the records carefully scrutinized. And if that was the case, one might as well put it out of mind. But suspicion of course tended to breed further suspicion: the thin end of *this* wedge being some Belgian ATA pilot by name of Vernet.

Patricia had told him: Suzie had told *her*, in strict sisterly confidence, and obviously not realizing at that time how close he and Patricia had become. Try Patricia again before dinner, he thought. He'd have been revelling in anticipation of doing so – even just hearing her voice over the wire – if the lack of a reply just now hadn't left him fearful that he might still *not* get to hear it: only listen again to the thing ringing – visualizing that empty flat . . .

Diana: why hadn't he let that girl find out for him where she was 'stuck out', so he could call her . . . Prime reason: he didn't want her thinking he was checking up on her. Second, the call to Suzie had priority, because for the last few days she'd have been living on her nerves and that would not, he imagined, go well with flying.

'Planning to spend the night in that tub, Rufus?'

He looked up at Charlie Ogden, CO of *Sepoy*.

'Getting out this minute, Charlie.'

Patricia was the emotional priority. The fear of finding she still wasn't there countered by that of leaving it too late, just missing her.

She had other friends, lots of them. No answer might only indicate that she was out dining, dancing, or at a theatre or the flicks. Towelling himself while the water gurgled out, he wondered whether the Marx Brothers' film *The Big Store* was still showing and whether she might already have seen it. An alternative might be Coward's play *Blithe Spirit*.

If he could get down there – with no first lieutenant to take care of the boat in his absence. On the face of it, he couldn't. But if she *was* there – might get one of the other COs to keep an eye on things, for just a day or two?

'Suzie – Rufus. I tried earlier, but—'

Listening: and catching the tone of disappointment – that it wasn't Chris. She'd had his message, had been intending to call him when she'd eaten ... Then the inevitable question: 'Where's Chris?'

'Well, that's why I'm calling ...'

He tried to break it gently: telling her there was nothing to worry about, but he was very sorry to tell her they'd have to postpone the wedding. 'Disappointing, I know – to put it very mildly—'

'Postpone?'

Explaining, then. Having – luckily – the excuse of an insecure telephone line and by this time well-ingrained habits based on the slogan 'Careless Talk Costs Lives'. Chris had gone on patrol in another boat: which for obvious reasons he couldn't name over the telephone. It would be a few weeks ...

'All right.' He heard her long intake of breath. 'All right. I understand . . .'

She was well, she told him – 'sparking on all cylinders'. And she'd let Chris's parents as well as her own know about the postponement of her wedding. He thought she was marvellous: a lot of girls in her position would have been in floods of tears by this time. Tears, recriminations: from Suzie, none of that. But she let him know that she knew about his relationship with her sister, and gave him to understand that at least she didn't *dis*approve of it: and changing the subject at that point – to the question of Diana's whereabouts – he had in the back of his mind the age-old question of which came first, the chicken or the egg? Diana and her Belgian, or himself and Patricia?

Suzie had said to Patricia once – quite recently, speaking of Diana, and Patricia had passed it on to him – 'I owe her a lot, I can't forget that. But my God, she can be as hard as nails!'

He finished – thankfully, grateful to her for having taken the bad news so well – 'Don't worry about Chris. No reason to, honestly . . .' But tense with worry himself by then – hanging up – thinking about Patricia, who was still away, Suzie had told him: adding, 'Certainly long enough, this time . . .'

He tried Pat's number again – obviously not expecting the call to be answered, but hoping for a miracle. Suzie had said something like 'Don't worry, she'll come back to you . . .' To *him*: that was how she'd told him she knew about their relationship. But it was a good point she'd made: Patricia *would* be gone, from time to time, absences of indefinite duration; it was only the coming back that mattered.

She definitely was not in her flat now, anyway. He cut off the plaintive, lonely ringing and put a call through to Betty.

He'd finished eating and had accepted a large Scotch from Charlie Ogden – a liar-dice session was about to get under way and he'd weakly consented to take part – when the steward on duty came through to tell him that he was wanted on the telephone.

'It's Mrs Chalk, sir.'

'Ah. Thanks.'

'Ah-*hah*.' Ogden grinned at the others. 'He's rung *all* his girlfriends, now he's got to face the music.'

'Smashing music, from what *I* hear.'

Tim Hart, captain of *Threat*. Chalk ignored him – he didn't like him much – and told Ogden, 'That last call was to my sister. The one before that, to Van Sommeren's fiancée – to tell the poor girl she's got to postpone the wedding. All right?' He went out to the anteroom, to the telephone receiver hanging on its cord.

'Diana?'

'Rufus! You're back, safe and sound! But I hear you've mislaid the bridegroom – Suzie called me, I was trying to get through to you there earlier, but – I don't know, lines engaged, or—'

'Right.' The *hell* she'd tried earlier. He'd been overdue by three days, for Christ's sake: why would she have called today, but not yesterday? Or the day before? If she *had*, there'd have been a message. He asked her, 'Where are you now?'

'Bristol. Flying some Blenheims from Filton to Cosford first thing tomorrow. I brought an Oxford into Whitchurch this evening, found I had to stay over for these Blenheims when two other pilots get here. Which they should have by now. But that's *my* worry . . . How are you, darling?'

'Well – all right. Fine. But I do want to see you, this time. Please?'

'Are you coming south?'

'Doubt it. I've no first lieutenant to leave in charge, you see.'

'Oh, well . . . So you're stuck there, and I'm stuck out here, there, everywhere . . . And I won't be getting any leave in the foreseeable future, unfortunately. We're really quite stretched, need twice as many pilots as we've got. The wedding's off, Suzie says.'

'Postponed.'

'That's what I meant. Any idea how long you'll be in, this time?'

'About the usual time, I suppose. I suppose you couldn't get yourself up this way? Get "stuck out" in Dundee?' She'd begun to laugh. At the sheer impossibility of it, he wondered, or at his making the suggestion even if it had been viable? He went on, 'Couldn't you deliver some 'plane up here? I could get away for twenty-four hours, say – we might meet in Edinburgh?'

'It's a gorgeous idea, darling – nothing I'd love more, but . . .'

But no. No soap – *darling*.

He only wanted to talk – talk this whole situation out. He thought she realized it too. Whether she knew that he knew about Jacques Vernet – as little as he *did* know – well, that was something else. As was the question of whether she could know about Patricia. Might *suspect*: she'd been jealous of her for years. Foresight, possibly – intuition?

He went back to the liar-dice game, feeling both frustrated and hypocritical.

'Four tens to beat, Rufus. Here – matches.'

He used one of them to light a cigarette with. They used match-sticks as counters: when you'd lost three you bought a round of drinks.

Ogden, who was passing it to him from his right, murmured, 'Four jacks, actually. Being kind to you, old chum.'

'That'll be the day.' He put his hand on the inverted leather cup. Staring at it, all of them thinking he was making his mind up whether to accept it or lift it, but actually thinking about Patricia, who *might* be back – well, tomorrow, say. Or next week . . .

'Looks like he's still dreamin' oh my darlin' love of thee.'

'Rufus, old horse?'

'Sorry.' Coming to, he shook his head. 'Four tens, you said. *I* say you can stuff 'em.' He lifted the cup, and found four kings under it. 'Well. Stuff *you*.'

'Clot.' Ogden scooped the five dice back into the cup, and pushed it towards him. 'I was gunning for Jake there. Come on, Rufus, finger out!'

'What I was thinking was I wouldn't want Johnny Mottram's job.'

'Special Op – canoeists?'

'In the land of the midnight sun.'

'Well—' Jake Sibbering, captain of *Sabre* – '– he's only got to sneak in dived, surface for a minute to send 'em on their way, get under again damn quick and move back in again at pick-up time. Uh?'

'So where and when does he get his box up?'

Meaning, how does he charge his batteries ... Ogden growled, 'Are you going to shake those bloody dice, or aren't you?'

'Going to roll 'em, are you, Chris?'

Matt Caulfield, the boat's engineer officer, peered at him across the wardroom table. *Tracker* was lying bottomed in a Norwegian fjord. Caulfield had broken into Chris Van Sommeren's thoughts in no more than a murmur, but in the pervading silence it might have been audible in the next compartment. It was dead quiet, and warm, the boat absolutely motionless, with all non-essential auxiliary machinery stopped and lights either switched off or glowing only dimly. In contrast to the semi-darkness in the gangway, the light over their heads in here spread a pool of almost dazzling brilliance. Caulfield added, 'She'll still be there when we get back, you know.'

'Rather obvious, Chief, but true enough.' Johnny Mottram,

the boat's scrawny, bearded skipper, watched as his replacement first lieutenant shook the cup and turned it over, then took a quick look under it. Mottram added, 'She's a pilot, Rufus Chalk mentioned? Delivers Spitfires hither and yon?'

He nodded. 'In the ATA – Air Transport Auxiliary. Rufus' wife is in it too.'

He hadn't talked about his wedding plans, or Suzie, in the two and three-quarter days he'd been on board. He'd got over his initial shock and resentment at the turn of events, but was still aggrieved enough to feel protective of his private life – that it wasn't any of their damn business. He knew these people – you did know just about all your brother officers, in your own flotilla – but he wasn't part of this team and he was as conscious of it as they were. Thinking more about this than about the game as he slid two aces from under the cup, shook the other three dice, peered at them under cover and left them hidden – glancing at Hugh Bellamy, then, the navigator, who was on his left.

'There's a third ace under here.'

'Oh, *bound* to be . . .'

Bellamy was RNR, a pre-war Merchant Navy cadet. Balding quite seriously, at twenty-two. It gave him a donnish look, and his quiet voice matched it. Although in fact they were all speaking in not much more than murmurs: partly because most of the ship's company were asleep, and partly from consciousness of sitting here killing time under about a hundred feet of water in enemy-occupied territory. Although it didn't make much sense to be whispering to each other, considering that in a few hours' time you'd be surfacing to run a charge – starting the submarine's two 2500 BHP diesels and keeping them at it all forenoon, charging her batteries. You'd have to shout then to be heard, anywhere near them, and the fjord would be fairly echoing with their racket.

Bloody lunacy, perhaps: but no option . . .

Bellamy had reluctantly accepted the proposition of three

aces. Chris asked Mottram, 'Did they *expect* to make it back to us in the one day, sir?'

The Norwegians, he was asking about, the three they'd brought here. One major, one lieutenant and one civilian, a doctor. On board, they'd kept to themselves, hadn't spoken much to anyone except the skipper. He'd shrugged: 'They hoped to. Hoped this chap they've come for might be so to speak wrapped up and ready for collection. In which case – depending on whether or not they run up against any Germans, I suppose . . .'

'Funny lot, weren't they?'

'You mean *aren't* they.'

'Yes. Of course . . .' The engineer asked Bellamy cynically, 'What d'you want me to believe you've got there?'

They'd bottomed her in Mursteinfjord, just inside the entrance. In position – according to Bellamy's navigator's notebook – 64 degrees 38' North, 10 degrees 54.3' East. Mottram had nosed her in close to the fjord's entrance at periscope depth a few hours ago, surfaced her within spitting distance of the islands out there – or rather semi-surfaced her, keeping her trimmed so low that only her bridge and periscope standards were awash – and brought her in slowly, still on main motors, between islands named on the chart as Lokoy and Bangoy, then passing even closer to other islands, islets and rocks, conning her through the narrowest of navigable channels and turning sharply to starboard into this very small bay off the east coast of Skjingen. It had been necessary to surface more fully then to get the canoes out through the fore hatch, but it was an evolution they'd practised before with these Norwegians in the Firth of Tay, and it had been completed in a very few minutes – during which time he'd been turning the submarine to point back the other way, ready for her exit. Being in the fjord at all was hair-raising enough, sitting in full view on the surface made it worse, and those minutes with the hatch open had been fairly heart-stopping. Mottram had been alone on the bridge

– knowing he might have had to dive in a hurry, once the fore hatch had banged shut – while Chris had been at his own action station in the Control Room, only able to guess at what was happening up top from the orders that came down the voicepipe. The Norwegians had been up on the casing, launching their folboats with the assistance of the boat's torpedo officer and the second coxswain and his winger: they'd embarked, two in one boat and one in the other – with an empty cockpit for the man they hoped they'd be bringing back with them – and paddled away, and as soon as the fore hatch had been shut and clipped Mottram had ordered main vents opened, and Chris had trimmed her down slowly to lie bottomed where she was now.

With a three-quarter used-up battery – hence economy with lighting – and in sixteen fathoms, with rocks and islands close all round and the nearest mainland coast about a mile to the east. The canoeists had headed southeast, aiming for some small fishing village in an indenture of that coast: how they'd proceed from there on was their own business. But the low battery was *Tracker*'s Achilles' heel.

Chris lifted the dice cup, under which he'd been told there reposed two more aces and a ten, but which in fact had been covering only two tens and a nine. Mottram was left holding *that* baby: muttering that he'd be glad to get his own first lieutenant back, he gathered the dice and prepared to start another round.

No rounds of drinks, in this game. At sea in submarine wardrooms there was no drinking, ever. Let alone in a situation like this one: although the known and accepted risks would have been sobering enough. Chances of getting away, if *Tracker* was caught inside the fjord, being roughly nil. Whatever the three Norwegians were up to, whoever it was that they were aiming to bring out, it had to be some issue or person of considerable importance – to be worth a submarine and fifty lives. Even getting this far had been due to luck as much as skill: with no darkness and no knowledge of German defensive positions, lookout stations or inshore patrols – or air patrols, which in the next few hours might become a major threat. The skipper had shrugged it off: 'Cross that hurdle when we come to it.'

Hurdles all along the way. Arrival here and entry to the fjord, for instance, had felt like Russian roulette: in a fairly calm sea – barely ruffled surface with very little white on it – German coastal lookouts with Zeiss binoculars might have been watching the periscope's white feather on and off for an hour or more before she'd surfaced and crept in between the islands.

Mottram had briefed him on the first evening out of Lerwick, with *Tracker* making fifteen knots northeastward on the surface. There were to be two days like that, then a single day dived, motoring eastward at periscope depth. (That was how they'd spent the day – yesterday: it was a little after 0400 now, 23 June.) So then – he'd explained – they'd enter the fjord, send the canoeists on their way and lie bottomed until they reappeared with their rescuee. Same procedure in reverse thereafter: leave the fjord on the surface but trimmed right down as before, dive as soon as she was clear of navigational hazards. Out of sight of land, surface and run for home.

'Only way to do it. What looked like the obvious way at first sight – when we first chewed this over, in Dundee – the obvious thing was to close the shore dived, surface to send the canoes away and then retire seaward, coming back in later. Well, if we had dark nights to hide in, that might have been the way to do it, but round-the-clock daylight changes everything.'

'Isn't the box a problem? After a whole day running in on the motors?'

'Of course it is. Even if there's just enough juice left to get us out to sea again.' Light-blue eyes probing into Chris', across the wardroom table: 'You with me?'

The point he was making was that if you ran into trouble – like having to evade anti-submarine craft – without adequate reserves of power you wouldn't be able to dodge, use bursts of high speed, and so on. Having to conserve the amps you'd be helpless – like a mouse for the cats to play with.

Mottram had nodded. 'The other way, the battery problem would have been worse. *Two* long trips inshore, an absolute need to run a full charge out there – in open sea, full daylight – and perhaps a bigger problem still if we came in the second time and our boys weren't there. What then – all the way out again – or hang around just offshore, either way exhausting the box *again*?'

'Right.'

'So the answer – don't faint, now – what we're going to do is put on a charge while we're inside that fjord and our passengers are doing their stuff ashore. It's hellish risky, but – no option, really. Well, there is – if for some reason we can't stay up, or run the donkeys – all right, we'll simply take a deep breath and play mouse. If we haven't stirred up the ants' nest by then we *might* even get away with it.' He'd got up from the table: 'Here, I'll show you.'

At the chart-table, then, he'd pulled out Admiralty Chart 3503, and pointed at its title – *Namsenfjorden*. 'This may be to our advantage. Mursteinfjord – see, right next door to Namsenfjord – here – and this is the big one. The Germans will obviously be making use of it – bags of room, numerous anchorages, and here at the top is Namsos itself – sizeable port, major centre for the whole area. With any luck they'll be ignoring Mursteinfjord – graciously leaving it to the fishermen, maybe.' He pointed with a pencil-tip: 'We'll enter by this marked channel, and lie bottomed in this little hole here.'

'Little hole' being a space about the size of Lerwick harbour, between the indented eastern side of an island called Skjingen and south of a smaller one, Lokoy, several minute islets and spurs of rock. When they surfaced to put on the charge, Mottram hoped that with the upper hatch only just clear of water the little of *Tracker* that would be showing might itself resemble a half-tide rock – to a passing air patrol for instance, or anything less than a deliberate search.

'We'll use the drowned exhaust, of course.'

Submarine diesels when running on the surface – the only way they could run, as they needed a huge intake of air – could have their fumes exhausted either above or below the surface. The so-called 'drowned' exhaust blew bubbles and slightly reduced efficiency, but it also reduced the noise and eliminated the exhaust haze which might otherwise attract attention.

In the liar game, Chris had lost a round. He'd lifted the cup on Mottram's claim of a high straight, and there it was. Glancing at the bulkhead clock, he saw that it was nearly four-thirty, and therefore a good time to duck out. 'I'll give French a break – and stay on till six, sir.'

They were going to surface and start charging the battery at six. Then – all being well – which was no *small* hope – dive at about midday and bottom again, wait until 2230, zero-hour for the Norwegians' return. Mottram had arranged with them that if they hadn't appeared by ten minutes past the hour he'd go back to the bottom and come up four hours later, continuing that routine for a second twenty-four hours; if by then they still hadn't shown up he'd assume they'd come to grief, and that would be the end of it. *Tracker* would withdraw, return to base.

But touch wood, Chris thought, she'd be on her way *tonight* – with the Norwegians and their prize on board. At the latest, anyway, by say midnight tomorrow, 24 June. Two days' passage to Lerwick, two more from there to Dundee – 28th. Or say 29th – to be on the generous side. And *Tumult* – allowing her a fortnight in harbour – wouldn't leave for her next patrol before about 6 July. So, if the wedding could be laid on at short notice, and Suzie could make it – first week of July?

He took over the watch from Harry French, *Tracker*'s torpedo officer. French had been sitting on the after 'planes-man's stool, engrossed in *Brighton Rock.* He was a sub-lieutenant, about twenty-one years old – ginger-headed, two days' worth of ginger stubble on his cheeks and jaw. Standing now, stretching: 'Jolly decent of you, Number One. Want to borrow this?'

'Thanks, I've read it.'

'Not bad, eh?' He sloped off, and Chris glanced around the Control Room. The watch, apart from himself, comprised an artificer, an asdic rating with his ears clamped to his skull by headphones, and one leading seaman. As much as you needed, when watchkeeping amounted only to staying awake and keeping an eye on the depthgauges and gyro compass, and an ear open for any movement like scraping along the bottom.

He'd checked those readings. There'd been no change, no hint of any movement. So far there'd been no evidence of any tidal effect in this small cove ... He sat down, where French had been, covertly glancing at the faces of his fellow-watchkeepers and putting names to them. He'd been making efforts in that area, in the past two or three days. The asdic operator's name for instance was Talbot. And the killick seaman was the gunlayer, name of – Clark. He'd nodded to him, murmured, 'Clark, isn't it?' Talbot if addressed would have had to remove an earphone and ask for a repetition. The ERA was reading, but he'd glanced up, a rather blank-faced stare: he was an older man than most – hair greying at the temples, and a ridged forehead: Chris, having searched his memory again, asked him, 'All right, Wilson?'

'So far we seem to be, sir.'

An educated voice, and a slightly dismissive tone; he'd looked down again already at the battered-looking Penguin book which he was having to hold tilted to catch some light. Chris wondered whether he knew that the penguin emblem had been designed by a man who was now a submariner, had survived a DSEA escape, was currently a first lieutenant tipped for early command. He almost surely didn't; by the look of him mightn't have given a damn either. But thinking about that – the grudging manner – he realized that if he'd been joining this boat as its permanent first lieutenant there'd have been quite a different attitude, on his own part to some extent but from the ship's company especially. Submarine crews were used to having officers they knew well. Whether or not they liked or disliked this or that individual, they'd know what to expect from him: whereas this Lieutenant Van Whatsit was an unknown quantity, a stranger who'd remain a stranger, and at the end of his patrol they'd be glad to revert to normality – to the devil they knew and might even like. Chris understood this, would have felt the same himself and didn't resent it in the least.

Didn't need anything to read, either. With Suzie to think about, he wouldn't have been able to concentrate on it anyway. Suzie, and getting back to her . . .

Thinking of the battery-charge, too. Maintaining the surfaced but very nearly submerged trim would be his own job, and with the top hatch only just clear of the surface he'd be watching points very, very carefully, from start to finish. Admittedly the prevailing calm would help – as long as it lasted. This close to the fjord's entrance, if there'd been any appreciable sea running you'd certainly have felt it here; Mottram would have his work cut out too, manoeuvring in an extremely confined space to keep her off the surrounding rocks.

With luck, it would stay calm. Please God, it would.

The reason for waiting until 0600 was that it was still technically night-time, and the locals – not excluding whatever German garrison there might be – would have their heads down even if the sun *was* shining. The diesels' racket ought to be less noticeable, too, at an hour when fishing-boats and other craft might be on the move.

Please God the Norwegians would make it by tonight's

2230 deadline. Then – out, away . . .

Six days to Suzie. Seven if they *didn't* make it.

She'd have been dumbfounded by Chalk's news – if he'd been able to contact her by this time. He would have, surely: *Tumult* should have got into Dundee yesterday afternoon, and calling her would have been his first priority. Wherever she was – 'stuck out', or not, he'd have got through to her. In fact if he'd had any sort of hold-up you could bet she'd have been on to *him* – she'd have been fretting already, without this. Chalk would have realized that, and broken it to her as gently as he could, but however carefully he'd handled it – well, poor kid . . .

He'd sighed, a long, hard intake of breath, and the artificer had glanced up, stared at him for a moment then looked down at his book again. Chalk's voice, meanwhile, like a recording in his brain: *Not the end of the world, Chris. Really should be only a couple of weeks' delay . . .*

He'd hung on to that. Still did: except that a couple of weeks had come down to *one*. Thinking about it – how you got used to things, found they weren't *so* bad after all – he was studying the white-enamelled deckhead with its labyrinth of pipes of various dimensions, tracing one visually – it was an HP airline – tracing it right through to the blow on number three main ballast – and remembering then having seen Chalk on board this submarine at a party they'd both been invited to, Chalk seemingly doing this same thing – pipe-tracing, which was a conscientious submariner's habit in idle moments – but then he'd realized that actually his skipper was in an entirely different kind of preoccupation: grim-faced, no party spirit whatsoever, and he'd seen it in a flash of insight: *Of course – Trumpeter . . .*

Tracker shifted, at that moment – such precise timing that for a moment he thought it was his imagination. A scraping – steel on rock – and a small lurch to port. He and the ERA were on their feet – seeing the for'ard depthgauge showing 95 feet – it had been at 94 – and the bubble now two degrees aft. She was motionless again: the scraping had lasted only seconds. Gyro heading hadn't changed, still read 141 degrees: it almost might not have happened. But Mottram had shot in, was making his own check of those telltale readings – which in fact told no tale at all beyond the fact that her hull was or had been in contact with solid rock at some point or points, and that she'd shifted on it or slipped off it.

'I'll have the bilges checked, sir.' He looked round at the gunlayer: 'Clark – shake the Chief Stoker, will you.'

Better safe than sorry.

Chalk woke early, although he'd been dog-tired the night before. He'd been the first to leave the poker-dice game, and before he'd gone up to turn in he'd resisted the urge to try Patricia's number again.

The point was, though, she had to get back *some* time: so what would be wrong with *now*, this minute? Or half an hour ago? He could see it: an SIS car dropping her at the door of her block of flats: she'd be entering the foyer, crossing it to the lift . . .

He'd dreamt of her. He couldn't remember any detail of where they'd been, or doing what, only that she'd been with him. He'd try again, he decided, before going into breakfast. If there was still no answer – forget it.

As if one could . . .

He'd have rung them at Glendarragh, in ordinary circumstances, but wasn't keen to do so because he knew that her parents – Lady C-G especially – disapproved of her seeing him as often as she did. *A married man, Patricia*! It was just as well the old girl didn't know the whole truth of it: even though she'd probably suspect it. Patricia had told him that for the sake of a quiet life she'd given up mentioning him at all, and Mama had taken to slipping in little questions . . . Which, since Patricia could run rings round her, probably saw the questions coming before her mother had thought of them, didn't get her ladyship very far.

He'd leave Glendarragh out of it, he decided. If she'd been going up there she'd have sent him a note anyway.

Christ – if she was back, *she*'d be on the 'phone, wouldn't be just sitting there waiting for him to call her, for God's sake!

He was shaving when he remembered the other dream. He'd been in *Trumpeter* again: same scene, same circumstances: he'd had a DSEA set strapped on and had been about to enter the after escape chamber; Chris Van Sommeren had asked him, 'Tell Suzie I love her – will you?'

He'd answered – he *thought* he had, but recollection faded as it came to mind – 'You can tell her yourself, Chris!'

It might have been his subconscious reaction *now* – a split second ago. What his answer *would* have been – and was now, in a sense, when he thought of *Tracker* up there on 65 degrees north, in those 24-hour days . . .

Mottram knew his business, though.

It was a few minutes past seven when he dialled Patricia's number again. If *she*'d been late last night, had thought – as he had – that it was *too* late to be calling . . .

Ringing.

Imagining her waking up: then giving her time to get her thoughts together, reach for the 'phone.

Still ringing. Even if she'd been in the tub . . .

Bathtowel wrapped around that lovely, slim, damp body: a bare arm reaching to the 'phone – *now*?

He let it ring three more times, then hung up.

Mottram called down, 'Start the charge.'

Twelve feet on the gauges. Her bridge was well up though, and the top hatch was open. Mottram had French up there with him. Chris, with his hand still on the trimming-order telegraph, glanced over his shoulder to check that Caulfield had heard the order: the engineer had vanished into his own domain, so you could assume he had. Anyway, this trim was all right: Chris turned the knob on the telegraph round to 'Stop pumping', and ordered, 'Shut "O" port and starboard.' At that moment the port-side diesel burst into action: you felt the draught at once, the rush of cold air which the diesel was sucking down through the tower. Noise increasing as the revs built up. They were using only one of the two diesels, leaving the starboard motor available for manoeuvring, as might be necessary to keep her clear of rocks.

Hazy-blue sky up there, a bright disc of it visible when he looked up through the lower hatch. There'd be some mist on the water, he guessed. Beautiful, no doubt, the kind of scenery described in travel books as 'rugged grandeur', but in his own capacity as first lieutenant, responsible for everything inside the boat while her CO was on the bridge, he'd never get to see it.

It was cold, in the flood of air; he shifted to stand just forward of the ladder, out of the mainstream of it. Leaning there behind the 'planesmen's backs – his left arm out to put some of his weight on the ladder's shiny steel, the coxswain's broad back was in front of him at the after 'planes, second coxswain at the fore 'planes to his right. Bellamy, who'd come from the chart-table for a quick look up through the tower, shouted above the diesel's pounding, 'If we can get away with this, anyone can get away with anything!'

Smiling contentedly, as he went back to his chart-table. One of those people, evidently, who seemed to come to life at times like this, seemed to thrive in dangerous situations. Chris felt a certain empathy: he supposed he might be rather like that himself. Or – second thoughts – might *have been* . . .

Having Suzie – the prospect of Suzie – to get back to now, might have changed him?

Checking the time – six-fourteen. Then the gauges: the trim was static. No worries on that score, with the upper hatch about three feet clear of water, which still had virtually no movement on it.

Bellamy was bloody right, though.

He crossed over to the voicepipe. 'Bridge!'

Mottram answered, 'Bridge.'

'Captain, sir – d'you want to stay at diving stations?'

'Yes. For the time being.'

The alternative would have been to relax to what was called 'patrol routine'. 'Diving stations' was the equivalent of what in surface ships was called 'Action stations', or 'First degree of readiness'. Which probably was the right degree of readiness to be in, in present circumstances. Although it would have been nice to have had a smoke – which at patrol routine, with the hatch open and fresh air rushing through the boat, would have been permissible.

'Control Room!'

The Control Room messenger answered it: 'Control Room?'

'First lieutenant on the voicepipe.'

Chris went to it, and Mottram told him, 'Remain at diving stations, as I said, but let them smoke.'

'Aye aye, sir!'

'And Number One—'

'Sir?'

'Send up my cigarettes and lighter, will you?'

At six-forty, the same call again: 'First lieutenant on the voicepipe.'

'Sir?'

'Be on your toes, Number One. Seaplane flying down-coast, looks like passing a bit close.'

'Aye, sir.' He left the pipe, and passed on the warning to the men around him.

'Fuckin' 'ell.' The coxswain, a Chief PO, turned on his stool and jerked two fingers upwards towards the hatch, the sky. He and the fore 'planesman were just sitting there, both smoking, ready for when the hydroplanes *might* be needed. 'Dive, will we, sir?'

'If he shows interest, I suppose.' Chris was under the

hatch, looking up. With the diesel's noise so close and in this confined, steel-enclosed space you wouldn't have heard any aircraft engine even if it was right on top of you. He glanced at Berkley, the 'outside' ERA at his station at the diving panel: figuratively speaking he was on *his* toes, all right – even his hands half-raised and ready to snatch the main-vent levers open if the 'dive' order came.

It would be possible to dive: but they could then blast the area with bombs. And whether she'd be able to get out of the fjord dived, twisting and turning – more or less blind – through that narrow channel . . . Mottram might be asking himself the same question, he guessed.

Six forty-two. Needles in the gauges still motionless at twelve feet. Diesel pumping away: the charge wouldn't be having any effect yet, but at least the battery wouldn't be getting any flatter. Mottram had used the port motor only once, running slow astern with some helm on; keeping her pointing the right way, probably.

'Control Room.'

Chris was there: 'Sir?'

'Our seaplane's continued down-coast. Perhaps we're invisible.'

'Hope so, sir.' He passed the news on, raising his voice over the diesel's racket. Bellamy muttered, shaking his head after a long draw at his cigarette, 'Beats everything.'

Just before 0700, when an LTO had come from the motor room to test the electrolyte in the pilot cells – the density should have begun to rise, by now – there was some kind of excitement in the bridge. Chris, with an ear to the voicepipe, heard French shout, 'Turning towards us, sir—'

Then after a moment, Mottram's voice in the tube: 'Control Room.'

'Van Sommeren here, sir.'

'Fishing-boat approaching. Chaps waving at us. Stand by for – whatever.'

'Aye aye, sir—'

French's voice: 'That's the lieutenant!'

'Control Room. Send one hand up to take this boat's lines.'

Chris told the messenger, 'Up top, quick!' Peters, his name was: his legs were already vanishing upwards through the lower hatch. Chris was back at the voicepipe, hearing confused shouting – at some distance, from the fishing-boat presumably – then Mottram's 'Go on down, Sub. And you, Peters.' Down on to the casing – which would be under water, they'd be wading. There was a heavy thump as the boat ran alongside: Chris wincing, realizing that the submerged bulge of the saddle-tanks must have taken the full impact.

The boat had pushed off and was heading out towards the channel. Two Norwegians were running it, a middle-aged one in a woollen hat and a boy of about fourteen. The man was in the shelter for'ard, where the wheel was, the boy in the open stern which was heaped with nets. Mottram asked the Norwegian lieutenant, 'What about them?'

'They – fishing. Maybe OK. *Maybe*.'

The major and the doctor were far from OK, apparently. The major had been shot, was either dead or badly wounded, and the other one, the doctor, was in German hands. In fact there were two doctors – the one left behind and this older man whom Kjellegard had brought with him on the boat – the man they'd been sent to fetch. Grey-haired, about fifty, ill-looking and – apparently – for God's sake – a German. In a soaked grey suit ... French had taken him below, guiding him down the ladder. Kjellegard had told Mottram he had no doubt at all the man who'd been taken prisoner – the civilian doctor who'd been one of the team – would try to save his own skin by telling the Germans whatever they wanted to know – which obviously would include how they'd got here. He mimed it, his English being somewhat limited – mimicking the doctor's answer to that question – 'In Royal Navy submarine, please!' – and then, as to where had they been expecting to reboard her – 'Mursteinfjord, island Skjingen if you please, Mein Herren!'

'Why bring that kind of man with you, for Christ's sake?'

'Was not Major Olsen choosing. Your people, I think. Doktor Heiden we know is sick, doctor is necessary. *This* one – Kjempe.' He spat over the side – looking up, watching the sky . . .

Mottram asked him, 'How come you and Heiden got away?'

'Our friends helping. Doktor Heiden with them – has been two month, I think. Kjempe—' the lieutenant mimed it again, throwing his hands up: '"Kamerad!" Major Olsen going back – shoot him, maybe, but—' another gesture, a sound like *poom* – 'dead. *Olsen* I'm telling you is dead. I *hope* . . . Me—' he pointed – 'in the boat, also Heiden. Captain – we go *now*?'

'Wait.' Mottram and the Norwegian eye to eye: one in doubt, the other frantic. 'I want a straight answer, now – understand? Are you *certain*? Not just guessing – out of panic or—'

'Panic?'

'Fright—'

'Fright – me, yes!' A jerk of the head: 'They *know* . . . *Certain*, Captain!'

'All right.' Mottram nodded. 'All right. God damn it.' Stooping to the voicepipe: 'Control Room. Break the charge. Out port engine-clutch, stand by main motors. Cox'n on the wheel.' He straightened. 'What should we expect – aircraft?'

'I think. Stuka, maybe. Also—' pointing eastward, as the diesel cut out – 'destroyers in Altfjorden. My friend tell me, in the boat. From here five miles, maybe. Airplanes also, sure—'

'Charge broken, engine clutch out, sir!'

'Very good. Lieutenant Bellamy on the bridge with the chart, please. Group down, slow ahead together. Steer—' he sighted over the gyro repeater – 'one-four-two.' All right for a start, but he'd need his navigator and the large-scale chart, to retrace the route they'd come in by, that narrow channel. At a pinch it might have been done submerged, but it would have been very tricky, and slower. Tricky enough as it was – which was why he'd put the coxswain on the wheel – and it couldn't be rushed. Get stuck, then have the Stukas over: you'd have dramatic proof then of the old adage *More haste, less speed.* Less *anything* ... He glanced at the Norwegian again – as Bellamy appeared, clambering out of the hatch with the rolled chart under one arm – wondering whether he was right to take the man's word for this. He seemed steadier now, must have begun to feel safe, or something ... Knowing nothing about the near-flat battery, of course, or that a single hour's charging would have made next to no difference to it.

Chapter 18

In mid-forenoon Chalk bumped into *Threat*'s CO, Tim Hart, in the corridor outside the flotilla staff offices, and Hart told him that 'young Van Sommeren's fiancée' had telephoned shortly after he, Chalk, had left the building on his way down to the dockyard. Hart had asked her if she wanted to leave a message; Suzie had asked him who he was, then said, 'Well, perhaps you could help. My name's Susan Cameron-Green, I'm engaged to Chris Van Sommeren—'

'Who's on temporary loan to *Tracker*. Wedding thus postponed, I heard. Rotten bad luck, Miss – er—'

'You said *Tracker*?'

'Shouldn't have, should I. Walls having ears, all that.'

'It's what I wanted to know. *Tracker*. Thank you so much. Goodbye . . .'

Clunk.

Hart told Chalk, 'No message, that's all there was to it.'

Chalk stared at him. '*All*, you say.'

'Not out of order, was I?'

He could have hit him. Minutes later, wondered why he hadn't. But why he of all people had had to take her call . . . He shook his head: he wasn't going to discuss Suzie or her problems or potential problems with Tim Hart. He told him,

'I'd suggest you leave it to the stewards to take messages in future, Tim. Mine, anyway.' He'd pushed on past him: he'd had a summons to report to Captain (S), who by this time would no doubt have read his patrol report, might also be able to tell him how long he'd have before the next one. Hart's voice sounded plaintive behind him: 'God's sake, I was only trying to be helpful!' He didn't look back. He had his own work to do and also his first lieutenant's – actually letting Sutherland, his third hand, do most of it, but having to keep a supervisory eye on him – and Patricia's absence, those ghastly visions which in the small hours had one sweating – and Diana, for whom he was beginning to feel a cold dislike – on top of all that, now, a gratuitous contribution from Tim bloody Hart.

The only hope was that the name *Tracker* wouldn't mean anything to Suzie.

He knocked on Captain Bertie Weaver's door, went in and shut it behind him. Still thinking about her: as anxious for her suddenly as he'd been nearly four years ago. 'Morning, sir.'

'Chalk. Morning. Sit down.'

He couldn't understand why she'd have telephoned like that anyway. She hadn't pressed him for the boat's name last night. He'd have to ring her – this evening . . .

Captain (S) finished reading the patrol report.

'Not your usual good luck, Chalk. But there you are, fact of life – if the targets aren't there, you can't sink 'em . . . Cigarette?'

'Thank you, sir.' He took one and lit it. Weaver had a pipe going.

'However – it was an ill wind, in the long run. If you'd fired all your fish and we'd recalled you early you wouldn't have crossed paths with Mottram. And as there's no Spare Crew first lieutenant at Lerwick at the moment, God knows what he'd have done.'

'Unusual to be going north at this time of year, sir?'

'Indeed. Quick trip, mind you – if it goes as it should. There was a lot of pressure on us to extricate this fellow. A lot of pressure on Northways, I gather – so you can guess where it came from.'

Chalk guessed he meant Churchill. Northways was the wartime headquarters of Admiral (Submarines), who wasn't exactly renowned for giving way to pressure from anyone at all. Winston, of course, would be the exception.

'Am I allowed to know who they're picking up, sir?'

'A Jerry – believe it or not. Anti-Nazi, scientist of international repute, potentially of value to us because he has inside knowledge of various projects and so forth. For your private information only, Chalk.'

He nodded. 'But if he's anti-Nazi, how would he have this inside knowledge?'

Weaver smiled his approval of the question.

'He has – or had – a Jewish wife, and they sent her to one of their loathsome camps. Perhaps he was for the chop then too, I don't know, but anyway he skedaddled – to Norway, for some reason or other, connections there I suppose – and since the bastards invaded he's been underground, as they call it. They'd have been out to get him, obviously, and recently our people got word that he wanted to be brought out and had this priceless intelligence to offer, and – and that's where *we* came in. Couldn't delay it, obviously – wait for the dark nights, for instance.'

'No . . . You say it'll be a quick trip, sir?'

'Quicker the better. Oh yes, I take your point – but hell, who'd want to hang around up there . . . Last thing *I*'d want . . . Now, let's talk about you and *Tumult*. And that's the first thing, of course – we'll see you get Van Sommeren back before we let you loose again, don't worry about that . . . Incidentally, isn't he supposed to be getting married soon?'

Suzie brought her Spitfire into the Cosford circuit on a wide, curving approach that gave her a view of the airfield which she wouldn't have had if she'd come in straight. She enjoyed flying Spits more than any other aircraft, but the one snag was the lack of forward visibility, especially during take-offs and landings, the flat-topped Merlin cowling completely shutting out your view ahead.

But in the air a Spit was tremendously exciting, immensely powerful. And so damned *easy* – so responsive ... As well as tolerant of minor examples of cack-handedness on a pilot's part. This was a Mark V, powered by a Merlin 45 and a four-bladed propeller. Stupendous ...

Touching down – *now*. One little bounce ...

Taxi-ing, you were *really* blind. You saw the ground to your right and left but not a damn thing in front.

There was a flap on, an urgent need to move a large number of Spitfires north to Prestwick in as short a time as possible. They were 'P1W' movements: abbreviation of 'Priority One, Wait', which meant that if the weather was unsuitable for flying the pilot had to wait beside his or her aircraft until conditions improved and take-off was possible. The last time there'd been this kind of operation with Spits it had been a consignment to be loaded on to an aircraft-carrier in the Clyde for transport to Malta. Only male ATA pilots had been involved – except for women flying the taxi 'planes shuttling them to and fro – because at that stage the women hadn't been allowed to fly operational aircraft. Suzie had read and heard about the Gibraltar–Malta convoy a few weeks later: they'd flown them off the carrier somewhere short of the island, and according to the report they'd all made it. This could be a repetition of the same stunt; and her own part in it – of which the Maltese would never hear – was to move half a dozen or more Spits from Henley to Cosford in Staffordshire. A team of girls from Hatfield were on the job, moving about thirty in this batch, and the Cosford ATA ferry-pool pilots would take them on north from here, very likely in one hop to Prestwick, while a taxi Anson would return Suzie and the other Hatfield pilots to Henley, to bring another lot up. And so on all day until sunset, possibly the next day as well. The Henley airfield was a small one to the south of the town itself, one of the fields – along with Challis Hill and High Post – to which Spitfires were dispersed from factories to be assembled and test-flown.

Parking her machine and climbing out of it, she was thinking again about Chris – who, she'd learnt this morning, was in a submarine called *Tracker*. She'd telephoned to Dundee to ask Rufus *please* to tell her the boat's name, but he'd already left the building and another CO had told her without any hesitation at all. Captain of *Threat*, he'd said he was – the boat Rufus had been standing by at Barlows' when she'd first met him.

Him, and Toby Dymock. And started Guy on his way to Spain.

If she'd had Rufus on the 'phone when she'd called this morning she'd have had to explain why she'd wanted that submarine's name. To him she *could* have explained it: that she'd been writing to Chris – primarily through her own need to do so, next best thing to talking to him – and she'd wanted to know the boat's name so she could mention it in her letter – be that much more *with* him – instead of shut out, forbidden to know this or that.

She wouldn't have told Rufus that she also wanted the name so she could mention it in her prayers. Prayers were private things, not for discussion over telephones. She prayed in the air sometimes, had done so this morning for both of them.

For Pat, too. Although she tried not to worry about her. There was enough, to be going on with. You had to take it for granted she'd just turn up, that some evening soon you'd hear her voice over the blower – 'Oh, have you missed me, Suzie pet?'

The taxi Anson wouldn't keep them waiting long, she guessed. As soon as all the pilots from Hatfield had touched down and signed in, the word would go round and they'd drift out to it. There were several Henley Spits to come in yet, though. Pushing into No. 12 Ferry Pilots' Pool's cafeteria, on her way to the bar she was looking round for friends and/or colleagues generally but in particular for the two girls from Hatfield who'd taken off before she had, had to be around here somewhere.

'Hi, Suzie!'

There they were. She waved back, veered off towards them – and almost collided with Diana. Diana Chalk.

Who'd been stuck out again last night. Suzie's eyes went past her, half-expecting to see Jacques Vernet and desperately hoping not to: he wasn't there, thank God.

'Suzie!'

'Hi. Where did *you* spring from?'

'Oh – Filton . . . Come and join me, Suzie. I'm *so* sorry about – you know, the postponement—'

'Damn bore, isn't it?' She grimaced. 'Really *is* . . . But – only a couple of weeks' delay, as Rufus said . . . Diana, actually I was on my way to join Harriet Shaw and Liz Cavendish – over there—'

'They'll keep, Suzie. *Won't* they.' Diana put an arm round her. To be sure she didn't just skid off, perhaps. She did like to have her own way – as Suzie and others were well aware . . . She was explaining, 'Haven't got long, actually, I've a Beaufighter for Prestwick, and then – well, never mind little old *me* . . . Suzie, I think you're *marvellous*, taking it so well. Want a coffee? Sandwich?'

'Well – all right. Yes. Both, please.'

'You and me too. I'm famished . . .' Holding her hand up, to get the attention of the steward behind the bar. 'It really is a *bloody* bore for you, Suzie.'

'Not only for me. Everyone else – the parents most of all, of course. And people who'd arranged for leave, and so on . . . Were you coming, Di?'

'If I'd found I could have – of *course*. Not sure, though – the way things are just at this moment—'

'Will you be seeing Rufus soon?'

'Oh – well. I *hope* so.' She looked exasperated for a moment: and as if she was about to say something else but then decided not to . . . 'Really, of all the times for him to send Chris off in some other damn submarine!'

'*Tracker*.' She'd turned away, was signalling to the two Hatfield pilots that she was stuck . . . Adding as she turned back, 'Rufus didn't send him off – wasn't anything he could have done about it. He's just as fed up as—'

'Did you say *Tracker*?'

Diana's hand on her arm: she seemed to have forgotten the coffee. Suzie looked at her, frowning. 'Just found out, this morning. Rufus wouldn't tell me last night, but—'

'I *bet* he wouldn't!'

'What?'

'Don't you *know*?'

'Know what?'

'That *Tracker* started life as *Trumpeter*?'

Tracker was bottomed again: in twenty-five fathoms, 128 feet on the gauges. Auxiliary machinery stopped, very few lights burning even here in the Control Room. The motor-room telegraphs had been disconnected: that had been done during the run northward – silent running, tiptoeing away . . .

Mottram glanced at his asdic operator: 'Same?'

A nod. Two destroyers were searching to the south of them, in the two-miles of open water between here and Skjingen; three others had continued westward on what had been *Tracker*'s course when she'd dived.

All five *should* have gone on westward. Leaving two behind here wasn't playing Mottram's game at all. If they found her – with a flat battery and surrounded by shallows, little islets and half-tide rocks, she wouldn't have a hope in hell. Mottram had picked this area in the belief that the destroyers would keep clear of its navigational hazards and that they'd assume he'd have done the same. Another hope was that when he did finally bring her to the surface she'd be less visible to observers on shore than she would have been in uncluttered sea.

As in the fjord – where at least one seaplane had passed without spotting her.

Chris was sitting on the corticene-covered battery-boards, with his back against the fixed self-destruction charge. As good a back-rest as any. He was thinking that the two destroyers still hunting for them in this neck of the woods could be a result of Mottram having botched his own perfectly good scheme. He'd expected the Germans to take it for granted that he'd continue westward – then south-west, the course for Lerwick, and he'd encouraged them in what was anyway a perfectly logical assumption by keeping her on the surface, conveniently under observation by a German seaplane, and diving her on a course of due west when a Junkers 88 had appeared from over the land, the Namsos direction. There'd been no bombs dropped – it had still been a long way off when they'd dived – and having done so he'd turned north, paddled quietly up into this area of rocks and islets.

Then, apparently having doubts about the boat's exact position and worried about the shallows and other hazards – his plan being to get around the western end of the foul ground and then right into it, as it were through the back door – he'd put up the small periscope, taken a couple of bearings very quickly, put it down again and taken the boat to forty feet. He'd used the small 'attack' periscope and had it up for probably no more than thirty seconds, but it might have been spotted. If the seaplane had been overhead by then, for instance. Overhead, and lucky; and might then have wirelessed a report that the submarine was steering a northerly course, not due west as it had been at the time of diving.

The senior destroyer captain would then have hedged his

bet: held on with three of his ships to search in the obvious direction – westward – but detached these two just in case the airman had known what he was talking about.

The air would last about thirty-six hours, Mottram had told his crew in a Tannoy broadcast an hour ago. So they could wait that long if they had to. He'd move when the destroyers had given up, surface here among the rocks and islands, and depart flat-out on the diesels. He'd ended his talk with 'Watchkeeping arrangements same as last night. Meaning most of you can get your heads down. Use up less air that way. And I want absolute quiet – they have very efficient listening-gear, remember. The heads, of course, are *not* to be blown . . .'

When they'd started out from the fjord Chris had no notion of Mottram's intentions: he'd wondered what he *could* do, with the battery in the state it was. He'd known of the seaplane's presence; also – soon after they'd started out – that from the bridge Bellamy had seen smoke over the land between themselves and Altfjorden, and this had been interpreted – correctly – as destroyers flashing-up their boilers in a hurry. When the order had come down the pipe for a ninety-degree turn to port – an indication that they were clear of the approaches to Murstenfjord – he'd been ready for the klaxon or the verbal order to dive, and he'd been surprised when it hadn't come.

Trumpeter's air, he recalled – from his own knowledge as well as Chalk's occasional – but rare – answers to the questions fellow submariners tended to put to him – had lasted less than eighteen hours. But she'd had twice as many men on board, and two compartments flooded: and the circumstances had been quite different, the most obvious thing being that *Tracker* could move, surface any time she wanted to. Not while the destroyers were up there, of course – in that sense the advantage wasn't all that obvious. But it did still give one certain options – other than drowning or suffocating, as had been the case in *Trumpeter*. For instance, that of surfacing, baling out, sending her down again with her main vents and the hatch open and the fuze running on this self-destruction charge.

Depending on circumstances, you might make a fight of it. A salvo of torpedoes, if the destroyers were close together, might produce very satisfactory results. Even taking *one* of the sods with you . . . What *Tracker* would *not* be able to do was get away. Dived, the battery would only get her a few miles – running economically, at that, and if the Germans knew their business they'd see she didn't get even that far. And surfaced, her flat-out speed on the diesels would be less than half that of her pursuers – five of them, armed as likely as not with five-inch guns.

The asdic operator nodded to an unspoken question from Mottram. He muttered, 'Still there, sir. Port quarter, both transmitting. Moving right to left, slow. Fifteen hundred yards, could be.'

'Among the rocks, then.'

A slight shrug. Knowing nothing of any bloody rocks . . . Mottram glanced at Chris. 'I think they must be.'

It wasn't *good* news. If they were among the rocks a mile east of here, there was no reason to assume they wouldn't be among *this* lot, in due course. Mottram had gone to the chart-table, switched on its overhead light; Chris glanced up at the dimly-lit bulkhead clock and saw that it was just after ten.

Lunch was corned-beef sandwiches and mugs of tea. The German, Heiden, declined food but accepted tea; and having got it, fell asleep again. Kjellegard had told Mottram he didn't know what was wrong with him but thought it might be heart trouble.

The engineer – Matt Caulfield – muttered, 'Fine thing to have him peg out on us, wouldn't it. Going through all this bloody effort—'

'What efforts are *you* exerting, Chief?'

Bellamy, with his quiet smile . . . Chief stared at him.

'None. As per skipper's orders, conserving oxygen. What do *you* do anyway – except toss yourself off several times a day?'

Chuckling, almost choking on a sandwich... He told Chris, 'At it all the bloody time. What's making his hair fall out.'

Mottram was conversing in whispers with their German guest, who apparently spoke some English. Chris had only come through to the wardroom to collect his rations: he took his two sandwiches and mug of tea into the Control Room, sat down on the boards on the starboard side where he had a clear view of the depthgauges. There wasn't the slightest movement on her. He asked Talbot, who'd taken over on asdics from PO Wootton, 'Anything new?'

A shake of the head: 'No, sir.'

'Reckon we'll be here long, do you, sir?'

The second coxswain, a young PO named Chisholm: on the helmsman's seat, mouth full, chewing ... Chris evaded the question, rather: 'Can't sit up there for ever, can they?'

Since the news that the destroyers had begun searching that end of the area of shallows and other hazards, he wasn't feeling quite as confident as he had earlier. There'd been no good reason for that confidence, anyway: beyond the fact that they *had* to get away with it, and that with Rufus Chalk in *Tumult* they always had.

'Sir—' Talbot's eyes had widened; showing more of their whites, so that in the half-dark it was as if he'd somehow switched on, suddenly ... 'Destroyers have stopped, sir. Transmittin', still – like they had a contact, sir.'

'Captain in the Control Room. Distance, roughly?'

You'd only get an accurate range by pinging on them: which would have been plain lunacy. But an experienced asdic man could make a guess. Talbot muttered, 'Thousand yards, maybe ...'

Mid-afternoon: she put her fourth Spitfire of the day down

at Cosford and taxied it over to the reception area. All the 'planes they'd brought up in earlier stages of this shuttle had already been flown on.

'Keeping you busy, are we?'

The ground-crew flight-sergeant nodded, handing her back the signed delivery papers. 'You are a bit, Miss.'

'Give it a fortnight, it'll be "You are a bit, *Mrs.*"'

'That so?' He smiled at her. 'I'll do me best to remember.'

Not to remember, was the thing. Keep busy – *frantically* busy – and remember *nothing*. Beyond such mundane things as take-off drill – starting with H–T–T–M–P–P: Hydraulics, trimmers, throttle friction, mixture, pitch, petrol – and so forth. Lots more of them like that. Walking to the office, telling herself, *Nothing else at all. Except he'll be back in a couple of weeks, I'll get a message that he's called, and ring him back, and—*

And he'd be *there*. Please God. Smiley brown eyes and all . . .

Submarines went out on patrol every day of the week, after all. Came back again every day of the week too. All right, not *always*, but ninety-five times out of a hundred, say?

She caught herself up again: *Don't think about it – idiot . . . Leave it to him – to them . . .*

'Hi, Suzie!'

'Mary. How are you doing?'

Mary Hastings was one of the Hatfield team. Before the first return flight to Henley she'd queried whether Suzie had been in a fit state to fly: Suzie being the senior pilot in the group, so that Jill Blessington who was the taxi pilot had offered her the Anson's controls. It was a matter of courtesy and an established ATA custom to invite a more experienced passenger-pilot to take over, and the offer was usually accepted. As it had been today, each time, Suzie assuring the rest of them that she was perfectly all right: she knew she looked like something the cat had brought in, but – 'I'm not worried, why should you be?'

The one thing that would *not* have done her any good was to sit and bloody think.

'One more each, is it?'

She'd nodded. 'About that. Unless they've brought more up.'

'If there aren't enough for all of us, *you* drop out, Suzie.'

'How you do go on!'

'Anyway, why not let Harriet fly the Anson this time, give yourself a break?'

'Don't want a break. Coffee's what I want. Coming?'

'Still holding the contact, sir.' Talbot moved the asdic set's training-knob fractionally clockwise. 'Other one's moving left to right, low revs.'

'Bearing?'

'Dead astern, sir. Red one-seven nine . . .'

Tracker was lying with her bows pointing due west, and Talbot's last guess at the range was three-quarters of a sea mile, fifteen hundred yards. Mottram said from the chart-table, 'Puts 'em close to the largest of the islets. So large it actually has a—'

A depthcharge exploded. It was nowhere close, but being completely unexpected it had some of the shock-effect of one much closer.

The booming echo faded, and Mottram finished what he'd been saying about the islet: '– actually has a name.' He came back into the centre of things. 'Harper.' The messenger: fair-headed, pock-marked. 'Go for'ard quietly, Harper, pass the order – whisper it – for diving stations. Nobody's to hurry or make a sound. All right?'

'Aye aye, sir.'

The ERA on watch offered, 'Pass the word aft, shall I, sir?'

'Good man . . .'

Depthcharges usually came in patterns, groups, normally about five close on each others' heels, not single explosions like that. Whether consciously or subconsciously you were waiting for the next one. Like waiting for a jab from a blunt needle, Chris thought. He'd moved to his own diving station, under the trimming telegraph. Mottram murmuring – half to himself – 'Must have a static target there. Or they think they have. Must think it's a bottomed submarine, in fact.'

'In other words – us.'

'Well . . .' A nod. 'As you say.'

It could be some old wreck. Or even not old at all: not every submarine loss had been accounted for. Could be a U-boat: during the Norway campaign *Troubadour* had sunk one not far from here. Chris watched men moving quietly to their diving stations: coxswain and second coxswain already on their stools, the helmsman now, and the communications number – who manned the telephone and kept the log – and Grant, the signalman. Electrical Artificer – Stavely, his name was. Expressions on the faces that showed any at all were of surprise or mild apprehension, or some degree of both.

Mottram ordered quietly, 'Without any noise, shut off for depthcharging.'

It meant shutting certain hull-valves: it was completed quickly, the reports came through to Chris and he in turn confirmed to Mottram that the boat was 'shut off'. PO Wootton, who'd taken over again on asdics, reporting meanwhile that one destroyer was still lying stopped but transmitting, and the other— he paused, concentrating . . . 'Stopping engines now, sir. Both of 'em's stopped.'

Nice easy targets, Chris thought. If you'd been up there. One fish in each . . .

But they *must* have been thinking they had a bottomed submarine there. Nothing else would explain their lying stopped now. Having dropped one charge on it – probably *right* on it, the two ships working together could have fixed its position within a yard or so. And they knew the charted depth – so often the imponderable factor that saved your life. A depthcharge had only to burst within ten feet of a submarine's hull to blast a hole in it. They'd be watching now to see what came up: oil, woodwork, clothing, bodies. Listening out meanwhile on their hydrophones for such sounds as it might make if by some miracle it had survived and was trying to move away: motors, propellers, or before that a ballast-pump running to lighten her, get her off the bottom.

And there, but for the grace of God—

'One's moving, sir. Red one-seven-eight, right to left.'

Mottram warned, 'Another charge due shortly, then.' He looked round, and told Bellamy – who was at his chart-table – 'Take a walk through the boat, pilot, tell 'em what's happening. They're attacking a wreck, probably. As long as they stick to it, then think they've sunk it – then bugger off – eh?'

'Aye aye—'

A second crash: even from that distance the boat felt it, the impact jarring her steel hull. Actually, *Trumpeter*'s steel hull ... Expressions around the Control Room might have become more wooden: but that was all. Wootton reported as the echo sang away, 'New HE on red two-five, sir. Fast turbines, closing. More than one, sir.'

'Three, probably.'

Coming back. Summoned back, no doubt.

A rather embarrassing phenomenon troubling Suzie now was that when she held a cup and saucer she couldn't stop them rattling: although on an aeroplane's controls her hands were as steady as they'd ever been. Lesson in it somewhere: such as the sky being her natural habitat, perhaps? The thought crossed her mind when she was trundling the taxi Anson towards the Henley huts and hangars, and had become conscious of a yearning for a cigarette and yet another cup of coffee.

One answer to the problem might be to remain permanently airborne. A more practical one, though, would be to ask for a mug instead of a cup. And for the mug not to be filled right up, so she wouldn't slop it and have them glancing at each other as if they thought she was drunk or something. She braked the machine to a halt, told Jill Blessington, 'Thanks. All yours now. See you at Cosford.' Looking back at the others: 'Beat her up on the way, shall we?'

When they overtook her in their Spits, she meant – but only jokingly, they'd obviously do no such thing. Trying to sound light-hearted, that was all. In fact one never did fool around: ATA rules were strict, and you'd be out on your ear if you did. *Safe* delivery of aircraft was the guiding principle. ATA pilots, for instance, didn't fly over cloud: it was all ground-contact flying, you were expected to have *terra firma* in sight all the time. Pilots did get caught out sometimes by bad weather – cutting it too fine, or misled by an erroneous forecast – and not having any form of communication with the ground it could be frightening when it happened. But 99 per cent of the time you had rivers, roads, railways, villages, even individual country houses in sight that you knew and recognized.

On the ground and heading for the huts, Jane Ascoli joined her – trotting up from the rear, then shortening her stride to match Suzie's. She was a tall, dark, angular girl, quite a bit older than her, and engaged to a major in Alastair's regiment – now in the Western Desert.

'Well, Suzie – last trip, huh?'

She nodded. 'Should be.' She wondered what might be coming next: something like *Why don't you take a breather, let the rest of us polish it off*?

'Awfully sorry to hear your wedding's postponed, Suzie.'

'Seems to be the topic of the day, doesn't it?'

'Why – I'd have thought it was quite *natural*—'

'Well, look – the Germans invaded Russia yesterday,

didn't they. You'd think that'd be of *slightly* greater interest. Or – closer to home – the fact they're still bombing all the ports. Which of them got it again last night – Portsmouth, was it?'

'You're even *closer* to home, Suzie. We're all quite fond of you – in case you didn't know.'

'Fond enough to do me a great favour?'

'No. Definitely not!' Liz Cavendish had joined them, on Suzie's other side. Jane asked Suzie, 'What kind of favour?'

'Just not to go on about my bloody wedding. Or my state of health, for God's sake. I'm perfectly all right, and the wedding's only off until Chris gets back from sea. Meanwhile, I'm trying not to think about it, so—'

'Point taken. Reluctantly.' Jane put her arm round Suzie's shoulders and squeezed her: *everyone* seemed to be doing it, today. Diana, for instance . . .'

It was like remembering being struck by lightning. About as near to it as you could get. That phrase one read in stories – 'her heart stopped' – her own heart *had*, she thought: had missed a few beats, at least. For *Tracker*, read *Trumpeter* . . .

None of these worried fellow-pilots knew anything about *that*, thank God.

She'd see them in the cafeteria hut, she'd said – after she'd checked in at the office.

'Suzie . . .'

Jane Ascoli had slowed – with that arm still round her, so she had to follow suit, while the rest of them carried on. 'Suzie, listen. Please, just for a moment?'

'Well—'

'I can understand that you want to keep going, stiff upper lip, all that, and I admire you for it – in a way. But you're *not* in a state to be flying, Suzie. God almighty, your hands are shaking like some old hag's!'

'Not on the control column, they're not.'

'I hate to drag this up, Suzie, but – remember Amy Mollison?'

'Of course I remember her! Drag what up – what's Amy got to do with anything?'

Amy Mollison had killed herself a few months earlier – in January. She'd been a long way off her course and over cloud: there were some peculiar circumstances, but the accepted conclusion was that she'd been lost, circling in the hope of finding a break in the clouds, and her Oxford had run out of gas and crashed. Into the Thames estuary.

Jane Ascoli told her, 'She had a lot on *her* mind, Suzie. Personal problems.'

'I see what you're driving at. I'd heard that, anyway, Diana Chalk told me. I'd forgotten. It's only speculation, isn't it.'

'Well – *either* way—'

'Nothing like that's going to happen to me, Jane.'

'Amy was the most experienced pilot we had, wasn't she? I don't expect she thought it could happen to her, either. Suzie, you could easily make sure it doesn't—'

'Report sick, you mean.' She shook her head, decisively. 'I'm *not* sick. And there's no similarity between me and my – my temporary *upset*—'

'There's a shake in your voice, at times—'

'– and Amy and whatever problems she may or may not have had ... Jane—' she pointed at the door marked OPERATIONS – 'I'll get this done, then I'll see you in the cafeteria – OK?'

'OK. I think you're wrong, but – I'll get you a coffee.'

'In a mug, please, not a cup?'

She knocked on the door, and went in.

'Oh—'

'Susan Cameron-Green, is it?'

She admitted it. She hadn't seen this one before. Dumpy, greying, with an engaging smile. 'I'm Sally Jordan – adjutant, standing in for Marge Verity – whom you've met three times today – or is it four? How d'you do ...'

They shook hands. Suzie had papers to hand in, delivery

receipts for the last lot they'd flown up to Cosford. 'Only this one batch to go now, isn't it?'

'That's correct. And only five aircraft – but there are six of you, aren't there?'

'Well.' Suzie shrugged. 'One of us can twiddle her thumbs in the Anson. I'll sort that out.'

'But there's another thing. I've been on to your pool about it, incidentally. There's a Hurricane here for Silloth – and with our local chaps all away, and you with a pilot to spare – would you help out?'

She checked the time. Silloth, on the Solway Firth, was an RAF repair and storage unit. She'd made deliveries there, also landed *en route* from A to B, several times. She nodded. 'Hurries take ninety gallons, don't they. So – one hop – should make it before dark, easily. Weather permitting?'

'The forecast's good. You'll do it yourself, will you?'

'Don't see why not. Will you tell Hatfield?'

'They know.' Sally Jordan had a nice smile. 'That's to say they guessed you'd take it on. But yes, I'll confirm it to them, and I'll tell Silloth to expect you.'

At the end of the working day Chalk rang the ATA at Hatfield and asked for Suzie, but the duty Operations Officer told him she was on her way to some place called Silloth, should have got there by now but hadn't rung in yet. She'd be stuck out for the night, obviously – probably in Carlisle, but until she heard from her she couldn't say for sure. If he'd call again in about an hour, say? With any luck she'd be able to tell him then.

He went up and bathed and changed, and listened to the news, read by Alvar Liddell. The Luftwaffe had hit both Plymouth and Portsmouth last night, the Finns had invaded Karelia, and the butter ration was to be reduced.

Patricia was constantly on his mind ... *Might* ring the Cameron-Greens, he thought: despite their reported disapproval of his friendship with Patricia. (Whatever suspicions they might have, that was all they could know it was.) In fact *he* wasn't supposed to know he was in their bad books, that Suzie had told him he was; so, with the postponement of the wedding and their future son-in-law being one of his own officers, it might seem a bit odd if he didn't get in touch. And Patricia might, conceivably, have told them before she left how long she thought she might be away. If one knew that she'd expected to be away this long, it would help a lot.

Downstairs, he called the Hatfield number again, and the same girl told him that Suzie had arrived at Silloth, where the RAF were giving her a meal and then laying on a car to take her into Carlisle. She gave him the number of the hotel where he could get her later on. Try at about ten, she suggested: Carlisle was quite a few miles from Silloth.

He got back to the exchange, and asked for the Glendarragh number. He was holding on, waiting for the connection, when Tim Hart brought him a gin and water: 'By way of apology for my indiscretion this morning, Rufus.'

He nodded. 'Thanks.'

'Better drink it while we've got it. Bastards hit the distillery last night. They say Plymouth gin was running through the gutters, matelots flat on their bellies lapping it up.'

'I don't believe it . . . Hello? MacKenzie? Is Sir Innes there? Rufus Chalk . . .'

They didn't talk for long, and Sir Innes wasn't able to tell him anything about Patricia's comings or goings.

'We've never heard from her as often as we'd like to. Any particular reason for – anxiety, at this stage?'

'Only that she's been gone what seems like an awfully long time. And the nature of her work – one *does* worry. I'm sure you must too. I expect you know that she and I see quite a lot of each other – whenever we can, that is, with our respective jobs. I'm *very* fond of her . . .'

'And how is Diana?'

'She *sounds* very well. Unfortunately, we rarely manage to see each other.'

'In my view that's a great pity.'

'Yes. It is. But it's – a fact . . . Any news from Alastair?'

'He writes occasionally. Those one-page forms they photograph or something . . . More frequently to Midge, I may say. Well – natural enough. And she keeps in touch, you know . . . When d'you think you'll have young Chris back?'

'Impossible to say, sir. But when I have any news I'll telephone again.'

It was getting noisy in the bar. There was a party getting under way: *Sabre* had got in that afternoon from a successful patrol in the approaches to the Jade – Wilhelmshaven – and her officers were celebrating. Having no doubt promised themselves early nights – as one invariably did. He went through, bought a round of drinks, heard the story about the Plymouth gin distillery again: it was a major blow against the war effort, everyone agreed.

Not that it was anything to joke about, in the wider sense. In the last couple of months all the ports had been heavily attacked, with very large numbers of civilian casualties. The Clyde, Mersey and Hull, as well as the southern ports, and London. In the Mersey area, he'd heard, something like a hundred thousand civilians had been left homeless.

After supper, he tried to ring Suzie at the Carlisle hotel, but its number was engaged, and when he tried again ten minutes later, he got through but was told Miss Cameron-Green had not yet arrived.

He was worried about her: had tried to convince himself he wasn't, that she surely would *not* know of *Tracker*'s origins: but it was quite possible that she did. The fact she hadn't ever mentioned it proved nothing: she wouldn't have *wanted* to talk about it.

He was caught up in the festivities then, couldn't get out of a game of *vingt-et-un* until about eleven. It hadn't worried him too much: rather than call every ten minutes, he'd thought he might just as well give her time to get there.

Actually, he realized now, it *was* a bit late. Hearing eleven strike, leaning against the wall beside the telephone, waiting for the connection to be made. Finally he was through to the hotel, asked for Miss Cameron-Green, and again had to wait. Lighting a fresh cigarette, one-handed. He was smoking too much these days, and knew it.

'Hello?'

'Suzie – Rufus . . .'

'Rufus! Oh God – you've had news—'

'No. I haven't – couldn't hope for it this soon. Are you all right, Suzie?'

'Did you hear I wasn't?'

'No – just that with Chris away—'

'It's damn late, isn't it?'

'I'm sorry. Worried for you, that's all. Did I wake you?'

'Not exactly, but I was half undressed and I'm downstairs now. You *shouldn't* worry about me. I've been telling people all day I'm perfectly all right – had a very busy day, as it happens?'

'I'm *very* sorry.'

'It's all right. I'll survive.' She laughed, added, 'Although I did have a bit of a narrow squeak today.'

'What kind of narrow squeak?'

'Problem with an undercarriage. Mechanical fault, not mine.'

'Well, take care – *please*. Chris'll want to find you intact, Suzie.'

'Which, thanks to you—'

'Enough of *that*... You tried to get me this morning, I heard.'

'Yes. I had to know which one Chris has gone in. Simply to *know* it. I write to him, when he's away, and—'

'Write the same as always – *Tumult*, care of GPO.'

'Not for *that*. To mention it in the letter, so he knows I know, and – oh, I suppose you think I'm nuts, but—'

'I think you're bloody marvellous. As you well know – or should do.'

'Well.' A laugh. 'You're entitled to your own illusions, I suppose. But – Rufus, I'm *sure* Pat'll just suddenly turn up—'

'Can't turn up *too* suddenly.' He drew in a breath. Every time his thoughts went back to her, it hit him . . . 'I spoke to your father this evening, by the way. He didn't know anything, either. Grousing that they hardly ever hear from her . . . So – fingers crossed. Say a prayer for me, will you?'

'Don't you think your own might be heard, when it's for someone else?'

'I'm in love with her, you know.'

'She is with you, too. As I'm sure you know. Rufus, I was about to say – I know about *Tracker*.'

'About – you mean—'

'*Trumpeter*.'

'Oh. Oh, Suzie . . . I'd hoped you might *not*. Not that there's any reason to feel – you know, superstitious, or – well, it was just that you *might*—'

'Rufus—'

'Huh?'

'It's all right – I *know* there's no – reason . . . I was nearly sick when I first heard, but – I'm worried now, but – you know, like I'm *always* worried. Perhaps a bit worse than usual because he's not with *you* . . . But don't hide things from me – please, from now on? If – when you do have news, *whatever* it is, *please*—'

'All right. I must say, you astound me. As I was saying a minute or two ago—'

'I know – I'm bloody marvellous. No – it's just that I don't want always to have to think there may be something you aren't telling me. Anyway – better hit the sack now. Early start, a Spitfire to deliver to Brize Norton. Bliss, but one does need to be more or less *compos mentis*. So – sleep well, darling Rufus, and – thanks for the call.'

'Chris, Suzie, is the luckiest man on earth.'

He thought wryly, hanging up, *At least his girl will be here when he does get back . . .*

'Layin' stopped mostly, sir. Both of 'em, must be.'

There were only two destroyers now because three had left at about midnight, the sound of their screws fading in the direction of Namsenfjord. It had seemed like good news at the time – three gone, only two left: step in the right direction.

But it was possible they'd only gone to refuel.

Just after five, now. This time yesterday *Tracker* had been in the fjord, with an hour to go before surfacing for the battery charge – and expecting to spend the day there, then quietly re-embark the landing party and creep away – undetected and unheard of. He'd been telling himself *Six days to Suzie. . .*

Mottram came back into the wardroom, having left Bellamy on watch in the Control Room. He said as he sat down, 'No other explanation for it, they think they've got *us* there. In fact they must think they've killed us. Question is, why should they still be hanging around?'

There'd been two more charges dropped – soon after the three destroyers had returned from their trip westward. Four charges in all, therefore, and if they reckoned that was enough they certainly did have to believe they'd made a kill. Chris wondered whether they might be fishing for evidence of it – proof of a submarine's destruction.

No. If you wanted that – something to float up that might serve as proof positive – you'd drop more charges, split her open so she'd spill her guts: and they'd have done it long ago.

The Norwegian, Kjellegard, was at the table. Mottram had told him his job was to look after Dr Heiden; he'd been in there with him, but the German was asleep now – audibly so, breathing in short gasps, under a blanket on that narrow bunk . . . He, surely, had to be the clue to this: he was the reason *Tracker* was here at all, he was central to the whole thing, so – surely ... He asked Kjellegard, 'Did you say the Gestapo were hunting Dr Heiden?'

A nod. 'Sure.'

'Well, d'you think the German navy might have to prove they've done him in?'

Chief muttered, stifling a yawn, '*That*'s a thought.'

'Done in?'

Mottram showed interest. 'You've a point there. Could be the answer.' He looked at Kjellegard. 'The Gestapo know Dr Heiden is – *was* – escaping by submarine. Is that what you told me when you arrived on board?'

A nod. Slightly puzzled expression, though.

'They knew he *might* be, or they knew he *was*?'

'Captain, sir.' Bellamy, in the gangway. 'One destroyer's leaving, sir.'

'*Is* it ...' Mottram pushed himself up, followed Bellamy into the Control Room. Kjellegard asked, pointing that way with his head, 'Is good?'

Chris nodded: he was listening to the voices in there. French muttered – he'd just woken from a doze – 'Better than a poke in the eye – at least, if I heard right—'

'Quiet a minute, Sub ...'

Trying to hear ... The asdic watchkeeper – a Glaswegian, name of Anderson – telling Mottram, 'Revs for twelve, fifteen knots, sir.'

'Nothing else near it? Nothing *coming*?'

A silence – he'd been checking on other bearings. Then, 'No, sir. Just the one. Range still opening.'

'What's *this* one doing?'

'Layin' stopped, sir. No – movin' one screw – dead slow ... Stopped again. He'd be just holdin' his position – would'n he?'

'Yes ...'

French muttered, 'Why can't he just piss off?' Glancing up, then: 'Hey, hear *that*?'

No-one could have failed to hear it: the destroyer's cable clattering out. And the asdic man's voice again, telling Mottram unnecessarily, 'Droppin' his hook, sir.'

Kjellegard asked Chris, 'What is that?'

'Destroyer's anchoring. Dropping anchor.'

Bellamy called to Mottram from the chart, 'Could be in quite shallow water there, sir.'

The Norwegian spread his hands. 'Is good?'

'No.' Chris told him, '*Not* good.'

It meant the German was going to stay a while. A 'while' being – well, open-ended. Chris was gazing upward, at the white-enamelled deckhead: when you heard underwater sounds it was natural to look in the direction they seemed to be coming from, but now he was noticing the sheen of condensation on that white paint – drips forming. Cork chips in the paint absorbed most of the condensation, but after you'd been down an unusually long time the cork tended to become saturated. So he'd been told – never experienced it before, only on several occasions had the chips come raining down like confetti when depthcharges had burst too close for comfort. But the air wasn't too good, either: his own breathing was shorter and harder than normal, and Chief was yawning almost continuously. *Tracker* had been dived for nearly twenty-four hours, he realized.

Chapter 19

There was still some cloud around, at Haywarden, but true to the forecast they'd given her at Silloth it was much lighter and more scattered. At Silloth it hadn't been so good. She brought the Spitfire down neatly enough to raise no eyebrows, and taxied it over to the fuelling point. Fuelling was the only reason for stopping here. She'd have made it from Silloth to Brize Norton in one hop, but an RAF maintenance engineer at Silloth had warned her that this machine had an above-average gas consumption – or was alleged to have; they'd checked it over and found nothing wrong, but were bound to recommend a precautionary stop along the way. Suzie would probably have accepted the assurance that the Spit was in good order and stuck to her plans – keeping an eye on the gauge, of course – if it hadn't been for visions of Jane Ascoli's 'told-you-so' if the machine had let her down.

As the Hurricane almost had, yesterday: and having come that close to it, she wasn't risking it again. What had happened was the selector lever which operated the Hurricane's undercarriage had jammed, wouldn't move when she was preparing to land at Silloth. She'd made several circuits, struggling with it; the same lever selected not only the undercart but also the flaps, so she'd been faced with a belly landing, flapless – considerably reduced control – with possibly dire effects on both 'plane and pilot. But on her third or fourth circuit of the field the lever had responded: and after a safe and normal landing she'd realized that her main anxieties in those minutes had been (a) the prospect of being crocked up when Chris got back, (b) the wagging fingers back at Hatfield.

At Haywarden a glamorous but rather snooty WAAF officer gave her coffee in their mess. Suzie's hands still shook, but she'd developed a way of handling a cup and saucer which cut out the rattling. It probably looked a bit strange, but it was less embarrassing than the castanets had been. A rather worse manifestation, though – of this state of nerves, whatever they'd call it – was that she'd found she couldn't sign her name. When she had to sign chits – for the fuel, for instance – her signature went haywire. She'd first noticed it at Henley; last night in her hotel room she'd practised for about half an hour and found no way of controlling it.

It would wear off, please God. When *Tracker* got into Dundee and she had that call from Chris.

She'd written to him last night, before Rufus telephoned. Her handwriting didn't seem to be affected: it went a bit wild occasionally, but she thought it always had. And to him she could just sign herself 'S'. But having poured out her heart to Chris, she'd dreamt of Toby Dymock: in the dream she'd been waiting for *him* to get back. Chris hadn't come into it at all, might not have existed.

The sleeping mind was *never* in one's control, she'd told herself about fifty times. Knowing damn well that there was no vestige of any such feelings in her waking thoughts, but still oppressed by a sense of guilt that they should have been lurking in her subconscious.

As if one chose one's dreams, for Christ's sake. She'd had some real beauties, in her time. Lighting another cigarette, and smiling at a remark the WAAF had made . . . She was on the ground at Haywarden for about an hour: two cups of coffee, two fish-paste sandwiches, four or five cigarettes. There'd been time to kill, her Spit hadn't been the first in line for fuelling and the ground staff had obviously been busy. The WAAF was really quite a pleasant girl – woman, years older than Suzie – but women flyers did tend to put a lot of such people's noses out of joint. She'd noticed it before. Envy, jealousy – whichever. She could understand it, too: in the WAAF's shoes *she'd* have been envious of First Officer Cameron-Green, ATA.

Airborne again, on course for the Midland Gap – to pass between Shrewsbury and Wolverhampton – she noticed that the Spit's oil-pressure was on the low side. It was all right – sixty pounds to the square inch – but she was fairly certain it had been higher than that on the way down from Silloth. *Had* been – surely ... The acceptable range of oil-pressure was between fifty and one-forty pounds to the inch: so there was no cause for panic, just that she'd have been happier to see it somewhere over the halfway mark.

Which it must have been, earlier on. Otherwise she'd have reported it at Haywarden.

Better watch it, she told herself. That *and* the fuel-gauge.

Just before noon the destroyer began to shorten-in her cable.

Nobody commented, in the wardroom. The engineer, Caulfield, rolled over on his bunk and pointed upwards, with a hopeful look on his now almost fully bearded face, and Bellamy muttered something; but that might have been in his sleep. The Norwegian lieutenant poked his head out of Mottram's cabin, looking from one to the other interrogatively: Chris came from the chart-table at that moment, saw the question on the soldier's face and shrugged – wordlessly answering, 'God knows ...' Nobody was speaking any more than they had to, now. He flopped down on to the padded bench and leant with his elbows on the table, face in hands.

Cable still clanking in. The Norwegian had retreated into the tiny cabin. He'd been dozing in there on the deck, on his back with his knees drawn up, beside the bunk in which the German – Heiden – was still comatose and breathing more erratically than before.

He wasn't the only one. Some were panting like dogs; and Chris felt as if he had a feather duster in his lungs. Thinking about it, he realized that he was panting too. He'd also been getting spasms of light-headedness, and had noticed symptoms of the same condition in others. It wasn't the syndrome of easy laughter under tension – taut nerves leading to reactions being more quickly triggered – but the beginnings of carbon dioxide poisoning producing an effect not unlike the early stages of drunkenness – the giggly stage, and waves of reckless optimism.

In effect, a kind of lunacy. The only justification for optimism – or for *hope*, say – would be if the destroyer which was about to leave was not replaced. And even that thought was – well, ludicrous, more of the same idiocy: he knew that another destroyer *would* take this one's place. Knew also, largely from research conducted since the *Trumpeter* disaster, that what followed the happy-go-lucky stage was a general lassitude, disinterest in – well, really in anything. Including survival, or steps that might be taken towards it. And to fend that off – apart from getting up into the fresh air – well, there wasn't anything. Except what he'd already seen to – the distribution of protosorb, a chemical substance that was supposed to absorb some of the poison from the air. It came in the form of white crystals, which were now spread on shallow trays on the deck all through the boat.

Reduction of CO_2 was the only hope. Letting oxygen into the atmosphere, for instance, got you nowhere, because the poison would still be present: you couldn't dilute it, and when its proportion in the atmosphere reached about 10 per cent, you were dead.

Then you wouldn't have any more worries. And *that* seemed funny. Remember it, to tell Suzie . . .

He remembered her telling *him* that Rufus Chalk was going great guns with her sister Patricia – whom Chris had met but didn't as yet know well. Very attractive: and smart, sophisticated. More so than Suzie. Although they were sisters and when you saw them together the likenesses were obvious, they were really quite different types. Chris smiled to himself, thinking *Good luck to old Rufus – but* I've *got the pick of the litter.*

She'd told him – he could hear her voice clearly, picture her as she'd said it – *'If I had to prophesy, I'd say he and Diana'll split up, and he'll marry Pat.'*

'Really think so?'

'*Really* hope *so. I'd* love *to have Rufus for a brother-in-law.*'

'Hey – he'd be mine, too . . .'

He thought, listening to the German's cable still coming in, that whether or not Rufus Chalk ended up as Suzie's brother-in-law, he'd be a big help to her, getting her over this.

As he'd done before, that other time. Well – Diana, of course, and the flying: that was the way they told it . . . But *Christ* – as if she hadn't been through enough. Poor kid. Poor *darling* Suzie.

Anyway, one wouldn't stay passively down here, as it were do a *Trumpeter*. Before it got that bad, Mottram would surface, obviously. Chris had thought quite a lot, off and on, about what they might do when the time came. There'd been some general talk about it too, at some stage – about torpedoing the one at anchor for a start, then running for it. There'd be lives lost, inevitably: but only *some*, not—

The cable's clanking stopped. He straightened, listening; heard Mottram's quiet, 'Damnation . . .'

'Drawing left, sir.'

It had started again. He understood that pause, could

picture events up there quite clearly. Whatever they called it in German, there'd have been a report from the destroyer's fo'c'sl of 'Cable's up and down' – meaning the slack was out of it, it was leading straight from the hawsepipe to the anchor on the sea-bed – and the skipper, being ready to move, would have ordered 'Weigh'.

Which they were doing now. Breaking the anchor out of the sea-bed, and heaving it right in.

Mottram put his head round the corner from the Control Room: Chris raised his head – he'd been resting it on his forearms – and stared back at him, blinking. Mottram told him, 'Changing the guard. Another one coming out.'

It wasn't any great surprise.

Earlier – several hours ago – they'd continued their debate on the Germans' motive in keeping a guardship over what they believed to be a submarine they'd sunk. Starting from the logical deduction that it had to centre on Dr Heiden, and the guess that the Gestapo might want proof of his death – well, that was *it*. The Gestapo would want proof of it for the simple reason that if Heiden wasn't in that submarine he'd still be at large in Norway, would still have to be hunted down: and it mightn't do them much good to go back and report, 'We *think* he's dead.' If he was still on the loose he might still get out, taking his knowledge with him. So they'd want a body. And – harking back to an earlier thought about dropping more depthcharges to blow the thing open – if they did that, they wouldn't necessarily have the right one conveniently floating up, in fact they might well destroy it – wouldn't then know whether it had been there or not. They'd want a *recognizable* corpse. And that wreck which they thought they'd done-in with a single charge – plus three others for luck – was in water shallow enough to anchor in, therefore shallow enough to get divers down: and *that* was what they'd be waiting for. A diver or a team of divers, and the necessary gear.

It made sense. Explained why one was facing suffocation.

But – he reminded himself again – that was *not* the case. The *Trumpeter* factor had to be kept out of mind: shouldn't even have got *into* mind, until now he'd hardly given it a thought. But conversely, the fact this was *Tracker* who'd started life as *Trumpeter* wasn't any guarantee of survival either. Something like twenty T-class submarines had been lost this far, and there was no reason *Tracker* shouldn't become the twenty-first.

At some point – it might have been an hour ago or twelve, one hadn't much grasp of time retrospectively – Mottram had murmured to him privately, 'Sorry about this, old chap. Damned unfair – when you don't even belong here.'

His way of apologizing for having put the periscope up, perhaps. He hadn't mentioned it, but he must have realized since then that if he hadn't done it *Tracker* might have been in the clear by now: on the surface, belting for home.

Some thought, that. *Really* some thought.

The noise had stopped again. Anchor close-up in the destroyer's hawse, no doubt.

Wootton's voice: 'HE on that bearing, sir. Slow.'

'And the new one?'

Chris heard a whimper from the German in Mottram's cabin. Like a child's, in nightmare. Wootton meanwhile telling the skipper, 'Red one-six-nine, sir, drawing left. Slowing, too.'

You'd hear that one anchoring, in a minute.

Mottram came through – leaving French, the torpedo officer, in the Control Room – and Chris moved further round the table to let him in.

'Listen, Number One. And you two. Decision time. Since we've got another of the bastards up there – and in due course no doubt *he'll* be relieved.' Meeting Chris's stare: neither of them needing to voice the thought that by that time – if they did wait that long – they might not be paying much attention to whatever came or went. He went on, 'Want to hear your views, see what you think of this. Point being that if they're waiting for divers—' he paused, getting it together, dragging a breath in too – 'and the diving starts soon enough, could be our best moment.'

'When they've got divers down – working—'

'Exactly. Up—' a forefinger pointing upward – 'and put a fish in him. Panic, confusion – surface, run for it.'

'Two things, sir—'

'One other point first. However obvious ... Either surfacing, or trying to put some distance behind us dived – hell of a long shot. Odds against getting away with it – Christ, we'll need miracles.' He looked at Chris. 'Sorry. Go ahead.'

'Two things.' He spoke carefully, taking his time over it. 'First is how long – to wait for that, I mean. Haven't got long – as we all know. Divers might be coming from Kiel – Hamburg – anywhere. Could be *days* ... Second – I doubt there'll be only one ship then. Diving-gear in one – salvage-vessel, maybe – and Gestapo observers, perhaps. Rest of the flotilla too, wouldn't be surprised. And if we hang on too long – well ...' He shrugged, left it at that.

'So—' Mottram was wiping his eyes, which seemed to be watering a lot – '– your vote's to chance it – *now*?'

'When this one's alone again, I'd say. Give the other one time to get into Altfjorden and anchor. Or if it's going to refuel – wherever ... But look – sir – they aren't expecting anything, won't be keeping a sharp lookout. They think we're *dead*.'

'That's a point. Good one.' Mottram stared at him, thinking about it. 'But—' he paused, glancing up as Kjellegard joined them. 'How is he?'

A shrug: 'Not good *before*. Need air, need—'

'Christ, who doesn't!'

Kjellegard protested, 'Captain ask, I only say—'

'Quite right. You shut up, Chief ... Number One – you're right. But we're also damn close to them, aren't we? And – hydrophone watch, surely. Even if not, and we torpedo him – hell, the others'll be on us before we get half a mile.'

Caulfield said, 'You told me to shut up, but if you want *my* view—'

'Let's hear it.'

'I agree with Van Sommeren. Have a go *now.*'

'Didn't say that, Chief. I'm saying let the one that's been relieved get well away – up to Namsos, or alongside a tanker, or wherever—'

'All right. An hour, *then* move.'

'Well.' Mottram thought about it for a moment. 'All right. All right . . . But – how to set about it . . . You see, if we could get off the bottom without—' he paused, shook his head – 'can't hope to, really, can we. If we *could*, I was thinking we might do better not to attack him, just – creep away, or try to. If we *don't* settle his hash, he'll be on us damn quick, and if we *do* – well, he's out of it but we've got four others after us. Can't have it both ways – *or* move silently—'

Chief muttered, 'Spin a coin', and Mottram frowned, repeated, '*Or* move all that silently. The minute you start that pump, Chris—'

'Hey.' He'd straightened, as a new thought hit him. '*Hey . . .*'

Three pairs of eyes on him. Bellamy hadn't joined in the discussion, but he'd been awake and listening, was up on an elbow now. Chris began – pointing upwards and astern – 'This fellow 'll be anchoring, any minute now – and he'll be stone deaf while he's doing it, won't he. Cable roaring out, hydrophones useless? If we're quick – now – and ready for it—'

'Crikey.' Chief muttered, staring at Chris, 'Man's a genius . . .'

'Perhaps he is, at that.' Mottram was staring at him too: Chris guessed, looking for reasons it wouldn't work. He could see only one snag – the short time it took to drop an anchor. You'd need to be *damn* quick – starting *now* . . . He was halfway to his feet: 'Go to diving stations, sir?'

The Spitfire's oil pressure was falling slowly but surely. In fact not all that slowly now, either. The gauge showed fifty pounds to the square inch: a few minutes ago the pressure had been fifty-five and she'd been thinking she might make Cosford. Certainly would not have got anything like as far as Brize Norton. Cosford had been a possibility though, and attractive by virtue of number 22 ATA ferry pool being based there.

It was no longer a possibility, however. The pressure had dropped below fifty, and she knew she was in trouble. The nearest fields would be Ternhill, Shawbury or High Ercall. A complicating problem, though, was that she didn't know precisely where she was. Cloud at this point was continuous. Hadn't been, only minutes ago, but was now, was *here*. Just a few minutes ago she'd left Shrewsbury to starboard – it had been clear to see – and then she'd had the Severn Gorge right under her; since then, she realized, she'd been pre-occupied with the damned oil-pressure.

Forty-five pounds to the inch. 'Emergency Minimum', that was called. Engine temperature and oil temperature were already high, and rising fast.

Next thing, the engine either seizes up or explodes. Or both.

Get down, find Ternhill or Shawbury. If possible, rather quickly. She was *in* cloud now, coming down through it, air-speed down to one-ninety. Thinking *Now I really have done it*. Oil pressure forty-two. Another fleeting thought: *When they're out to get you they don't damn well let up, do they?* The Hurricane yesterday, now this. Out of cloud, but not a damn thing she recognized. On a route which she knew so well she could have listed landmark after landmark with her eyes shut ... Must have gone off course: been over cloud and off-course, mesmerized by the bloody oil-gauge.

Nothing like that's going to happen to me, Jane ...

The hell it wasn't. Pressure was down to forty: it'd go at any moment ...

To the left, ahead, a big, recently-cut hay field. Might make *that*. Hay-stooks dotted here and there, but—

Glycol – hydraulic fluid – bursting out of the 'plane's nose lashed the perspex in front of her – painting it a dirty white – and streamed over her head. Visibility now zero except over the side of the cockpit. She'd switched off the engine – averting that explosion anyway – and trimmed the Spit to gliding speed – 110 mph. Petrol cock – off. Now the hood: released, it flew away. Undercarriage – no, no hydraulics, darn it. So no wheels. Check the harness: OK, locked. The glycol had mostly gone, but there was still a residue plastering her goggles. A hedge flashed under: she held off as well as she could, with her feet jammed against the rudder-bars – as ready for the impact as she'd ever be: she thought in that final second *Oh, Chris, I'm such a fool . . .*

Waiting – still – at diving stations. The faces around the Control Room were quite familiar to him now: sick and exhausted, but not the strangers' faces they'd been only a couple of days ago. All breathing open-mouthed: eyes dim in dirty whites and sockets like dark holes in skulls. Most of them were leaning on things, or squatting . . . The German should have anchored fifteen or twenty minutes ago: it had seemed like touch-and-go, to get the ship's company closed up in time, ready to open the main-line suctions on 'O' port and starboard – and open up from depthcharging, so the depth gauges were functioning again – and a stoker in the machinery-space ready to start the ballast pump. Chris would have also to blow 'Q', the quick-diving tank: he'd flooded it after they'd bottomed, to hold her virtually anchored with its five-ton flooded weight. An advantage being that it *could* be blown – instantly, more or less.

Noisily too, unfortunately. The destroyer *had* to be anchoring, when he blew it. Which was what they'd been waiting for, for about twenty minutes now.

'Red five-oh, sir. Turning again.'

PO Wootton – white as linen, eyes bright pink – knew the German was turning because the bearing had been shifting from left to right and had now become steady. When he'd made his turn the bearing would start moving the other way, right to left.

As it had now. The sickening fact was that the destroyer was patrolling up and down, *not* anchoring, conceivably wasn't going to. A snag he had *not* foreseen.

Mottram muttered, 'Someone ought to tell him he's wasting fuel.' He looked at Wootton again: '*Sure* he's not transmitting?'

'Sure, sir.'

Because they wouldn't be expecting any submarines to be around, other than the one they thought they'd sunk.

'He'll be listening out, though.' Mottram looked over at Bellamy, at the chart-table. 'How far would he be from us on that bearing, pilot?'

'Five hundred yards, sir, roughly.'

'Christ. Spitting distance.'

'Red one-one-oh, sir.'

Anchor? Please – anchor?

Mottram had gone over to the chart-table. Murmuring to Bellamy, 'Twenty-five fathoms ... Due west, patch here's only six. So – we'll steer a course of two-nine-oh.'

'Two-seven-five should clear it, sir.'

'Not worth the risk. Two-nine-oh for half a mile, let's say. No – we won't. We'll steer three double-oh – and stay on it. Priority's to put distance between us and this coast. Course for home after we surface.'

'But – could be what they'd expect, sir?'

'We don't have to consider that, do we?'

He left him to work it out for himself. Bellamy wasn't in any better shape than the rest of them – a few minutes ago he'd seemed to be asleep, half-lying across his chart-table – and the point *his* oxygen-starved brain was missing now was that this whole gambit depended on the Germans not having even a suspicion that there could be a live submarine within a hundred miles.

Wootton reported, 'Moving again, sir. Right to left, very low revs.'

'Bearing?'

'Red – one-two-four, sir.'

'The other one was right astern when he anchored, wasn't he?'

Bellamy told him from the chart-table – alert now, proving he *wasn't* all that slow-witted – 'He was on red one-seven-six, sir.'

Near enough right astern. So if this one was heading for the same spot he'd have maybe a thousand yards to go yet. A few hundred anyway. The fact he'd cut his revs justified the hope that he *might* be nosing in to anchor.

Condensation wasn't only gathering on the deckhead now, it was beginning to fall – here and there, sporadically – like spots of warmish rain. Leaning on the slanting steel ladder with his forehead resting on one of its higher rungs, Chris wondered whether the deckhead had dripped like this when it had been *Trumpeter*'s – and if it had, whether anyone had been alive to see it. Probably not: they'd all been dead long before this stage ... He focused on Mottram: 'Might be as well to change the Protosorb, sir.'

'All right.' Looking up, seeing the sweat on the white paint. 'Go ahead.'

'Where is it, cox'n?'

''Fore ends, sir. Want me to—'

'No. Harper.' The rat-faced messenger: pink-eyed, more like a ferret ... 'Ask the TI for the Protosorb, then replace all the stuff that's on the trays.'

'Aye aye, sir.'

It might help, a little. Had damn-all to do with condensation: the dripping had only reminded him about it – that the stuff already spread around might have absorbed as much CO_2 as it could take.

Mottram muttered, 'Wonder what this bugger's at.'

There'd be a variety of explanations to choose from. A trainee helmsman on the wheel, for instance. Or giving a midshipman a lesson in pilotage, or the engineer wanting to run the engines at low revs for a while, for some reason ...

Chris could *see* the damn thing up there. Sliding through the dark-blue water, a small bow-wave rolling away to wash around the nearer islets: the men in its bridge breathing fresh air, taking that blessed luxury for granted . . .

'Red one-seven-oh, sir. Still moving right to left.'

'Revs?'

'Dead slow, sir. Manoeuvring speed.'

And very nearly in the right spot, Chris thought, still picturing the scene up there. He felt dizzy, now and then – *now*, for instance – and slightly sick. He rested his forehead against that double steel rung again: thinking – incongruously – *Wedding day – tomorrow*?

Ought to send Suzie a telegram: *Sorry, can't make it, all my love, darling—*

'Stopped his engines, sir.'

Back to earth: to hope . . . Thinking that if the German was going to anchor he'd most likely put his screws astern shortly, to take the way off: and you'd hear it, get some warning . . . Mottram raised a hand, crossed two fingers. His face above the now untrimmed, straggly beard glistening with sweat, eyes red-rimmed, sore-looking. Well – most were – his own too, probably, one hadn't been looking in any mirrors. He asked Mottram, 'What depth, sir – when we get going?'

'Make it forty feet.'

'Forty. Aye aye, sir.'

The question had been somewhat premature. But less counting chickens than keeping oneself awake, one's mind on the job. Getting it *back* on the job. Reflecting, though, that if the destroyer turned and headed back westward again, it wouldn't be easy or even rational to go on with this. If you didn't surface reasonably soon, he knew – from his own rapidly worsening condition as well as from the appearance and obvious lassitude of most of the men around him – was pretty sure that even another hour might be too much . . . Leave it too long, he thought – coining an aphorism – might be leaving it for ever.

But if you surfaced here, the Germans would have her at point-blank range.

Answer: move *now*, chance it, don't wait any longer for the bastard to drop his hook. Get her off the putty, blow 'Q' and start the motors, say your prayers . . .

The noise of the destroyer's cable rushing out took him by surprise. After all the waiting – he'd almost jumped out of his skin. Then: 'Start the pump!' – simultaneously switching the electric telegraph to 'pump from for'ard'. Actually to suck ballast from the midships compensating tanks, but the pump was further aft. The word PUMPING appeared, lit up, and he glanced round at the ERA on the diving panel: 'Blow "Q".'

'Blow "Q", sir . . .' He already had a wheel-spanner on the valve, had only to wrench it round: you heard the high-pressure air thump through the pipe, and its impact in the tank. '"Q" blowing, sir.'

The German's cable was still rattling out. When it stopped, you'd carry on: bloody *have* to. 'Q' tank had a light that switched off when it was empty, and it flickered out now: Berkley shut off the air and reported '"Q" blown, sir.' His face was so white under the stubble that it almost glowed. But *Tracker* was moving. Even before 'Q' had been empty there'd been a slight lurch and the needles in the gauges had begun to inch around their dials. 124 feet: 122 . . . Looking over the 'planesmen's shoulders he saw that the bubble was near-enough amidships. So her whole length had to be off the bottom. 120 feet, rising on an even keel: he reached to the trimming telegraph, clicked it to 'Stop pumping', and told Mottram: 'Clear of the bottom, sir.'

'Group down, slow ahead port.'

'Grouper down, slow ahead port, sir . . .' The order was passed aft to the motor-room by telephone. In the same instant the cable's noise ceased: it left a silence that seemed to double *Tracker*'s own output of sound.

Chris told the 'planesmen, 'Forty feet.'

'Forty feet, sir.' The coxswain glanced to his right, at Chisholm's fore planes' indicator, which showed that that pair were at hard a-rise. He put some more angle on his own – dive-angle, to pull the stern down, get the bow up. As she gathered way, the 'planes would begin to take affect.

'Port motor running slow ahead, grouped down, sir.'

'Very good.' Mottram told the helmsman, 'Steer three double oh.'

'Three double oh, sir . . .'

Cable noise again. As reassuring as the motor's low hum. Laying out more cable, he guessed: wouldn't take them long, but they wouldn't have been doing it at all if they'd thought there was any reason to use their hydrophones. Needles in the gauges swinging past the 100-foot marks: he switched the trimming telegraph to 'Flood for'ard'. She'd be getting lighter as she rose, so he had to put some weight back into those midships compensating tanks; otherwise the trim could become uncontrollable and she'd rocket to the surface.

Which was *not* desirable.

Silence again. Only *Tracker*'s port motor and screw disturbing the underwater stillness.

'Course three double-oh, sir.'

'Slow ahead starboard.'

Hoarse whispers: nothing louder.

Eighty feet. He moved the telegraph to 'Stop flooding', and ordered 'Shut "O" suctions and inboard vents.' She might be a bit light for'ard, he thought: in which case the ballast he'd let in as she rose to the ordered depth of forty feet could as well go into 'H' compensating tank, which was halfway towards the sharp end.

'Both motors running slow ahead grouped down, sir.'

'Very good.' Mottram glanced round: 'Messenger . . .' He told Harper – who was clutching a container of Protosorb to his chest, had been coming through on his way aft – 'Pass the word – we'll remain at diving stations, but I want everyone to settle down, keep quiet and still. All being well, we'll surface in about two hours.'

If air and battery lasted that long. Battery might, with the motors driving her at only about two and a half knots, but air probably would not. Even if it did – which presumably you'd find out only by *not* falling into a coma – after two hours' run you'd still be surfacing within sight of the coast.

Chapter 20

In *Tumult*'s wardroom, during the course of the afternoon Chalk had written a long letter to Patricia. Up to now all their communications had been by telephone, but Suzie had put this in his mind when she'd told him over the 'phone from Carlisle, 'I write to him, when he's away.' He'd also foreseen the prospect of taking *Tumult* out on her next patrol, around 5th-6th July, with Patricia still away; having that on his mind during the two or three weeks at sea – not even knowing whether she'd be there when he got back. A total void, complete ignorance of where, or when ... He'd put it this way in the letter, *Where or When* being one of their favourite songs – with Pat's own words substituted for one couplet: *The clothes you aren't wearing/You weren't wearing then ...*

The tune ran through his mind now, reminding him of one particular time and place – how he'd wanted her in his arms but also to stand back and feast his eyes on her, and she'd told him, 'It's called having your cake and eating it, my darling.'

In the Mess, alone, he sat at the bar and asked for a beer. It was thin, watery stuff, but a half-pint cost only twopence and one acquired a tolerance of it. Thoughts of Patricia running on, meanwhile – how dreadful it would be if she wasn't back by the time he had to push off again, so that he wouldn't know what to expect when *he* got back – whether there'd be an answer to this letter, or a message that she'd called.

Or nothing, and still no answer to the telephone.

Might ring Betty, he thought. He should have done so anyway – to ask how she and the children were, and whether Mama was still hanging on, and all that – and it was remotely possible that she'd have seen Patricia before she'd left. She went down to Betty's for weekends sometimes: *might* have been there and said something like 'Won't be seeing you for a month or so' – something of that kind . . . But he thought he would not telephone Suzie this evening. He'd have no news for her, and by this time tomorrow he might have. The flotilla's Staff Officer (Operations)'s estimation was that midday tomorrow was the earliest one could hope to hear; there was to have been a deadline for the landing-party to be back on board, and it would be at least twelve hours after that before Mottram would risk breaking wireless silence. Perhaps longer. Give it another twenty-four hours or so, the SO(O) had suggested, before we start any serious worrying.

Consciousness of *Tracker*'s previous existence as *Trumpeter*, Chalk recognized, was an entirely personal thing. A personal aberration, even. Others seemed not to give it a thought. Chris Van Sommeren, for instance, had only been concerned about it for Suzie's sake – knowing about Dymock and the ordeal she'd been through then. For himself though – when he let it into his mind at all – and in dreams, very much *un*invited – he saw their faces – groups as well as individuals – and heard their voices: saw fear, hope, resignation, courage. Dymock's courage, in particular, and Andrew Buchanan's spectre presented itself more often than most. Most clearly of all, the statements he'd made about his wife: *She's so straight; there's no question . . .*

Zoe, *straight*?

Buchanan must have had his doubts, Chalk had realized since. To have talked about it at all. He'd either have been trying to convince himself, or as it were testing the water, looking for some reaction from Chalk that might have told him something, one way or the other.

He'd seen her once – about six months ago. He'd been with Patricia at the Café Royal, and she'd been one of a party of about eight men and women; one of the men was not in uniform. He'd only seen them when he and Patricia had been leaving, and Pat had confirmed – with obvious delight – that the rather fat civilian who'd had Zoe on his right was George Lindsay, Lord Spynie's son: he did have a porcine look, as Patricia had once said he had – referring at the same time, he'd remembered, to Buchanan's 'tarty' wife. Lindsay was undoubtedly of military age, had presumably to be in what was known as a 'Reserved Occupation' – meaning exempt from the general call to arms. It would be on the grounds of running a business or businesses vital to the war effort, perhaps. Chalk had wondered how it would feel to be a civilian – male, and his own age roughly, and although overweight seemingly able-bodied – in London in the winter of 1940.

At that stage he hadn't been sleeping with Patricia. On *that* crucial night – it had been his last before returning to Dundee – he'd taken her to the restaurant in Wardour Street where they'd dined on numerous occasions, and earlier in the evening she'd introduced him to an establishment called *Le Petit Club Francais*, in a mews behind St James's Street, packed with Free French and run by a Welshwoman called Olwen; Patricia knew it through her job, had been taken there by Frenchmen. It was the closest Chalk had ever come to her SIS environment; he hadn't liked the place, and they'd never been there again. About – three months ago, this had been. They'd finished their meal and he'd paid the bill, and he'd put his hand on hers amongst the coffee-cups:

it was about the tenth meal they'd had there, perhaps the twentieth time they'd been out together in London. They were looking at each other, not saying anything at that moment, and her hand had turned, the rather long, smooth fingers caressing, intimate, so clearly symbolic of physical contact in a deeper sense that to him it was instantly, powerfully arousing. She'd known it too: asked quietly, 'Home?' Meaning that little flat of hers – where she'd asked him as he followed her in and pushed the door shut behind them, 'Want a drink?'

'Don't think so. Do you?'

'No.' That smile of hers: Dietrich would have given the world to be able to smile like that. 'I don't think there is any, anyway.'

'We don't have to waste time, then.' She'd been in his arms: no waste of time at all. No sense of time either, or location – no sense of anything but – amazingly – *Patricia*.

Later – in the dark, all of London blacked out around them and for some reason no raids that night – she'd murmured, 'This isn't going to be a casual affair, is it?'

'Most certainly is not!'

'Truly? How *you* feel?'

'I don't know how to describe how I feel. I could *burst*, with the – the *strength* of it, the – I simply can't *begin* to—'

'That's *exactly*—'

'You're more beautiful even than I thought you were. Too beautiful to be real. Pat – darling – I never *dreamt*—'

'Oh, *I* did.'

'Really?'

A soft laugh in the darkness. 'Once or twice.'

But he hadn't really considered the possibility until just recently, when he'd had finally to accept that his marriage had gone *phut*. By that time he'd already been in love with her: fooling himself that it was something from which he could extricate himself without tears on either side when he had to – when he and Diana patched things up, had been the rather vague assumption.

He'd told her earlier that he hadn't much liked *Le Petit Club*, and he'd sorted out the reasons by this time. The first was that he'd disliked the *ambience* of intrigue, different groups of French obviously loathing each other – she'd explained some of the basic politics to him – and two – much more personally – because it had felt like an anteroom to another world, the one she vanished into, where he couldn't follow her and where his imagination put her in the most appalling danger.

He'd asked her, 'Do you have to go on with it?'

A sigh . . . Then: 'Do you have to go on with *your* thing?'

And later, in the dawn – when he'd mentioned it again, his dread of her next departure – 'I can't talk about it, Rufus. Simply *can't*. In any case, you're off on patrol again – when, this next week?'

Shades of Mrs Nat Eason: his own recognition then that it was those left behind who suffered.

He touched the letter in his reefer pocket. He hadn't stuck it down, intended to add to it from time to time, whenever there was something worth adding – like news of *Tracker* and Van Sommeren . . . Sipping at a second half-pint of beer-flavoured water, leafing idly through the day before yesterday's London *Evening News*: someone returning from leave must have left it here. The front-page headline was BLITZ OVER: MOSCOW'S TURN NOW. Because Hitler had invaded Russia, which had been his ally. Perhaps, he thought, the British communists – the *Daily Worker* in particular – would stop referring to it as 'a boss's war' now.

'Wotcher, Rufus.'

Tim Hart, *Threat's* CO, with his own first lieutenant. Chalk glanced at them. 'Off tomorrow, aren't you?'

A nod. 'Bosch is already trembling in his jackboots. Have another?'

'No, thanks. Going up for a bath, in a minute.' He looked down at the paper again, paging over. An item about the garrison in Tobruk still holding out against encircling Germans only emphasized what had already become fairly obvious, that General Wavell's recent offensive had ground to a halt.

'Lieutenant-Commander Chalk, sir.' A Wren stewardess, in the doorway. 'Telephone, sir . . .'

'Thanks.' He threw the paper down, asked the Wren as he passed her, 'Male or female?'

Prim little smile: 'A lady, sir.'

Patricia?

'It wasn't her, of course.'

Chalk was knocking his pipe out on the palm of his left hand, tilting it for the wind to blow the ash away. It was a stiffish southwesterly which had been coming up during the past hour and was now creasing the sea down there in white ridges, the spray flying like smoke where it broke against the rocks.

He blew through the pipe, and pushed it into a pocket.

'It was an ATA girl, calling to tell me that Suzie had had what she called "a slight mishap" with a Spitfire. She was in a hospital in St Albans, suffering from mild concussion, a sprained ankle and all-over bruising. No lasting damage, anyway; she'd been *very* lucky. And she'd asked this girl – whom I'd met at that party Suzie and her chums gave at White Waltham – to let me know that her father was on his way down and would be taking her home to convalesce in Scotland. Would I please contact her there, at Glendarragh, when I had news for her.

'She shouldn't have been flying, this girl told me: she'd been in a highly nervous condition, several of them had seen it and begged her to report sick. All on account of the postponed wedding, was their view, it seemed.' He shrugged. 'I told Miss Who'sit that there was a great deal more to it than just that. As indeed there was. Suzie'd given no indication of stress of that order, mind you, when she'd been talking to me – not a quaver. But that was Suzie, you see. Dare say I should have known better, added my persuasive efforts to her ATA friends' urgings. Wouldn't have made any difference, though. She'd gone through a truly hellish period, during and after the *Trumpeter* business: and I suppose she'd seen a repetition coming – perhaps even subconsciously – or just wouldn't give way to it. Point of fact, it was what I'd been frightened of, I should have been more perceptive – not just impressed by her stamina, as I had been ... Anyway – I got the number of the hospital, and spoke to the matron: Miss Cameron-Green was flat out, she told me, and would remain so – in purdah, *not* taking telephone calls – until her father came for her next day. I asked her to tell Suzie I'd rung and I'd be in touch with her later at her parent's house.

'Then I rang Glendarragh and spoke to Lady C-G. Sir Innes was on his way south, she told me, by the overnight train, would be collecting Suzie from the hospital at about noon next day and bringing her back with him that night. Night of the 25th – the wedding day, as it would have been – and she asked me whether I couldn't even guess at when the wedding *might* take place. Damn-fool thing to ask, in the circumstances ... I asked her in return whether they'd heard anything of Patricia, and she told me no, they hadn't. "We're rather concerned for her, you know. Actually, Innes is going to speak to some man to whom he has an introduction – in London tomorrow, see if he can't find out *something* ... Rufus, may I ask you – while I have the chance – whether you're *serious*, about Patricia?"

'"I can't tell you how serious. Never more so in my life. Never anywhere *near* so."

'"What of Diana?"

'"To all intents and purposes, that's over. Will be formally, legally, in due course. As soon as I can tie her down to it. She hasn't given me a chance to discuss it with her – she knows I *want* to—"

'"I see. Well . . . I'll tell Suzie you telephoned."

'Not the most enthusiastic of potential mothers-in-law. But I suppose one couldn't expect much else, in the circumstances. What I'd said about Diana was the truth of the situation, though: she seemed to be happy enough with things as they were – me as husband-in-waiting in the background – whom I'm sure, knowing Diana, she'd expect to be able to call to heel whenever she wanted to – boyfriend Jacques Frogface in the foreground, and of course her beloved flying. She qualified to fly four-engined bombers, by the way, at about this time. As Suzie did too, later on. Only about a dozen of them did. Oh, I told you this, didn't I? Imagine, though – those damn great machines, and a slip of a girl at the helm – eh?'

'Yes.' I glanced at my watch. 'But—'

'I know.' Checking *his* time. 'We've got half an hour or so, anyway. Even though she *does* drive like a maniac . . . Where was I? Oh, yes . . . After the Glendarragh call, I got through to Betty – whom I'd failed to reach when I'd tried before – and as I'd more or less expected she didn't know anything about Patricia. But her children were well, and her husband – Dick – was in Crete, she told me. We'd pulled out of Greece by then. And our mother was pretty well on her way out, I really ought to get down and see her as soon as I could, etcetera.

'And that was that. No news of *Tracker*, not a whisper of Patricia's whereabouts – well, easy to guess *where*, it was the *when* that mattered, when would she reappear – oh, and Suzie crocked up. Not on the whole the happiest set of circumstances.' He shrugged, gazing out to sea. 'Then at lunchtime I was given news that *really* put the kybosh on it.' He turned to face me. 'Emanating from Lord Haw-Haw. The night before, apparently, he'd come on the air from Berlin with his "Jarmany calling" programme, and claimed that a

British submarine, HMS *Tracker* – he'd named her – had been sunk off the coast of Norway. She'd landed a party of "Norwegian communist saboteurs", he called them, all of whom had been killed or captured.

'Imagine. Not so much "news", as a bombshell. I had it from the SO(O), who sent his messenger asking me to drop in at his office – before lunch, this was . . . D'you remember those Haw-Haw broadcasts? Sometimes there was a factual basis to his sneers, but a lot of it was absolute tosh. For instance, by that time he'd two or three times announced the sinking of the carrier *Ark Royal* – which was still going strong, then. So there was a chance this was yet another load of bull. On the other hand, if it wasn't true how had they identified the submarine as *Tracker*? The SO(O) had an answer to that one – they'd caught the Norwegians and screwed it out of them. It was possible, obviously, but at the time he and I both felt he was grabbing at straws.

'However – Lady C-G had said Sir Innes would be home with Suzie at about midday. I was in our Mess by about one – lunchtime – and I rang Glendarragh expecting to get Sir Innes and warn him – prime him with the hope of it being a lie. They might not have heard, you see, but on the other hand they *might*. One listened now and then to Haw-Haw, primarily for laughs – you didn't have to believe his rubbish, but it still somehow got around, didn't it. You'd be asked "Hear what Haw-Haw had to say last night, old boy? Sunk the *Ark* again, no less!" So they *could* have heard, and for Suzie it could be the straw that broke the donkey's back. This ATA colleague of hers had reckoned she mightn't be far off a nervous breakdown: and that's not like catching a cold, you know, there can be lifelong damage done. *Their* real concern had been that she'd crash – which she had, although she told me it was an engine fault, not hers – and the ATA accepted her accident report, when she sent it in . . . Anyway – I rang Glendarragh – half my pay was going on telephone calls, but there wasn't much I could do about it – and got

Lady C-G again. The others hadn't arrived yet: MacKenzie had taken the brake to meet them at Tyndrum, but the train was probably running late. Often did – you'd have bombing somewhere along the line during the night, and consequent hold-ups. Trains took shelter in tunnels, sometimes . . . But why, she asked me, was I ringing? Did I have news? I told her no, I didn't, but there'd been this enemy propaganda claim of a submarine being sunk on that coast, and if Suzie happened to hear of it it might do her no good at all. So I'd telephoned only to warn her that if it did come to their ears, it wasn't necessarily the truth.

'"But—" she asked me – "it *may* be?"

'"I doubt it. They landed some Norwegians, for a certain purpose, and if they were rounded up that could be how the Germans got to know they'd come by submarine. The boat's name, even."

'"Did they give the name?"

'"I think they did. I've had this information second-hand, mind you, I don't listen to enemy broadcasts all that much."

'"Was it Haw-Haw?"

'"Yes. And as you know—"

'"He tells the most blatant lies!"

'"Exactly. So if they haven't heard about it, there's no need to mention it at all."

'"Quite. I understand."

'"One other thing. If the worst comes to the worst—"

'"If it's true, you mean."

'"*If* it is, may I come over to you and break it to her myself? I introduced Chris to her, you see, I feel – responsible. Not for the first time either."

'"All right. I – appreciate your suggesting it, Rufus. I'm sure Innes will too. It's good of you. But please God—"

'"Yes. Please God . . ."'

Chalk paused: refilling his pipe. He went on – after checking the time again – 'Not such an awful mother-in-law-to-be after all, I thought, after that conversation.

When the going got tough, she seemed to come up trumps. Didn't escape my notice that I seemed to have done myself a bit of good, too. But on the *Tracker* issue I didn't have any great hopes of a happy outcome. The Haw-Haw claim coming on top of the fact they'd sent her north at the wrong time of year: and that the Germans must at least have caught the landing-party – in which case, once they knew there was a submarine in the vicinity, how could Mottram possibly get out of it, with no shred of darkness to surface into?

'Anyway – I had lunch, went down to the boat, saw that everything was happening that should have been, dealt with a few queries from young Sutherland, and so on. Routine chores. But also, facing the stark realities of the situation, I had to think about how I'd replace Chris as first lieutenant, if I had to. I think – to be honest – I was *expecting* I'd have to. Then – mid-afternoon – another message from the SO(O): would I call in to see him at my earliest convenience, please.

'I think I probably ran. I don't remember. What I do remember, clear as anything, is that bugger saying absolutely nothing, giving nothing away in his expression either, simply handing me a pink signal form. Pink for secret – as you'll remember: in this case Top Secret, and it would have come in cypher of course. From *Tracker* – time-of-origin less than an hour earlier – addressed to Senior Submarine Officer Lerwick and repeated to Uncle Tom Cobbley and all, giving her position, course and speed, ETA Lerwick 1800/Z June 26th, and adding *Request ambulance and doctor for removal of sick passenger Doctor Heiden to hospital.*

'Oh, and something about two Norwegians having been left behind, killed or captured. I looked up at the SO(O), who'd cracked a smile by that time. Personally, I *just* managed not to weep. Instead I borrowed his telephone – he courteously left me to it – and I rang Glendarragh. Got MacKenzie this time, then Lady C-G. She told me, "I've put Suzie to bed. I told her you called, Rufus. Does this mean – you're coming here?"

'"In a few days' time I will, if I may. But meanwhile – any champagne in the cellar?"

'"Champagne . . ." She'd caught her breath. I was enjoying this – as you can imagine. I told her, "Get a bottle up and open it, take a glass up to Suzie, tell her *Tracker*'s on her way back and I'll bring Chris over to her in about four days' time. Five at the outside. Would it suit you to lay on the wedding for – oh, a week from today?"'

EPILOGUE

'Wedding went off well.' Chalk qualified that statement with 'Ruined for me personally by still having no news of Patricia. Whoever Sir Innes had seen in London had only given him a bland assurance that "as far as he knew" she was all right. Oh, and "very highly regarded". But as I say – good wedding. Bride and groom ecstatically happy. *Tracker* had surfaced in full view of the Norwegian coast, by the way, and nobody'd taken a blind bit of notice of her . . . What else – I've got to be quick now, haven't I? Well, the Cameron-Greens made me very welcome; the inference was that there'd be no problems once I was free – and Patricia home and of like mind, of course . . . Astonishing, you know, the blind faith one had: worried stiff for her, but no real doubt she *would* be back . . . Oh, one small thing – Sir Innes mentioned that "the Buchanan woman's" engagement to George Lindsay had been all over the gossip columns, photographs and all, quite recently. While I was on patrol, it must have been. So she'd got what *she*'d been after – if the old great-aunt had been right, our Zoe was all set to become extremely rich. And – what else . . . Well, Suzie and Chris had a 48-hour honeymoon – she was still using a crutch, by the way – and a slightly longer, supplementary honeymoon after our next patrol. Thanks to an extremely well-disposed commanding officer. It'd be nice to say they lived happily ever after, but – as you'll remember—'

'He commanded *Sepoy*, in the Trinco flotilla.'

'Left me for his COQC course in late '42, had a training boat at Campbeltown for his first command, then as you say, *Sepoy.* She was refitting – at Dundee – and he took her out to Trinco in '44. Lost with all hands in the Malacca Straits a few months later.'

'Yes. Poor Suzie.'

'As you say . . . And – speak of the devil—'

A car had crashed over the cattle-grid: would now be trundling up the 400 yards of dirt track which Chalk referred to as a drive and the Irish call an avenue. I was staring at him: it was a question which I'd had in mind – obviously – but hadn't asked: it was very much his private business, and I'd left it to him to tell me when he saw fit.

'Suzie . . .'

'Hadn't you guessed?'

'But – Patricia—'

He'd been sitting: was on his feet now, big hands flat on the wall, eyes on the sea. He told me, 'I never saw her again. The story we were given – eventually – was that she'd crashed on take-off in a Lysander, in some French wood – clearing in a wood, I suppose – shot down just as it left the ground by machine-gun fire from a German patrol. In other words she'd *just* missed getting out. And – staying alive . . . But to tell you the truth it was almost a relief, when I heard it. She'd been gone for months by then, we *knew* she must have – come to grief – and at least it hadn't been the kind of horror that had – obsessed one's dreams.'

At least she hadn't died in a Gestapo cellar, he meant.

I said – at a loss for any comment that might have sounded less *banal* – 'I'm awfully sorry. Even taking that point – all those months not knowing, must have been – hellish.'

'Well.' That small shake of the head. '*One* word for it.' Turning back then, as it were cocking an ear, and I heard it too – a car rounding the bend, about a hundred yards away. He told me, 'Hang on here, will you. We'll be with you in two shakes.'

He came out alone, though. I turned from the sea expecting to see both of them, but it was only him, and for once the setter wasn't at his heels.

'Loose ends, now. While Herself is squaring herself off.' He sat down. 'That thing switched on, is it?'

'Question first – would the two of you dine with me tonight? I'll do the driving, pick you up – I'd thought Youen's at Baltimore, if you like seafood?'

'Love it. Very kind.' He'd nodded. 'Better see how she feels, but – I'm sure . . . Now then – *which* loose ends?'

'Diana?'

'Living in Connecticut. Married a Yank. Has the bloody nerve to send us Christmas cards. But that's all, about her. Obviously we got divorced, but – no details, story's finished – right?'

I'd nodded. He asked me, 'So what else?'

'Well – Alastair?'

'Lost a leg in Italy in '43. Farming at Glendarragh now – the C-G parents were under the ground long ago, incidentally, he's *Sir* Alastair. Has a prize herd of Aberdeen Angus and lets out the shooting and fishing. We visit him there occasionally – he married Midge, and she's still going strong. They've been here a few times . . . My sister – Betty – died of cancer just after the war; Dick – her husband – finished up as a brigadier, but he's been dead for some years now. He was older than the rest of us, of course. By the way, we have a son and a daughter – both of 'em breeding like rabbits, hence the spate of grandchildren, up to now all female. Son called Guy – not unlike him, either – daughter Patricia. This was Guy's son that just arrived. Pat's in Sydney, married to an Australian. What else . . . Oh – must tell you this. In 1945 – I was a commander – I was at Barlows' again, for the launching of one of the new "A" class. They were too late for the war, none of 'em saw any action, but they were real state-of-the-art submarines at that time. Museum piece now, they've got one at the Gosport submarine museum, open to the public. Well – you'd know . . . But who should be presiding at the launch but Lady Spynie. Zoe, no less. Frightfully smart, gowned and hatted, agleam with bloody diamonds. I had a few words with her – had to – took her aback a bit, but she couldn't get out of it either. But my God – gracious as hell on wheels . . . Oh – here's Herself.'

Suzie.

In slacks and a sweater, hair grey instead of the dark brown I'd been picturing all week, but otherwise – trim figure, vivacious, really very attractive – *still* . . . In fact exactly as one might have hoped she'd be. Even the dog at her side: it almost tripped her as she came down to us, and I remembered Chalk's description of his first sight of her, when the overweight labrador had cannoned through the door with her and she'd reminded it that it was a dog, not a hippo . . .

She'd dropped a yellow envelope of snapshots on the table, and told her husband, 'Here he is – your grandson.' Her hand was in mine, then – small, warm, firm: 'He's been telling you a whole pack of lies, I'm sure.'

'Just told him about Zoe at that launch.'

'Oh, *her*.' Suzie sat down. 'I suppose he conned you into believing they only exchanged telephone calls – huh?'

'Well – that's how it is on the tape.'

'And you really believe it?' Laughing, pointing at him: '*This* old rogue?'

'*Young* rogue, then.' Chalk had glanced quickly through the snaps. Shaking his head as he pushed them back into the envelope. 'Old Grandpa, now.' Nodding towards Suzie: 'And that's old Grannie.'

'Balls.' Her smile had faded. '*Bollocks*, Rufus. You know who you are – and *what* you are. And I know *me*, damn it!'

So did I – more or less. Watching them, seeing the challenge in her vividly blue eyes, and his slow smile growing – the smile of an old man enjoying the sight of his pretty, younger wife – I thought I knew them, well enough. All I had to do was work out how to frame their story.

AUTHOR'S NOTE

In June 1939, HM Submarine *Thetis* was lost during her acceptance trials in Liverpool Bay. There were 103 men on board and only 4 survived. She was salvaged and refitted as HMS/M *Thunderbolt*, which after distinguished war service was lost with all hands in the Mediterranean in March 1943.

The idea for *Not Thinking of Death* stemmed from the *Thetis/Thunderbolt* history, and the chain of mistakes contributing to the loss of the fictional HMS/M *Trumpeter* closely follows the detail of the *Thetis* tragedy as set out in the Report of the Tribunal of Enquiry into her loss. (The Report, in some basic respects inconclusive, was published by HM Stationery Office and presented to Parliament by the then prime minister Neville Chamberlain in April 1940.) But nobody who was involved in those tragic events is represented in any way in this novel, in which all the characters are fictional.

A.F.